With All My Heart

With All My Heart

Barbara Dawson Smith

St. Martin's Paperbacks

ISBN: 0-7394-2881-0

Printed in the United States of America

St. Martin's Paperbacks are published by St. Martin's Press, 175 Fifth Avenue, New York, NY 10010.

CONTENTS

Chapter One

The Man in Black

Captain Lord Joshua Kenyon was prepared to die. Having settled his mind on the matter during the dark hours of the night, he felt quite calm as Harrington proffered the long-barreled pistol.

"Trouble's afoot, Cap'n," Harrington said in a gravelly undertone. He darted a glance through the murky predawn mist at Josh's opponent, a fashionably clad gentleman huddled in conference with his stout retainer. Tendrils of fog lent a ghostly illusion to their shadowy figures. "There be somethin' peculiar about them two," the servant went on, his eyebrows drawn together into a single bushy gray line. "I can feel it in me bones."

"That's the brisk sea breeze you feel," Josh said.

"Huh. That Mr. Pankhurst, 'e wouldn't speak nary a word to me just now. An' after sayin' plenty t' the both o' us yesterday eve."

"Perhaps he's as peevish in the mornings as you are."

"Or mayhap 'e's 'ad second thoughts," Harrington said doggedly. "Mayhap 'e regrets challengin' ye. If ye'd jest go over there and talk t' the gent—"

"Give up, Harry. There's nothing to be gained by bandying words."

Keeping a cold, clear head, Josh focused his attention on the dueling pistol provided by his adversary. The finely tooled mahogany grip fitted his ungloved hand perfectly. Well balanced and lightweight, the weapon felt like an extension of his arm. It was sleeker—though no less deadly—than his government-issue pistol. "A magnificent piece," he said, wondering where Pankhurst had come by such a fine pair of weapons. "The carving looks to be prerevolutionary French."

"Could've belonged to Nappy 'isself fer all I care." Harrington planted his short, sinewy form in an obstinate pose, his arms akimbo, his craggy face set in crusty disapproval. "Blinkin' fool notion, this duel. Ye're too good a shot to miss. Ye'll 'ave the law on yer tail in a twinklin'."

"I won't shoot to kill." Josh kept silent about his true intentions; Harrington would try to talk him out of that, too. "Do your duty now. That's an order."

"I don't have t' take yer orders. We ain't in the cavalry no more."

"But you're still in my employ."

Muttering a string of blue curses, Harrington gave in and sketched a grumpy salute. Never content unless he had the last word, he said, " 'Ave it yer way then, Cap'n. But if ye're exiled, I ain't fleeing t' the Continent wid ye. 'Ad enough of them bloody frog-eatin' Frenchies t' last me a lifetime." Wheeling around, he stomped off, his gait awkward from his game leg. The battle at Waterloo in June had aggravated the older man's chronic injury.

That same battle had left Josh heartily sick of bloodshed. With the war over at last and Napoleon exiled to the remote island of St. Helena, Josh had sold his commission in the cavalry and returned to England.

How he loved being back here! From out of nowhere, the thought struck him hard. He had disembarked from the transport ship a week ago and tended to military matters in Portsmouth before setting out for the green hills and quiet forests of Stokeford Abbey. Though impatient to reach home, he'd made a detour to Brighton to complete one last duty by calling on David Pankhurst and his father, Baron Timberlake. He'd ended up in this deserted place near the sea, facing death at the hands of an angry man.

A man who had waited a long time to have his revenge.

Gripping the pistol, Josh disciplined himself to feel nothing but hard purpose. He remained standing in the copse of ash trees as Harrington met Pankhurst's second in the center of the misty clearing. The two men stood back to back, then counted off ten paces apiece. The tramp of their footsteps added somber notes to the distant symphony of the surf.

An animal alertness vitalized Josh. It was the same keen awareness he'd experienced before countless battles, the sense of standing on the edge of a precipice, the knowledge that he might not live to see the sunset, the desire both to rush time and to wring every last bit of pleasure out of it.

To the east, the pinkish-gray of the sky heralded the approach of sunrise. Snakes of vapor coiled around the scrubby trees. He could smell the scent of salt from the ocean a hundred yards beyond the dunes. With a curious detachment, he noted that the sandy soil would readily absorb any spilled blood.

His blood.

No surgeon hovered by the black carriage that had borne Pankhurst and his retainer here a short time ago. Odd that, for Josh knew David Pankhurst to be somewhat fastidious in his habits, a typical aristocratic civilian who fussed over a cut finger, who would flee in horror from the carnage on a battlefield. Yet Pankhurst had brought only his second.

With expert efficiency, Pankhurst checked his firearm and took practice aim. Josh couldn't remember him having an interest in guns. But David Pankhurst had had seven years in which to nurse his grudge. Seven years to hone his skill with a pistol . . .

A horse snorted, pawing the ground. Josh barely glanced at his restless black gelding tethered to the slender trunk of an ash tree. He kept his attention trained on the man stepping into position.

The Honorable David Pankhurst.

From a span of twenty paces, his face gleamed, a pale oval beneath a wide-brimmed beaver hat. Unlike Josh, who stood in his shirtsleeves, Pankhurst had kept on his coat to ward off the early morning chill. The misty dimness blurred his features, though Josh well remembered the smooth-shaven cheeks, the blue eyes stark with fury in the candlelit foyer. It was an image at odds with the genial fellow who at one time was to become Josh's brother-in-law.

But on the night before the wedding, Josh had ended his betrothal to Lily Pankhurst. He'd gone off to war, and shortly thereafter, Lily had languished and died.

Her heart had been broken, people had whispered. She'd taken her own life, others said. The thought made Josh's skin crawl as if icy fingers touched him.

At the edge of the clearing, Harrington clutched a scrap of pale fabric in his gnarled fist. " 'Ere's the signal," he said, his gruff voice sounding hollow in the foggy air. "Keep yer guns lowered till the cloth touches the grass." The valet paused, glaring from Pankhurst to Josh. "Unless one of ye young hotheads wants t' call it off."

Silence veiled the air, a silence invaded only by the singing of the sea and the twittering of a sleepy bird. Pankhurst's second hovered off to the side, wringing his hands while nervously shifting from one hobnailed shoe to the other. In stark contrast, David Pankhurst stood unmoving. There was an almost waiflike quality to his slender form; then Josh blinked and the odd illusion vanished. It wouldn't do to forget that Pankhurst harbored an intense, unforgiving hatred.

Josh held the pistol at his side, his forefinger tensed around the half-moon curve of the trigger. "Get on with it," he commanded.

" 'Tis yer blood," Harrington muttered. Scowling, he

opened his fingers and let the white square flutter downward.

The descent seemed to take an eternity. Josh felt the damp chill in the air. Pinpricks of mist struck his face, and an acrid fear soured his tongue. He steeled himself for the impact of the bullet.

The instant the cloth met the scrubby grass, he raised his arm skyward and squeezed the trigger. With a deafening boom, the ball discharged harmlessly into the air.

Simultaneously, another blast echoed as Pankhurst fired at Josh. The bullet whined past his ear. Then incredibly, Pankhurst staggered sideways. He collapsed to the ground and lay still.

Dumfounded, Josh stared. He'd aimed up into the trees. Had his bullet ricocheted off a limb?

A garbled shout burst from Harrington. "Stop 'im! The murderin' blighter shot Pankhurst!"

Josh spun in the direction the servant pointed. In the mist beyond the trees crouched a black-cloaked figure. His shadowed features were indiscernible at a distance of some twenty yards. In his grip, he brandished a smoking musket.

The man took off at a run. His cloak flapped as he bounded onto a nearby horse, wheeled around, and galloped away in a thunder of hooves.

Harrington charged toward his own mount, moving with a swiftness that belied his infirm leg.

Josh dropped the spent weapon and sprinted after Harrington. He caught up to the valet as Harrington was untying the reins of his roan gelding from a holly bush.

"Stay," Josh ordered. "I'll catch the bastard."

The valet shook his grizzled head. "Ye're the better of us at doctorin'. Ye must see t' Pankhurst."

Though he burned for the chase, Josh forced himself to accept the logic in that. Harrington could ride like the wind, a skill retained from his long-ago days as a jockey. With the agility of a much younger man, he hopped nimbly into the saddle and took off into the patchy fog.

The sky had grown lighter, casting a pearly glow over the scene. In the branches overhead, a lark trilled. Moisture dripped from the towering oaks and glistened on the shrubbery.

Josh cursed himself for missing the intruder's stealthy approach. No wonder his horse had been skittish, whinnying a warning that Josh had failed to heed. The stranger must have fired his pistol at precisely the same moment as Josh and Pankhurst. By the grace of God, Josh should be the one lying on the ground.

Pivoting on his heel, he stalked across the clearing to his fallen adversary.

David Pankhurst lay sprawled on his side like a broken puppet, his body half-twisted and one arm draped limply across his face. His portly retainer crouched nearby without making any attempt to give aid. His floppy brown hat hung awry, and his shoulders shook with sobs.

"Sweet heaven . . . sweet blessed heaven . . ."

Josh occasionally had witnessed such a reaction on the battlefield. The hardiest of soldiers could wilt in the face of bloodshed. But at the moment he had no patience for womanish wailing.

He dropped to his knees beside Pankhurst. As he bent over to examine the limp form, the servant gave a loud gasp.

"Nay, m'lord! 'Tain't right. Ye mustn't touch—"

"I only want to help him," Josh snapped. "I'm a trained doctor."

As he spoke, he unfastened the brass buttons on Pankhurst's greatcoat. The unconscious man wore a loose white shirt and plain brown breeches more suited to a stableboy than a man of fashion. Odd, but perhaps Pankhurst hadn't wished to ruin a good set of clothing. Odder still, Pankhurst appeared far less robust than Josh recalled. Or was it merely a trick of the dim light?

Spying no obvious blood, he untied the stiff white cravat and inserted his fingers, locating the artery in Pankhurst's throat. The skin was smooth, warm, soft. To his relief, a pulse throbbed, swift and thready.

Glancing up, he said tersely, "He's alive."

"Praise be!" the servant blubbered, tears streaking down his plump, country-bred face. "Oh, praise be to God!"

A certain falsetto tone to that voice distracted Josh. But having long ago suspected Pankhurst's predilections, he wasn't entirely surprised at the man's choice of a minion.

Taking care not to jostle Pankhurst, he gently grasped the man by the shoulder and rolled him onto his back. The limp arm fell away from his face, the movement dislodging the wide-brimmed beaver hat. It was then that Josh received his second blow of the morning.

Frozen in place, he stared down in shock.

An abundance of long, golden-brown hair spilled out of the hat. Blood stained one side of the tousled mane. But it was the face that snared Josh's attention. Those distinctive, fine-boned features didn't belong to David Pankhurst.

Cursing, Josh loosened the shirt and pushed his hand inside. He encountered satiny skin, a slim waist . . . and a band of cloth that wrapped the upper portion of the torso. As he explored the binding, there was no mistaking the small hills and valley of a feminine bosom.

He had dueled with a woman.

Chapter Two

An Unwelcome Guest

Alarm catapulted Anne to the surface of slumber. She had been dreaming of the dark figure of a man standing in the mist . . . the devil incarnate. The image faded under the vicious pounding in her head.

Lifting her lashes, she squinted against the brilliance of full sunlight. The radiance intensified the throbbing in her skull. Her head burned as if she'd fallen into a vat of fire. Feebly, she brought up her hand to shield her eyes.

Her fingers met the smoothness of linen covering her brow. To her puzzlement, she discovered a neatly tied bandage that encircled the top of her head. Had she hurt herself?

In a swift, excruciating glance, she recognized her spartan bedchamber: the battered armoire that held her clothing, the framed painting of wildflowers done by Mama, the wingback chair with the stuffing poking out of the cushion from a hole she'd never had the time to mend. The ordinary surroundings should have calmed her, yet her skin prickled from a latent uneasiness.

Why did she lie abed so late in the morning? Papa might want her to go to the lending library. Mama might be too preoccupied with painting her latest work of art to fetch his newspaper and coffee.

Shuttering her eyes against the infernal light, Anne struggled to draw herself up into a sitting position. She felt as weak as a newborn babe, all floppy limbs and uncoordinated movements. The simple act of lifting her chin made her dizzy.

Near the window, fabric rustled as someone drew the drapes. A blessed dimness shrouded the room, yet even that minimal light hurt. Then the muffled tramp of footsteps approached the bed.

As she turned to see who was there, a peculiar giddiness affected her vision. The bedposts doubled in number, as did the fireplace and the washstand with its chipped china pitcher, a hand-me-down from her youngest brother, Isaac, newly wed and living in town.

Anne shut her eyes again in an effort to control her nausea. She couldn't be ill. Papa always said she was as healthy as a prime mare. She took pride in never suffering fevers and sniffles like her brothers, in always being the reliable one, nursing her siblings through their childhood illnesses and caring for her aging parents.

She *had* to be well. Too many people depended on her.

Anne pushed back the coverlet that she had embroidered long ago for Abelard, the eldest, now an important barrister who disdained sentimental castoffs. As Anne prepared to stand up, a broad masculine hand settled onto her shoulder. "Easy now. You need to rest."

That low-pitched male voice startled her. It didn't belong to any of her nine brothers; they were all gone now, either married or adventuring in far-flung lands.

She turned her head too fast, battled another wave of dizziness, and lifted her blurry gaze to the tall man standing beside the bed. Twin images of him shifted back and forth. The gorge rose in her throat. For one horrible instant, she feared she'd died and gone straight to hell.

It was *him*. Lord Joshua Kenyon.

Memory slammed into her. The furtive ride through the darkness. The cold weight of the pistol in her perspiring palm. The hard knot of hatred inside her as she'd faced him across a misty field.

Why was he in her bedchamber?

She couldn't think, could only stare at him in suspended disbelief. Although she'd long known him by hearsay, Lord Joshua Kenyon was so much more than she'd expected. More handsome. More intense.

More intimidating.

His closeness struck her with a deep, resonant jolt. She had last viewed those forceful brown eyes from a distance of twenty paces. Now she could see flecks of gold glinting in his gaze. With his black hair mussed and the plain white shirt clinging to his muscled torso, he looked like the devil's gift to womankind.

"You—" she said, her voice weak and wobbly. "Get out . . . of my house!"

"Not until I have some answers."

His expression ruthless, he bent down as if to grab her. She scrambled toward the other side of the bed. But an upsurge of queasiness waylaid her and she doubled over, gagging.

Lord Joshua snatched up the empty chamber pot and thrust it in front of her. Just as she lost the remnants of her breakfast.

As the vile reflex subsided, she lay curled into a miserable ball, uncaring whether she lived or died. He fetched a glass of water from the bedside table and held it to her lips. "Rinse your mouth."

Too shaken to refuse, Anne obeyed and after a moment felt marginally better. Drawing gulps of air, she forced herself to sit up cautiously and hugged her knees to her bosom. The awful nausea remained at bay so long as she didn't make any sudden moves.

Lord Joshua strode to the door to deposit the chamber pot in the outer passageway. To her vague surprise, he exhibited no squeamishness. Her brothers would have held their noses and made rude comments. Not that she would say anything in his favor.

She felt humiliated by her weakness and appalled at her vulnerability. What did he intend to do to her? He wanted to punish her, of course. Men despised being tricked by women.

"I should have been sick all over you," she said in a raspy whisper.

Joshua Kenyon calmly replaced the glass on the table. "At least you're awake. You were out for nearly an hour. Your head must hurt like the very devil."

"I feel fine," she lied, though a rhythmic throbbing made it difficult to think. "You've no right to enter my chamber. If anyone finds you here—"

"You should have thought of that when you came after me with a gun." He leaned closer and displayed his open hand. She braced herself to evade his blow, to strike one of her own in retaliation. But he merely said, "How many fingers am I holding up?"

Anne blinked. His sleeves were rolled to the elbow, revealing strong forearms, the skin darkened by exposure to the sun. He had a large, well-shaped hand that might have been elegant if not for the calluses on his palm. His fingers were long, square-tipped, powerful.

Capable of throttling a woman.

Swallowing the sour dryness in her throat, she cast a desperate glance at the door. Her vision dipped and swayed. Mama and Papa couldn't know he was here. They would never leave alone with a strange man. "My father could walk in at any moment. Then you'll be in terrible trouble."

"How many fingers?" he repeated.

"Six," she said, only to keep him from bobbing his hand in front of her face. "No . . . four."

"Two," he corrected. "The bullet creased your skull, Miss Neville. You've suffered a concussion."

Anne gingerly touched the bandage that swathed the

crown of her head. She staved off a premonition of disaster. "So you know . . . who I am."

"I know you're not David Pankhurst." He flattened his palms on the bed and scrutinized her with the dark eyes of a scoundrel. "Tell me why he let you take his place."

"Why should I? You're the intruder here."

"And you're the imposter. I'm not in the habit of meeting women on the dueling field."

"I don't suppose you are," she said scathingly. "You prefer to break their hearts and abandon them. As you did Lily."

His face tightened. But when he spoke, he made no reference to the woman whom he had killed as surely as if he'd put a gun to her head and pulled the trigger. "Pankhurst is a puling coward for letting a female fight his battles."

"David is no coward! He didn't even know I took his place."

"Then tell me why you were there, pretending to be him."

How easily Lord Joshua had maneuvered her with his taunting. He'd forced her into a corner where the only way out was to give him the information he wanted, else he would believe the worst of David. "He lacks experience with guns," she admitted. "I feared for his life, so I put laudanum in his tea yesterday evening."

"But you didn't fear for *your* life."

"I never miss—or at least I haven't until now," she said bitterly. "Cyril taught me how to use a gun. He wins every shooting competition he enters."

"Cyril?"

"My brother." She paused, then added, "One of my *nine* brothers. If you don't leave immediately, I'll call for them. They'll thrash you to within an inch of your life. And I'll cheer them on."

Lord Joshua looked singularly unimpressed as he

straightened to his full, menacing height. "Bloodthirsty, aren't you?"

"Yes." He didn't need to know that she'd only meant to wing him, to teach him a lesson. "Benjamin outweighs you by two stone. Dorian took boxing lessons in London. Hugh has never lost a fistfight."

"Don't forget Cyril, the expert marksman."

Was Lord Joshua laughing at her? He was a narcissistic fool, then. "If I were you, I'd avoid tangling with any of us Nevilles. I'd leave here at once. And never return."

He lifted an eyebrow as if pondering her advice. She felt a fleeting relief when he turned and walked away. But he merely headed to the washstand and dipped a cloth in the water, wringing it out. Over his shoulder, he said, "Your brothers don't live here anymore."

Her heart sank. How had he seen through her ruse?

"Peg," Anne said on a stifled groan. She'd forgotten all about the loyal serving maid who had dressed in male costume and accompanied her to the duel. Of course, Peg must have led Lord Joshua here. No doubt she'd also blurted out Anne's rather humdrum history: that she had been born and raised in the village of Merryton-on-Sea on the outskirts of Brighton, that she'd never lived anywhere but this big, rambling house with its steep gables and narrow rooms, that she was an old maid of eight-and-twenty who, after helping to raise her brothers, now devoted herself to the care of her aging parents.

Lord Joshua would believe her to be easy prey.

"Yes, Peg," he confirmed. "If you're referring to that sniveling creature who was also garbed as a man."

As he returned to the bed, his keen gaze raked over Anne, making her aware of the shabby shirt and breeches she'd found while cleaning under Geoffrey's old bed. She glanced down to see several brown blotches on the rumpled linen shirt. Bloodstains, she thought, her insides contorting. Only then did she notice that someone had removed her coat and boots.

Him.

While she'd been insensible, Lord Joshua had put his hands on her. He'd had free rein to touch her as he willed. The thought of being at his mercy stoked a smoldering heat in the pit of her stomach. The heat of anger, the fire of vengeance.

"Where is Peg?" she demanded.

"I sent her on an errand."

"Blast you. You can't order my servants about."

"I'll do as I see fit."

"So you'll tramp on anyone who stands in your way. If there were any justice in this world, you would be dead."

"I'm sorry to disappoint you, then." Something glimmered in his eyes, but his smile was smooth, his tone commanding. "Lie down."

She stared at him, distracted by the way a mere curving of the lips could impart a devilish attractiveness to the harsh lines and angles of his face. That look fed the unwanted warmth in her secret parts. She wasn't so weak-spined as to feel an attraction to him, of course. But at least now she could see how he charmed gullible women.

Then she realized what he'd said.

Lie down. Did he mean to ravish her?

She leapt onto all fours and lunged away from him. But Lord Joshua caught her by the shoulders and used his superior strength to press her backward against the mound of feather pillows. Though her senses reeled and her head pounded, she remembered the self-protection skills taught to her by her brother Francis.

She jerked her knee up to catch her attacker in the groin.

He hissed out a curse. Instead of releasing her, he trapped her with his hard body against the mattress. She grabbed a hank of his hair and twisted hard. "Oaf! Let me go."

He didn't budge. When she tried to sink her teeth into his bare forearm, he caught both her wrists and imprisoned them above her head.

"Calm yourself," he grated. "I've no intention of hurting you—unless you force me to it."

With his free hand, he draped the wet cloth across her bandaged brow. The unexpected coolness soothed her aching temples but failed to ease her agitation. She was intensely aware of him as a man, his subtle spicy scent, his solidly muscled form, the measured beating of his heart against her bosom. The heat of him seeped through their clothing, and again she felt flushed and disoriented.

With all the firmness she could muster, she said, "Release me."

"Only if you promise to stay put."

"Why should I make any promises to the man who shot me?"

He stared down at her for another moment. Then he eased his hold on her and stood up, his face grim. "You're mistaken. That wasn't my bullet."

Anne pushed up on one elbow. "Do you take me for a fool—" Yet an elusive memory took shape in her mind. Once again, she stood in that misty clearing, seeing the handkerchief drop to the ground, her gaze intent on him as they brought up their pistols. "You fired . . . into the air. I saw you raise your arm."

He gave a curt nod.

Why had he done so? Had he been prepared to die? Why hadn't he wanted to defend himself against David? Those questions vanished under the onslaught of another, more important one. "Then I don't understand . . . whose bullet struck me?"

"There was another man. He was hiding in the underbrush."

Holding the cloth in place on her brow, Anne tried to absorb the unbelievable statement. She had no recollection of seeing any man but Lord Joshua Kenyon and his second. "You're saying . . . this man deliberately shot me?"

"Yes."

"How absurd. Who would do such a thing?"

"That's precisely what I intend to find out."

His purposeful tone chilled her. The last thing she wanted was for Lord Joshua Kenyon to linger here. Then her parents would find out the risk she'd taken. As it was, she'd have some nimble explaining to do when they saw her bandaged head. "He was a hunter gone astray, I'm sure. It was an accident."

"We'll see," he said. "My servant has gone after the man."

"Then you'd best hurry back to where we dueled. Else he won't know where you've gone."

He smiled slightly as if amused by her obvious attempt to evict him. "I sent your maid to wait for Harrington. I'm staying right here until I know you're out of danger."

"Danger," she groused, flinging aside the cold compress. She sat up so quickly that spots swirled before her eyes. By force of will, she concentrated her gaze on Lord Joshua. "The only danger is *you.* So leave this house at once. You aren't welcome here."

"Anne Aurora Neville!" a familiar voice cried out. "My gracious, whatever is going on here?"

Chapter Three

Mrs. Neville's Invitation

A sense of doom struck the breath from Anne's lungs. She looked over to see her mother standing in the doorway of the bedchamber. Rosy color suffused those plump cheeks. Mrs. Lenora Neville clutched a tea tray and the china rattled, evidence of her agitated state of mind.

"Mama! I—I can explain . . ."

Anne swung her legs off the bed. Her stockinged toes curled against the cold floorboards, and her head swam with dizziness. She groped for the bedpost to steady herself.

By the time she could see straight, Lord Joshua had taken the tray from her mother, set it on a table, and offered his arm to her. Mama leaned trustingly on him as if he were a true gentleman rather than a cad of the worst ilk. A white cap of fine Brussels lace perched atop her gray curls. She had discarded her usual paint-spattered apron and old dress in favor of her Sunday-best maroon gown.

There could be only one reason for her faultless attire— and for the tea tray laden with her most precious porcelain pot, the one with the tiny pink roses that Papa had given her on the occasion of their twenty-fifth wedding anniversary. Mama must have already known that Lord Joshua Kenyon was here.

Dear heaven, what had he told her?

"I should like to sit near my daughter," Mrs. Neville said to him. "I've been ever so worried about her."

"Of course." Lord Joshua moved the old wing chair closer to the bed. "May I say, she's going to be fine. You left her in good hands."

Hah, Anne thought. She burned to voice her scathing opinion of him, but hesitated to upset her mother any further. "I'm on the mend, Mama, really I am. You mustn't distress yourself."

Stout as any woman who'd borne ten children, Mama settled down, wheezing a little as she gazed worriedly at Anne. "How can you say that, darling? You've suffered a horrid injury. Your poor head . . ."

"Never mind me," Anne said, noticing her mother's labored breathing. "You're flushed. Is your dyspepsia bothering you? I can fetch your tonic."

"Stay right where you are," Lord Joshua commanded, glaring at her. "Your mother is only weary from walking up the stairs with a heavy tea tray." Turning, he gave Mrs. Neville a cordial smile that masked his treacherous nature. "The pot of tea would have been sufficient. You needn't have bothered with those extra plates of sandwiches and cakes."

"Nonsense, men are always hungry," Mrs. Neville said, her face brightening as she looked up at him. "I should know, for I raised nine boys."

Watching her mother simper, Anne perched on the edge of the bed. Had he told Mama about the duel? Surely not. Then what explanation *had* he offered her? "You must be wondering why there's a strange man here in my chamber," she said. "I can't blame you for being distraught when you walked in—"

"Nay, 'twas your manner of speaking that shocked me. To hear you tell his lordship that he isn't welcome here." Mrs. Neville cast another worshipful look at Lord Joshua. "Pray excuse my daughter's harsh words, m'lord. She must not realize the kindness you've done for her."

All charm and graciousness, he bowed. "No offense taken, Mrs. Neville. I'm sure that crack on the head temporarily addled her senses."

Anne opened her mouth to assert that her senses were in perfect order when her mother said, "Anne, dear, have you two been properly introduced? This is Captain Lord Joshua Kenyon, brother to the Marquess of Stokeford. Lord Joshua is a hero of our triumphant victory over Napoleon. He saved your life this morning."

Hero? Savior? Anne gripped the bedpost. "What exactly did he tell you?"

"I had no choice but to relate every unfortunate detail." Lord Joshua's mouth bore the hint of a smirk. "Forgive me for revealing your secret."

"Secret?"

"Don't you remember?" her mother said. "You went out riding early this morning in all that nasty fog. And in boy's clothing, no less. I thought you'd outgrown the need to behave like your brothers."

"It's . . . easier to ride in breeches," Anne improvised.

"But what if the neighbors had seen you? I can only imagine what that pesky Mrs. McPhee would say. Or that busybody Mrs. Tinniswood."

"I—I'd planned to return before anyone was up and about."

"You returned sorely injured, that's what." Mrs. Neville fanned herself with the lace edge of her fichu. "Mercy me, you gave me quite a start. I rose early so that I might paint by the morning light"—she smiled at Lord Joshua—"I like to dabble in oils and watercolors. You can see one of my works on the wall over there."

He walked over to view the painting that hung above the fireplace. "You've captured the harebells with superb accuracy."

"Why, thank you," Mrs. Neville said with a modest blush. "Well, then, back to my story. That's when I happened to look out my window. I nearly swooned with fright when I saw his lordship striding up the front steps, carrying you in his arms, Anne. He told me that you'd . . ." She paused, her face stricken.

Anne's head whirled with suspense. "That I'd what?"

"That you'd neglected to have a groom accompany you," Lord Joshua said smoothly. "You took a tumble from your horse. It was sheer good luck that I happened to be riding past."

"A tumble," Anne murmured in relief. "I see."

"You struck your head on a rock." Mrs. Neville clasped her hands to her generous bosom. "Gracious, there was so much blood. You were so limp and pale that I feared you might be . . . oh, I can't say it . . ." Her voice caught on a sob.

Lord Joshua passed her a folded handkerchief from his pocket. She dabbed at her watery hazel eyes, then loudly blew her nose.

Anne floundered in guilt and remorse. She wanted to get up and embrace her mother, but the effort of letting go of the bedpost seemed too strenuous. "I'm sorry, Mama. I never meant to worry you."

"Nor did she mean for you to find out about her foolish behavior," Lord Joshua added. "I trust she's learned her lesson."

He sent Anne a pointed scowl, and she scowled back. Blast him for treating her like a naughty child! If it hadn't been for him calling on David yesterday, offering his sham condolences, none of this would have occurred.

"I don't usually behave like such a watering pot," Mrs. Neville said, twisting the handkerchief in her paint-spotted hands. "But I can't bear to think of losing my only daughter. Whatever would Papa and I do without you, Anne?"

"Shh, Mama. It won't happen again. You have my word on that."

But her mother continued to fret. "Who would mix my colors? Who would search out flowers for me to paint?

Who would remember to return your dear papa's books to the lending library?"

"I would," Anne said. "I'm not going anywhere."

"You're my dearest companion, the only one of my children left to me. The boys simply don't come to visit as often as they ought."

"They're here every Sunday for dinner," Anne patiently reminded her. "And all the holidays, too. During the week, Hugh sometimes comes by to see us—"

"With his mending, because no one can sew as cunningly as you."

"—and Benjamin often brings his children to visit—"

"Because they love the stories you read to them."

"—and Cyril joins us for tea whenever he's in town—"

"Whenever he runs out of that delicious damson jam you make." Mrs. Neville sighed. "Indeed, you're a treasure beyond compare. There's nothing like a daughter's touch around the house. Don't you agree, m'lord?"

Was Mama trying to do some matchmaking? The possibility boggled Anne's mind. Surely she was mistaken.

"I bow to your superior experience," Lord Joshua said, pouring a cup of steaming tea. "I've only brothers, and my parents are deceased."

Anne felt an involuntary clutch of curiosity. How many brothers did he have? As swiftly as the thought had arisen, she stifled it. She already knew the essentials of his character—that he was a knave who would abandon his weeping bride, that he had a knack for beguiling women from London to Luxembourg.

Glowering, she watched that charm in action as he handed her mother the cup of tea. "For you, ma'am."

"Thank you," Mama said, "but truly, you mustn't wait upon me. What sort of hostess will you think me?"

"I think you're a devoted mother who's suffered quite a shock."

Anne compressed her lips. Mama would have far more urgent need of her smelling salts if she knew that he was the man who had left Lily Pankhurst standing at the altar.

Mrs. Neville took a sip from the fine china cup. "Tell me, m'lord, how long will it take for Anne to recover?"

"She has an ugly gash, but it's clean and should heal nicely. I recommend that she be confined to bed for a fortnight."

"A fortnight! That's ridiculous!" The outburst made Anne's head throb anew. "I'll be up and about by this afternoon."

His arms folded across his broad chest, Lord Joshua fixed her with a stare. "You'll do as I say. Head injuries are not to be taken lightly."

"Who are you to tell me so?"

"Why, didn't you know?" Mrs. Neville said, a smile wobbling past her melancholy. "Not only is he a war hero, he's a trained physician."

"All that and a nobleman, too," Anne said acerbically.

"Why, yes," her mother said with bright-eyed interest, "and isn't it a marvelous coincidence that he of all men would have found you? We owe your life to his medical skills."

Coincidence, indeed. It was a diabolically clever lie, the perfect way to entrench himself in her bedchamber. No wonder Mama hadn't objected to his presence here. A doctor was supposed to be trustworthy, respectable, sincere.

"So you've devoted your life to healing," Anne said, letting sarcasm creep into her voice. "Where did you study?"

"In field hospitals on the Continent. Although I served in the cavalry, I also pursued the practice of medicine."

"Then you're both a killer and a healer." In the same breath, she was shocked at her callousness. For all that she disliked him, he had fought to preserve the freedom of their country.

Lord Joshua stood watching her for a moment of charged silence. Anne had learned the hard way from dealing with her brothers that if she showed any sign of weakness, they would take swift advantage. But she apologized anyway. "I'm sorry. That remark was uncalled for."

He inclined his head in stone-faced acceptance. "It's a dichotomy that can't be understood by those who haven't gone to war."

Against her will, she felt the tug of shame and compassion. "I'm sure you're right. Now, you must have places to go. Don't let us keep you."

"Quite the contrary. I'm at loose ends at the moment." His cool gaze warmed as he turned to her mother and said, "Ma'am, my patient should be kept under strict observation for the next few days. If it's agreeable to you, I intend to find lodging nearby in order to keep an eye on her."

"You're the soul of kindness," Mrs. Neville gushed. "But I insist that you stay with us as our guest, m'lord. I won't hear of you renting a room when we've so many empty ones now that my sons are gone."

"Thank you," he said. "I accept your offer."

The bargain was made before Anne could form a coherent protest. "That's . . . that's impossible," she stuttered. "We can't be entertaining while I'm ill. Who will prepare a room?"

"Why, Peg, of course," Mama said as she heaved herself out of the chair. "If ever I can find the lazy chit."

Anne wished her mother luck. "But what about Papa? He's busy with his studies, and he doesn't care for visitors."

"Nonsense, 'tis only our rambunctious grandchildren who drive him into his study for a bit of peace and quiet. But he does enjoy learned company." Mama looked brightly at Lord Joshua. "Do you know much about history? It's a particular interest of my husband's."

"I studied at Oxford," Lord Joshua said. "It would be a pleasure to talk to him."

Anne feared that Lord Joshua would slip and reveal the truth to her father. "Nevertheless, I'm sure our humble house isn't up to lordly standards."

Lord Joshua's expression held an edge of irony. "My

needs are few, Miss Neville. You see, I spent the past fifteen years in the military. Any accommodation with a roof
will seem like a palace to me."

Mrs. Neville beamed. "Excellent. Oh, just wait until
Mrs. McPhee and Mrs. Tinneswood hear the news. Fancy,
the brother of the Marquess of Stokeford staying in *my*
house."

Agog with excitement, she hastened to the doorway,
where she paused to add, "Do heed his lordship, Anne.
He'll have you feeling well again in no time. But mind,
you leave the bedchamber door open. The proprieties must
be observed." Smiling at Lord Joshua with unwarranted
trust, she left them alone.

He strolled to the table, poured another cup of tea, and
stirred in a pinch of sugar. A sense of unreality worsened
the pounding of Anne's head. She felt floored by his deft
maneuvering of her mother, aghast at the prospect of
having him as a houseguest, and angered by his presump-
tuousness.

Nothing had gone according to plan. By all rights, he
should have been the injured party, groaning in pain from
the wound inflicted by her pistol. He should be far away
from here, too, and unaware that he'd been shot by a
woman. Instead, her scheme to avenge David's beloved sister had taken an unforeseen and dangerous turn.

What purpose could Lord Joshua have for insinuating
himself into this household? He must be plotting revenge.

Holding the cup, he walked toward the bed. A quiver
skulked down her spine, but she concealed her uneasiness
behind a show of scorn. "That performance of yours was
quite cunning," she said. "Shall I address you as m'lord?
Or Dr. Kenyon?"

"Call me Josh. All my friends do."

"No, thank you, *Doctor*. You may go now. Your very
presence makes me ill."

"A pity for you, then. Your mother would be vastly disappointed by my departure."

"My mother doesn't see your true nature. She's always had a blind spot for the male of the species."

"Or perhaps she sees the truth—that I wish only to help you." He stopped directly in front of Anne, hunkering down so that she had little choice but to meet his bold, dark gaze. He lifted the cup to her. "Have a sip, Miss Neville."

She slapped at his hand. "I want nothing from you."

Too easily, he averted the cup without spilling a drop. "It isn't poison. Would you reject tea made by your mother with her own two hands?"

"Take it—and yourself—away from here."

He made a sound halfway between a snort and a chuckle. "I must say, I've had some irascible patients before. But none to match you."

With that, he lifted the porcelain cup to her mouth. She was taken aback by his sheer audacity. Steam from the tea warmed her upper lip. A faint, delectably sweet aroma drifted to her nose. She could almost taste the liquid on her tongue, easing the dryness in her throat, soothing her headache.

Then he smiled. That slow arc of his lips brought a gleam to his eyes and sincerity to his countenance. Thick lashes lent a touch of softness to his bluntly masculine features. He had a thin blade of a nose, high cheekbones, and a wicked-looking scar that she hadn't noticed before on the underside of his jaw. His shaven cheeks bore the hint of dark whisker growth, and she had the shocking impulse to touch that bristly roughness.

"Go on," he murmured, his voice smooth as silk. "It'll help you feel better."

Had he read her thoughts? Did he want her to touch him?

The tea, she realized. He meant for her to take a sip.

Her head burned abominably, making mincemeat of her willpower. Despite her best efforts, the resistance flowed out of her like water through a sieve. A treacherous lethargy came over her as she was drawn to the comfort he offered.

Ever so slowly, she tilted her head and parted her lips. The fragrant vapor fed her senses just as the hot liquid met her mouth.

The slamming of a door downstairs intruded. The hollow sound of voices came from the foyer. A man's sharp, urgent tone carried upward on a draft of air.

Anne gripped the bedpost. Her heart lurched against her breastbone as that voice brought her sharply back to reality.

Crouching before her, Lord Joshua turned his dark head in a listening pose. His smile died, sapping all warmth from his harsh features. How could she have forgotten, even for a moment, that he was the enemy?

Footsteps pounded up the stairs. On a rush of panic, she said, "Blast you for not going away. Now David's here."

Chapter Four

The Promise

Josh set aside the teacup and vaulted to his feet as David Pankhurst stalked into the bedchamber.

Pankhurst stopped short. His fair, curly hair was disheveled and his cravat dangled loosely from his collar. Golden stubble marked his square jaw. Usually a meticulous dresser, he looked as if he'd donned his unbuttoned yellow coat and gray pantaloons while dashing out of the house.

His wild blue eyes sought out Anne. "My God! Are you all right?"

Using the bedpost as a lever, Anne stood up. Her face had an unhealthy pallor beneath the bandage, and the bloodstained shirt and boy's breeches enhanced her willowy stature. "David," she said in a mollifying tone, "I'm fine, really I am. Let me tell you what's happened."

But Pankhurst was no longer listening; he glowered at Josh. "What have you done to her?"

"I brought Miss Neville home," Josh said. "She shouldn't have been out fighting your battles."

"Knave! You shot her." His face contorting with fury, Pankhurst launched himself across the bedchamber.

In a nimble sidestep, Josh evaded the attack. He caught Pankhurst's arm in mid-swing and wrenched it backward. Pankhurst fought hard but inexpertly, getting in a wild

punch that glanced off Josh's cheekbone. Ignoring the explosion of pain, Josh tightened his grip. He wrestled the
man facedown onto the bed and planted his knee against
the small of Pankhurst's back.

It was over in a matter of moments. Pankhurst squirmed
in vain, panting for air. "Damn you!" he said, his voice
somewhat muffled by the bedcovers. "Damn you to the fires
of Hades."

"Guard your mouth. There's a lady present." Josh gave
that wiry arm an extra twist.

Pankhurst yelped.

Anne uttered a strangled sound. "Beast! You're hurting
him!"

"So I am." Josh glanced over to see her swaying on her
feet, her face as white as the linen that wrapped her brow.
"Sit down. Now."

She didn't obey, of course. Rushing at him, she leapt
onto his back and locked her arms around his neck in a
chokehold.

Josh staggered, thrown off-balance by the unexpected
burden of her. Despite her impairment, she gripped him
with throttling force, cutting off the air to his lungs. With
his free hand, he grabbed her forearm while maintaining a
grip on Pankhurst. The three of them struggled in silence,
Pankhurst against Josh, Josh against Anne.

Caught in the middle, Josh fought for breath. Spots
swam before his eyes. The rules of gentlemanly conduct
drilled into him by his grandmother prohibited him from
using brute force on any female.

So he employed a gentle touch instead. He reached
around and caressed the flattened curve of one breast. When
she gasped and flinched away, he took instant advantage.
He tilted sideways and flipped her beside Pankhurst on the
bed.

She lay limp and panting. Her golden-brown hair spilled
around her shoulders and down to the waistband of those
ridiculous breeches. Within her thin stockings, her toes

were curled in a curiously vulnerable pose. From his view straight down at her, he caught a glimpse of the small, swathed bosom inside her gaping shirt.

His body responded with a surprising surge of lust. For an instant, fantasy filled him with the craving to take her on this bed, both of them naked, their hot flesh joined in wild, uninhibited lovemaking.

Just as quickly, he discounted the image. He preferred his women to be lush, feminine, biddable. He felt a strong attraction to this hellion only because it had been months since he'd taken his pleasure between a woman's soft thighs. Months of hard campaigning, catching sleep when and where he could, drilling his troops for the final battle. There had been neither the time nor the opportunity to indulge his base instincts.

He wouldn't do so with Anne Neville, either. She was far more likely to cut off his cock with a dull blade than welcome a romp with him.

Her cheeks flushed, she glared up at him. "You . . . *lout.*"

"I've been called worse."

"That move always worked with my brothers."

"I'll wager your brothers never used *my* move." He knew she remembered him touching her breast, and he relished the outrage that sparked in her eyes. "I'll release Pankhurst if you both promise to relax and listen."

She regarded him with livid distrust. Josh expected her to quarrel further, but she merely rolled onto her side, facing his prisoner. Reaching out, she brushed back a lock of Pankhurst's hair. In a softened tone, she said, "We may as well let him speak, David. It's the only way to get rid of him."

Pankhurst gritted his teeth. "All right."

She lifted her gaze to Josh, and her warm manner cooled again. "There, m'lord. You've managed to subdue a wounded woman and a man recovering from an overdose of laudanum. Are you satisfied?"

"Hardly," Josh said with a jab of dark humor. He was

struck by the display of affection between her and Pankhurst. Was there more to her interest in Pankhurst than mere
friendship? Mulling over the thought, he released Pankhurst
and stepped back, keeping a watch on the younger man.

Pankhurst sat up on the bed and attempted to tidy his
crooked cravat and wrinkled coat. Indignation underscored
his rigid movements, and high color tinged his cheeks.
While Anne helped Pankhurst straighten his collar, Josh
was struck by their similarity in coloring and physique. It
pacified him somewhat for failing to see through her cha-
rade on the dueling field. Superficially, they shared a closer
resemblance than even Pankhurst and Lily, for his sister
had had dark hair and a slight, though curvaceous form that
had attracted hordes of men.

"Please don't be angry at me," Anne said gently to Pankhurst. "When I tell you what's happened—"

"Why should I listen? You drugged my tea last evening."

Her face came alive with emotions: regret, tenderness,
pleading. So her feelings for Pankhurst *did* delve deeper
than friendship. His tumbled gold curls and moody countenance gave Pankhurst the sort of tragic air that would
appeal to impressionable young ladies. From the adoring
look Anne cast at him, she ranked first among those misguided legions. Her naïveté nudged forth an unwelcome
sympathy in Josh. She didn't know Pankhurst as well as
she thought she did.

As if Pankhurst were the injured party, she leaned closer
to him, laying her hand on his forearm. "Pray forgive me.
I only wanted to help you. To guarantee that Lily's death
was avenged."

"That was *my* right, not yours."

"But I've had more experience with guns. Cyril tutored
me, remember?"

"Little good it did you," Pankhurst said with an offended
air. "Even your perfect marksmanship was no match for the
devil himself."

"But that's what I'm trying to tell you, David. Lord Joshua didn't shoot me. He fired into the air."

Pankhurst flashed a frosty look at Josh, who leaned against the washstand and regarded them with disdain. "He deloped? Impossible."

"Believe it," Josh said, knowing how implausible it sounded. He wouldn't have accepted it himself had he not been there to witness the event. "A man concealed himself in the bushes—"

"He might have been a hunter," Anne broke in. "His bullet struck me by accident."

"Balderdash." Jumping to his feet, Pankhurst brushed the wrinkles from his breeches. He spoke to Anne while glaring at Josh. "I'm sure that's the story he told you."

"Miss Neville took a bullet meant for you," Josh stated. "I would think you'd want to do everything in your power to track down the gunman."

"Track him? He was *your* minion, no doubt. You ordered him to ambush me in the event you missed."

Keeping a tight rein on his temper, Josh propped one foot on a stool. "On the contrary, I was hoping *you* could tell me his identity."

"I?" Pankhurst imbued the word with supreme skepticism.

"Yes. Whom did you tell about the duel?"

"No one."

"Miss Neville knew."

"His servant came to borrow a brace of dueling pistols," Anne said. "I insisted he tell me why David needed them."

"There, you see," Josh said to Pankhurst. "If she heard, so might someone else. Someone who wanted to ensure your death."

"What twaddle," Pankhurst said. "This is a shabby attempt to divert suspicion from yourself."

"People often have secrets," Josh persisted. "The question is, what are *you* hiding?"

That ill-tempered blue gaze flickered away. The pause

lasted for a mere three ticks of the small clock on the bedside table. Then Pankhurst tugged at his uneven cravat.
"May I remind you, I'm not the one on trial here."

"Neither am I. Yet surely you'll cooperate with me in
finding the sniper."

"Stop badgering David," Anne said heatedly. Propped
against the bedpost, she appeared wan and defenseless in
the dimness of the drawn draperies. Her hands clenched the
coverlet so hard that her knuckles went white. "We've been
the best of friends for five years. I assure you, he has no
secrets from me."

Josh bit back a snort. "Then explain how a hunter happened to fire at the exact moment we did," he said. "A
hunter wearing a black hooded cloak."

"Perhaps he was a poacher."

"Poachers don't ride fine steeds. Nor do the gentry hunt
alone and so near the beach. No, this was a deliberate act.
By someone who knew Pankhurst was meeting me this
morning." He directed his attention to the angry young
man. "The question is, who?"

Pankhurst remained stubbornly silent.

"Someone on your staff must have overheard your foolish challenge to me yesterday," Josh mused. "The news
could have been spread over all the neighborhood by nightfall."

"Perhaps your servants gossip, but mine are loyal."

"David and his father lead a quiet country life," Anne
added. "Their few retainers have served Lord Timberlake
for many years."

"If you believe they don't gossip," Josh said, "you know
little of human nature."

"I certainly know more than you!"

"Then you'll agree that the desire to pass along news is
a powerful stimulus. You yourself said that a servant told
you about the duel."

"Only because I'm a close friend of David's."

Seeing he would get nowhere with the argument, Josh

said, "Then allow me to suggest another possibility. Perhaps the gunman knew *you* were disguised as Pankhurst."

Pankhurst bristled. "See here now, Kenyon. You've gone far enough."

For once, Anne paid him no heed. Her widened eyes latched onto Josh. "Are you suggesting . . . he wanted to kill *me*?"

"It's a prospect we can't ignore."

"How absurd! Who would wish me harm? The dairyman for neglecting to leave our empty milk bottles on the stoop? Or perhaps the greengrocer for bruising one of his apples?" She snapped her fingers. "No, I'm sure it was the curate because I skipped church last Sunday when Mama was ill."

Josh cleared his throat to cover a chuckle. Indignation lit a flare of beauty over Anne's unadorned features, but he doubted she'd welcome him saying so. Nor did he truly suspect her of being the object of murder. She was too ingenuous to lead a secret life.

"There's another probability," Anne stated. "Perhaps the gunman was aiming for *you,* m'lord."

He'd already considered—and rejected—the possibility. The men under his former command bore him goodwill for bringing them safely home. And he'd been back in England for only a few days, hardly long enough to have incurred the lethal wrath of any civilian.

Except for Pankhurst himself.

"The bullet struck *you,* Miss Neville. You, in the guise of David Pankhurst."

Pankhurst peeled off his glove and advanced on Josh. "I know what you're about, Kenyon. You're hoping I'll forget your cruelty to Lily. For that, I demand satisfaction—again. We shall meet at dawn tomorrow." Then he lifted his hand as if to slap the glove against Josh's cheek.

Josh seized Pankhurst's wrist in a bone-crushing grip. "Have a care whom you strike."

"Enough, both of you!" Anne pushed to her feet. She stood, swaying, her fingers pressed to her bandaged brow.

In a strained tone, she went on. "David, I won't let you risk your life . . ."

Shoving Pankhurst aside, Josh crossed the room in an instant, his bootheels thudding on the bare wood floor. He slipped his hands beneath her arms to steady her. She was tall for a woman, and her muscles quivered as if she struggled against collapse. "You've had enough excitement for one day," he said. "Lie down."

"No . . . more . . . duels."

"As you wish."

Anne blinked, her gaze quarrelsome in the pale oval of her face. "Do you mean that?"

He stared straight into those disquieting violet-blue eyes. "Yes. The fool can slap me all day and I won't fight him."

He could feel the doubts radiating from her, surrounding her like a fiery nimbus. Her enmity intrigued him. He'd always had his pick of women, a fact that had made him the butt of ribald amusement in the cavalry. While he took shameless advantage of the benefits of having a handsome face and an impeccable lineage, Josh had had to work harder to earn the esteem of the men under his command. Now he found himself strangely drawn to the challenge of winning Anne Neville, too.

"Cad!" Pankhurst burst out. "Unhand her."

To Josh's surprise, she waved him away. "It's all right, David. He's a doctor."

Pankhurst snorted. "He's a killer, that's what."

Ignoring him, Josh deftly maneuvered Anne to the bed. "You're not to get up any more today. That's an order."

She plunked down on the edge of the mattress and repeated, "So long as you'll fight no more duels. I'll have your promise, too, David."

"Don't be ridiculous," Pankhurst blustered. "Kenyon abandoned Lily. He broke her heart and sent her to her grave."

"I haven't forgotten," she said, flashing an aggrieved

look at Josh. "But shots already have been fired. That should be the end of it."

"Lily's dead, and he's alive. It's far from over."

"You must set aside your vengeance," she said fervently. "Don't you see? I couldn't bear it if you were hurt . . . or killed."

"Dash it all," Pankhurst grumbled. "You shouldn't ask such a promise of me."

"Nevertheless I must."

When she reached for his hand, Josh intercepted her outstretched arm. It irked him to see such a strong and self-reliant woman cater to Pankhurst's patronizing manner.

He placed his thumb against the tender flesh of her inner wrist. Then he took out his pocketwatch, flipped open the gold cover, and timed her heartbeats. "Do as she says, Pankhurst. Her pulse rate is far too swift."

Anne wrested her hand free. "And you, sir," she said, scowling at Josh. "I hope I can trust your word."

"My time is better spent finding our mysterious gunman," he said, closing the pocketwatch and putting it away. "But if you like, I'll give you my promise—again."

After searching his face, she nodded. "Now you, David." She lowered her voice to a throaty murmur. "Please, I'm begging you."

To his credit, Pankhurst appeared affected by her heartfelt sentiment. He dipped his chiseled jaw and let out a huff of breath. "All right, then," he said grudgingly. "Though only for the sake of your health."

Her face lit up with the hopeful smile of a besotted woman. "Thank you."

That glow caused an unwanted tenderness in Josh. She wanted what she couldn't have, he thought cynically. A pity she didn't understand why her regard wasn't returned. But it wasn't his place to tell her.

"M-m'lord?" The cautious voice came from the doorway. It was Peg, garbed in an untidy brown frock and voluminous white apron that made her resemble a giant turnip.

Wringing her stubby fingers, she bobbed a curtsy. "Please, sir, ye must come down to the kitchen at once. Yer man, Mr. Harrington, he's come back. He says he's got somethin' for ye."

A surge of purpose swept through Josh. With any luck, Harry had discovered the sniper's identity.

Josh flashed David Pankhurst a quelling glance. "You have five minutes. Then I want you gone. My patient needs her rest."

Chapter Five

The Ultimatum

Anne watched Lord Joshua stride out of the chamber. As the click of his footsteps faded, she felt gripped by a curiosity that outweighed her anger. Had his servant caught the gunman? She wanted to get up, to follow Lord Joshua and find out, but her head ached too badly and she dreaded a return of that awful nausea. It had been mortifying enough in front of Lord Joshua.

"Audacious devil." David smacked his fist into his palm. "He's giving orders as if he lives here."

"He does," she admitted in frustration. "At least temporarily."

For several heartbeats, David gawked at her. "I beg your pardon?"

"It's true, I'm afraid. Mama invited him to stay while I recuperate."

"Blast it all! Didn't you tell her he's a cad?"

"She wouldn't listen. You know how Mama admires the nobility."

"Kenyon is lower than a worm. I'll set her straight on that matter." Pivoting on his heel, David started toward the door.

"No, please!" As he turned back, frowning, Anne tried to fathom her reluctance. "I'm sure Mama has already told half the neighborhood. I—I couldn't bear to disappoint her."

"She must know the truth. Kenyon is a menace to decent women."

"It's only for a few days. Then he'll be gone for good."

David gave her a look that conveyed his disappointment in her, a look that made her feel abashed and somehow guilty. "I cannot abide his presence. Nor would you if you knew all that he's done to my family."

"I do know! It makes me furious, too."

He continued as if she hadn't spoken. "You never witnessed his shabby treatment of Lily. The rascal promised her eternal love. He charmed her, wooed her, won her. And then—"

"Then he abandoned her," Anne recited, having heard the story many times before. "He ended their betrothal on the eve of their wedding. It was utterly reprehensible of him."

"Yes," David bit out. He gripped the edge of the battered desk she used for paying bills and writing her mother's correspondence. "I found my sister weeping in her bedchamber, trembling from shock. She told me that Kenyon had shattered her heart and left her to face the shame of being spurned."

Sympathy and rage twisted inside Anne. If only she'd been there, perhaps she could have helped Lily overcome her despair. But the blow had been struck in London seven years ago, before David and his family had moved to Brighton. Before Anne had met David at church and discovered they both enjoyed singing in the choir, collecting seashells along the beach, and taking rides through the countryside.

"Lord Joshua is indeed a callous man," Anne began.

"Callous! He might as well have held a gun to her head. It would have been a more merciful end."

David's agitation alarmed Anne. Even though Lord Joshua had fired into the air that morning, he might turn vicious if another duel were fought. She shuddered at the image of David lying in a cold, misty field, blood soaking his white shirt, his beautiful blue eyes closed forever. "Please, David, set aside your anger. He'll be gone from here soon, never to trouble us again."

David paced in long, furious steps. "I can't forget so easily," he said through clenched teeth. "There's something I haven't told you. Something about Kenyon and my sister."

"You can tell me anything."

"All right, then. It's imperative that you understand just how vile he is. He made lewd advances toward my sister. When she refused him, he set out to seduce Lily's companion, her dearest friend, Catherine."

The unspeakable act stunned Anne. On a quick, indrawn breath, she whispered, "You can't mean . . ."

"Yes, my sister discovered them together on the day before the nuptials. He had the gall to blame his actions on Lily for refusing to share his bed before they were properly wed."

Anne's stomach curdled. Lord Joshua had attempted to dishonor his bride-to-be. When that had failed, he'd turned his carnal attentions to Lily's good friend. How could he have had the effrontery to commit such an offense? And on the eve of his wedding, no less!

Recalling the illicit brush of his fingers on her breast, Anne felt flushed from head to toe. Yes, he was a man who would dare anything.

David surged around the room as if driven by a storm of emotion. "I've shocked you," he said tersely. "Such a tale is too indelicate for a lady's ears. But telling you the truth is the only way to convince you of Kenyon's base nature."

She had thought him foolhardy for instigating the duel. Now, she could see why he'd sought Lord Joshua's blood. "I can't blame you for being distraught."

"Distraught, bah. I'm outraged." Flexing his fists, he made another circuit of the dimly lit bedchamber. "While

Kenyon fled to the Continent, Lily was left to hang her head in shame. To endure the whispers, the speculation, the ghastly fate of being abandoned. He'd broken his vow to her, yet she was the one who suffered."

Anne felt a rush of ill will toward Lord Joshua. "Lily shouldn't have mourned the loss of such a contemptible man. She should have held her head high."

"Lily wasn't like you," David said, stopping at the fireplace and staring down at the cold hearth. "She wasn't robust and courageous. She was sweet and delicate. Like her namesake bloom."

"The perfect woman," Anne murmured. Instantly she bit her lip to silence her sarcasm. What had gotten into her to be so callous?

But if David noticed the vinegar in her voice, he showed no reaction to it. He looked lost in memories, and she acknowledged a bitter envy in herself. She wanted to be sweet and delicate, too, rather than tall, outspoken, pragmatic, capable of handling any crisis. Growing up, she'd had to be forceful in a household of unruly brothers who were all bigger and stronger than she.

If only she knew how to be more biddable, agreeable, feminine. Was that why David had never regarded her as more than a friend?

Burying her selfish thoughts, she groped for understanding. "I can only imagine the torment Lily must have endured. And how difficult it must have been for you, too."

"My sister sank into a decline. Day after day, she didn't eat or sleep. Zounds! If you could have seen her . . ."

Anne had to close her eyes; his pacing made her dizzy. But he had a need to voice his volatile thoughts, so she encouraged him. "She must have grown steadily weaker."

"Yes," David said, and by the sound of his voice, he stood near the curtained window. "She became listless, so painfully slender I could see her bones. She had no interest in parties, the *ton,* the London scene. At last, I knew I had to take drastic measures. I convinced our father to purchase

Greystone Manor in the hopes that a sojourn in the sea air might stir her back to life."

"Greystone is indeed a beautiful home." Against her closed lids, Anne pictured the thickets of oak trees that shaded the stately, secluded house. The lush setting like an oasis in the stark landscape of the coast.

"We were lucky to procure such a jewel. Father and I gave Lily everything that might restore her happiness." David made a sound like the long, mournful sighing of the wind. "But in the end, it didn't matter. Nothing mattered."

Anne felt an unexpected twinge of impatience that David could not conquer his grief. Appalled at herself, she said, "You made her final days happy. Lily loved the house and the grounds, the sound of the surf. You said so yourself."

"Yes, she did seem to rally for a time. On warm days she liked to sit outside on the verandah. Or I'd carry her up to the hill overlooking the gardens."

"There's a marvelous view of the house and the ocean."

"Lily thought so, too. But by then, she had wasted away to nothing. She could scarce lift her head to smile at me. When the end came . . ." His voice deepened, throaty with emotion. "Father and I had her buried on that hill. So that she would rest eternally overlooking the sea."

A tightness in her throat, Anne opened her eyes. David stood in the shadowy corner, his head bowed and his shoulders sagging. How she wanted to brush back the fair curl that drooped onto his high brow. How she wished he would take her in his arms and let her comfort him. But she could give him only words.

"You did your best," she murmured. "Your sister has gone to her heavenly reward, to a place where she can be happy, free of pain, infinitely loved. Now you must let her rest in peace."

Averting his face, David drew a shuddering breath. "You're right, of course. I shouldn't let it make me so angry."

Aware that he needed a moment to master himself, Anne

waited in silence. Her head throbbed mercilessly, but that physical pain was nothing compared to the emotional agony David must be feeling.

She had thought him recovered from the loss of his younger sister, for in the past months he'd seldom mentioned her, though he kept fresh lilies on her gravesite. Now, Lord Joshua Kenyon had ripped open the old wound. He had gone to Greystone yesterday to offer his belated condolences to David and Lord Timberlake. What had been his true purpose? To gloat? Or to create the pretense that he was a kind and honorable gentleman?

That must be it. Now that he was back in England, he wished to resume his exalted place in society. But after the callous way he'd treated his bride-to-be, his reputation lay in tatters. Not even his insidious charm or heroism on the battlefield could save him—unless he showed amends for his misdeeds.

The sight of David's distress lit a fire inside Anne. In her desire to please Mama, she had taken the easy road. She hadn't argued hard enough to prohibit Lord Joshua's stay here. How could she have neglected to consider the effect on David?

She pushed herself up from the pillows and swung her legs over the side of the bed. The room tilted as if she rode a floundering ship. Regardless, she braced her palms on the mattress in preparation to rise.

David stepped to her side. He stared in consternation as if noticing Anne's injury for the first time. "Aren't you supposed to be resting?"

"I must speak to Mama again . . . warn her against Lord Joshua."

"But you look as if you're about to swoon. Are you?"

The image of him divided, causing a lurch of queasiness in her belly. "I . . . hope not."

"As do I." He wrung his hands. "Here I am going on and on about my own troubles when you've been hurt . . . and on my behalf."

"I've no regrets about that."

"Silly girl," he said affectionately as he picked up the teacup from the bedside table. "Drink this. It'll restore you."

He held the cup to her lips, and she sipped the now-cool tea. His caring manner stirred none of the turmoil that Lord Joshua had aroused in her. If only David would touch her, stroke her cheek, perhaps even take her in his arms and lower those finely molded lips to hers. Instantly, she was ashamed of herself. He'd never attempted any such impropriety in the five years they'd shared a comfortable—if somewhat sedate—companionship. And why should he? David treated her with respect; he was a gentleman with exquisite manners.

Unlike Lord Joshua.

"Perhaps . . . I should lie down." Aware of a vague discontent, Anne sank back against the cool pillows. Her head throbbed abominably. "Will you fetch Mama for me?"

David awkwardly patted her shoulder. "Certainly. If you'll forgive me for unburdening myself."

"I'm always happy to listen," Anne rallied to say. "Truly I am." Friends made the best marriages, she knew that from her parents and her married brothers. If only David would see that, too.

He bowed farewell, and a golden vial of sunshine poured past the curtains to anoint his fair hair. "I'll bid you adieu, then. And leave you with a caution: beware of Kenyon. He can be very persuasive."

The image of that ruggedly chiseled face flashed in her mind. It was a face stamped by experiences no lady should care to know. "Never fear," Anne said firmly. "He's the last man on earth who could charm me."

Preceding Peg into the kitchen, Josh had to duck his head to avoid striking the doorframe. The large, low-ceilinged room held gleaming copper pots hanging from hooks and a kettle bubbling on the hob. Sunlight streamed through the

single window with its jaunty yellow curtains and the pots
of red geraniums on the sill. In the center of the kitchen, a
long wooden table held rolled-out dough and pie pans,
along with a wooden bowl half full of blackberries.

Harrington stood there, scooping fruit into his mouth
with his stubby fingers.

"Did you catch the man?" Josh asked.

Harry looked up, his whiskered chin stained by the dark
juices. "Nay, the blighter got away, but—"

"Thief!" Peg roared. "Rotter! I picked them berries me-
self!"

She snatched up a frying pan and rushed at him. Despite
his bad leg, Harry spun around with his fists brandished.
Half a head shorter than Peg, he circled her like a pugilist
in the boxing ring.

"If ye'd fed me a decent breakfast," Harry grunted, "I
wouldn't've had to forage."

"I ain't servin' th' enemy."

She went after him, but he dove under the table and
popped up on the other side, chortling at his escape. "Mag-
pie! I liked ye better as a man. At least ye kept yer trap
shut."

"Bonehead! If ye'd kept *yer* trap shut, I'd still have berries."

"Serves ye right fer tryin' t' starve me."

"I'll serve ye all right. On a platter fer dinner." She
hurled the frying pan at him. He ducked, and the pan
crashed into the dry sink, knocking over a pile of pots in
an explosion of noise.

Josh considered letting the two of them fight it out. The
stocky maidservant was more than a match for the wily
valet. But Josh was impatient to learn what—if anything—
Harry had discovered.

He removed a bowl of eggs that Peg was about to hurl
at Harry. "You should know that Mrs. Neville has invited
me to stay here."

"Stay?" Peg repeated dumbly.

" 'Ere?" Equally horrified, Harry lowered the pot lid that he was using as a shield. "Wot about our room at the inn?"

"You'll fetch our things after you give me your report." Turning to Peg, Josh added, "You're wanted upstairs by your mistress."

She bobbed a reluctant curtsy. "Aye, m'lord." She glowered at Harry, then snatched up the bowl of berries and trotted out the door.

"Good riddance," Harry called after her. "Ye'd likely burn them pies, anyhow." Going to the hob, he poured hot water into a pot and then tossed in a pinch of tea leaves. "Grumpy female. Don't know 'ow t' treat a man."

Josh settled himself on the edge of the table. "Whenever you're ready, you can tell me about the gunman."

Harry looked up sheepishly. "Righto, Cap'n, though 'tain't much t' tell. I followed the mucker into town, then lost 'im in the fog near Prinny's Pavilion. 'E must've ducked down an alley."

"Could you find the spot again?"

"Aye, sure's me name's 'Arry A. 'Arrington the third. An' the fellow dropped somethin'."

"What?"

Limping toward Josh, the valet reached inside an inner pocket of his nondescript brown coat. He withdrew a card and slapped it into Josh's palm. "Don't know if 'tis of any use or not. But 'tis all I got."

His thoughts racing, Josh stared down at the black print on the pasteboard rectangle. Trivial perhaps, but with the devil's luck, it would give him a direction in which to commence his search.

Chapter Six

The Brothers

"Why are you wearing that silly hat, Auntie?" With the baffled innocence of a four-year-old, Mary stared at Anne, who reclined on the chaise in the parlor.

Smiling, Anne touched the binding around her head. "Do you like it, dearest? It's all the fashion in London."

"It's not a hat, it's a bandage," six-year-old James said with boyish relish. "Papa said you fell off your horse and almost got smashed to bits and *killed*."

"I believe your papa was teasing," Anne said lightly. "As you can see, I'm all in one piece."

But Mary's blue eyes filled with tears. She threw herself at her aunt and clung with chubby arms. "Are you going to die, Auntie Anne?"

"Gracious, no, darling. You mustn't worry yourself." But even as she hugged the little girl, Anne shuddered to think of the risk she'd taken. What if she *had* died? What if the path of the bullet had shifted half an inch? In her blind determination to help David, and an even blinder belief in her own infallibility, she had nearly caused her family immeasurable grief.

Anne tilted up Mary's chin and gently wiped away her tears. Then she ruffled James's blond hair, for he too looked more concerned than he'd let on. "I only need a bit of a rest, that's all. In a few days, we'll be playing hopscotch again in the park."

Mary brightened at once. "I like hopscotch!"

"I'd rather play jacks," James said.

"Then we shall. We have yet to determine who's the jacks champion of Merryton-on-Sea."

"That's enough, children," Benjamin said from his chair opposite Anne, where he sat talking to his brothers. A no-nonsense man with short, dark hair, he was beginning to show the creeping paunch of middle age. Only four of her brothers had come to visit today; the other five were out of town, Abelard living in York, Cyril in London, Emmett in India, and the twins, Francis and Geoffrey, enlisted in the infantry.

"Run along now," Benjamin added. "You two mustn't be bothering your aunt."

"They could never bother me," Anne said. "I enjoy their company."

"We love you, too," Mary piped up. "You're the bestest auntie in the whole world."

Tears pricked Anne's eyes as she returned the little girl's hug. How she craved having a family of her own, to enjoy the simple pleasures of raising a brood of cherubs with blond hair and blue eyes. Her brush with death had focused her mind on that goal. As soon as she was well, as soon as Lord Joshua left this house for good, she intended to find a way to make David see her as more than a friend.

Stern-faced Benjamin shooed the two little ones toward the other children, who were toasting bread on forks over the hearth fire and elbowing one another for the best position.

Seeing Mary's dejection, Anne said, "Perhaps you'd like to go up to the nursery. I found a dollhouse while I was cleaning the attic last week." To James, she added, "And a whole brigade of tin soldiers."

A smile spread over James's chubby cheeks. Wheeling

toward the older boys, he yelled, "Let's have a war! *I* get first pick."

"Last one there plays Bonaparte," shouted a wiry lad named Stephen, Dorian's eldest son. He dropped his fork and dashed for the doorway. In a mad clamor, the other boys followed, their faces dotted with purple jam and their laps leaving a trail of crumbs. Mary joined hands with Dorian's daughter, Eliza, as they scampered after the boys.

The shrill of their voices made Anne's head throb, though she was careful not to wince. Her brothers would send her straight back upstairs if they knew of her pain, and she'd go mad if she languished another moment in bed, staring at the four walls and thinking of all the things she could be doing—delivering a basket of food to old Mr. Pettigrew, stretching new canvases for Mama's paintings, mixing a tonic for Mrs. Hobbs, who had been feeling poorly since the birth of her last child.

Listening to her brothers talk, Anne plucked a shirt at random from her basket of mending. With her head hurting, it took an effort to thread the needle, but at last she began sewing a rip in the collar.

Isaac drew up a footstool. All long arms and legs, her youngest brother resembled a gangly spider. "If you're feeling better," he ventured, "perhaps you'd give me some advice."

"Let me guess," Anne said as she stitched. "Nell is out shopping again." Benjamin and Dorian had brought their wives, who had gone upstairs with Mama to inspect the box of family mementos that Anne had also found in the attic.

"She's off to the shops for the third time this week," Isaac said glumly. "Don't know how I'll pay the bills."

"You must tell her so. A new bride doesn't always understand the importance of keeping to a strict budget."

"But she weeps piteously whenever I speak of money." He hung his head. "I confess, I give her whatever she wants just to make her stop. I don't know what else to do."

The pampered only child of doting parents, Nell could also be sweet and generous—although Anne wished the girl could be a little less generous with Isaac's salary as a clerk in a law office. "I know it's difficult, but you must be firm with her."

"She'll turn into a watering pot. I just can't bear it." A faint sheen of sweat glistened on his brow. "I was hoping . . . perhaps *you* might . . ."

"Have a word with her?"

"When you're feeling better, of course."

Anne let her mending fall to her lap. Eight years his elder, she had watched out for Isaac all his twenty years. She couldn't ignore his appeal this time, either. "If you think it will help—"

"It will, indeed!" he said, his blue eyes brightening. Grasping her hand, he gave it a squeeze. "Thanks ever so much, Annie."

"Don't vex her with your troubles, Isaac," Benjamin scolded from his seat near Dorian and Hugh. "You're worse than the children."

Isaac straightened his bony form. "This is a private conversation. It's rude to eavesdrop."

"I'll do as I see fit. Whenever Mother and Father aren't present, it's my duty to see to the care of this family. Your duty is to obey me."

Recognizing Benjamin's dark frown, Anne braced herself for the inevitable lecture. Ever since Abelard had moved to York last year, Benjamin had taken on the role of bossy elder brother. "My duty," she countered tartly, "is to obey our parents, not you."

"Hear, hear," Isaac said.

"I'll second the motion," Hugh said, waving a chocolate biscuit with a desultory flick of his wrist.

Dorian chuckled. "Looks as if you're outmaneuvered, Benj."

"Quiet, all of you," Benjamin commanded. "We should be keeping Anne company, not pestering her with our problems. After the fall she suffered, she must have a thunderous headache."

Anne picked up her sewing to prove she felt normal. "I'm well enough. Really, you needn't fuss."

Benjamin glared at her. "I don't fuss. Fussing is for women and infants."

"Oh? What about last week, when you called me to help your dog deliver her pups?"

Dorian, Hugh, and Isaac snickered.

Benjamin shifted his large form in the chair. "It was Duchess's first litter. Females understand these matters."

"Then Genevieve could have helped," Dorian said slyly.

"My wife is far too delicate for such a matter. Anne is more practical about these things."

"Genevieve swoons as easily as you do," Hugh observed. Always possessed of a good appetite, he sat in his customary position beside the tea tray with its load of cakes and sandwiches.

Benjamin shot him a black look. "I beg your pardon."

"Duchess did fine on her own," Anne said, taking neat, automatic stitches. "I should think after siring five children yourself, Benjamin, you'd know that birth is a natural process—"

"Enough." His face paling, he held up his hand. "Kindly withhold the details."

"She's baiting you," Dorian called out. "Because she doesn't want to talk about how much her head hurts."

"Oh, hush," Anne said. Dorian had always been too astute for his own good. "The state of my health is a dull subject, indeed."

"How the devil did you fall off your horse, anyway?" Hugh drawled, brushing the crumbs from his lap.

"I can answer that," Isaac said. " 'Twas you who taught her to ride."

Hugh landed a playful punch on his brother's arm. Isaac gave him a shove that nearly sent him tumbling to the ivy-patterned carpet. The two youngest brothers started a tussle that threatened to knock over a vase on a nearby table.

"Stop that at once," Benjamin said. Then he gave Anne a speculative stare. "Whatever you say, I mean to have a talk with that physician fellow—Lord Joshua Kenyon."

Anne's heart lurched over a beat. *She* meant to have a talk with Lord Joshua. But she hadn't seen him since early morning when he had come into her chamber to check on her. He had brought Peg along—for the sake of propriety, he'd claimed. But Anne suspected otherwise. He'd wanted to keep Anne from asking too many questions about his search for the gunman. He had examined her with swift, clinical efficiency, then departed the chamber.

Without telling her his plans for the day.

"You'll have a long wait," she said. "His lordship has gone out, and heaven only knows when he'll return."

"Perhaps we should check the local gaming den," Hugh remarked. "Mama says he's a rogue of the first order."

"She seemed rather delighted by the prospect, too," Dorian added dryly.

"I shouldn't think so," Isaac said with youthful indignation. "The cad left his bride standing at the altar. Then she died of a broken heart."

"She was Pankhurst's sister, was she not?" Benjamin asked in a ruminating tone. "That acquaintance of yours, Anne. What's his name? Daniel?"

"David," Anne corrected. "And the story is true. David told me so himself." It pained her that she hadn't seen him in two days, not since the morning of the duel. Dismally, she knew he wouldn't pay her another visit so long as Lord Joshua was in residence. And it looked as if Lord Joshua were here to stay, for her denunciation of him had had little effect on her mother.

"Your papa was a scoundrel, too, in his day," Mama had said.

"Papa?" Anne had scoffed at such a description of her dear, innocuous father who spent his days happily puttering in his study.

Mama giggled. "My John was a naughty one, indeed. Broke hearts from Brighton to London, so dashing and handsome he was."

Indignant, Anne said, "Lord Joshua is nothing like Papa. A true scoundrel cannot be reformed."

"Quite the contrary, my dear girl. If ever you can tame one, they make the very best of husbands."

Anne snapped out of her reverie to realize that an unnatural silence had fallen over the parlor. Her brothers were quiet. Too quiet. She caught them exchanging secretive glances as if they were privy to an indelicate jest.

Though they'd been remarkably mum about her ugly bandage, Anne smoothed back her hair. "What is it? What's wrong?"

"Wrong?" Benjamin said too quickly. "Nothing's wrong."

"Not a thing," the others chorused.

"Nothing fit for feminine ears, anyway," Hugh added, biting into another pastry from the tea tray.

Anne pursed her lips. They were banding together to shut her out, and though she knew the futility of trying to wrest the truth out of them, she made the attempt anyway. "Tell me. Is it something to do with David?"

They exchanged another round of glances.

"That *is* who we were just talking about," she prodded. What could they possibly know about David that she didn't already know?

Benjamin cleared his throat. "We merely wondered about his intentions toward you. He hasn't . . . er . . . shown any signs of a matrimonial bent, has he?"

So that was it. They were concerned about her happiness.

Longing ached in her breast. But she had no wish to expose her secret dreams to her brothers—or to anyone. She pretended an interest in her mending. "No, he hasn't."

Benjamin lifted an eyebrow. Dorian shifted his gaze to the window. Isaac stared down at his brown leather shoes.

Hugh plucked another sandwich from the tea tray.

"What is it now?" Anne asked sharply. "There's something more. Something you're keeping from me."

"You sound testy," Dorian said. "Is your head hurting again?"

"No, but yours will if you don't tell me—"

"Speaking of hurt heads, dear sister," Hugh cut in, "reminds me of the time Dorian pushed you out of the tree fort."

"That was an accident," Dorian objected, rising to his feet to move the tray. "And kindly leave a little food for the rest of us."

"My point is that if anyone can take a knock, Annie can," Hugh said between bites. "She's always had an exceedingly hard head."

"And you've always had an exceedingly impudent mouth." Anne hurled a fringed blue pillow at him and knocked the sandwich out of his hand.

Hugh squawked a protest. A large, heavy-muscled man, he dropped to all fours to retrieve the tidbit while Anne and her brothers burst out laughing.

"She also has an exceedingly accurate aim," spoke a gruff voice from across the parlor.

Anne's smile died. Her widened gaze shot to the doorway.

Lord Joshua must have just come in from riding. A dark green coat covered broad shoulders that were squared with a military precision. He wore a crisp white shirt, buckskin breeches, and gleaming black riding boots. His fine appearance sparked the tinder of resentment in her. She resisted the urge to smooth the skirt of her plain gray gown, to tidy her hair. Due to the bandage, she'd had to secure her tresses at the nape of her neck in a style more suited to a young girl than a mature woman of eight-and-twenty.

He was staring straight at her.

Her heart beat madly. But only because of what he'd said. Would he tell her brothers about the duel? "Lord

Joshua," she said, afraid she sounded breathless. "Do come in and meet my brothers."

He obliged, and she saw the parlor through his critical, aristocratic eyes: the fussy, rose-flowered wallpaper, the comfortably frayed blue upholstery on the chairs and chaises, her mother's collection of ceramic dogs on the mantelpiece, a few of them chipped from encounters with her rambunctious brothers.

Benjamin shot to his feet. His thinning brown hair framed a weathered face that showed the deep creases of laugh lines around his eyes and mouth. But he wasn't laughing now.

His cool blue stare assessed Lord Joshua. "Benjamin Neville," he said crisply. "I understand you're a guest here."

"Not for long," Anne called out. "Now that I'm better, there's no reason for him to stay."

But her brothers weren't listening. They gathered around to flay Lord Joshua with pointed commentary.

"So you're our sister's rescuer," Isaac said.

"Mama says you carried Annie home and laid her in bed yourself," Hugh added.

His face stern, Dorian put his hands at his waist. "You must tell us your version of this mishap that befell Annie."

Lord Joshua shrugged. "I'm sure you've already heard the tale from Mrs. Neville and Miss Neville."

"Not everything," Benjamin said. "I wonder where you were heading before dawn."

"I was on my way to Devon," Lord Joshua lied without blinking an eye.

"But you're recently discharged from the cavalry, are you not?" Dorian observed. "Did you come from Portsmouth? You've gone far out of your way."

"I had business to attend to in Brighton."

The brothers exchanged another glance. "I for one am thankful you were out and about," Isaac said. "Our mother called you a knight in shining armor."

Anne ended her pinch-mouthed silence. "Don't be dramatic, Isaac. Anyone would have stopped to help."

"Don't be so certain," said Benjamin, settling his large frame into a chair and propping his chin on his steepled fingers. "You've seen little of the world, dear sister. Not everyone plays the good Samaritan."

"Annie thinks everyone is like her," Dorian said with a chuckle. "Responsible, benevolent—"

"Bossy," added Hugh, offering the last gooseberry tart to Lord Joshua. When he waved away the tray, Hugh claimed the tidbit for himself.

"And she's very good at dueling—" Lord Joshua said.

Anne's fingers tensed around her mending. Dear God, was he mad?

"—with words," he finished. "A very articulate lady, your sister."

Her brothers chuckled knowingly.

Anne gritted her teeth. "And you, m'lord, are very poor at social graces."

"Forgive me," he said lazily. "I've been out of society for quite some time."

Lord Joshua strolled toward her and leaned down to inspect the bandage. His scent enveloped her . . . leather and horses and man. His touch light, he settled his warm hand against her cheek, making her tingle all over. "No fever. Although your face is a bit too pink."

She batted his hand away. "Stop that."

Isaac sprang to his feet. "See here now. What d'you think you're doing?"

Lord Joshua slanted a look at her brothers. "Examining Miss Neville. Surely you'd prefer for me to do so in your presence."

To Anne's chagrin, Benjamin nodded crisply. "Proceed," he said.

With his thumb, Lord Joshua lifted her eyelid, put his face close to hers, and peered deeply into her eyes. A protest lodged in her throat; she was afraid her voice would sound weak if she dared to speak. "No enlargement of the pupils," he observed. "Any dizziness today?"

She felt giddy from his nearness. "No."

"Headache?"

"No."

Still leaning over her, he placed his hand on the back of the chaise. "It's wise to know when to admit to the weakness of injury, Miss Neville. You might do yourself harm by denying it."

He sounded so rational, so concerned, that she could almost believe he cared what happened to her. But it was all a façade for the benefit of her brothers. "Sitting in my own parlor can't possibly do me harm."

"You've been sewing," he said, scowling at the shirt in her lap. "You'll overtax yourself. I'll escort you back to your chamber."

"Don't bother. My brothers will do the honors—when I'm ready."

But he had already turned away to address Benjamin.

"She suffered a mild concussion. To heal properly, she needs quiet and bed rest. In fact, I left her strict orders not to leave her chambers. She was to take a dose of laudanum if she had trouble sleeping."

Benjamin frowned. "She never told me so."

"Of course I didn't," Anne said. "I'm not an infant who requires a nap."

The brothers closed in on her. "You said your wound wasn't serious," Isaac accused.

She patted his arm. "It isn't. And I didn't want to worry you."

"We only meant to pop in for a quick visit," Dorian said. "You should have sent us away."

"And I shouldn't have brought the children," Benjamin said gravely.

"Nor I my mending," Hugh said. He snatched the shirt away and tossed it into the basket beside her. "Don't you dare touch a needle and thread until Kenyon declares you fit."

"We'll get you upstairs straightaway," Benjamin said.

She started to object, then looked at the ring of reproach-ful faces and fell silent. She wouldn't win this argument. And her head truly did throb in beastly, rhythmic strokes.

Resigning herself, she accepted Benjamin's arm on one side and Isaac on the other. To her chagrin, she needed their support as they made their way to the staircase. Hugh and Dorian followed, peppering Lord Joshua with questions about his service in the war. When he declined to talk about Waterloo, they didn't press him. Instead, they related the experiences of the twins, Geoffrey and Francis, as described in their letters.

Their affable male camaraderie incensed Anne. Her brothers acted as if they were old friends of Lord Joshua's, when in truth, they should scorn him for his foul reputation. Had they so quickly forgotten what he'd done to Lily Pank-hurst?

Men, she thought in the throes of headache and ill hu-mor. They were so fascinated by blood and gore, it blinded them to reason and heart. If, indeed, they were even capable of reason and heart.

But she would never forget what he'd done. Lord Joshua Kenyon was the last man on earth she could ever regard as a hero.

Chapter Seven

An Unexpected Visitor

Anne had lied to Lord Joshua.

Slipping out of the house through a side door, she glanced from side to side, her gaze sweeping the rambling garden with the old oak tree, where her brothers had built a fort many years ago. The platform was still there, though a pirate's flag no longer fluttered from the pole. When her brothers had barred her from entering their domain, she had had her revenge. Sneaking out one night, she had painted the fort pink and hung festoons of lace salvaged from Mama's old gowns.

Those days were long gone, Anne thought as she hurried through the neat garden filled with the rosebushes and hollyhocks and phlox she grew for her mother to paint. Right now, Mama was pottering in her attic studio while Papa read aloud to her from one of his history books. Her parents had shared that comfortable arrangement for years, and with luck, they wouldn't notice her absence.

But Lord Joshua might notice. Anne hoped to accomplish her plan before he returned from wherever he'd gone this morning.

The gate creaked under a push of her hand, and she took note that the hinges needed oiling. That was another chore neglected during her convalescence. She had spent the past five days at rest until she wanted to scream from the inactivity. The awful dizziness was gone at last, and she could ignore the lingering discomfort in her head. Today, she'd even left off the bothersome bandage and had gingerly covered the healing wound with her best bonnet of brown straw with a jaunty pheasant's feather. In her Sunday gown of mustard-yellow muslin, she felt girded for battle.

As she stepped along the rutted dirt road heading out of Merryton-on-Sea, the wind blew off the waters in the distance. The tang of salt revitalized her. Anne realized just how much she'd missed being outdoors. Despite her grim intentions, she felt exhilarated, as if she were setting off on a grand quest. Always, it had been her brothers who'd had the adventures, her brothers who had gone off to study at university or to work in London or to travel exotic lands.

Thunderclouds piled in the distance, but she had only a short walk into Brighton. She hurried up a grassy slope, her feet finding the familiar path. All the while, she rehearsed what she would say.

Yes, she had lied by omission to Lord Joshua, but the sin was justifiable. Over the past few days, she'd had time to mull over the extraordinary duel. And she had arrived at an appalling conclusion: there might, indeed, be one person who bore a grudge against her.

Someone who would profit from her death.

However, she saw no reason to reveal that fact to Lord Joshua. He was a stranger, an outsider, and he had no right to meddle in a private family matter. She far preferred to solve the problem in her own fashion.

A proliferation of houses marked the approach into Brighton. The sea glowed in the sunlight like a maiden in repose, spreading shimmery blue skirts along the horizon while the town knelt in supplication.

On any other day, she might have stopped to admire the scenery. But this morning, she plunged onward and took the road that led into the east end of the city. The cobblestone streets were thronged with drays and carts and carriages. Servants scurried here and there on errands. Workmen banged and sawed on the skeleton of a new building. Ever since the Prince Regent had embraced Brighton as his favorite seaside resort, construction had boomed. Each summer, more and more fashionable folk flocked here from London, requiring an even greater influx of tradesmen and servants to fulfill their every need. Though Anne appreciated the ever-increasing variety of shops, she sometimes missed the quaint town of her girlhood.

In an old section, a gray stone mansion presided over the row houses that encircled a leafy green square. The residence looked deserted, forlorn, a relic of the past. There was no sign of activity, no gardener weeding the flower beds, no maidservant scrubbing the dingy front steps, no coachman waiting with a fine carriage to carry the master off to the shops or to the races.

Marching up the front walk, Anne kept her spine straight, her shoulders back. If Edwin Bellingham had had any hand in this business, she would box his fool ears.

She thunked the knocker three times, and the noise echoed inside the great hall. Amid a rattling of bolts, the door opened to a narrow slit. From out of the gloom emerged the flared barrel of a blunderbuss.

Terror swamped her. She dove behind a column. "Don't shoot! It's me, Anne."

The blunderbuss wavered, then withdrew. In its stead appeared a pair of squinty dark eyes in a craggy face. The stooped form of an old man barely showed through the crack. "Eh, what's this?" he said, his voice as dry as bones. "What the devil are you doing here?"

Without awaiting an answer, he motioned her into the dimly lit hall. Then he swiftly banged the heavy door shut as if the legions of hell thronged outside. He threw the bolt and turned the massive iron key. All the while, he muttered to himself. "Harebrained hooligans. Thought 'twas them again, knocking and then running off like cowards. Enjoy giving me heart palpitations, they do."

Gathering the shreds of her aplomb, Anne leaned down slightly to kiss his wrinkled cheek. "You gave me a terrible fright, Uncle. Have the neighbor boys been pestering you again?"

"Ruffians, the lot of them." He shook the blunderbuss. "Next time I'll pepper their backsides with buckshot."

"They're just silly boys playing silly pranks. But *this* is serious." Her movements brisk, she took the blunderbuss from him and placed it on a nearby chair.

"Bah. Young folk need to be taught a lesson. You've no respect for your elders."

"I respect you, Uncle. Enough to stop you from earning the wrath of your neighbors."

Cocking his balding head, Sir Francis Bellingham scowled at her through the gloom. Tufts of white brows formed a shelf over his black pebble eyes and beaked nose. "Why haven't you brought me a damson cake? You know how I like it with my tea."

"I've been busy—"

"Why are you up and about, anyhow?" he interrupted. "Lenora sent a note. Told me you'd fallen off your horse and cracked open your head and almost died."

"Mama does exaggerate."

"My sister always did." He cleared his throat, a raspy sound like rustling leaves. "I didn't believe her, else I'd've come to call."

Anne hadn't really expected him to visit. Sir Francis Bellingham hadn't left this moldering mansion since the death of his wife so long ago. To spare his pride, she said, "I must thank you for the lovely nosegay. I placed the flowers on the mantelpiece where I can see them every day."

He grunted disagreeably, but she could tell he was pleased. "Sent Grafstone out to pick 'em in the square. No sense in squandering good coin on something that'll wither and die."

Anne smiled. She had decided long ago that it was better to find humor in her uncle's miserly nature than take offense. His blue satin coat was forty years out-of-date and sadly frayed at the cuffs and elbows. She had offered many times to refurbish his wardrobe, but he stubbornly refused to accept anything new.

"Speaking of Grafstone, why didn't he answer the door?" she asked. "Is he suffering from rheumatism again?"

"Nay, I sent him upstairs," Sir Francis said, waving a gnarled hand at the staircase. "To awaken the slug."

"The . . . oh, Edwin." Dismay nipped at the heels of her amusement. "Does my cousin have an appointment so early? I was hoping to speak with him."

"You, too? I thought at least *you* had come to see me," Sir Francis complained. "That worthless son of mine gets all the visitors. Though this time, it's a bill collector."

So Edwin had been served another dun notice. In commiseration, Anne patted her uncle's sloping shoulder. "I enjoy your company very much, indeed. I promise I'll come back soon and finish reading *Gulliver's Travels* to you. But today, I do need to see Edwin."

"Huh. You're too good for the likes of him. What could you want with that wastrel?"

"To ask his help in gathering contributions for the missionary fund," she fibbed. "He knows so many wealthy people in society."

"Bah, they're all cheats and cardsharps and drunkards. Not a philanthropist among 'em."

"Then perchance *you* would make a generous donation. That would save me the trouble of soliciting funds."

Predictably, a look of horror enveloped his age-seamed features. "Come to think, p'raps Edwin does know a rich gull or two. Wait in the library, and I'll see what's keeping the boy."

Like a crab seeking shelter, her uncle scuttled toward the staircase. Anne subdued a twinge of guilt over her falsehood. There had been no other way. Uncle Francis mustn't overhear her conversation with Edwin.

Nor must anyone else.

As she headed toward the library, her shoes whispered over the scuffed floor, a sound that echoed in the colossal foyer. A shadowy chandelier hung from the domed ceiling, the crystals dulled by dust. Though immensely wealthy, Sir Francis kept only a married couple on staff, old Mrs. Grafstone in the kitchen, and her doddering husband as combination valet and butler. Even if they'd been young and spry, the Grafstones alone couldn't have kept the household running smoothly. This gargantuan mansion required a staff of twenty or thirty at least, footmen and maids and under-butlers.

As always, Anne fought back the urge to throw open the shutters and let light into the gloomy mausoleum. To roll up her sleeves and scrub the accumulated grime from the woodwork and floors and furniture. But she mustn't think of that now. She must focus her mind on a more momentous matter.

The library held the musty scent of old books, leather bindings, and accumulated bric-a-brac. Rigid with tension, Anne turned toward the age-speckled mirror fastened to the wall inside the doorway. In the murky light, her odd violet-blue eyes looked dull and lifeless against her plain features. At least the brisk walk had brought a rosy tint to her skin, though the feather on her hat hung at a crazy angle. Licking her fingers, she did her best to tame the adornment.

Perhaps she should remove the bonnet entirely. No, her hair looked like a rat's nest, for her scalp was too tender to endure a decent brushing. Better to keep the healing wound concealed anyway, to appear strong and controlled, ready to outfox a devious male—

A movement in the mirror caught her attention. Against the reflection of book-lined walls and oak tables, a dark shape shifted in the gloom.

She whirled around to see a man rising from a wing chair near the unlit hearth. His face was shadowed, his large form partially hidden behind a globe of the world.

But she recognized him at once.

"What's that thing sticking out of your hat?" Lord Joshua asked in distaste. "A cock's feather?"

"Pheasant."

The blow of his presence made her voice thin. Her heart thrummed as rapidly as her thoughts. Had Lord Joshua found out the truth? Had he probed for family secrets and turned up this one?

He must have. Dear, trusting Mama would have answered all his questions.

Still, Anne had to make certain. "Why are you here?"

"Your uncle told me to wait in the library." One corner of his mouth tipped upward. "He thought I was a dun collector."

"And you find it amusing to dupe an old man?"

"I merely played along with his assumption. He said he'd cut off his son's pursestrings if he didn't come downstairs and face me himself."

"You've no reason to be here."

"I've the same reason as you, I'll venture."

"I'm visiting my uncle and cousin," she said icily. "As you don't know either of them, you must be up to no good."

Lord Joshua moved stealthily toward her as if he were stalking an enemy. "Better *I* should interrogate *you*," he said. "What are you doing out of bed again?"

She felt a quivery disorder in the depths of her belly. The reaction was fast becoming familiar to her. Over the past few days, whenever he was near, she experienced a rush of warmth, a tingling awareness of him.

It was not a sensation she relished.

Anne veered to a window and made a show of opening the blinds. The wooden slats clattered a protest; then sunshine poured into the library, illuminating the shabby furniture and moldering books. Over her shoulder, she said, "I'm in perfect health. So you may return to my house, pack your bags, and depart Brighton for good."

"You'd like that, wouldn't you, Miss Neville?" he said, his breath warm against her ear.

Gasping, she spun around to find him standing directly in front of her, crowding her against the window. Her hands came up to form a shield, though he made no attempt to touch her. Like a subtle note of danger, his male scent disturbed the air. He stood so close she would be forced to brush against him if she fled.

She wouldn't give him the satisfaction.

She tilted her head back to glare at him. She was a tall woman, yet he stood half a head taller. "I'll thank you not to startle me like that."

"You seem on edge today. Tell me what's the matter."

"I find your presence annoying."

The corner of his mouth quirked upward. "Do you always blush when you're annoyed?"

"I've been out walking. It's the natural result of exertion."

"Ah, but you shouldn't have exerted yourself. You could suffer a relapse."

"I'll do as I see fit."

His smile deepened. "Willful and insubordinate. You wouldn't survive ten minutes in the military."

"If I were under your command, I'd start a mutiny."

"And I would enjoy conquering you."

The pitch of his voice lowered to a slumberous rasp that held secret meanings beyond her limited experience. Without conscious intent, she found herself staring at his mouth. The rakish tilt of his lips promised something more than physical subjugation, something that stirred a confusing welter of longing inside her. To conquer her, Lord Joshua would have to lay his hands on her, and the shocking prospect stirred excitement inside her. She had the mad urge to touch him, too, to explore the warmth of his sun-burnished skin, to run her fingertips over the scar along his jaw and ask him if he'd earned it in battle.

Was this how he had seduced Lily's companion, Catherine? With smoldering looks and wicked smiles? Had Catherine too felt drawn to him against her will?

Pressing her fingers into her palms, Anne returned her gaze to his. Sunlight gleamed on the flecks of gold in his brown eyes. His knowing smirk told her that he'd read her thoughts and was amused by her inner turmoil.

She returned his stare. Never before had she met a man like him, a man who possessed a feral animal magnetism. Little wonder that sweet, innocent Lily had fallen under his spell. Or that her friend Catherine had succumbed to his advances.

But Anne knew better.

She stepped away, risking the brief contact of his arm in exchange for the safety of distance. Stopping in the shadows beyond the reach of the sunlight, she assumed a haughty demeanor. "I've had quite enough of your nonsense. You aren't welcome here. Please be kind enough to depart."

His eyes narrowed to the watchful look of the hunter. "After I've asked a few questions of your cousin."

"This is a family matter. It doesn't concern you."

"Oh? Your mother told me some interesting facts. I could only conclude that Edwin Bellingham has ample reason to want you dead."

The ominous statement hung in the air like the dust motes that danced in the sunlight. Anne felt pierced by the worry that had brought her here. Had her own cousin really tried to kill her? Did he hate her so much?

The slapping of footsteps yanked her gaze to the doorway. Clad in a wrinkled shirt and trousers, Edwin stomped into the library. His black curls were tousled, his cravat untied, his feet bare. Though he was only twenty-seven, spidery veins of dissipation already marked his ill-tempered features, and half-moon shadows underscored his gray eyes. He winced against the strong sunlight.

Scowling at Lord Joshua, he said, "Did you raise those blinds? Stupid oaf, how dare you take such liberties after you've rousted me out of bed—"

"Good morning, Edwin," Anne said. Determined to control the interview, she emerged from the shadows and took up a stance in front of Lord Joshua. "You can thank *me* for opening the blinds."

Edwin's startled gaze landed on her. He brought up his hand to shade his eyes. "What the devil . . . Anne?"

"I'd like a word with you. In private."

"Why are *you* here? Father said you'd fallen off your horse and cracked open your skull."

Under normal circumstances, his sneering tone would have irked her. But this time, she felt a stab of suspicion. Was his remark meant to cover up his guilt?

Lord Joshua stepped around her. "Things didn't happen quite that way. I'm wondering if you know how she was really injured."

"Know what?" Edwin said testily. "Begone, you son of Satan. I haven't the funds to pay you."

"I'm Lord Joshua Kenyon. I've come to collect answers, not bills."

Edwin gawked first at him, then at Anne. "Kenyon? Is he a friend of *yours*? What is this nonsense?"

"I can explain." She took up a position in front of Lord Joshua again. "However, I'd prefer that you and I talk alone in another chamber."

"Talk! Don't want to talk," Edwin grumbled. "All this jabbering is giving me a headache." He shuffled over to a sideboard and picked up a dusty crystal decanter. Uncorking it, he peered inside and sniffed it, then tipped the rim into a glass and cursed when it came up dry. He tried each of the five decanters in turn. All the while, he groused to himself, sounding remarkably like his sire.

Anne crossed the room and snatched the last decanter just as he was about to pour.

"Give that back!" he said, grabbing for it. "There's a finger of brandy left, the last in this godforsaken mausoleum."

She turned and dumped the contents into a dusty vase.

Then she replaced the decanter on the sideboard. "It's too early in the morning for spirits."

"Curse you!" He peered into the vase as if desperate enough to accept grime and cobwebs in his drink. "You can't give me orders. This is *my* house, *my* liquor, *my* everything."

"Quite the contrary," Lord Joshua said.

To Anne's displeasure—and there could be no other reason for her sudden coil of tension—he stood at her side. How did the man move so quietly?

"Everything here belongs to your father," Lord Joshua continued in that smooth, hard tone. "According to his last will and testament, when he dies, the whole lot goes to Anne."

Edwin jerked upright like a puppet on strings. "How do you know—? You're a meddlesome rascal."

"Yes, he certainly is meddlesome," Anne said, frowning. "I'll manage this matter, Lord Joshua."

But neither man was listening. She might as well have been addressing the bedraggled, stuffed grouse on the pedestal nearby.

His thick eyebrows lowered, Edwin stared at Lord Joshua. "Who told you about my father's will?"

"It doesn't matter. What does matter is that Anne didn't fall off a horse. Someone took a shot at her."

Edwin blinked rapidly. "What? Who?"

"It happened nearly a week ago while she was out on an early morning walk. A man hid in the bushes. He fired at her, then galloped away."

"Bah. A poacher."

"No. I came upon the scene just as it happened. I caught a glimpse of the gunman. Judging by his fine clothing and mount, he was a gentleman."

"A hunter, then." Edwin threw himself into a leather wing chair and slouched with his arms dangling over the sides. He yawned without bothering to cover his mouth. "A pity what's happened, Anne. But you can tell me about it another day. At present, I'm in desperate need of a nap."

His eyelids drooping, he settled more comfortably in the chair.

Thanks to Lord Joshua's interference, the time for subtlety had come and gone. Anne marched to her cousin and boxed his ear.

"Ow!" Edwin jerked away, putting up his hands to block her attack. "Leave off, you harridan. I'm not ten years old anymore."

She shook her finger at him. "You're still playing your nasty games, though. When you were ten, you'd put worms in my bedclothes and vinegar in my tea. But at least back then, you never came after me with a gun."

He sat up straight. "A gun—? *Me?*"

"Are you so dense, Edwin? Let me make myself perfectly clear. You have every reason to shoot me."

"But . . . you can't possibly believe that *I* would . . . would . . ." He sputtered to a stop.

She wanted to acquit him of the crime. For all that Edwin Bellingham was a drunkard and a disgrace, he was still her cousin, the only son of her mother's elder brother. She hoped that look of horrified surprise was genuine.

"Debt can make a man desperate," Lord Joshua observed.

Edwin glowered at him. "I beg your pardon! You can't accuse me without serving any proof—"

"Where were you on Tuesday morning?"

"Why . . . asleep in my bed, of course."

"Not according to Grafstone. He said you didn't drag in until after dawn."

"What? Why, that insolent—Oh, I remember now. The dice match." Shifting in the chair, Edwin gave a rusty laugh. "We played all night. If you don't believe me, you can ask John Cryer or Sir Phillip Madison. Or Lord Timberlake."

"David's father?" Anne asked in astonishment. "He isn't a gamester."

Edwin curled his lip. "A quiet chap, I'll vow, but he likes a good wager as much as any gentleman."

Lord Joshua gave him a hard stare. "If you're lying, you'll answer to me. Only a craven villain would shoot a woman."

"I didn't shoot her, I say. Tell him, Anne. I don't even own a gun."

"Uncle Francis does," she said. "He has quite a collection of antique firearms."

Leaping to his feet, Edwin advanced on her, his fists clenched. "Bloody female. You still haven't learned when to keep your mouth shut—"

In a blur of motion, Lord Joshua caught him by the throat and shoved him against a bookcase.

Chapter Eight

A Cry in the Night

With one powerful hand, Lord Joshua throttled her cousin. The bookshelves rattled. Several ancient volumes thunked onto the carpet, stirring puffs of dust. Edwin uttered a garbled sound of distress. His face flushed beet-red, and he grappled ineffectually with his assailant.

"That's an ill-mannered way to address a lady," Lord Joshua said in a deceptively pleasant tone.

"Let . . . me . . . go."

"Apologize, and I'll consider it."

"I meant . . . no offense . . . to you."

Lord Joshua tightened his fingers. "Tell Miss Neville, not me."

Edwin's eyes bulged out. "So . . . sorry . . . Anne," he choked out. "I beg . . . forgiveness." The last word emerged as a humble squeak.

Anne rushed toward them. "Release him, for pity's sake. You'll strangle him."

"It's no less than he deserves." But Lord Joshua unclamped his hand and stepped back.

Edwin drooped against the bookshelf, panting for air and rubbing his neck. "Ye gods," he gasped out. "I should call the law down on you for that, Kenyon."

Lord Joshua gave him a contemptuous look. "I suspect

the magistrate would be more interested in *you*."

To Edwin, Anne said, "You should know, I've told Uncle Francis many times that I don't want his money. But he refuses to rewrite his will."

"Bah. Everyone wants money. Don't pretend you wouldn't enjoy traveling the world, buying fancy clothes in London and Paris, wearing jewels and attending parties. You might even trap yourself a husband."

An unbidden yearning enveloped Anne. She imagined herself clad in a fashionable gown, whirling around the dance floor, relishing the surprise and admiration on Lord Joshua's face.

No, *David's* face. Perhaps the prospect of a rich dowry might entice him into making an offer for her hand. Not, of course, that she intended to buy his love.

"I really don't want this inheritance," she said firmly. "Not when it will cause a rift in our family."

Edwin regarded her with patent disbelief and open resentment.

Shaken by that look, she fell silent. It made her ill to think that her cousin could wish her harm. But did his animosity extend to murder?

She didn't resist when Lord Joshua took her arm. "I'll be watching you, Bellingham," he said.

Then he drew her out of the library. They went outside in the sunshine, and she breathed in the cool, cleansing sea air. Yet nothing could wash away the memory of that ugly encounter.

"Nasty sot," Lord Joshua said. "I should have choked the life out of him."

She rallied at that. "You can't kill someone on suspicion alone. It's possible that Edwin is innocent. He did look aghast when he heard I was shot."

"Of course. He could be jailed for attempted murder."

She swallowed. "You never answered his inquiry. Have you proof of his guilt?"

"No. But I'll find out the truth."

Lord Joshua's eyes were cold and flat, and a secretiveness lurked in his grim visage. Was he telling her everything? Or did he withhold evidence for some nefarious purpose of his own?

And why did she expect him to admit anything to her, anyway? He'd made it clear that she was to have nothing to do with the investigation.

A bandy-legged groom waited by the front walk. No, not a groom, she realized. It was Lord Joshua's manservant. The one who had chased after the gunman. From her bedchamber window, she'd seen him in the yard.

Perhaps she could coax information from him that she couldn't pry from the tight-lipped Lord Joshua.

She smiled at the servant. "Mr. Harrington, I presume."

Whipping off his cap, the grizzled man bobbed his head. "At yer service, miss."

"I haven't thanked you for risking your life on my behalf. It was very brave of you to pursue that man."

" 'Tweren't nothin'." He slid an admiring look at her. "Might I say, ye're a master o' disguise, miss. Fooled me, ye did. Who'd've believed ye were naught but a pretty lass?"

Anne decided to take that as a compliment. She glanced at Lord Joshua, who was preoccupied with stroking the horse's sleek black neck. In a lowered voice, she said, "Since his lordship will be riding, perhaps you would be so kind as to walk me home." And she'd interrogate him on the way.

Harrington cocked one end of his caterpillar brows. "The cap'n will 'ave somethin' t' say about that, I trow."

"I will, indeed," Lord Joshua said in the pleasant tone she'd begun to recognize as more ominous than a shout. "Harry has other duties."

"Can't he postpone—?" she began.

"Don't be quarrelsome, Miss Neville. *I* shall escort you home."

" 'E do like t' give orders, miss," Harrington said. "Just

remind 'im 'e ain't in the cavalry no more." Nimble as a
leprechaun, he sprang into the saddle, flashed Anne an imp-
ish grin, and set off down the street.

"Harrington is right," Anne said coolly. "You act as if
I'm incapable of making my own decisions."

"I'm sure you're capable of many things," Lord Joshua
said. "Nevertheless, I'll accompany you."

Keeping his arm linked with hers, he guided her down
the drive to the cobbled street. She could not pull away
without creating a scene for the amusement of all the pas-
sersby. And did she want to pull away?

Awareness of him transcended her pique: his muscled
arm brushing against hers, his pensive profile holding untold mysteries ... and the innate air of command that
caused those around him to leap at his bidding.

She raised her chin. "I'm not a cow to be led about by
a halter."

A gleam in his dark eyes, he looked her up and down.
The wind tousled his black hair and lent a rakish quality to
his rugged handsomeness. "No, you're a spirited filly in
need of a master's firm hand."

"Should I need guidance, m'lord, I wouldn't seek it from
you."

"But I'll give it anyway." His smile vanished. "You did
a foolish thing today, Anne. Edwin Bellingham might have
drawn a gun on you."

Her stomach tightened. Ignoring his unsanctioned use of
her name, she said, "Edwin would not have dared. Not with
Uncle Francis nearby."

"A desperate man will dare anything."

He spoke with the certainty of experience. Had he witnessed such desperation during his years in the military?
Had he himself teetered on the brink of death? He must
have. Perhaps more often than he cared to remember.

But his past shouldn't interest her. "What have you
found out thus far?" she asked. "I want to know everything."

"There's little to tell."

"Then tell me that little."

He narrowed his eyes as if weighing the wisdom of confiding in her. Unlike her talkative brothers, he had a closed quality to his features that prevented her from reading his thoughts. "The gunman eluded capture, as you know. But as Harry gave chase, he saw the fellow drop a paper. It was a calling card stamped with the name of a prominent bootmaker in town."

"And?"

"And that's all. The tradesman has compiled a list of his customers for me. I'm checking all of them out."

"Is Edwin on the list?"

Lord Joshua nodded. "Along with a number of other gentlemen."

"Who are they? Give me their names."

Patronizing as ever, he patted her hand. "There's no need for you to know."

"I beg to differ! I should know which men to watch out for."

"I'll do the watching. You can hardly go around Brighton knocking on the doors of strange gentlemen."

"Then I'll get one of my brothers to accompany me. Hugh or Isaac would oblige."

"You'd have to tell them the truth about the duel."

She fell silent, stymied by the need for secrecy. If her brothers got wind of her folly, they'd flay her alive. And then they'd flay Lord Joshua.

It might almost be worth the price to witness his downfall.

She stepped around a coin-sized slug and decided it resembled Lord Joshua's black soul. "I shan't sit home mending linen and baking cakes. I can corroborate Edwin's story—by questioning those men who played dice with him."

"Leave them to me."

"And what of Lord Timberlake? He was there, too. Do

you really imagine you'll ever again be allowed in David's house?"

This time, she had Lord Joshua by the strings.

His fingers tightened almost imperceptibly, although his expression remained bland. "I'll handle it."

"How, pray tell? The servants will have orders to refuse you entry."

"I have my ways."

He had once served as a reconnaissance officer, or so he had told her brothers. From his obstinate expression, Anne knew he would offer no more information about his search. Blast his reticence. She vowed to find out more on her own.

Passing beneath the shade of a rowan tree, she asked a question that had been nagging at her for days. "Why did you fire into the air?"

He sent her an enigmatic stare, then returned his gaze to the rutted dirt road ahead of them. "It was David Pankhurst who wanted the duel, not I."

"So you would have just let him shoot you?"

"He's a poor shot. He would have missed."

"Hah. You were a fool to take such a chance."

"There's no excitement in life unless you take chances, Miss Neville."

She had the frustrating impression that he'd handed her an outrageous answer to stop her questions. He allowed her to see into only the shallows of his thoughts, without illuminating the depths she sensed below the surface. The trouble was, she didn't know how to probe those depths when he kept his thoughts hidden from her.

Having been caught up in their conversation, she was surprised to see they had left the hustle and bustle of town. The thunderheads still lurked on the horizon, not yet close enough to block the sunshine. Sheep dotted the lush green meadows on either side of the path. They passed a hedgerow, where crimson spindleberries intertwined with the green foliage. A peacock butterfly flitted over the flowering thyme that grew wild on the rolling landscape. In the distance stretched the narrow shingle of the beach and the endless, shimmering sea. In spite of her ill humor, the glorious vista soothed her frazzled nerves and filled her with an irresistible joy.

She was weary of quarreling. Perhaps it was time she came to know her enemy, all the better to put him off guard. As her mother liked to say, it was easier to catch a fly with sugar than with vinegar.

"You grew up in Devon, did you not?" she asked.

"The family seat is Stokeford Abbey. My elder brother lives there now." He slanted a glance at her. "But no, I'm not leaving yet."

Determined to be pleasant, she ignored his sarcasm. "Tell me about the place. Is the countryside very different from here?"

"More hills, more trees, and no view of the sea. It's been a long time since I was there."

"How long?"

"Seven years." He stared as if challenging her to notice that he hadn't been back since he'd betrayed Lily. "Why the inquisition?"

"I don't wish to spoil such a lovely day with harsh words. So tell me about your family."

He regarded her skeptically, but said, "Michael is the eldest. He's married to a Gypsy girl."

"A Gypsy?" Anne exclaimed. "They're tinkers and thieves. And he's the Marquess of Stokeford."

Lord Joshua shrugged. "Vivien is a fine woman. Their marriage caused something of a scandal, but she and Michael are happy together. At last count, they'd produced three children."

"You have a younger brother, too, do you not?"

"Gabriel. He spent four years traveling through Africa. When he returned home and married, he and his wife, Kate, wrote a book about his travels. Apparently it made them rather famous in academic circles."

When he spoke of his brothers, his face held a hint of

pride and warmth that belied his callous nature. "What an unusual family you have," she said.

"Go on, say it. I've achieved my own brand of notoriety."

"I would, had I not resolved to be civil."

They reached a wooden stile, which Lord Joshua leapt in a nimble bound. As she climbed over, careful of her bothersome skirts, he caught her waist to steady her. That brief pressure sizzled through her, scorching her hard-won calm. Awareness of him lent a vibrancy to the day. Though it mortified her to admit it, Anne could no longer deny she was immune to his substantial allure.

He took her arm again. "Then there's my grandmother," he went on as if unaffected by the contact. "She's one of the famous Rosebuds."

Anne made an effort to match his composure. "Rosebuds?"

"The Rosebuds are Grandmama and her two friends. They've been cohorts for over half a century. And meddling the entire time."

"Grandparents have earned their right to meddle."

He snorted, though without rancor. "If ever you met my grandmama, you might change your mind about that. She raised me and my brothers."

In spite of herself, Anne felt a softening of compassion. "Your parents died when you were young, then?"

"No," he stated. "They were merely incompetent."

Shocked, she asked, "What do you mean by that?"

"My mother spent all of her time in prayer, while my father languished in a drunken stupor. They're both dead now."

"I'm sorry," Anne murmured with sincere feeling. "Every child deserves good parents."

"Save your sympathy. I've put the past behind me, where it belongs."

"You can't have forgotten them so easily." She thought of her own parents, so warm and loving. "It must have been difficult for a young boy to understand their human frailties."

"It doesn't matter anymore," he said. "Let it be."

Judging by the sharpness of his tone, he would tell her nothing else. Yet questions burgeoned in her, the desire to know more about his troubled childhood. She wanted to put her arms around that lonely, hurting little boy and console him.

Then she gave herself a mental shake. Better she should wonder if the man's lack of moral conscience had sprung from the flawed seeds of his upbringing.

They reached the pond at the edge of Merryton-on-Sea, and only a short walk remained to her house. Lord Joshua bent down to whisper in Anne's ear, "We're being watched."

Anne looked over to see a white curtain twitch in one of the cottages. Mrs. McPhee peered out, straight at them.

"Drat," Anne muttered, lifting her hand in a friendly wave to the middle-aged busybody. "The news will be all over the village that Miss Neville has been spied walking with a scoundrel."

Flashing a devilish grin, Lord Joshua stroked her arm. "A pity we can't give her something more to gossip about."

He was gazing at her lips in a way that caused an involuntary clench of response in her. For one mad moment, she wanted him to lower his mouth to hers, regardless that they were under observation by the sharp eyes of the village gossip.

Annoyed with herself as much as him, she reached up and gave his ear a twist. "Then let her talk about this."

"Ow!" he said, flinching away and scowling. "Why did you do that?"

"I could always tell when my brothers were plotting mischief. That move made them think twice."

Just then, a brown-haired man strode out from behind the tall hedgerow that bordered the churchyard. His sober black suit was tailored to fit his short, wiry form, and he carried a prayerbook in the crook of his arm.

Seeing them, the clergyman faltered to a stop.

Anne hoped he couldn't read the impure thoughts that had held her enthralled. Forcing a stiff smile, she said, "Reverend Cummings, what a pleasure. Have you met Lord Joshua Kenyon?"

A shadow of distaste crossed the clergyman's face. Then his boyish features relaxed into a forced smile. "I've seen you about the village, my lord."

"I've seen you around the churchyard, Reverend."

A curious tension shimmered in the air. Of course, Anne realized, the vicar must have heard Lily's story from David.

"Reverend Cummings is rather new to our parish," Anne said to make conversation. "His father is Arthur Cummings, a Member of Parliament, so our humble congregation is especially honored."

"It's a blessing to serve such a faithful flock," the vicar said. "And may I add, it does my heart good to see you out and about, Miss Neville. You must be on the mend."

"Yes, I hope to attend choir practice this evening."

"That's out of the question," Lord Joshua said. "As your physician, I won't allow you to overexert yourself."

"Singing is hardly exertion," Anne objected.

"You could walk or you could sing. You made the choice to walk. That's all you can do for one day."

She swallowed another protest rather than squabble in front of the vicar.

"Perhaps you'd best heed his good advice," Reverend Cummings said with a regretful look. "Er . . . do you know if David will be at practice?"

A pang of remorse speared her. "I can't say. I haven't spoken to him in several days."

"If you'll excuse us now," Lord Joshua said. "Miss Neville needs her rest."

He tugged on Anne's arm, and she had no choice but to accompany him down the path that led to her rambling, timbered house on the outskirts of the village. "You're giving too many orders again," she said as soon as they were out of earshot.

"Then let me give you another. You're not to stroll the countryside alone anymore."

"I can take care of myself, my lord."

"It's time you called me Josh."

"It's time you went away, *Lord Joshua*. Once and for all."

With cynical amusement, he shook his head. "Give up, Anne. You're saddled with me until I find the sniper."

"Why are you so persistent?" she asked in frustration. "I was the one who was shot. You should leave the matter to me and go on your merry way."

His expression turned grim. "No. The bastard nearly killed you. He won't get away with that."

His tone sent chills down her spine. He had the single-minded resolve of a soldier intent on defeating the enemy. Pursing her lips, Anne knew that further argument was futile. She was stuck with him until they captured the gunman.

The cry came from out of the night.

Jolted awake, Anne sat halfway up in bed and peered into the darkness of her chamber. The black shapes of furniture sat in the gloom. Outside, thunder rumbled and lightning flashed. Rain pelted the windows like tapping fingers. Surely she must have imagined that agonized moan.

As she was settling back down, gingerly positioning her head on the pillow, the sound came again. It was a far-off groan, distinctly different from the noise of the storm.

Dear heavens. Was Mama ill? Or Papa?

Then an unnerving thought gripped her. Perhaps the murderer had crept into the house. Perhaps he had attacked her parents.

Heedless of the ache in her skull, she scrambled out of bed. Her feet met the icy bare floor, but there was no time to hunt for her slippers or dressing gown.

Taking a heavy candlestick as a weapon, she went down the darkened corridor and had her hand on the doorknob to her parents' bedchamber when another muffled cry echoed. With a shock, she realized it emanated from the opposite direction.

From Lord Joshua's bedchamber.

Anne stood paralyzed, waiting for the cries to awaken her parents. But from inside their chamber came the loud, rhythmic snores of her father, accompanied by the whistling breaths of her mother. They were making too much racket themselves to notice any other noise.

She could fetch his servant, the odd little man named Harrington. But he slept in the stables, and Anne was loath to venture out of doors at night in the pouring rain. She was on her own.

Had Edwin come to finish her off? No, her cousin wouldn't make the mistake of going to the wrong room. He had played here with her brothers often enough as a lad.

Then the ghostly echo of another cry chilled her to the marrow.

Perhaps Lord Joshua had been attacked. Or perhaps he'd been overtaken by illness. Perhaps he lay dying.

That would serve the rascal right. For what he had done to Lily, he deserved to suffer a slow, agonizing death. And yet . . . the pain of that cry tugged a chord deep inside her.

Gripping the candlestick, she headed along the darkened passage to the rear of the house. Floorboards creaked beneath her feet. Struck by the impropriety of the situation, she hesitated another moment outside his closed door. A lady never entered the bedchamber of an unmarried man in the middle of the night. Especially not the bedchamber of a man as notorious as Lord Joshua Kenyon.

Then a drawn-out moan drove all logical consideration out of her mind. She twisted the knob and entered the darkened chamber.

The absence of moonlight made the room as black as its

occupant's heart. But she knew the layout of the furnishings and turned her gaze to the left side of the chamber, past the washstand and plain oak wardrobe, to the narrow bedstead that had once belonged to Geoffrey. Straining to see through the deep shadows, she could hear Lord Joshua tossing and turning on the mattress.

"Are you all right, my lord?" she called softly. "May I fetch you anything?"

She could hear only the drumming of the rain.

Was he in such pain that he could not speak? Indecisive, she stood waiting.

Then he loosed a long, guttural moan. The sound sent goosebumps skittering over her skin and straight into her soul. She could no more ignore that cry than she could will herself to stop breathing.

Hurrying to the bed, she leaned down. A flash of lightning illuminated his harshly handsome face. His eyes were closed, his expression rigid with pain. Moisture glistened on his cheeks. Tears?

The sight wrenched her heart. Was he dreaming, then? What events in his past would cause nightmares in such a cynical, arrogant man? Something from his childhood? Or his wartime experiences?

He moaned again, leaving no doubt of the depths of his torment.

She set down the candlestick. Intending to awaken him, she touched his shoulder. Her fingers met bare, muscled flesh. With a shock, Anne realized he was naked—at least what she could see of him in the occasional flicker of lightning. The sheets were twisted at his waist, affording her a measure of modesty.

Not that modesty should rule her. She had nine brothers, and he was just another man.

Her heart beat unnaturally fast, and her fingers trembled with the unthinkable urge to run her fingers through his tousled hair, to place her hand on the hard-hewn sculpture of his chest and offer comfort to him.

Anne gave his shoulder a shake. "Wake up, m'lord. It's only a dream."

Through the darkness, his arms lashed out to seize her. He thrust her facedown on the mattress. It happened so fast, she had no time to react.

His heavy weight pinned her to the bed. Her head swam; her lungs emptied. She bucked and twisted, but his iron muscles held her trapped beneath him.

A growl rumbled in his chest. Hot breath seared the back of her neck, and his teeth nipped her earlobe. He was like a wild beast that had pounced on its prey. Anne jerked her head to the side and screamed.

But the sound wasn't a scream; it was a feeble, choked squeak. She couldn't even draw enough air to call for help. Panicked, she made another violent attempt to break free. With all her might, she stabbed her elbow into the hard flesh of his midsection. "Joshua! Let me go!"

His muscles tensed. A low, feral curse sounded in her ear. He ground his hips against her bottom in a move that made her entire body prickle with heat.

In the next instant, he levered himself from her and sat up. His tone rough and incredulous, he said, "Anne?"

She gulped one breath, then another. Her head pounding and her senses reeling, she scrambled off the bed and groped for the washstand. "You . . . *oaf*."

"What the *hell* are you doing in here?"

"Idiot! I tried to help you . . . you thick-skulled . . . over-weening . . . *man*."

"Help me?"

With shaking hands, she untwisted her nightdress. She could still feel the imprint of him, hard and muscled, against her back. "You were moaning . . . I thought you were hurt."

For a long moment, there was only the beating of the rain. He sat on the edge of the bed, his head lowered, his face averted from her. In a burst of lightning, she saw tension in the stiffness of his posture. "I'm fine," he said tersely. "Get back to your own chamber."

"Fine? Is that *all* you can say after attacking me?" Incensed that he offered no explanation, and in particular no apology, she went on. "You obviously had a nightmare. The least you can do is to tell me about it."

"I don't remember. Now get out."

Something vibrated in his voice, the hint of suppressed emotion. Anger? Or did he fear to admit to any human weakness?

No, he was not a man who cared what others thought. But she knew instinctively that he was lying to her. A person didn't experience such a terrible dream without just cause. Geoffrey had suffered nightmares for months after he'd been bitten by a vicious dog. And Joshua had had tears on his face . . .

"I only wish to help you—" she began in a softened tone.

"Get out," he shouted. *"Now."*

His voice struck like a thunderbolt, blasting her compassion and igniting her ire. "With pleasure," she snapped. "Go ahead and suffer alone. But next time, keep quiet so you don't awaken me."

As she stalked out into the corridor and jerked the door shut, Anne chided herself for feeling any charity toward him. She had been on a fool's errand to offer her help. Lord Joshua Kenyon was too callous to harbor any deep emotions.

She would have no answers from him tonight. Or any time.

Chapter Nine

The Love Letter

"Were either of you awakened by the storm?" Anne asked as she joined her parents at the breakfast table the next morning.

Mrs. Neville added a pinch of sugar to her tea. "Storm? Why, no, although I stayed awake for a time planning my next painting. What do you think of an autumn arrangement of rowan berries and orange balsam painted in oils? Perhaps a cunning little mushroom or two and a few late-blooming field roses . . ."

"It sounds lovely." At least Mama didn't know of that midnight visit to Joshua's bedchamber. "And you, Papa?"

His round spectacles perched on the bridge of his nose, Mr. Neville peered absently over the top of the newspaper. "What? Rowan berries are fine, I'm sure."

"I asked if the noise last night had disturbed you."

"Noise?"

"The rain and thunder. It was quite fierce."

" 'Pon my word, I didn't hear a peep." Mr. Neville cast a sly glance at his wife. "Except for your mother's snoring, of course."

"Now, John, 'tis you who snore, not I," Mama said.

"Hmmm. Remember the time the Tinneswoods heard a racket and came racing over here in the middle of the night?

Thomas had his sword and Phoebe a frying pan. They'd thought we'd been beset by burglars."

Mrs. Neville slapped him playfully on the wrist. "Isaac had fallen out of bed and wailed to high heavens, that's what. For goodness' sake, a lady never snores."

"So you say, my love. *I* would say we're a well-matched pair."

Their familiar banter eased Anne's mind. They were unaware of her nocturnal visit to Joshua's chamber. Yet a discomfiting agitation lingered inside her, a reaction to that scandalous, breathtaking encounter.

Afraid that her parents might notice her blush, she affixed a slice of bread to a toasting fork, rose from the table, and went to the hearth to brown the bread over the flames. She kept her back turned for a moment while she indulged in the memory of Joshua's heavy weight on her, the hard heat of his body, his masculine scent. It was foolish, it was shameful, but she couldn't stop thinking about the matter. And wondering how the cad could have such a profound effect on her.

Returning to the table to butter her toast, she studied her father. He had thinning black hair and a decided paunch from the hours he spent reading in his study. The years had carved clefts in his cheeks, yet his blue eyes had a rakish sparkle that she had taken for granted before now.

Had he once been a rogue?

Surely Mama had exaggerated. Anne couldn't imagine her sedate, kindly father pursuing hordes of females. But even if he had behaved so rashly, Papa had too much integrity to have abandoned a gullible girl at the altar.

"Has Lord Joshua come down for breakfast?" she asked tersely.

"He rode out shortly after dawn," Mama said. "An admirable custom of his, I trow. He doesn't lie abed till noon like so many young men these days."

"His military training, no doubt," Papa said absently,

turning the pages of his newspaper. "Let us hope Francis and Geoffrey come home so disciplined."

Reaching for the jar of orange marmalade, Anne hid her relief that Joshua had left the house. She wanted that list of gentlemen who had frequented Quincy's Bootmaker shop. Chances were, he'd taken the list with him, but she meant to search his bedchamber anyway.

"I wonder where his lordship goes each morning," Mama mused, arranging the saltcellar and dishes of bacon and bread as if pondering another still life oil. "He professes not to know many people in town. La! Nor do we, me with my painting and your papa with his historical studies. But I've been thinking. Perhaps we might ask Edwin to introduce Lord Joshua to Brighton society."

"No!" Anne spoke sharply, and at her mother's startled look, she made an effort to moderate her tongue. "I'm sure Lord Joshua will be departing soon, so there's no need to bother my cousin."

"Why, Edwin won't mind. He's a member of the best circles."

"And also the worst circles," Anne tartly reminded her mother. "Anyway, I'm much improved now, so I don't need a physician. There's no reason for Lord Joshua to stay here."

Mama let her cup clatter back into its saucer. Distress tugged her plump features. "Why, there's every reason for him to stay. He has a place in our hearts for saving your life. Isn't that so, John?"

"Mmm?" Glancing up from the newspaper, Papa mumbled, "Yes, of course, darling."

Smiling again, Mama turned back to Anne. "See? Your papa agrees with me. His lordship must remain our guest for as long as he pleases."

"But what of his family? They must be anxious for his return."

"A few more days won't matter. The Marquess of Stokeford will see his brother soon enough. As will his grandmother, the illustrious dowager." Her face alight with awe, Mama clasped her hands to her ample bosom. "Perhaps Lord Joshua will mention us to them. Wouldn't it be marvelous if they took an interest in us? Why, if we became friendly, I might prevail upon them to sponsor you for a London season."

Anne froze with her knife in the orange marmalade jar. "I've no interest in high society. Besides, I hardly think Lord and Lady Stokeford would take notice of our rustic family."

"Whyever not? My brother is Sir Francis Bellingham. And your dear papa"—Mrs. Neville touched the sleeve of his blue coat—"is a gentleman of impeccable breeding. His family goes back to King Henry the Sixth."

"Alas, the impoverished branch of the Nevilles," Papa said drolly, rattling the news sheet as he turned the page.

With jerky motions, Anne slathered marmalade on her toast. "My point, Mama, is that you mustn't expect too much of Lord Joshua. Remember what he did to Lily Pankhurst? He tried to seduce her best friend!"

"Yes, it was a dreadful deed," her mother said on a sigh, "but young men will sow their wild oats. He redeemed himself when he rescued you."

"He also fought for his country," Papa interjected. "Where would England be without our brave soldiers? Throughout history, they've been our heroes."

"Well said." With a nod of her mobcapped head, Mama added, "Anne, dearest, I can understand your antagonism toward his lordship. However, seven years of hardship can change a man for the better. It isn't like you not to see the good in a person."

"Good, bah," Anne said waspishly. "He's proven himself to be a rake. And I find it very peculiar that he'd stay among strangers when he could go home and visit his family." She sank her teeth into the toast. The excess of marmalade was as unpalatable as her thoughts.

Laughing fondly, Mama reached across the table to pat her hand. "My dear, isn't it obvious?"

"Pardon?"

"Why, his lordship is taken with you." Then her mother delivered the coup de grâce. "If all goes well, perhaps he'll make you an offer of marriage."

Marriage? The notion of Joshua as her husband, lying with her in bed each night, shook Anne with a shameful longing. Denying the reaction, she retorted, "I'd sooner marry Mrs. Peavy's billy goat."

"Slanderer!" Arthur Cummings proclaimed, shaking his fist. "How dare you make these foul allegations about my son? I'll have the law on you."

With steely calm, Josh lounged in a chair and waited for Cummings to finish his tirade. The parody of a dignified statesman, Cummings paced the sumptuous library. He had a full-bodied, resonant voice from years of elocution lessons and delivering speeches in the House of Commons. But his tailored coat and brilliantly white cravat couldn't fully disguise a stocky form rough-hewn as if carved by a pickaxe. With his ruddy features and close-set eyes, he looked more suited to driving a dray than serving in Parliament.

Arthur Cummings had recently purchased a pair of boots from Quincy's. His name on the list had led Josh to uncover a deadly motive for him to hide in the bushes on the morning of the duel. Arthur's son, Richard, was involved in a carnal relationship with David Pankhurst.

"You won't call in the law," Josh said. "The scandal would ruin you."

"I would gladly relinquish my own life in the pursuit of justice!" Cummings proclaimed, his nostrils flaring. "My son is a man of God, a veritable saint who has dedicated himself to the pursuit of prayer and the sanctity of the soul. Neither he nor I shall bow to your filthy lies and evil innuendos."

"I've a letter in my possession that proves my claim beyond a shadow of a doubt," Josh said. "It was written by David Pankhurst."

Cummings froze. The redness in his cheeks paled to stark white. Only the muffled crashing of the surf outside broke the unnatural silence. Again, Josh waited, searching those coarse features for a sign of guilt.

"I don't believe you," Cummings said roughly. "Show it to me."

"The letter is hidden away in a safe place. Where you'll never find it."

A vicious anger flared in those beady eyes. It was masked quickly by a façade of dignified displeasure. "I beg your pardon," Cummings intoned in his mellifluous baritone. "I am a respected Member of Parliament, a servant of the Crown, and a pillar of this community. I won't tolerate these unfounded insults toward me and my family."

"I won't tolerate a would-be murderer."

The politician's jaw dropped. "Murderer?"

"Yes. Did you shoot David Pankhurst?"

"What—No! Is he dead?"

The note of hope in Cummings's voice disgusted Josh. Bastard. He tried to imagine that loutish face inside the concealment of a dark, hooded cloak. But it had been too damned foggy the morning of the duel to make out the man's features.

Besides, Cummings could have hired a felon to do his dirty work.

"Pankhurst is very much alive," Josh said. "But someone took a shot at him on Tuesday last. And you have ample reason to want him dead."

"This is an outrage," Cummings blustered. "Good God, I'd scarcely recognize Pankhurst if I passed him on the street."

"You're both members of society. I'm sure I can find witnesses to prove you wrong." Rising to his feet, Josh started toward the door of the library.

Cummings strode after him. "Wait. You mustn't leave just yet."

Josh turned around to find Cummings behind him, a conciliatory smile pasted on his face. "We've both served our great country," the politician said in an affable tone. "You in our glorious victory over Napoleon, and I as an elected official of the English people. There should be accord between us, not these ludicrous accusations."

"Go to hell."

A red flush stained Cummings's face. Josh half expected him to keel over in a fit of apoplexy. Clearly, the man was accustomed to success when using rhetoric to talk his way out of trouble.

Those wily eyes assessed Josh. He could almost see the workings of that crafty mind as Cummings considered and discarded ways to convince him.

Abruptly, the politician marched to a desk near the tall windows that overlooked the sea. Sitting down, he unlocked a drawer and drew out a small leather sack that clinked when he set it on the shiny mahogany surface. "There's two hundred guineas," he snapped. "It's yours when you bring me that letter."

"Keep your bribe. That's not what I want from you."

Cummings made a harsh sound in his throat. "There's more where that came from. But you'll have to wait a few days. Until I can contact my banker in London and liquidate some holdings—"

"No." His neck stiff, Josh shook his head. "The letter isn't for sale. Consider it my insurance policy to keep you from harming Pankhurst."

Leaving the older man fuming, he strode out of the house and into the fresh, clean air. Plato cropped the lush green lawn alongside the cobbled street. Untying the reins, Josh stood for a moment in the cool sea breeze and stroked the animal's silken mane.

A fist of anger gripped his gut. Not so much because of the bribe offer, but because Arthur Cummings had equated his oily politicking to Josh's service in battle. Against his will, his most recent nightmare returned to plague him.

A shadow world with rivers of blood . . . his feet slipping as he tried in vain to reach a dying comrade . . . the boom and crash of cannonfire . . . the enemy attacking from behind . . .

He'd snapped awake to find himself crushing Anne Neville to the sheets. He'd been too overwrought, too disoriented, to question her presence in his bed. Instantly aware of her soft, feminine form struggling beneath him, his body had reacted with explosive heat. All of his agitation had metamorphosed into a powerful craving for her. For one mad moment, caught between the horror of his dream and the promise of paradise, he'd nearly taken her innocence.

She had no inkling of how close she'd come to being ruined.

A veneer of sweat coated his palms. Anne had seen him at his worst: weak and terrified, crying out like a frightened child. He hoped to God she hadn't noticed the tears of anguish wetting his face. He despised the thought of her—or anyone else—probing the experiences he kept under lock and key. She wouldn't understand the atrocities he'd witnessed in the patriotic hell of war.

He had to find the sniper, to stop him before he tried to kill again. Josh knew that only then could he leave here with a clear conscience.

How he longed to visit his brothers and meet their families, to parry Grandmama's wit and trade jests with the Rosebuds. Afterward, he would go to Wakebridge Hall, his estate in Hampshire. He felt a desperate need to find sanctuary in the humdrum details of an ordinary life. The solitude of that calm and orderly setting was his only hope for putting his nightmares behind him.

He glanced back at the mansion with its tall columns and ornate scrollwork, as ostentatious as the man who lived there. He couldn't shake a prickly uneasiness. Arthur Cummings would stop at nothing to keep himself free of scandal.

Swinging into the saddle, Josh decided it was time to find a better hiding place for that letter.

The bedchamber looked innocuous in the light of day, Anne thought as she quietly closed the door. Last night, the darkness had been thick and impenetrable, fraught with peril. Looking at the bed, she felt an involuntary thrill. How vivid was the memory of Joshua covering her. Afterward, she had lain awake for hours, alternately praying for the cessation of sinful temptation and aching with compassionate curiosity about the source of his nightmares.

Delving into his mind would be extremely imprudent, she told herself. Especially now that she had seen the vulnerability in him. Somehow, the glimpse into his tortured soul had made him all the more irresistibly attractive. It stirred the need to comfort him, to heal his wounded spirit.

Foolish, foolish thoughts.

She firmly turned her attention to an inspection of the bedchamber. When Geoffrey and Francis had shared these quarters, piles of rumpled clothing had scattered the bare wood floor along with a clutter of slingshots, books, and toy soldiers. Now the place was neat as a parson's soul from the perfectly made bed to the tidy row of shaving supplies on the washstand.

Of course, Joshua had a valet to keep things in order. Anne had nearly collided with Harrington in the passageway half an hour ago. As the odd little man had entered this chamber, she had been forced to tarry in the next room. At last he'd finished his duties and, from the window, she had seen him limp out to the stables. Aware that he might return at any moment, she made haste in her search.

She headed across the bedchamber and threw open the doors of the armoire, where Joshua's garments hung from hooks. For a moment she stood there, struck by a pang of conscience. She mustn't feel guilty about looking through his personal belongings. It wasn't as if she meant to steal anything; she only wanted a peek at that list, to find out the names of the men who might have shot her.

If the list was here.

For a man of his lofty means, Joshua had a modest wardrobe—probably because he had been absent from civilian life for so long. There were several shirts of white muslin and breeches of black cloth. His two coats were sewn of ordinary wool. She probed the pockets and found only lint and a folded handkerchief embroidered with what looked like his family crest. Next, she examined the cavalry uniform with its dark blue jacket adorned with epaulettes and gold braid. She imagined him resplendent in military finery, a decorated war hero mounted astride his black horse.

And then she imagined him in battle, fighting for his life, witnessing men under his command falling dead from enemy bullets and cannonfire.

Swallowing against the tightness in her throat, she closed the armoire and approached the bed. There was nothing remarkable about the narrow mattress with its brown wool blanket tucked over white linens. Yet she had the most curious urge to press her cheek to the pillow where his head had lain. Leaning closer, she saw a long, brownish-blond hair lying on the covers. She snatched up the strand and hid it in her pocket. Heaven help her if anyone found evidence of her presence in his bed last night. Not only would she shame her parents, she might lose David, too. He would be appalled to hear that she had lain there with Joshua in the dark of night. And Joshua had been half-naked . . .

Her face hot, Anne refused to dwell on that episode. It had been a mistake, that was all. She mustn't wonder about his nightmares or feel any need to unearth his secrets.

Repeating that dirge to herself, she lifted the covers and probed beneath the mattress. Her fingers encountered a piece of paper. She quickly drew it out and unfolded it. To her exasperation, she was looking at an old essay of Geoffrey's with the schoolmaster's stern commentary penned in the margins.

At least now she knew where her brother had hidden his failing grades. Crumpling the paper, she stuffed it into her pocket.

Anne tidied the bed, then looked around the chamber. Where else might a man keep his valuable papers?

A valise was stowed behind a chair. Crouching down, she unbuckled the strap. As she opened the top of the case, the scent of leather and shaving soap brought another disturbing reminder of Joshua.

Something gleamed dully inside, and her fingers brushed against cold metal. Her breath catching, she drew out a military-issue pistol.

The piece weighed heavier than the one Uncle Francis had lent her for target practice. To her, shooting had been a sport designed to increase her accuracy. It had been a game, not a deadly business.

How many enemy soldiers had Joshua killed with this gun? The thought made Anne shudder, even as she admitted to a reluctant admiration of him. He had done his part to safeguard the freedom of England. That awareness had been brought into sharp focus the previous night.

Months after the end of the war, he still suffered from terrible dreams that disturbed his sleep. She had long considered him to be cold and callous . . . until now. Surely an unfeeling man would not have been so deeply affected by the horrors of the battlefield. She felt drawn to talk to him, to hear his stories and to offer the comfort of a listening ear.

But it was dangerous to feel compassion for him. She mustn't lose sight of her goal, to find the gunman and thereby banish Joshua from her life.

Upon replacing the pistol in the valise, Anne made a thorough search for a hidden compartment. Her efforts were rewarded when she discovered a flap along the inside of the case. It concealed a pocket containing several papers.

The first one was for the sale of his commission, the next a letter of commendation from Lord Wellington himself.

Apparently, Joshua had comported himself well on the battlefield, if not in his private life.

The last paper rustled as she hastened to open it. To her disappointment, she found herself gazing not at a list from the bootmaker, but at another letter. She was about to replace it in the valise when she recognized the elegant penmanship. Glancing down at the signature, she experienced a deep jolt of surprise.

David.

Why in heaven's name had David Pankhurst written to Joshua?

Then she glanced at the top of the page and realized the letter was addressed to a man named Richard. Sitting back on her heels, she veered between confusion and outrage. How had Joshua obtained David's personal correspondence?

Anne knew she ought to refold the letter without reading it. But because she burned to know why Joshua had it in his possession, she scanned the neatly penned words.

You understand me as no one else does . . . I beg of you, do not speak of forsaking our arrangement . . . I miss the touch of your hand and count the moments until we can meet again . . .

More bewildered than ever, Anne read the text again, then lowered the paper to her lap and stared unseeing at the wall. It was the sort of impassioned love letter she had always dreamed of receiving from David. But he had written these ardent words to another man. To Richard.

Richard Cummings, the vicar?

She grappled with a profound perplexity. For some time, she'd been aware of a camaraderie between the two men, for she'd seen them together in church. As the director of the choir, David often had to consult with the Reverend Cummings on the music selections for Sunday service.

But could that explain the intimate tone of this letter?

An uneasy perception lurked at the edge of her mind, yet she shied away from examining it. For David to convey such fervent language to another man made no sense. No sense at all—

Sounds broke through her reverie. The approach of footsteps. The rattle of the doorhandle. A muttered curse.

Still kneeling, she turned to see Joshua walk into the bedchamber. He wore his riding clothes, buckskin breeches and a dark green coat. The wind had mussed his hair so that a black strand lay upon his brow.

Her thoughts disjointed, Anne felt only a blank surprise at his presence.

He stopped abruptly, his gaze jerking from her to the opened valise. Black fire flared in his eyes; then his lips curled in a sneer. "Snooping, Miss Neville?"

Chapter Ten

Secrets

Joshua shut the door with a definitive click. "I'm afraid meddlers often find out more than they want to know," he went on. "That letter is quite a testimonial, wouldn't you agree?"

His cold, mocking tone struck Anne like a slap. Abruptly, her inner turmoil was funneled into an intense resentment for him.

She sprang to her feet, the missive clutched in her hand. "Why do you have this letter?"

"Better you should ask what it means."

"Did you steal it? Of course you did. You're a thief as well as a bounder."

He didn't bother to deny it. "I borrowed it as evidence," he said, tossing his leather gloves onto the bed.

"Evidence! Of what, pray tell? A close friendship?"

He stared at her for a long, measuring moment. "Yes, a *very* close friendship. I don't believe you realize what's going on between the two of them."

Anne wanted to claw that shrewd, worldly expression from his face. She wanted to run from the horrifying suspicion that lurked in the shadows of her mind. With jerky motions, she refolded the letter. "Don't try to divert attention from your own guilt. You had no right to take someone else's private property. I'm returning this to David at once."

She stalked past Joshua, but he stepped in front of the door and blocked her exit. "I didn't procure the letter from Pankhurst. I found it yesterday afternoon when I called on the Reverend Cummings."

"*Found* it? You *robbed* a man of God."

"Every man has his flaws. So does Pankhurst."

"David is a fine, upstanding gentleman. Who are you to judge him, a cad without honor or principles?"

His face frighteningly serious, Joshua clasped her shoulders. "Listen to me, Anne. You've led a sheltered life. You know little of the darkness in the human soul."

"I know more than you think! My brothers tell me quite a lot."

"Do they? In this case, I doubt they'd tell you the truth."

"The truth is that you're not fit to breathe the same air as David. Yet you'd spout vague innuendos against his character."

"If you want candor, then I'll give it to you. David Pankhurst and Richard Cummings are lovers."

The blunt statement struck the breath from her. She felt dizzy and cold, awash in unreality. Spots swam before her eyes. What he suggested was unthinkable. Impossible. Unbearable.

Yet her mind leapt to the logic of his words. Such a relationship would explain the intense, secretive looks she'd intercepted between the two men. It would explain why David sought out the vicar's company more often than necessary. It would explain why he'd never asked for her hand in marriage.

But . . . two men together? *Touching?* Like . . . *that?*

Her cheeks hot with horror, she vehemently shook her head. "I don't believe you," she choked out, her throat thick. "You're telling wicked tales."

"Read the letter again if you need proof." His tone gentling, he added, "I'm sorry, Anne. I know you have an affection for him."

His pretense of regret broke the dam of emotion in her. Dropping the letter, she lashed out at him with her fists, striking his chest, his arms. Her slippered toes connected with his shin, but she hardly noticed the pain. "You *aren't* sorry, blast you! You *wanted* to ruin him. Just as you wanted to ruin Lily!"

Joshua turned his head to the side to avoid her blows. His hands on her shoulders, he blunted her attack by holding her at arm's length. Otherwise, he made no attempt to stop her from battering him. She felt as if another person inhabited her body, a raging, uncontrollable fanatic.

In the midst of her frenzy, her vision blurred and a warm wetness trickled down her cheeks. Tears. Her arms falling limp, she wept in great, heaving sobs that consumed her completely. She felt wilted and shivery, unable to deny the death of her dreams. David! If he had paid court to another woman, she might have had a chance to win him back. But she could never bring herself to fight his preference for a man. The thought of him touching her with hands that had touched the Reverend Cummings brought the sourness of bile to her throat.

He was lost to her. Forever.

A firm arm encircled her waist, and she found herself supported by Joshua. Slumping against him, she buried her damp face in his shirt and breathed in his disturbing, masculine scent. His fingers stroked her hair as if she were a child.

But she didn't feel like a child. As her tears dried, she grew aware of his hard muscles beneath her cheek, the heat of his body against her bosom and hips. She wanted to snuggle closer, to seek comfort in his arms, to hear his voice whispering tender words in her ear.

No, it was David she wanted. David, whom she could never have.

Joshua led her to the chair by the hearth and made her sit down. Then he crouched before her, rubbing her hands between his. "You're cold as ice."

"Of course," she said crossly. "I can thank you for that."

A smile flirted with his mouth. "That's my girl. Fight back. Strike me again if it makes you feel better."

Anne balled her fingers into a fist. But without the fire of anger she couldn't bring herself to hit him anymore. The wild outburst and subsequent tears had left her drained and embarrassed of her loss of control. In her frostiest tone, she said, "I am *not* your girl."

"That's your misfortune."

"My misfortune was meeting you."

"Undoubtedly so." Seemingly unfazed by her acerbic tongue, he brought out his handkerchief and dabbed at her cheeks. The gentleness of his touch gave rise to a disobedient warmth inside her. She snatched the folded cloth and finished the task herself, conscious that she must look all red-eyed and blotchy.

In all fairness, though, she couldn't pin her anger on Joshua. It was David who deserved her ire. She felt betrayed, bereft, and more than a little mortified by her own stupidity. Now she understood why her brothers had asked pointed questions about his intentions toward her, then shared those meaningful glances. "I suppose everyone knew about David but me."

"Hardly. Sodomy isn't discussed in polite society."

"Then how did you discover his . . . eccentricity?" Struck by a stomach-curdling thought, she blurted out, "Did he ever . . . did you . . . ?"

He gave her a sullen look of distaste. "God, no! I like women."

She didn't doubt that. He had tried to seduce Lily's closest friend. Despite the impropriety of the topic, Anne forged on. "Then how *did* you find out?"

"It's the way Pankhurst looks at other men. And the way he doesn't look at women. I suspected it years ago."

"He might have told me. We're friends."

Friends. Could they still be friends? Did she even want to continue their acquaintance, knowing of his secret predilection? The shock was still too raw for her to find the answers.

Then another shock hit her. Perhaps all this time David had been using her. Using their casual courtship as a cloak so that no one would guess the truth about him and the Reverend Cummings. The possibility left a bitter taste in her mouth.

Joshua hunkered down on one knee before her chair. "For what it's worth, I never meant to tell you."

Did he expect her to be pleased by that? She had been left in the dark by too many members of his gender. "Typical man. You'd pat me on the head, then go off alone as if I'm incapable of finding the villain who shot me."

"I certainly wouldn't pat you on the head." His mouth tilted in a lopsided grin. "Your scalp is still tender."

She flung the crumpled handkerchief at him, but he dodged easily and it fell to the floor. "I want that list of names," she said.

"You won't find it by searching through my things. I have it right here."

He patted his chest, indicating an inner pocket of his coat. For the span of a heartbeat, she considered thrusting her hand inside and groping for the paper, and Joshua tussling with her, trapping her against his hard, muscled form—

She sat up straight, her fingers tautly laced in her lap. "You shouldn't have taken that letter. It has nothing to do with the shooting."

His tolerant expression hardened. "Quite the contrary. There's one man who would rejoice if Pankhurst were killed. A man by the name of Cummings who recently purchased a new pair of boots from Quincy's."

She gasped. "The vicar—"

"No. His father, Arthur Cummings."

"But . . . he's an elected Member of Parliament."

"And if the truth comes out, his career would be in

shambles. Not to mention, his son would be ousted from the clergy and tossed into gaol."

From time to time, Anne had seen the politician in church, a pompous, patronizing man full of self-importance. His one redeeming grace was his pride in his son. "Doesn't Mr. Cummings spend most of his time in London?"

"He's been in Brighton for the past few weeks, drumming up votes for the next election. I spoke with him not an hour ago."

Rising to his feet, Joshua stepped across the bedchamber to pick up the letter from the floor. He folded the paper, then tucked it into an inner pocket of his coat—probably the same pocket as the list she coveted. His closed manner had already shut her out.

Anne sprang up and marched into his line of view. "Well? What did Mr. Cummings say?"

"He denied any knowledge of the shooting." Joshua reached down into his valise and fetched the pistol. He tucked the weapon in his waistband so that his coat hid it from view.

Watching him, Anne shuddered as if touched by a ghostly finger. "Why do you need a gun? Did Mr. Cummings threaten you?"

Joshua brought out a handful of bullets, which he also placed in his pocket. "No, I'm merely taking precautions."

"Who will you interview next?"

"Another of the men on my list."

"Tell me his name."

He gave her an assessing look. "He's no one in your social circle. He's a moneylender."

She started toward the door. "I'll fetch my bonnet and go with you."

Joshua caught her arm. "No. He's unfit company for a lady. You'll hamper my investigation."

"Then I'll call on Lord Timberlake instead. To see if he can corroborate Edwin's story about the dice game."

And if she ran into David? A hollow pang of loss struck her. But she couldn't let herself think of that now.

"The devil you will," Joshua said. "I told you to leave Timberlake to me."

"I told *you* he won't allow you to enter his home." Anne took grim delight in mimicking, "You'll hamper *my* investigation."

His mouth twisted in a classic display of male pique. He stood close, and as always, her disobedient body responded to his nearness with the weakening warmth of awareness. The rugged beauty of his face and form made her common sense scatter. Even when he scowled, this man wielded a perplexing power over her.

Joshua blew out an impatient breath. He glanced up at the ceiling as if seeking guidance from the plain white plaster. Then he looked back at her with steel in his dark eyes. "If I have to bind and gag you, you aren't traipsing around the countryside without an escort. I'll take you to Greystone Manor."

Anne opened her mouth to disagree when a rap sounded on the door. In a panic, she glanced around for a place to hide. She had time only to dart behind the door as Joshua drew it open.

"Beg pardon, m'lord, I didn't know you were here," said a familiar male voice. "Mama said you'd gone out."

Isaac. Hugging the wall, Anne stifled a groan as she glimpsed her brother's lanky form through the crack in the doorway. What was he doing here in the middle of the morning?

"I returned to fetch something I'd forgotten," Joshua said.

"You're alone?" Isaac asked in puzzlement. "I could have sworn I heard voices in here. Er . . . I don't suppose you've seen my sister?"

Anne imagined Isaac craning his long neck, trying to peer past Joshua's large body. She stood unmoving, scarcely breathing. If Isaac discovered her here, he'd tattle to their brothers, even though she had practically raised him from an infant. On matters of importance, her brothers always closed ranks.

"If I see her, I'll be happy to give her a message," Joshua said.

"Tell her . . . she promised to speak to my wife." Isaac lowered his voice. "About Nell's spending habits, you see."

That promise had been made nearly a week ago, Anne thought guiltily. She vowed to make amends—then Joshua's strong voice distracted her.

"Isn't that just like a woman?" he said, affable amusement in his tone. "They'll bleed a man dry with their appetite for fancy hats and fashionable gowns. I can offer you some advice, though."

Anne considered the advice she'd like to dish out to Joshua. How did he know how to handle a spendthrift wife?

"Anything," Isaac said dejectedly. "I'm at my wit's end."

"Don't despair, man. Give Nell a small monthly allowance, then inform the shops to refuse her credit. She'll soon learn the value of prudence."

"But whenever I suggest a budget, she weeps."

"Crocodile tears, my fellow. Always a favorite female tactic." Anne heard him clap Isaac on the back. "Come along, I'll tell you how to handle a woman. There's nary a one in the world who can't be managed."

The door clicked shut and their muffled voices vanished down the corridor, leaving Anne fuming in the bedchamber. Handle a woman, indeed. Joshua would soon find out that she knew how to manage a man.

A short while later, Josh paid the price for teasing Anne.

He had intended to escort her to Greystone Manor straightaway, but counseling Isaac had delayed him. When he finally escaped outside, he took a deep breath of air scented by the aroma of fresh bread from the bakehouse. A hired man was digging up potatoes in a field, while cows grazed the adjoining meadow. Josh found himself actually looking forward to a gallop through the countryside. He hoped Anne could sit her horse well enough for a run.

Striding toward the stables, he spied a rather dingy curricle waiting in the yard. Anne sat in the high front seat and talked to Harry, who held the bridle of the horse.

The horse.

A black rage choked Josh. He charged across the yard, scattering a flock of chickens that squawked noisily. "What the devil's going on?" he demanded. "Unharness Plato at once."

A sheepish contrition on his grizzled features, Harry glanced at Josh, then at Anne. "I told ye the cap'n would be fit to chew nails."

Her pleasant expression vanishing, she fixed Josh with a cool stare. She sat up straight, her lips thinned and her spine like a poker. "My mare has thrown a shoe," she said. "I didn't wish to delay our trip, so I instructed Mr. Harrington that we would take your horse."

"Plato is a highly trained cavalry mount," Josh said through gritted teeth. "I won't have him denigrated to the task of pulling a lady's carriage."

"But the old boy likes it," Harry said unhelpfully. "Look at 'im, Cap'n. 'E's as keen as a racehorse at the startin' gate."

Harness jingling, Plato tossed his black mane and pawed the earth with his front hoof. He eyed Josh and snorted as if to say, *Hurry, let's go.*

The sight failed to pacify Josh. Plato had carried him through hailstorms of bullets, into the very midst of enemy forces. Without flinching, the gelding had endured the stink of blood and smoke, the shrill cries of the dying, and the boom of the cannon. Plato had the battle scars to prove his valor.

Harry ought to understand that. But Harry was gazing admiringly at Anne.

"I won't tolerate insubordination," Josh snapped. "Unharness him at once."

"Don't listen to him," Anne said to the servant. "We're only going for a short drive. Plato doesn't mind at all. You said so yourself."

"So I did." Harry's eyes twinkled beneath his caterpillar brows. "Methinks ye should bow t' the lady's wishes, Cap'n. 'Tis a small enough favor t' grant 'er."

The wretch was enjoying himself, rot his treacherous soul.

"Move aside," Josh growled. "I'll do the job myself."

For a moment he thought the cantankerous man would stand his ground, and he'd have to use physical force. Then the servant stepped back and observed the scene with his arms folded.

By way of apology, Josh stroked Plato's silken mane. "Got you trussed up like a Christmas goose, do they? Never fear, I'll have you free in a moment. You'll get an extra serving of oats for suffering this indignity."

"Don't be silly, m'lord," Anne said. "Climb up here before someone notices that you're sulking like a schoolboy."

"Afraid the neighbors are watching us again?" he taunted, reaching for one of the buckles that fastened the traces.

She eyed him with cool superiority, the effect somewhat spoiled by her ugly brown bonnet with the pheasant's feather that bobbed in the breeze. "Actually, it's Mama. She's coming straight this way."

Pivoting on his heel, he spied Mrs. Neville hurrying from the house, her plump arm lifted in a wave.

"Lord Joshua, wait!" she trilled. "I must give something to Anne."

Hellfire and damnation. All Anne needed was another ally. Unless he could win Mrs. Neville over to his side.

As the older woman came huffing and puffing up to him, he took her paint-stained hand in his and patted it. "I'm glad you're here, Mrs. Neville. Perhaps you can talk some sense into your daughter."

"She's a sensible girl already," Mrs. Neville said. She had a paintbrush tucked behind her ear and a rainbow splatter on her white apron. "And she's quite advanced enough in years not to require a chaperone."

"I've ordered her to stay home and rest. She mustn't risk a relapse."

"Surely the fresh air will do her wonders."

"Then she may sit out on the terrace and read a book," Josh said. "The jolting and rattling of a carriage will only give her a headache."

"For heaven's sake, we aren't going all the way to China," Anne said. "Only to Greystone Manor to visit David. You were willing to let me ride on horseback."

That was before she had absconded with his horse.

"You'll enjoy the nice, scenic drive," Mrs. Neville said, clasping her hands to her pillowy bosom and beaming at Josh. "You two must stop at the cliffs and enjoy a view of the ocean, too. Peg is preparing a small repast. There she is now."

Lugging a wicker basket, Peg lumbered toward them. She wrinkled her piggy nose at Harrington as she went to strap the basket to the back of the carriage.

"I've had second thoughts about this trip," Josh said sharply. "I won't risk Miss Neville's health—"

"But dear Anne couldn't be in safer company than that of her own physician." Mrs. Neville made a shooing motion toward the curricle. "Make haste now, m'lord. You're squandering a fine, sunny day. The sky is the perfect color of harebells."

She looked delighted at the prospect of sending her spinster daughter for a ride with an eligible bachelor. The hell of it was, Josh didn't have the heart to disappoint her. He also had the sense to know when the battle was lost.

"Harebells," he said in lieu of a curse. As he stepped up and took his seat beside Anne, she handed over the reins with an uncustomary meekness. He snapped the leather ribbons, and Plato launched into a trot, black mane swinging jauntily.

Traitorous nag. Both of them.

As soon as they had waved goodbye to the others and headed down the dirt lane that led out of the village, Josh said, "Don't think I approve of your tactics. Far be it from me to repay your mother's kindness with discourtesy."

"This isn't pleasant for me, either. Mama believes we're courting."

He had suspected as much, but hearing Anne say it aloud filled him with a morbid aversion. God save him from matchmaking mothers . . . and tart-tongued spinsters.

Despite her waspish tone, Anne glided her teeth over her lower lip in an unconsciously feminine gesture of uncertainty. He caught himself staring at her mouth. Then he clenched his jaw and glanced back at the road. "I trust you set her straight on the matter."

"I did my best. But I could hardly tell her the real reason you're overstaying your welcome."

"At least we agree on that."

"Yes, we do."

He looked at her again, and their gazes held for a moment. She wore that look of prim superiority again, her lips thinned and her chin elevated as if to mock the notion that she could ever be attracted to him. She looked more like a woman on a mission than a potential paramour.

Her violet-blue eyes were pretty, he allowed, except when she wore a contrary frown, which was most of the time. The bonnet hid her single redeeming glory, the golden-brown hair she wore in a tight, unbecoming twist. Although Josh was no expert on ladies' fashion, he'd wager that her unsightly mustard-yellow dress was at least five years outdated.

So why did he feel the insane urge to soften those pinched lips with a kiss?

She turned her gaze straight ahead, folding her gloved

hands in her lap. Perversely, her touch-me-not manner intrigued him. As he drove the open carriage along the winding road, he let himself wonder about her. She should have married and had a family of her own, instead of catering to her parents and her brothers.

After that one sobbing outburst, she had taken the news about Pankhurst with a stiff upper lip. Any other young lady would have retired to her chambers with a fit of the vapors. But Josh wasn't fooled. Her heart had been shattered.

Remembering her weeping in his arms, he felt the stirring of an unmanly softness. She had clung to him like a bewildered child, burying her face in his chest, her tears dampening his shirt and her body trembling. He would never forget the tenderness that had washed over him, or his helpless desire to comfort her.

Uneasy with his response, he turned his mind to David Pankhurst. He hoped to God that Anne wouldn't weep if they encountered the blackguard. Pankhurst had led her on a string all these years. Because she was too innocent, too naïve, to recognize the darkness in a man's soul.

Out of the blue, Anne asked, "Will you tell me about the war?"

Josh almost dropped the reins, and Plato responded by launching into a teeth-jarring canter. Urging him back into a trot, Josh said gruffly, "It's over. That's all you need to know."

"I don't mean to pry, of course—"

"Then don't."

"But I was hoping for an explanation after what happened last night." Point-blank, she stated, "Mr. Harrington said the war caused your nightmares."

His hands went sweaty inside his leather gloves. He fought back the ever-present darkness that lurked at the edge of his consciousness. "Harry shouldn't be gossiping about me," he said through gritted teeth. "Let that be the end of it."

A small, earnest indentation appeared between her eyebrows. Again, she rubbed her teeth over her lower lip in that ingenuous, disarming manner. Then she murmured, "I understand, and I'll respect your wishes. Though I do want to be prepared when the twins come home on leave from the infantry. Geoffrey, in particular, has a tendency toward nightmares."

She'd yanked the rug out from under Josh with her mild manner, and he resorted to stiff-necked antagonism. "I won't change my mind on this, Anne."

"Then you may listen while *I* talk. Did you know that both Geoffrey and Francis have attained the rank of corporal? They'll be insufferable when they return, probably tell me to salute them before sitting down to breakfast." She smiled, and the twinkle in her eyes made her appear younger, more carefree. "Do you know, in his most recent letter, Francis already put in his order for my plum cake and Peg's steak-and-kidney pudding? He said that if we refused, he'd see us both court-martialed and drummed out of the family."

"He's been subsisting on hardtack, beans, and gruel," Josh found himself admitting. "Though when we reached France, the quartermasters managed to find cheese and beef more often."

"With the meat cooked over a makeshift fire out in the field," she said. "The twins made a jest of it in their letters, but I can see where a man would miss the comforts of home."

"You can't even begin to imagine," he said, not bothering to keep the bitterness from his voice.

"I would like to hear about it." Her expression solemn, she placed her hand on his arm. "Please. As little or as much as you like."

Her gloved fingers looked dainty against his sleeve. He was nonplussed by her offer of feminine support. Deciding there was no harm in speaking of conditions out in field campaigns, he related a few amusing stories, one about a priggish officer who had had his servant make him a bed of foliage and branches each night rather than deign to lie on the bare earth. Josh went on to describe sleeping in the saddle during long marches, trying to train recruits whose only experience with a horse was behind a plow, and disciplining a nervous ensign on sentry duty who had sounded the alarm upon seeing dark shapes moving toward him in the night.

"We all sprang awake and groped for our sabers and rifles," Josh said. "We might have been bleary-eyed, but we were ready to battle the French to the death. Then we found ourselves facing a herd of cows."

Anne laughed, and the sight struck him deeply. With her head tilted back and her mouth relaxed in a smile, she radiated a beauty that transcended conventional standards. How had he thought her plain? Her complexion was flawless, her eyes an unusual shade of violet-blue. But it wasn't mere physical attributes that charmed him. It was her transformation from pinch-mouthed prude to free-spirited woman. She made him feel mellow inside, the burden of the past somehow lightened, at least for the moment. And she made him wonder if she'd respond with the same warmth and abandon in bed.

Would she lower her guard more often with him if the specter of Lily didn't stand between them?

As if Anne had heard his thoughts, her smile vanished, and she shaded her eyes with the edge of her hand. "Look. We're here."

As they emerged from a thicket of trees, he realized he'd forgotten their purpose, at least for a short while. He had been distracted by Anne, so distracted that he'd lost all sense of time and place. That in itself disturbed him.

He concentrated on Greystone Manor, which nestled in a lush setting overlooking the sea. Immaculate green lawns stretched to the edge of the cliff. Ivy twined over the aged gray stones of the stately house, but no smoke puffed from the many chimneys. For a moment, Josh had the odd fancy that the place was deserted, the gardens tended by some magical force.

Then, out of the corner of his eyes, he saw something move in one of the attic windows. A curtain twitched and a face peered out, only to vanish a moment later. He stared, but the white curtain remained in place. That would be the servants' floor up there. He wondered if Timberlake knew that someone on his staff was shirking his duties.

But if the rumors in town were true, Timberlake had far more serious problems than one recalcitrant employee.

Josh brought the carriage to a halt in front of the house. No groom came to offer assistance, so he secured Plato's reins to an iron post. With Anne at his side, he rapped on the door and heard the deep booming echoes inside.

Anne stood very still, too quiet. In a glance, he noticed the tension in her face. Gone was the beautiful, lighthearted girl. Now, her lips were thinned, her eyes somber, her brows hooked into a frown.

Wanting to spare her this ordeal, he said gruffly, "You needn't come inside. You can wait in the carriage."

"It's best to take one's medicine, no matter how vile the taste."

Josh wanted to shake sense into her. "This isn't a nasty potion to swallow. It'll be awkward if you encounter Pankhurst."

She sent him a chilly glance. It was as if that lowering of barriers in the carriage hadn't happened. "You needn't worry about me falling into hysterics again, m'lord. I'm no mawkish fool."

Despite her brusque tone, a sense of protectiveness lingered in him. Not because he cared about Miss Anne Neville and her predicament—but because he had an innate aversion to injustice. Pankhurst must have known she harbored tender feelings toward him. Yet he had used her as a smoke screen to mask his secret life.

Josh would welcome the chance to plant his fist in the selfish bastard's face.

The front door swung open. A sinewy, sour-mouthed woman in a white cap and apron scowled out at them. He'd known her seven years ago, when she had served Timberlake in London. "Good morning, Mrs. Oswald. It's a pleasure to see you again."

She glowered at him, then at Anne. "Mr. Pankhurst has gone out, miss."

"That's quite all right," Anne said. "We're here to see Lord Timberlake."

Those disapproving brown eyes narrowed. "The master isn't expecting anyone. Nor will he see you."

She started to close the door, but Josh thrust his palm against the thick oak panel and gave her his most charming smile. "Miss Neville and I would like a word with him. We won't take more than a moment of his time."

Mrs. Oswald's peevish look could have curdled milk. She seemed to take perverse pleasure in saying, "If you must know, I've been given especial orders never to admit you to this house, m'lord."

"But it's a matter of grave importance," he said cajolingly. "You don't want to lose your post by turning us away, do you?"

She made a tut-tutting sound. But she grudgingly opened the door and allowed them into a large foyer decorated with delicate French furniture and soft-hued landscape paintings. For all its beauty, the place held a hollow, tomblike silence.

"Wait right here," Mrs. Oswald said, pointing at two straight-backed chairs that flanked the entryway. "And don't go wandering about the place."

The ring of keys jingling at her waist, the housekeeper marched down a marbled corridor, twice casting a suspicious glance at them over her shoulder.

Anne sat down on the edge of the pink upholstered seat. Her fingers trembled slightly as she retied the bonnet ribbons beneath her chin. "I do hope he'll see us," she said. "His lordship isn't the friendliest of men. In truth, I've met him only a few times over the years."

Only half-listening, Josh craned his neck to watch the housekeeper's progress. The moment she turned a corner and vanished, he seized Anne's hand and pulled her to her feet, drawing her toward the passageway.

"What are you doing?" she asked, trying to tug free. "Mrs. Oswald told us to wait here."

"I've a plan to ensure that Timberlake will see us. So keep quiet and do as I say."

Just like a woman, she kept talking, albeit in a whisper. "*This* is your plan? To trespass where we aren't invited? You'll have us thrown out of the house."

"Chances are, we'll be thrown out, anyway." He cast a pointed look at her. "And before you condemn me, consider your own actions today, poking through my belongings."

She had the good grace to fall silent.

Exerting light pressure on her back, he hurried Anne along the corridor, rounding the corner as the housekeeper had done. They passed an array of doorways that opened into sumptuous chambers designed as formal receiving rooms. In one, a maid on hands and knees polished the baseboards. According to Josh's inquiries, Timberlake never entertained guests here, likely because his wife was deceased and he had no hostess. Instead, he sought out his amusements in town—in gaming hells and petticoat parlors.

Anne put out a hand to stop him. "Listen," she murmured.

The muffled sound of voices came from one of the rooms ahead. She started toward the noise, but Josh thrust her into a small alcove behind a cluster of ferns and draperies. "What are you—?" she began indignantly.

"Shh." Sliding his arm around the front of her waist, he brought her tightly back against him and put his hand over her mouth. She went rigid, and he might have been holding a plank of wood. But at least she made no move to escape.

She too must have heard the approaching footsteps.

The danger of discovery heightened Josh's awareness of

her. He relished the softness of her lips against his palm.
As for the rest of her . . . she had curves in all the right
places. Those curves tempted him to run his hands over
her, to see if he could make her melt. She had a strong,
lithe form that made him think of energetic sessions in bed.
His cock stiffened like a soldier on parade.

Fool. He must be more starved for female company than
he'd thought. Next time he went into town, he'd find a
lightskirt and end his abstinence. A long, lusty night was
all he needed.

The loutish Mrs. Oswald reappeared. She marched toward the front of the house, glancing neither right nor left
as she passed the alcove.

The moment the sound of her footsteps vanished, Josh
released Anne and peered out into the corridor. It was clear
in both directions. He beckoned to her as she smoothed her
ugly skirt. A pink flush suffused her cheeks, adding a touch
of beauty to her sallow features.

His momentary attraction ended when she spoke. "Was
it necessary to smother me?" she hissed. "I'm intelligent
enough to know when to keep silent."

"Are you? Then prove it."

He stalked down the corridor, leaving her to scurry along
in his wake. Arriving at the doorway that Mrs. Oswald had
vacated, he stepped into an enormous dining room.

Blue draperies framed a bank of windows that looked
out over the cliffs to the sea. The rest of the gilded, elaborate room lay in gloom. At the end of the long, linen-
draped table, a man sat alone, his hands wrapped around a
crystal goblet of wine. His head and shoulders sagged in a
picture of melancholy.

Then he looked up and spied them. An expression of
alarm crossed his gaunt features, and his wine glass tipped
over, spilling a pool of crimson over the white linen. Just
as swiftly, his face settled into noble disdain. "What the
devil—? I told Oswald to send you away."

"Please don't be angry, my lord," Anne said, stepping

around Josh. "It's important that we speak to you."

"Miss Neville. Why are you in the company of this rascal?"

"Because I knew you wouldn't consent to see me," Josh said smoothly.

Timberlake focused that morose glare on him. "So I wouldn't. How dare you enter my home and interrupt my breakfast?"

It was noon and he ought to be at his luncheon. But the bags under his eyes and his pallid skin bespoke a dissipated nature. "I've a few questions to ask you," Josh said. "Answer me truthfully, and I'll be gone from here."

"By God, you'll be gone without any answers," Timberlake said, rising to his feet in an attempt at authority. "After what you did to Lily, you ought to be horsewhipped."

Torment vibrated in his voice, and Josh felt a mixture of pity and anger. But he knew it would serve no purpose to dredge up the past. "I've made my apologies to you, Timberlake. Henceforth, I hope we can at least be civil."

"Civil? If you had any notion of what I go through each day—" Timberlake slumped back into the chair and passed his hand over his face. A sparse array of graying sandy hair sprinkled his balding pate.

Anne sent Josh a quelling frown, then hurried forward to touch Timberlake's arm in a sympathetic gesture. "We don't mean to distress you, m'lord. Perhaps you'll allow me to ask the questions."

Timberlake slowly raised his head as if seeing her for the first time. "You're a kind girl. Have I ever told you that? I always had high hopes for you and my son."

Her posture stiffened almost imperceptibly. By reflex, Josh took a step toward her, then stopped. Better he should stand unobtrusively at the other end of the dining table. Anne was right; the mere sight of him would close up Timberlake tighter than a clam.

She drew over a chair and sat down beside the baron. "M'lord, I must speak to you about the duel."

"The duel," he said in a scathing tone. "Kenyon came to see us last week. The knave was ready to shoot my son, to rob me of my only remaining child."

At that, Josh broke his silence. "It was your son who issued the challenge."

Gripping the edges of the table, Timberlake glared at him. "You knew he was a poor shot. You should have refused to fight."

Josh turned away to pace, lest he retort that he'd never had any intention of firing at Pankhurst. Timberlake would never believe him.

With a delicate cough, Anne redirected Timberlake's attention. "Pay no heed to him, m'lord. He's a very rude man."

Timberlake's thin face settled into its haggard lines again. "So you say, Miss Neville. I haven't had the chance to thank you."

Josh stared through narrowed eyes. Had David Pankhurst told his father about Anne's role in the duel?

"Thank me?" she said cautiously.

"For preventing a tragedy, of course." Timberlake managed a faint smile. "It's quite all right. I was glad that you drugged David's tea."

Anne sat back in her chair. "You knew?"

"Oswald saw you. Later, we couldn't wake him up. Quite clever of you, my dear."

She released a breath. "May I ask, what did you do later that night? Did you go out?"

He blinked warily. "I went to visit friends in town, I believe."

"My cousin Edwin claims that you played dice all night with him. Is that true?"

"Er, yes. Not that he should be telling a lady of such things."

"If you please, think back carefully. Was Edwin there all night? Or did he leave before dawn?"

"Can't say for certain. Had a few glasses of Madeira,

you know." Timberlake rubbed his brow. "By Zeus . . . I do remember the chap vanishing for a while. He went off with a—" He loudly cleared his throat. "A lady friend."

Josh pressed his fingers into the carved oak back of a chair. Had the whore been a ruse? Had Edwin left for long enough to don a hooded cloak and lie in wait for his cousin? He wanted to ask, but forced himself to let Anne do the talking.

She leaned forward, her gaze on Timberlake. "Who was she?"

"I would never speak of such a female to you, Miss Neville."

"Never mind propriety. This is important. Can you tell me her name?"

"Name? How should I know?" Timberlake shrugged. "I was concentrating on the game. One must shake the dice just so, blow on them, then throw with a spinning twist of the wrist. Like this." With a flourish, he pantomimed making an imaginary toss down the long table.

"Please, m'lord," Anne said, "think. Was the hour perhaps near dawn?"

"Is the old boy in trouble again?" the baron asked with a sly grin. He shook his finger at her. "You mustn't play nursemaid to your cousin, Miss Neville. No man likes a nag."

Josh bristled. He'd had enough of Timberlake's patronizing manner. The time had come for a more direct approach. "No more insults. She has every reason to want an answer out of you."

The baron lifted his weak chin. "I beg your pardon—"

"Beg hers instead." Josh strode forward, untied her bonnet, and removed it. Ignoring Anne's squawk of protest, he gently tilted her head so that the healing gash could be seen against the golden-brown strands of her hair. "She drugged your son so that she could take his place that morning. And no, I didn't shoot her. There was a sniper hiding in the bushes. He rode off before I could catch him."

Timberlake's mouth opened and closed. His wide-eyed gaze flitted from the wound to Josh and then back to Anne. "What? Do you mean . . . someone wanted to shoot my son? This can't be true."

"Believe it," Josh said. "I'm curious to know if you sank deeper into debt that night."

"I hardly think the state of my finances has anything to do with . . . that."

"The word in town is that you've squandered your fortune. That you can no longer afford to live in such style." Josh waved a hand to encompass the house.

Anne gasped. "You've gone off the subject. We were speaking of Edwin."

"There are other possibilities, too." Turning back to Timberlake, Josh said, "Tell me, did you owe someone money, someone who might try to punish you by threatening your son?"

Timberlake's face went pale. He righted the wine glass and groped for the decanter. But his hands shook badly, causing crystal to clatter against crystal. A few more drops stained the table linens.

Anne took the implements and poured for him. She held the goblet to his lips so that he could take a few sips. When he was done drinking, the baron swiped his hand across his mouth and slumped back in his chair.

At that moment, Mrs. Oswald burst into the dining room. Her face was flushed red beneath the voluminous mobcap. Panting, she stopped, her wild eyes fastened on Anne and Joshua. "I bade them wait in the hall, master, truly I did. I've been dashing all over the house, upstairs and down, looking for them."

"Never mind," Timberlake said, lifting a trembling hand. "You may go."

"Begging your pardon, m'lord, shouldn't I see these two to the door?"

"No. I'll ring for you when I'm ready."

Eyeing Josh as if he were planning to purloin the silver,

the housekeeper backed out of the dining chamber. Her manner radiated suspicion—and something else. Something he couldn't quite fathom. Of course, she had been devoted to Lily. It was conceivable that Mrs. Oswald had channeled that loyalty into an intense hatred for the man who knew Lily's secrets.

The little interlude had restored a bit of pink to Timberlake's face. He still appeared distressed, but was no longer on the verge of apoplexy. He let his chin sink to his chest. "I must make a confession," he said in a heavy tone. "I borrowed money from a man . . . to pay my creditors. Fifty thousand guineas, to be precise."

Josh resisted the urge to whistle. Most people never saw that much money in a lifetime. Even in high-stakes games among aristocrats, it was a notable amount. And more than enough to induce someone to murder. "Go on," he said tersely.

Timberlake lifted his head. "He's charging an exorbitant interest rate, but I had no other place to turn. Last week, I told him how low in the pockets I was . . . and I begged for more time to repay the debt. But he warned me . . ."

Anne laid her hand on his sleeve, stroking his arm as if he were a child. "Warned you?" she prompted softly. "Of what?"

His eyes hollow, Timberlake looked at her beseechingly. "He said . . . he'd ruin me. I thought he meant to take me to court and seize the house, all my belongings. I never imagined . . . he would do bodily harm to you."

Planting his palms on the table, Josh demanded, "Who is he?"

Timberlake scowled. "I'm speaking to Miss Neville, not you."

Anne flashed a warning frown at Josh, then returned her attention to the baron. "We know you could never harm anyone, m'lord," she said in that soothing tone. "But this villain must be brought to justice. You do understand that."

"Of course." Timberlake scrubbed his hands over his gaunt face. "Of course."

"Will you tell me his name, then?"

He hesitated a moment longer, then gave a jerky nod. "He's a businessman, a member of society by virtue of his wealth. His name is Samuel Firth."

Chapter Eleven

A Grave Matter

"Before we leave here, there's something you need to see," Anne said in a clipped tone. "Follow me."

Josh knew he was in trouble. Wary and annoyed, he tramped after her as she headed along a flagstone path through the gardens at Greystone Manor. Her uptilted chin and stern expression showed nothing of the kind, caring woman she had been with Timberlake or the high-spirited girl she'd been in the carriage. She had donned that ludicrous bonnet again, and the pheasant feather wagged with each cantankerous step.

Josh caught up to her and matched her strides. "Out with it," he said. "You're miffed because I didn't tell you about Timberlake's gaming debts."

"Miffed? That's how a silly girl reacts to losing a hair ribbon."

"You're angry, then," he amended. "But you shouldn't be."

Stopping on the path, she planted her hands on her hips. "We're partners in this inquiry, whether you approve or not. That requires sharing all information."

"This partnership exists only in your imagination," he muttered.

It was the wrong thing to say.

She released a huff of indignation, compressed her lips, and resumed her march through the formal gardens. Bees buzzed among a scattering of late-blooming flowers. Although the beds were well tended, there was no gardener anywhere in sight. Again, he felt a vague disquiet, as if he were missing something he ought to notice and heed. With a sweep of his gaze, he took in the low stone wall that held back the wild desolation of the downs.

He had a bad feeling only because he disliked trailing after Anne like a recalcitrant schoolboy. But this once, he'd let her have her way. Perhaps after she'd stewed for a while, he could talk sense into her.

He couldn't understand the woman. She ought to thank him for protecting her. That was a man's role, to face danger, to guard the female of the species. So why the hell didn't Anne behave the way nature intended? It would certainly make his life easier. For a moment he imagined her kneeling at his feet, gazing up at him in adoration. And then he imagined her naked, her face soft with yearning . . .

"This way," snapped the real Anne.

She diverted from the garden path and climbed a low hill to a small, Grecian-style temple that resembled a quaint ruin. Tall Ionic columns supported the roof, and the surrounding thicket of beech trees created the illusion of a woodland setting. The leaves whispered in the cool breeze off the sea.

Anne mounted the three marble steps that led into the shrine. Tramping in her wake, he tried to fathom why she would bring him here. Perhaps she wanted to berate him in private. Or perhaps—God forbid—she was distraught and would lapse into tears again. He didn't think he could endure that.

"There's a temple similar to this one on the grounds of Stokeford Abbey," he said quickly. "My brothers and I used to play pirates . . ."

At the top of the steps, he paused, struck by a peculiar foreboding. Statues of nymphs filled niches in a charming grotto. The air inside was hushed and peaceful. In the center of the chamber, Anne gazed at a long block of carved white marble.

A sarcophagus.

An icy sword pierced his gut. He didn't have to ask who was buried here. Numbly, he said, "This is Lily's grave."

"Yes," Anne said, glancing over her shoulder at him. "I thought you should see it. You've never had to face the reality of what you've done."

On leaden feet, he walked closer. A spray of white lilies lay on top of the coffin, carefully arranged by David Pankhurst's loving hand, no doubt.

The sight struck Josh harder than he could have expected. His throat rigid, he reached out to touch the cold stone that was carved with fanciful scenes from mythology. In his mind's eye, he saw Lily at their first meeting, a lovely, dark-haired girl with the face of an angel. He'd been on a fortnight's leave from the cavalry, lonely for feminine companionship, and Lily had stolen his heart.

Regrets poured from a hidden spring inside him. Bowing his head, he uttered a silent prayer for the repose of her soul.

"She shouldn't have come to such an end," he said gruffly, almost to himself. "She was beautiful, vibrant, full of life. Her laughter could ring like musical chimes. When she accepted my proposal, I was ecstatic, madly in love."

That had been the woman who'd captivated him—and a hundred other gentlemen. With her shapely figure and alluring smile, she'd led them all around by the nose. If only he hadn't been so besotted, if only he'd been able to see past his obsession for her, he might have prevented the ensuing disaster . . .

"If you loved Lily," Anne asked on a note of perplexed anger, "why did you forsake her?"

Josh looked up to meet her inquiring gaze. He couldn't tell her what she wanted to know. He could never tell anyone. Wheeling away, he prowled to the front of the temple.

"It's over with and done," he said harshly. "The past is buried, so leave it lie."

Contrary as ever, Anne walked to his side, her eyes intent on him. "I only want to understand. David said you made lewd advances toward Lily. When she refused to submit, you tried to seduce her closest companion, a lady named Catherine."

Sweat prickled over Josh. "Give up, Anne. I won't talk about it."

She firmed her mouth. "Every now and then, I find myself wanting to believe there's a decent man in you. But I can't reconcile that with your rejection of Lily. What happened? Did you tire of her? Or decide that you didn't wish to be leg-shackled? Perhaps you didn't want to give up your freedom as a bachelor."

"Yes, you're right. I'm a selfish cad." He *had* been selfish. But not for the reasons Anne suggested. He'd wanted a wife and children, a life filled with love and laughter. Fool that he had been, he'd hoped to find happiness with Lily.

Now he wanted only to live his life alone. In peace.

Anne tilted her head to the side. "Why do I sense that you aren't telling the whole truth?"

"Because nosy people are never satisfied. You poke and pry without any respect for a man's privacy."

She parted her lips as if to retort. Then her gaze shifted beyond him, and the widening of her eyes made him swing around. Every muscle in his body tensed.

A fair-haired man in a blue riding coat and doeskin breeches stalked up the grassy slope. He gripped a riding crop in his gloved hand. The sunlight illuminated the angry, rigid features that so resembled Lily's.

David Pankhurst looked ready to kill.

Anne stood perfectly still as she watched David approach. Fleetingly, she noted the long, swinging stride that lent him an aura of vigor. His classical features might have been chiseled by a master sculptor. She often had wondered why such a handsome, eligible bachelor would befriend her when he could have courted any woman he wanted. She'd harbored the secret hope that in time, he would fall in love with her.

Now she knew the truth. He didn't want her. He didn't want any woman. Small consolation, that.

In the telltale letter, David had poured out his heart to another man, his lover. A vision of him clasped in an embrace with the Reverend Cummings flashed sickeningly through her mind.

You understand me as no one else does . . . I beg of you, do not speak of forsaking our arrangement . . . I miss the touch of your hand and count the moments until we can meet again . . .

Those passionate words burned like acid into her heart. She couldn't face him. She wanted to flee, but her feet felt nailed to the marble steps, her bosom crushed by a weight of emotions. Sorrow for the loss of her dreams. Resentment that he could pay court to her for five years without ever intending to offer marriage. Fear that she might shame herself by sobbing again.

Joshua moved to her side. His presence gave her a certain sense of relief. Strange how she could view him as her protector.

David stopped at the base of the temple steps. His furious blue gaze whipped from Anne to Joshua. "Why are you here?"

"To visit your sister's grave," Joshua said in an uncharacteristically mild tone. "I apologize for trespassing."

"You also invaded my home and badgered my father. He's in there now, drinking himself into oblivion." David waved the riding crop toward the house. "You shouldn't have told him that Anne had been shot."

Leaning his shoulder against a pillar, Joshua crossed his arms. "He might know something about the man who did the deed."

David slapped the riding crop against his gloved palm. "Balderdash! Isn't it enough that you ruined Lily's life? I won't let you do so to my father, too."

"He's doing a fine job on his own. I presume you're aware of his financial situation."

David's gaze wavered. "I want you off this property at once, Kenyon. You aren't welcome here." To Anne, he added, "You needn't endure the company of this knave. I'll escort you home myself."

His gallant manner was almost her undoing, and she took a deep, steadying breath. "Thank you, but that won't be necessary. I'll go with Lord Joshua."

Scowling, David bounded up the steps to her side. "How can you say that? You're standing by the tomb of the woman he scorned. When he abandoned Lily, he might as well have cut her throat."

Taking her arm, he attempted to draw her away. But Anne extracted herself from his grasp. She felt no flutter of attraction anymore, only the bittersweet ache of loss. "Please, don't."

"Don't?"

"She knows about you and Richard Cummings," Joshua said.

David's face blanched. He stood unmoving, a deer frozen by lamplight, his lips white and his gaze stark. Then he jerked his head from side to side. "There's nothing to know. The vicar and I are friends."

"More than friends," Anne said softly. "I read the letter you wrote to him."

"Letter?"

"The one in which you begged him not to forsake your arrangement. You said . . . you missed his touch, that you were counting the minutes until you two could be together again."

He opened his mouth, then closed it. She could see the denial that he wanted to voice, the frantic need for deception. "No!" he said on a note of forced laughter. "You misunderstood. He wanted me to step down from my post as music director. I refused to do so. We were going to meet again to discuss the matter, that's all."

A part of her wanted to accept the wild story. But logic wouldn't let her. "David," she said gently, "you're a gifted conductor. Reverend Cummings would never dismiss you."

"Yes he would." He clutched at her hands. "You must believe me. We quarreled over the music selections."

Desperate fear flickered in his gaze. She saw the truth there, and unexpectedly, it calmed her. Despite her own distress, his pain was the greater. It was a pain of the spirit, the agony of knowing the world would revile him for the path he had taken.

She gave his hands a reassuring squeeze. "You've no cause for alarm, David. I'll keep your secret. You can trust me in that."

He backed away from her, sank down on the top marble step, and closed his eyes. He breathed heavily as if struggling to absorb a shock. When he opened his eyes again, he stared straight at Joshua. "You," he bit out. "It was you who stole the letter."

"Solely for the purpose of finding the gunman," Joshua said. "There are those who despise you for what you are. Those who would seek your death."

"Yes, *you* would. You couldn't shoot me through the heart, so you'll destroy me any other way you can."

His venom lashed Anne. She sat down beside him and touched his sleeve. "David, listen. Arthur Cummings bears a grudge against you. And he cannot account for his whereabouts at the time of the duel."

David turned an aghast face to her. "You've told Richard's father—? How could you do that to me?"

"He already knew," Joshua said. "I spoke with him myself just this morning."

"You can help us," Anne said urgently to David. "Call on the Reverend Cummings. See what the two of you can find out about the shooting. If he . . . truly loves you, he'll want to protect you from harm."

Shaking off her hand, David stood up. His glacial blue eyes showed no sign of the affectionate friend she had known for so many years. "Help you? Never. So long as you've aligned yourself with Kenyon, I'll have nothing to do with you."

Chapter Twelve

On the Beach

"This looks like a good spot," Joshua said.

Anne blinked, realizing he had stopped the carriage along a narrow strip of rocky beach between a break in the cliffs. She had been deep in the doldrums, reflecting on the painful interview with David and mourning the easy camaraderie they'd once shared. His rejection had cut deeply, yet she could understand the fear and panic that had provoked it. If only she could make him realize that she wouldn't betray him.

If only she could understand *why* he had turned to a man.

Joshua helped her down, then fetched the picnic basket that Peg had strapped to the back of the carriage. Anne balked at spending any more time in his company. He disturbed her and frustrated her when she craved calm and quiet in which to sort through her conflicting emotions.

But she was weary of quarreling, so she followed him along a trail that led through the scrubby underbrush, past furze bushes and wild thyme. He stopped near some boulders that provided shelter from the chilly breeze. Spreading out a blanket on a clump of sea grass, he set down the basket, then opened it to survey the contents.

"By God, I'm hungry," he said.

"I'm not," Anne said. "You may eat if you like. I'm going for a stroll."

Sweeping past him, she went down to the seashore and took several deep, invigorating breaths of salty air. Gulls wheeled against a backdrop of scudding white clouds and blue sky, their cries an accompaniment to the muted roar of the waves. The peaceful scene was a balm to the wound in her soul, calming her inner disquiet.

Until Joshua caught up with her.

In his stealthy manner, he appeared out of nowhere. One moment, she was alone, relishing the restorative powers of nature. The next, she felt a different sort of disquiet as she discovered him walking beside her. The rugged angles of his face, his keen brown eyes, and sun-burnished skin over-turned her preconceived notions of handsome. There was nothing pretty or polished about him; he was all hard, un-compromising man from the slash of his cheekbones to the scar that marked the underside of his jaw.

His presence awakened an unwanted warmth in the pit of her belly. More so now that he had unbent and told her a bit about his war experiences. Why had she never felt so powerful a reaction to David? Perhaps because David had been safe, uninterested in her as a woman. But Joshua made her aware of her femininity in a new and compelling way. Yet now, more than ever, he remained a mystery to her.

By his own admission, he had been enraptured by Lily. There had been no mistaking the torment in his voice, the agony of regret. *She was beautiful, vibrant, full of life. Her laughter could ring like musical chimes. When she accepted my proposal, I was ecstatic, madly in love . . .*

He made Lily Pankhurst sound like the ideal of womanly perfection. And he made Anne yearn to have a man speak of *her* in such glowing terms.

Ashamed to realize she felt jealous of a dead woman, she turned her attention to the beach ahead. What had happened to make him leave Lily? Anne knew that any further attempt to find out would be futile. He had declared the topic forbidden.

They strolled side by side for several minutes until he stopped abruptly and pointed down at the rocks. "That shell is walking."

"There's a hermit crab inside it."

"So you say."

It seemed natural for them to crouch down together and watch the little creature scuttle among the rocks, antennae waving and claws moving swiftly.

"It looks rather like a lobster," Joshua said. "Why is it carrying that shell?"

"That's where it lives. As it grows, it will have to scavenge to find a bigger shell in which to make a home." She looked curiously at him. "Have you never seen a hermit crab before?"

He shook his head. "Stokeford Abbey lies inland. Other than disembarking from a transport ship, I've never been on a beach."

So he had missed out on the wonders of the seashore, where she had spent so many happy hours on outings as a child. On impulse, she said, "Come along, then. We must see to your education."

"With pleasure."

At the warmth in his eyes, she had to steady herself against a sense of vertigo. Shifting her gaze downward, she scanned the rocky beach. She nudged a strand of green seaweed with the toe of her leather shoe. "This is *fucus saccharinus*," she said. "It's commonly called sea belt. The local people use it as an herb for cooking."

"It looks like the slimy green stuff Harry has been complaining about. He says that Peg has been mixing it into his soups and stews."

Anne laughed. "It's quite healthy and nourishing, I assure you."

"Tell that to Harry. He thinks she's trying to slowly poison him."

As they walked, Anne pointed out various types of shells, periwinkles and whelks, limpets and sea eggs, and a stinging sea nettle that resembled a lump of clear jelly. She removed her gloves to touch the whorls of a seashell. When they spied a stranded starfish, Joshua scooped it up and cradled it in his palm. Heedless of the salt spray on his shiny black boots, he waded out into the waves and released the marine animal.

He returned to Anne, his hands dripping. "There, I rescued the poor creature. Perhaps that will raise your opinion of me a notch or two."

His smile struck her breathless. The wind tousled his hair in a way that made her envious. She longed to have the freedom to play with those thick black strands.

Curling her fingers at her sides, she said primly, "Only a loudmouth proclaims his good deeds to others."

"I stand rebuked, then. I hope you'll forgive me my sins."

His penitent look was spoiled by that faintly wolfish tilt of his lips. She couldn't help laughing again, surprised by how much his teasing lifted her spirits. "I rather doubt that you view yourself as a sinner, m'lord."

His gaze dipped to her mouth. "You're always so formal. Call me Josh."

"I mustn't. You're not a member of my family." She repeated the social rule by rote. But she had thought of him as Joshua since the previous night in his bedchamber, when he cried out from a soul-deep pain. That experience had altered something between them. Did he feel it, too?

Or had he been so caught up in his nightmares that he scarcely remembered pressing his half-bare body to hers?

"You call Pankhurst by his first name," Joshua said.

"I've known David for five years."

"But I'll wager you've never entered his chamber in the middle of the night. Nor have you ever lain beneath him in bed."

So he hadn't forgotten. The vividness of her own memory made her blush, and while she was caught off guard, Joshua took her hand, his fingers cool from submersion in the sea, large and solid around hers. Anne told herself to pull away. She shouldn't imagine him clasping her close again. Nor should she desire the brush of his lips against hers or the touch of his hand on her bosom. Those wild, wicked thoughts had taken hold in her like a stubborn root.

They returned to the blanket spread out in the lee of the rocks. Anne busied herself with unloading the contents of the basket. Peg had wrapped cold roasted chicken, a small wheel of cheese, and a crusty loaf of bread. Nestled in the bottom were a flask of water and a bottle of red wine, which Joshua took from her.

"Water for you, I surmise," he said.

"Yes, please."

He looked at her consideringly. "On second thought, after the morning you've had, you need something stronger." He poured an ample measure of wine into two glasses, then handed one to Anne.

"I never drink spirits during the day." Recklessly, she took a sip and let it slide warmly down her throat. "Peg knows that."

"Then your mother added the wine. It must be part of her plot."

"To encourage a romance." Why had Mama never conspired for her to wed David? Unless she too had guessed the truth about him. Looking at Joshua, who sprawled comfortably against a boulder, Anne took a longer drink. "But you would never court the one woman who sees all your failings."

He lifted his glass in a salute. "You know me so well."

Was he mocking her? She should leave matters at that. But the wine emboldened her. "I've been thinking . . . perhaps we should encourage Mama."

"Pardon?"

"We can pretend to be courting. It's the perfect way to explain why we're always together."

He lowered his eyebrows. "Absolutely not. That's a ridiculous idea."

"Why?" she said defensively, taken with the notion. "It makes perfect sense to me. We'll need an excuse to tell people why we've joined forces."

"We haven't joined forces. I made an exception today in case Timberlake wouldn't speak to me."

"I beg your pardon. Since I was shot, I have every right to be a part of this investigation."

Joshua shook his head decisively. "I won't be drawn into another quarrel. The sea air has me feeling far too lazy."

He lounged against the boulder, bit into a chicken leg, and proceeded to enjoy his meal. Anne too felt disinclined to argue any more. She cut a slice of cheese and bread to nibble on in between sips of wine. The hiss of the surf and the brilliance of the sun had a somnolent effect on her, and her cares drifted away like wisps of smoke.

Or perhaps it was the wine. She felt remarkably at ease in Joshua's company, almost as if they were friends sharing a pleasant outing. In truth, she couldn't remember ever feeling so relaxed with David. Always with him, she had been anxious to please and on her best behavior.

A cloud shadowed her heart. Though she never drank more than one glass of wine, she held out the crystal stemware for a refill. Gathering her courage, she blurted out, "Do you suppose David turned to the Reverend Cummings . . . because of me?"

Giving her a blank look, Joshua poured another round of wine. "What do you mean?"

"I thought perhaps because I'm too proper . . . or too ignorant of fashion . . . or too unschooled in how to attract a man . . ." Her cheeks hot, she gulped down half her wine at once.

His gaze sharpened. "Don't blame yourself. It isn't your fault."

"But if I'd tried harder . . . if I'd let him know how I felt . . ."

"It would have made no difference. I suspected his nature long before you even knew him."

A thought boggled her. Gripping her glass, she leaned forward and whispered, "You mean to say David has had other affairs . . . with other men?"

"It's a likely assumption, yes."

Torn between relief and lingering uncertainties, she leaned her elbow on the picnic basket, needing its support. "Then you don't think there's something wrong with me? Could a man really find me . . . attractive?"

Sweet heavens, she had to be tipsy to pose such a question to a rogue. To confess her deepest, darkest insecurities to Lord Joshua Kenyon.

Arching a black eyebrow, he studied her intently, making her suspect the worst. If he had to think about his answer, then she didn't want to hear it. "Never mind," she said stiffly. "I withdraw the question."

"No, you don't. Take off your bonnet."

"Pardon—? Why?"

"For once, do as I say."

In her fuzzy state of mind, it was easier to oblige him than to refuse. She fumbled with the ribbons and lifted the hat from her head, placing it on the blanket. Before she could comprehend his intention, he picked it up and sent it sailing toward the narrow strip of beach.

"My bonnet!" She jumped up, tangled her feet in her skirts, and swayed for balance. The slight delay was long enough for the wind to catch the hat and roll it toward the waves, where it bobbed along the surface of the water and then vanished beneath the churning surf.

In a huff, she whirled around so fast her head spun. Sinking to her knees to steady herself, she accused, "You ruined my best hat. Why?"

"I couldn't have a good look at you with that ugly cock's feather wagging at me."

"Pheasant. It was a lovely pheasant's feather, and it cost me four pence at Piper's Emporium." Realizing she still

clutched her glass, she took another drink and stared resentfully at the water where the bonnet had disappeared.
There was only the blue-green sea capped by white curls
of foam.

Anne turned back to find Joshua had moved to her side.
Her heart tumbled over a beat as she breathed in his spicy
scent along with the saltiness of the air. She could see the
faint, dark growth of whiskers on his jaw and wondered
dreamily if he had to shave twice a day like her brother
Hugh. Then her gaze focused on Joshua's lips, so close, so
intriguing.

No doubt he had kissed Lily with passion. He had whispered sweet words in her ear and caressed her body in an
effort to coax her into his bed . . .

When he reached out to her, a thrill quickened Anne's
blood. Dear sweet heaven, perhaps he would kiss her, too.
Perhaps she would let him . . .

Something tugged on her scalp. Aghast, she realized he
was plucking the pins from her hair. "Stop that!"

She shoved at his arm—too late. Her untidy hair un-
furled down her back and around her shoulders. Hastily she
put aside her empty wine glass and scrambled to find the
tortoiseshell pins on the green plaid blanket.

Joshua held out his hand to show the pins lying in his
palm. "Looking for these?"

She lunged, but he closed his fingers and put them behind his back. Scowling, she eyed his muscled form and
considered wrestling with him, then settled for indignation.
"I want my pins. Emmett sent them to me from India."

"You'll get them back when I'm through."

"Through?"

"Taking a good look at you. You asked me to appraise
your assets."

His keen scrutiny made her aware of her disorder. She
had never liked wearing her hair down, not even as a child.
Once, when she was nine, she had hacked off her long
tresses with the gardening shears in an effort to fit in with

her brothers. Now, she considered using the cheese knife.

No, she'd use the cheese knife on *him*. On his most vulnerable part. "I told you, I've changed my mind."

"It's too late for that."

"*I* asked the question, so *I* can retract it."

When she gathered up her hair and tried to twist it into a knot, he caught her arms. "Don't," he murmured. "I like it loose."

Her hands stilled. "It's untidy."

"It's beautiful." He idly combed his fingers through her hair. "Soft and tousled. As if you've just awakened."

The stroking of his fingers melted her bones. Against her better judgment, she imagined opening her eyes and seeing him lying beside her in bed. Dangerous, impossible, *sinful* thought. If it weren't for the effects of the wine, she might summon the strength to push him away. "I don't understand," she whispered. "Men always admire women who spend hours primping."

"Because they like to fantasize about undoing it all."

Anne puzzled through that disheartening information. "With all my brothers to care for, I never learned how to primp. So I suppose I shall never attract a real suitor."

His eyes were dark and mysterious on her. "Never say never."

Then he leaned forward and touched his mouth to hers.

The light caress of his lips brought all of her senses to life. Awash on a wave of vertigo, Anne closed her eyes. She was falling, and she *wanted* to fall, so long as Joshua was there to catch her. His kiss ignited a pleasurable response that drizzled through her like warm honey. When he started to draw back, she caught the lapels of his coat and held on to him, maintaining the delicious pressure of their mouths.

His breathing altered and deepened, and he put his arms around her, nestling her bosom against the hard wall of his chest. His embrace felt exactly as she'd imagined in her dreams—only far better. To her amazement, the tip of his tongue nudged the seam of her lips. Then he delved inside. *Inside,* savoring her like a fine wine, enhancing the heat that tingled through her breasts and settled low in her belly.

A moan emanated from her inner depths. Never had she known a kiss could be so intimate, so all-consuming. While their mouths were still joined, he moved his hands over her, sliding one around the curve of her breast, his thumb idly stroking in a way that made her flushed and restless. She wanted him to increase the contact, craved it with a madness that made her wriggle against him in an effort to get closer.

"Joshua," she murmured into his mouth. "Oh, Joshua."

His grip tightened for a moment; then he set her firmly away from him.

Disoriented, she opened her eyes to see him watching her with deep concentration. His mouth curled into a moody, aloof smile. "That's enough education for one day."

His pronouncement invaded her dreamy haze. Joshua had been tutoring her? Was he really so controlled, so calculating? Yes. His casual manner proved that nothing tremendous had occurred. At least not for him.

He'd been toying with her. He probably found her naïveté amusing.

Her cheeks burning, she gathered the shreds of her poise. "How kind of you to share your vast experience."

"It was my pleasure." He dropped the tortoiseshell pins in her lap. "And you needn't have any fears in regard to your womanly charms. Your response to me was perfectly natural."

His cool analysis of their earth-shaking kiss stung her. "I should have taught *you* a lesson. Francis once showed me exactly how to maim a man."

"I'll heed the warning."

"Don't bother. You won't get near me again."

"I'm glad we've settled that."

Looking somewhat annoyed, he gathered up the remains of their picnic while she pinned her hair into a bun so tight it pinched her newly healed wound. She welcomed the pain as a distraction from the turbulent emotions inside her. She was angry at him for being so unaffected by that kiss. And mortified that she could feel such a wild yearning for him. Still.

After stowing the basket, he helped her into the carriage. Plato perked up his ears and set off eagerly at one light snap of the reins.

With a pretense of indifference, Anne folded her hands in her lap and gazed straight ahead. The cool breeze blew sense back into her brain. She had allowed Lord Joshua Kenyon to kiss her. A man she knew to be a cad and a scoundrel. It was a disturbing revelation, to discover the fragility of one's willpower. If he hadn't drawn back, she would have let him do with her whatsoever he pleased. She couldn't blame her lack of resistance on the wine, either. Even now, the memory of his embrace aroused a softening warmth in her depths.

Her gaze strayed to his hands as he deftly handled the reins. He had strong, skilled fingers with the devil's own touch. How could she have forgotten that he had attempted to dishonor his innocent bride-to-be right before the wedding? Or that he'd then romanced Lily's closest friend?

Dear heavens. How had Lily Pankhurst resisted the wonders of his hands and mouth?

Stop, Anne scolded herself. In a moment she'd convince herself that he was irresistible. But he was only a man, and after living with nine brothers, she knew all their slovenly, brainless foibles. She had been in shock from learning the truth about David, that was all. In a vulnerable moment, she had sought comfort from the nearest person.

Henceforth, she would keep her mind on her purpose— to find the gunman and see him punished. Then she could rid herself of Joshua for good.

Turning her gaze to him, she asked, "Where do we go from here?"

"Home."

Realizing they neared Merryton-on-Sea, she kept her voice brisk. "I was referring to our inquiries. I suggest we interview Samuel Firth straightaway. Do you know where to find him?"

"Yes."

"Then proceed. There's no point in delay."

Instead of answering, he scowled straight ahead at the rutted road that meandered past the green to her house at the far end of the village.

She would not be discouraged by his opposition to their partnership. Sometimes, the best way to handle a recalcitrant male was to outstubborn him. "I've been thinking," she said. "I believe our investigation would best be served by our entering Brighton society to watch these men."

That caught his attention. Swinging his dark gaze to her, he scanned her from head to toe and laughed. *Laughed.* "You, in society? They'd eat you alive."

Self-consciously, she adjusted her skirts. "I realize my wardrobe is rather outdated, but I can borrow some fashion books from Mrs. Tinneswood and spruce up my gowns."

"It's more than pretty dresses. You're too direct. One needs subtlety to survive the legions of snobs."

"You should practice what you preach, then," she retorted. "*I* was far more effective in eliciting the truth from Lord Timberlake than you were. *Your* brand of subtlety involves threats and browbeating."

There, not even a man of his insufferable arrogance could deny the truth in that. But he didn't seem to have heard her. He frowned at the dirt lane ahead, his lips compressed and the oddest expression of consternation on his tanned features. Curious, she turned her gaze in the same direction.

Outside the stone fence that surrounded her rambling house stood a fine black coach drawn by four matching white horses. A coachman stood conversing with two tall footmen in crimson livery.

"Who in the world is visiting Mama and Papa?" she

wondered aloud. "We don't know anyone who owns such expensive equipage."

Under his breath, Joshua uttered a sound suspiciously like a curse. "I do," he said grimly. "It's Grandmama."

"Your grandmother?" Anne said in astonishment. "Lady Stokeford?"

"The dowager Lady Stokeford," he corrected in a gravelly tone. "I'd planned to go home and surprise her. I'd like to know how the devil she even knew I'd sold my commission."

"Mama," Anne guessed in mortified awareness. "She went on and on about her ladyship at breakfast this morning. She must have written to your grandmother a few days ago and invited her. I'm so sorry."

Joshua shrugged. "This will put a crimp in my inquiries, that's all. You'll understand when you meet my grandmother. She's a social whirlwind."

With that, he drew the carriage to a halt behind the coach, hopped down, and helped Anne descend. He greeted the coachman and footmen like old friends, clapping them on the back and exchanging a few quips with them.

A slender, white-haired woman emerged onto the porch. Her head held majestically high, she stood waiting, her hands folded in front of her elegant blue gown.

When Joshua saw her, a grin broke on his face. He strode swiftly up to the porch and enveloped her in his arms, lifting her off her feet. She chided him, laughing all the while.

Anne stood on the flagstone walk and smiled wistfully at their joyous reunion. How silly of her, but she was happy for them. And it was somehow reassuring to know that Joshua wasn't always cold and calculating, that he could welcome an old lady even when he knew she might interfere with his investigation.

Their investigation, Anne amended to herself. And in a flash of brilliance, she conceived a plan to force him to accept their mock courtship.

Chapter Thirteen

Gather Ye Rosebuds

"So you're the girl who's kept my grandson from returning home," Lady Stokeford said to Anne, who sat beside her on the chaise.

Josh shifted in his chair. This wasn't how he'd intended to spend his afternoon, ensconced in the parlor at Neville house. He should be out asking questions, not facing his own inquisition.

Regal in ice-blue silk with a crown of snow-white hair, Lady Stokeford had brought her two aging cohorts: plump, smiling Lady Enid Quinton in her ubiquitous turban, and the formidable Olivia, Countess of Faversham, her clawlike fingers wrapped around the ivory knob of her cane. The trio had been dubbed the Rosebuds some fifty years ago, in their debutante days. They had been escorted here by a dapper, elderly gentleman named Nathaniel Babcock, who sat chatting with Anne's father.

"Miss Neville hasn't kept me here," Josh said, determined to take charge of the conversation. "I had a business matter in Brighton. The Nevilles were kind enough to offer me a room during my stay."

Perched on a spindle-backed chair, Mrs. Neville beamed at her illustrious visitors. "Such a modest gentleman he is. But as I said in my letter, he saved dear Anne's life. He found her lying half-dead on the path and brought her back here, then tended to her dreadful wound. We'll never, ever be able to repay him."

"Quite so," Mr. Neville said gruffly as he aimed a stern look at Anne. "And I trust my daughter has learned her lesson about riding alone at so early an hour."

Anne dipped her chin in uncharacteristic meekness. "Yes, Papa. It won't happen again."

"I never did care for horseback riding," Lady Enid said with a shake of her orange-turbanned head. "I vow, you might have broken your neck."

"But you must be on the mend," Lady Faversham said, giving Anne a keen stare. "You went for a drive with Joshua."

"I'm feeling better every day, thank you," Anne said. "May I add, Lord Joshua has been most helpful in my recovery."

She sent him a demure smile that caused a combustive reaction in his groin. By gad, the minx was flirting. She intended to pull him into that cursed courtship scheme, whether he liked it or not.

"You exaggerate," he said with a taut smile. "I did nothing more than any other physician would have done."

"You took me for an outing to the beach." To his grandmother, Anne added, "We shared a lovely picnic luncheon. I showed him crabs and whelks, and he showed me . . . wonders I'd never imagined."

Lady Stokeford arched an eyebrow. "Above and beyond the call of duty, I must say. But then, my grandson has many heroic qualities. Wouldn't you agree, Miss Neville?"

"She scarcely knows me—" Josh objected.

His grandmother waved him into silence. "Do allow the girl to speak for herself."

That was precisely what he feared. Making a fist on the arm of the chair, he glowered at Anne. It had been a mistake to get rid of that hideous bonnet. Without it, she looked younger and charmingly wind-tousled, with tendrils of golden-brown hair softening her prim features. Her cheeks had a pink glow of health, and her lips were full and red.

It had been a mistake to kiss her, too.

He had acted on a whim, touched by her naïveté and intrigued by her uninhibited chatter after a glass or two of wine. How well he remembered the surprising pleasure of those lips, so sweet and untutored, eager for him. Her ardent response had caught him off guard. Forgetting he was on a public beach with a respectable virgin, he had been ready to lift her skirts and take his pleasure of her.

Even now, in the company of visitors, he had to discipline an insubordinate lust. God help him if his grandmother guessed how thoroughly he had kissed Anne.

Or how foolishly he burned to take her to his bed.

"Lord Joshua is indeed an admirable man," Anne replied, casting a modest glance at him. "But I mustn't be so *unsubtle* as to dissect his finer qualities. He tells me I'm far too opinionated already."

Grandmama's blue eyes held a sparkle of amusement. "Excellent. I approve of a girl with opinions."

Leaning forward on her cane, Lady Faversham gave a brisk nod. "There is nothing more tedious than a milk-and-water miss who cannot think for herself."

"Indeed," Lady Enid said in her babbling manner, "the young girls seem to grow sillier each year."

"And prettier, too," added Nathaniel Babcock. The old fellow winked broadly at Josh.

Lady Stokeford slapped his arm with her closed fan. "So. Were you gawking last week when we went shopping in Salisbury?"

"'Pon my word, ribbons and lace can't hold a man's attention." Nathaniel's eyes twinkled at her. "But all teasing aside, 'twas you I was looking at, my dear."

He gallantly kissed her hand, and their shared, intimate smile distracted Josh. His brothers had mentioned in their letters that Grandmama had a devoted gentleman friend, the great-uncle of Gabe's wife, Kate. But perhaps there was more to the matter than Josh had thought.

"I'm pleased to know that my grandson has been so obliging," Lady Stokeford said, reaching over to pat Anne's hand. "And it's a happy coincidence that he should be here at the same time as the Angletons' soirée."

"Mr. and Mrs. Freddy Angleton?" Mrs. Neville asked with a note of awe. "Gracious, they're leaders of Brighton society. And quite wealthy, I hear."

"Coal," Mr. Neville pronounced. "The fellow has made a fortune off his holdings near Newcastle."

"Their parties are the talk of England," Lady Enid said. "Why, I heard they rode in on elephants from India at their last ball."

"Nouveau riche," Lady Faversham said with a sniff. "They are hardly appropriate acquaintances, but the party will be amusing, I suppose."

"How lucky you are to have received an invitation," Anne said wistfully. "Will all of society be there?"

Only then did Josh notice that she was bending forward, her gaze intent on Lady Stokeford. Damnation, the chit was plotting again. "I'm sure my grandmother doesn't wish to answer a lot of questions after such a wearying journey," he said smoothly. "Grandmama, are you staying with the Angletons? I'll be happy to escort you there."

Lady Stokeford gave him a fond smile. "You'll be pleased to know that I'm staying right here, at Mrs. Neville's generous invitation. She thought you might like to be near me since we haven't seen one another these past seven years."

"You're generous to accept our humble accommodations, my lady," said Anne's mother. "It shall be wonderful to have a full house again."

While Josh scrambled to think of a way to avert this new disaster, Lady Stokeford made it worse. "As I was about to say, the Angletons' party is tomorrow evening.

here. I've been tending to a business matter."

"What sort of business could be more important than your loved ones?"

"It's nothing of interest to a lady." Except Anne. She was far too interested in sticking her nose where it didn't belong.

"Well, let me see. You wouldn't do anything illicit— despite all your mischief-making as a child, I could always count on you to be honest. I do hope that hasn't changed."

"I assure you, I'm not involved in anything illegal. You can safely pack up your things and return home."

"Be mysterious if you wish. But since we're on the topic of secrets . . ." With her index finger, she tapped her dainty jaw. "I understand Lord Timberlake has purchased a home in the area. Have you gone to pay your respects to him yet?"

His gut clenched. How had Grandmama managed to strike so dangerously close to his purpose? It had to be luck. Not even with her uncanny ear for gossip could she have learned about that thwarted duel.

"I've called on him," he said tersely. "Nothing more need be said."

But Grandmama followed her own counsel. "It was a tragedy that Lily died so young. I do hope you don't blame yourself."

"It's over with and done."

"Not entirely." She placed her hand on his arm, her gaze soft with sympathy. "My dear boy, you must be prepared when you attend the Angletons' party. The vicious rumors will start again. They'll whisper that you betrayed your bride-to-be by consorting with another woman."

"Let them babble as they like. It matters little to me."

"It matters to *me*. Perhaps now you'll tell me what really happened between the two of you."

He gave a firm shake of his head. "The subject is closed."

But his grandmother went on. "Lily was a charming girl,

beautiful and admired by the men. Pardon my bluntness, but did you find out she was having an affair?"

"No," he exploded. "I did not."

"Certainly you must have had cause for abandoning her. It was a whirlwind courtship, and it's understandable that you might have panicked on the eve of the wedding—"

"I didn't panic," Josh said through gritted teeth. "That's all I'll say on the matter. To you or to anyone else."

Grandmama pursed her lips. The suspicious look she flashed at him cut him to the quick. His jaw taut, he turned his gaze out the window. God, if only she knew the truth. But he had sworn a vow of silence, and he would guard that secret to his dying day.

"Forgive me for dredging up the past," Lady Stokeford said with a stiff note of apology. "Better we should speak of your future."

"As you like." He seized the diversion. "I intend to settle at Wakebridge Hall. With my training as a doctor, I'll practice medicine, too."

He expected her to object, but she nodded thoughtfully. "With your inheritance, you needn't pursue a profession. However, I can see that you feel compelled to do something worthy with your life."

"It's something to keep me occupied, that's all."

"I hope you'll turn your mind to marriage, too," she went on. "It's past time you took a bride. Miss Anne Neville would suit you quite admirably."

Poked by the pin of her audacity, he sprang up from the chaise. "Devil take it, Grandmama. I've no wish to marry."

"It isn't natural for a man to be alone." She gave him a look that was part compassion, part determination. "I don't know if you're wallowing in guilt or grief or both, but I do know that you can't mourn Lily forever."

For a moment, he felt too strangled to speak. The mere thought of marriage made him sweat. Losing his heart to Lily had been enough for one lifetime. Now he craved only solitude. He wanted to put his memories of the war behind him, to ride the peaceful land of his estate without bracing himself to meet the enemy over the next hill.

The last thing he needed was an outspoken, meddlesome wife.

"You don't even know Miss Neville," he snapped.

"I haven't lived for over seventy years without having learned something of human nature. Anne is clever, strong, and honest. And I do believe I detected a mutual regard in the way you two were looking at each other."

Stifling a curse, he paced the small sitting room. He wanted to deny it again. But then Grandmama would badger him about why he was staying in Brighton. If she found out the truth, she and the Rosebuds would meddle, and he already had one foolhardy female to protect.

"All right," he forced out gruffly. "I'll admit to having an interest in Anne. But that's the extent of it."

A brilliant smile spread over Lady Stokeford's finely wrinkled face. "I suspected as much. She's a fine, feisty girl, and she won't bore you once the lust has worn off."

He pivoted on his heel to glower at her. "Blast it all! What can you know—"

"About lust?" She lifted her gaze heavenward. "Oh, you young people. You can't imagine your elders knowing anything about intimate relations. As if you babes were found beneath cabbage leaves."

Not letting her see him cringe, he resumed pacing. "You needn't make it a topic of discussion."

"I should, indeed, when an innocent girl comes in without a bonnet, her hair mussed, and her lips reddened. Now, I won't ask you what you two were doing on that beach, but I will say, what precisely are your intentions toward Anne?"

"I won't seduce her, if that's what you mean." Seeking a diversion, he said, "I'd rather hear about Nathaniel Babcock's intentions toward you."

His grandmother blushed. *Blushed.* "Pish-posh. We're

merely friends. We've known one another since I was a debutante."

More curious than ever, he pressed, "What exactly is the nature of your relationship?"

"Really, Joshua! How rude of you to pry into the affairs of your elders." She rose from the chaise and swept toward the door. "It's high time I went to the aid of Mrs. Neville. She'll want advice on the latest fashions." A high color in her cheeks, Lady Stokeford departed the room, leaving a trace of her lilac perfume.

Chuckling, Josh shook his head. He should have gone for that plan of attack from the start. He would have spared himself the inquisition.

And the damnable lie of declaring a romantic interest in Anne.

Chapter Fourteen

Gilding Lily

Seated in the luxurious Stokeford coach, Anne peered out the window and tried in vain to catch a glimpse of Joshua on horseback. She could see only the throngs of pedestrians and carriages, the cobbled courtyards in between the old stone buildings near the marketplace.

The narrow streets of Brighton prevented Joshua from riding alongside the vehicle, she reminded herself. He'd promised his grandmother that he'd escort the small party into town since Nathaniel Babcock had departed to stay with friends nearby.

Surely Joshua wouldn't abscond, though.

Lady Stokeford had taken charge with tact and charm and a steely resolution rather like that of her grandson. After surveying the meager contents of Anne's wardrobe, the dowager marchioness had conferred with Mrs. Neville in private and then announced that a trip to the dressmaker was in order.

Now, as Lady Stokeford sat gossiping with her two elderly friends, Anne twined her gloved fingers in her lap. Mama and Papa had been surprisingly happy to send her off to the shops with the Rosebuds. She felt a moment's chagrin. Were her parents so eager to see her wed and gone? They had never encouraged—or discouraged—an alliance with David. Had they known that he could never make her happy? From time to time, they had pressed her to enter society and seek a husband. But they had always respected her declared disinterest in primping and preening. Until now.

She was still pondering their reaction when the Stokeford coach came to a stop and the footman handed them down. Shops lined both sides of the fashionable street, chemists and milliners, shoemakers and confectionaries. Footmen toting towers of parcels trailed behind elegant ladies with parasols.

Flawlessly masculine in a dark green coat and buckskin breeches with gleaming black boots, Joshua dismounted. The sight of him filled Anne with a giddy memory of his kiss. She felt short of breath at the thought of his large hand cupping her bosom. And the wicked longing to experience it again.

He bowed to his grandmother. "Here you are, safe and sound. I trust you won't mind if I make myself scarce for a few hours."

Lady Stokeford waggled her fingers in a dismissing motion. "Certainly not."

"But where are you going?" Anne exclaimed in dismay.

One corner of his mouth quirked upward. He stepped forward and raised her hand to his lips. Ignoring her question, he posed one of his own. "Dare I hope you'll miss me?"

The rascal was flirting. A thrill bedazzled Anne even as she reminded herself the courtship was merely a ruse. She forced a smile. "Of course. But I thought you'd want to stay with us, to visit with her ladyship."

"And watch you ladies compare buttons? No, thank you."

"I quite agree," Lady Stokeford said, linking arms with Anne. "Do run along, my dear boy. We've work to do, and you'll only get in the way."

The dowager drew Anne toward the dressmaker's shop.

Overhead, a sign decorated with fleur-de-lis displayed the name Madame Daumier. Lady Enid and Lady Faversham, who had been examining the display in the bowfront window, fell into step behind them.

Anne had one last, frustrating glimpse of Joshua swinging onto Plato. He looked at her and grinned, bringing his hand up in a mocking salute. Then he rode away down the busy street.

He intended to interrogate Samuel Firth. Without her.

"I've just remembered an errand for Mama," Anne said, balking at the door. "She needs ocher pigment to complete one of her paintings. I'll dash down to the chemist's and be back before you know it—"

"Nonsense," Lady Stokeford said crisply. "Your mother told me quite clearly that you must have the proper attire. Come along."

Anne acknowledged that she was well and truly trapped. By Mama's wishes, by Lady Stokeford's command, by her own desire to successfully mingle with the suspects at the ball.

A little bell tinkled overhead as they entered the shop. Decorated in the lavish grandeur of the old French court, the place had an elegance and style that surpassed the more modest Piper's Emporium, where Anne usually made her purchases. Here, gold cords anchored swags of burgundy draperies, and gilded chairs lined the counter where dapper salesmen showed bolts of cloth to fashionable ladies. Feeling awkward amid the opulence, Anne lagged behind the Rosebuds.

A tall, handsome woman clad in tasteful dark blue came sweeping toward them. "*Bonjour.* I am Madame Daumier. May I be of assistance?"

Lady Stokeford introduced herself and the Rosebuds, then brought Anne forward. "Miss Anne Neville will require a full wardrobe for her launch into society."

Madame's eyes lit up. "*Oui,* my lady. You will want

many gowns, then, for morning, for visiting, for tea, for walking, for parties."

"No," Anne said. "I need a ballgown, that's all. The expense—"

"Will be borne by your father," the dowager said crisply. "He has already approved the matter."

"But—"

Her protest was lost as the fawning Madame ushered them into a large, private dressing chamber where Anne found herself surrounded by an army of assistants. Two women stripped her down to her shift while another circled her waist with a tape to take her measurements.

Several other women brought in bolts of fabric and lengths of lace. The Rosebuds sat in gilt chairs and perused books of fashion, discussing which styles would best suit Anne.

The abundance of fine textiles boggled Anne. There were silks and cambrics, linens and satins, in an array of pretty colors. For a moment, she lost herself in the fantasy of wearing such finery, of savoring Joshua's reaction to her. Then she sternly reminded herself that a new gown or two were merely the means to an end.

The seamstress held out a length of white cloth. "Mademoiselle will need a special gown for her debut. This sarcenet is popular with the young ladies in London."

"Miss Neville has character unlike those silly girls just out of the schoolroom," Lady Stokeford said, fingering a roll of vivid pink silk. "This one will enhance her complexion and make her stand out in a crowd."

Anne eyed it askance. "Pink is too . . . feminine. I favor this yellow. Or perhaps the brown over there."

"They don't favor *you*," Lady Faversham said bluntly. "That gown you were wearing today is an example."

"Pardon?"

"Oh, dear, I'm afraid Olivia is right," Lady Enid said with an apologetic look. "That particular hue turns your skin . . . sallow."

"It does?" Holding up her best gown, Anne examined herself in the full-length mirror. She'd always considered the mustard color to be bright and cheerful. But here, with the late afternoon sunlight streaming through the tall windows, she took a closer look at herself. "Good heavens," she said faintly. "You're right."

Lady Stokeford glided to her side. "You're a handsome girl," she said. "You must trust in my judgment to dress you properly."

Handsome? With her strong features, too-tall form, and odd, purplish-blue eyes? She did want to be handsome . . . to know how to attract a man. The memory of that episode on the beach made her weak at the knees. Would Joshua kiss her again if she learned how to behave like a lady of fashion?

No. She must charm the suspects, not him.

"All right, then," Anne said decisively. "I'll have the pink ballgown and perhaps another for daytime. But that's quite sufficient. I will not beggar my parents." Not only that, she would have little use for an extravagant new wardrobe once she and Joshua exposed the gunman. Once Joshua left Brighton forever.

"Such a sweet, considerate child you are," Lady Enid said, a smile warming her plump features.

Lady Faversham nodded in approval. " 'Tis rare to find one so unselfish these days."

"Nor one so able to stand up to my autocratic grandson," Lady Stokeford added. "I do believe you're the perfect girl for him."

Anne's rib cage squeezed, leaving her breathless. Without thinking, she said, "But I'm not at all like Lily. *She* was perfect."

The Rosebuds exchanged a glance. Lady Enid let the fashion book in her lap fall shut. Lady Faversham tightened her knobby fingers around her cane. Lady Stokeford tilted her head sympathetically.

Lady Stokeford waved Madame and her assistants out

of the dressing room. When they were gone, she said in a soft voice, "I presume you're referring to Lily Pankhurst?"

Anne realized she had committed a *faux pas* in bringing up the scandal. Swallowing her questions, she said, "Forgive me, my lady. I was wrong to mention her."

The dowager shook her head. "You've every right to be curious about my grandson's broken betrothal. May I ask, did you ever have occasion to meet Lily?"

"No. But I am—or was—fast friends with her brother, David. He's told me many times how wonderful Lily was. Even Joshua said she was beautiful, vibrant, full of life."

The memory of his words haunted Anne. *Her laughter could ring like musical chimes. When she accepted my proposal, I was ecstatic, madly in love . . .*

Lady Stokeford came forward and took Anne's hands. "You're most certainly all those things, too," she said with conviction. "When you enter society, you'll have men fawning at your feet."

Anne felt like a giantess beside the dainty dowager. "But I'm not small and delicate."

"Thank heavens for that," Lady Faversham said, thumping her cane on the carpet. "Some girls these days look so frail, they'd blow away in a brisk breeze."

"Joshua admires you already," Lady Enid declared. "Only think how enchanted he'll be when you're arrayed in the lastest fashion."

Anne walked restlessly to a table and plucked at a bolt of sea-green silk. Unable to contain her dogged curiosity, she said, "If only I could understand why he betrayed Lily. How could he have been so cruel to her?"

"I too wish I knew the answer to that," Lady Stokeford said on a sigh. She sank down onto a gilded chair. "My grandson refuses to speak of the matter."

Lady Enid and Lady Faversham murmured in commiseration.

Anne bit her lip. The Rosebuds didn't know what he

had done. They didn't know that he had turned his amorous attentions from Lily to her friend Catherine.

Anne couldn't bring herself to tell them the truth, either.

Lady Faversham patted Lady Stokeford's hand. "Whatever happened, my dear, he's paid for his sins. And it's admirable that he's never spoken a single harsh word about Lily."

"Not a syllable," Lady Enid declared. "Why, a true knave would have cast all the blame onto the woman."

"After all," Lady Stokeford added, "Lily isn't here to defend herself."

Anne hadn't considered that. When she'd questioned him at the gravesite, he'd had ample opportunity to denounce Lily. He could have claimed that she'd betrayed him with another man. But he'd said nothing. Why? Was it possible that the war had taught him something of honor?

"I'm convinced that Joshua had good reason to act as he did," Lady Stokeford went on. "Even as a boy, he had a keen sense of integrity. Why, he once walked five miles to return a nail he'd absent-mindedly taken from the village blacksmith."

Lady Faversham gave a crisp nod. "He was quite skilled at mediating the quarrels between your eldest grandson and mine."

"And he was so kind to poor Charlotte when she burned her arm," Lady Enid said, her plump face solemn beneath the iridescent green cloth that wrapped her head. "He was the only one who could persuade my granddaughter to take her medicines."

That didn't sound like the aloof, callous man that Anne knew. The seducer who had scorned his bride-to-be in favor of another woman.

As the Rosebuds returned to the task of selecting fabrics and styles, Anne felt more confused than ever. Surely their opinions of Joshua were embroidered by family loyalties. It was natural for Lady Stokeford to view her grandson in the most favorable light. Yet what if the Rosebuds were right? What if there had been extenuating circumstances that had brought about the end of the betrothal . . . circumstances known only to Lily and Joshua?

And Joshua wouldn't talk.

Much to Anne's frustration, she was no closer to answering the biggest question of all: How could he have spurned the woman he'd professed to love?

Josh declined the secretary's offer of a seat in one of the leather chairs flanking an unlit fireplace. He remained standing as the diligent little man opened a polished mahogany door and vanished into the next room.

The antechamber had tall windows with dark green draperies, decorative potted plants, and a table with the latest newspapers. But Josh was too restless to relax with the London *Times*. It was a relief that he'd managed to duck out of the hen party at the dressmaker's, though Anne would make him pay for his defection later. She had no qualms about standing up to him, and he rather enjoyed her quick-witted mind.

He had also enjoyed kissing her. Her passionate response had surprised him. That had to be the reason he couldn't stop thinking about her—and imagining what else he'd like to do with her.

He'd like to soften that sharp tongue of hers again. He'd press her up against a wall and kiss her until she melted in his arms. This time, he'd caress her shapely curves, undress her slowly, look at her naked. He'd weigh her breasts in his palms and taste the rosy tips. Then he'd move lower, savoring her satiny skin until she writhed and moaned with pleasure—

"M'lord?" The sober secretary stood by the door, a hint of startled curiosity in his obsequious manner. "Mr. Firth will see you now."

Cursing himself for fantasizing instead of plotting strategy, Josh cleared his mind of all but his cold purpose. He must be alert and vigilant, prepared to wrest answers from a slippery predator.

The office within was more functional than sumptuous, showing little trace of the wealth of its occupant. Clearly, this was a place of commerce from the ledgers on the bookshelves to the plain wooden shutters that were thrown back to admit the afternoon light.

Samuel Firth sat behind a vast mahogany desk. He was a surprisingly suave, handsome man in his early thirties, with clean features and groomed black hair. Though his rolled-up shirtsleeves exposed muscled forearms, he looked more like a gentleman rogue than a ruthless moneylender.

Those intense blue eyes assessed Josh with a flash of something else he couldn't identify. Something akin to agitation. No, animosity. A blot of ink stained the paper in front of Firth as if he'd flung down his quill pen in anger upon hearing of his visitor.

Odd that he would feel malice toward a stranger. Or perhaps not so odd.

Firth made no attempt at the social amenities, neither rising from his chair nor extending his hand. "Kenyon," he acknowledged with a curt nod.

"Firth." Josh responded to the man's rudeness by seating himself without invitation. "I took a chance on finding you here so late in the day."

"I'm a businessman, not a noble dilettante. So state your purpose. I've little time for chitchat."

"I've a few questions to ask of you," Josh said. "About a matter you'll find quite worthy of your time."

Firth tightened his fingers on the arms of his chair. A muscle worked in his jaw, and again, the impression of raw hostility fed Josh's suspicions. Was Firth merely an impatient, mistrustful man? Or did the tension in him betray guilt?

"Go on," Firth growled.

"I understand you lend money to those who sink too deep at the gaming tables. Is this true?"

Firth stared for another long moment, then gave a bark of laughter. "Are you saying you came to me for a *loan*?"

"Hardly. My inquiry concerns someone who is indebted to you. Lord Timberlake, to be precise."

"I don't discuss my clients."

Steepling his fingers, Josh leaned back in his chair. Either Firth had a twisted integrity, or he was hiding the truth. "Timberlake admitted the debt to me. He also said that he lacks the means to repay the fifty thousand guineas."

His face stony, Firth said nothing.

"Eight days ago, you threatened to force him to pay," Josh went on. "One way or another."

"The matter has nothing to do with you."

"That remains to be seen. Tell me your whereabouts at dawn on Tuesday of last week."

"Tuesday?"

"You heard me. It was only a week ago, so it shouldn't be so difficult to recall."

Lounging in his chair, Firth cocked a black eyebrow. "I was here in my office as I always am at that hour."

"So early? Can your secretary corroborate that?"

"Higgins doesn't arrive until eight o'clock. Now, tell me what this interrogation is about."

"Someone took a shot at Timberlake's son, David."

Firth frowned. "At dawn? Are you saying that David Pankhurst was involved in a duel?"

"Yes." Josh kept silent about Anne's masquerade. The fewer who knew about that, the better. "But his opponent didn't shoot him. There was a man hiding in the bushes. He fired at Pankhurst and then rode away."

Picking up the quill pen, Firth idly turned it in his fingers. "How can you know all this? Unless you were the other party in this duel."

"That isn't important."

"It is, indeed." Firth's mouth formed a knowing sneer as he looked Josh up and down. "Were you two quarreling over a lover?"

The implication strained the limits of Josh's restraint. He fought back the urge to plant his fist in that insulting face. Tightly he said, "I ended my betrothal to his sister seven years ago. The day before the wedding."

"I hear she took her own life."

Josh returned that frosty blue stare. So the gossip about Lily's death had reached even the ears of this moneylender. Deliberately, he resumed the topic of his visit. "Have you no one who can testify to your whereabouts on Tuesday?"

"If you're accusing me of attempted murder, then show me your proof."

"You've ample reason to shoot David Pankhurst—or to hire someone to do so—as a warning to his father. That should be cause enough to interest the magistrate."

Looking obliquely amused, Firth tapped the desk with the pen. "Feel free to report me. The magistrate owes me a few favors."

It came as no surprise that Samuel Firth paid bribes to a corrupt legal system. Or that he believed he could get off free after shooting Anne.

In a blaze of memory, Josh saw her sprawled on the cold ground, her eyes closed and scarlet blood staining her brownish-blond hair.

He sprang to his feet, pressed his palms to the desk, and leaned forward. "No one is above the law, Firth. Not even you. If you're responsible for this shooting, then by God, I'll make you pay."

Samuel Firth stood at the window and gazed down at the busy roadway. For once, he paid no heed to the glitter of the sea or the wharves that lined the commercial section of town. Every muscle in his body tensed as Lord Joshua Kenyon strode out of the building and untied the reins of his magnificent black gelding.

Cold hatred knotted Samuel's gut. For many years, he had thought about this meeting, when he would come face to face with one of the hallowed Kenyon brothers. He had planned what he would say, how he would act.

But the moment had arrived out of the blue, and he had said nothing. He had held his tongue and heeded the inner instinct that warned him the time was not yet right.

In the street below, Joshua Kenyon swung onto his horse and rode away. He had the aura of a cavalry officer, square-shouldered and arrogantly commanding. He was the middle brother, a captain who had earned accolades from Wellington himself. Like his brothers, he had been blessed from birth with wealth, authority, and privilege.

Samuel had spent his youth on the wretched streets of Covent Garden. The riches he enjoyed now had been acquired through his own blood and sweat. He had clawed his way to the top and carved out his place in the glittering world of society.

For one purpose.

Soon, he promised himself. Soon he would set his plan into motion.

And then he would enjoy his revenge.

Chapter Fifteen

The Jealousy Ploy

"Behold, our pièce de résistance," said Lady Stokeford, making a sweeping gesture toward Anne at the top of the stairs. "Do come down, my dear. Your coach is waiting to whisk you to the ball."

Feeling rather like a fairy-tale princess, Anne started slowly down the steps. She pretended not to notice Joshua standing with her parents, the Rosebuds, and Nathaniel Babcock in the hall below. A guilty pleasure filled her at the softness of silk against her skin, the sheer cambric undergarments finer than anything sewn by her own two hands. For once in her life she actually loved being a woman instead of envying her brothers their freedom. Who would have thought that a new gown and an afternoon of primping could make such a difference in her?

Conscious of her manners, she made a dignified, ladylike descent. As a child, she'd dashed up and down these polished wood risers many times chasing her brothers; she had even slid down the banister on occasion. But back then, she hadn't been wearing high-heeled slippers and a form-skimming gown that had cost nearly as much as the household expenses for a year.

She was still shocked by the sum that Madame Daumier had charged for the overnight order. But Papa hadn't even flinched. With characteristic insouciance, he had paid the dressmaker a deposit on the new wardrobe, the rest of which would be delivered in the coming week. The extravagance troubled Anne, for her entry into society was founded on pretense. Her parents believed she and Joshua were courting.

Gripping her brocaded reticule, she reminded herself of the necessity of the ruse. She was ready to confront the man who had shot her, if indeed she found him. Tonight would be the test of her abilities to charm the suspects. Not Joshua.

Yet, halfway down the stairs, she could no longer resist savoring his reaction. Let him laugh now and say she wouldn't fit in with the nobility!

He was staring at her with unsmiling attention.

Standing apart from the others, he looked dashing in his cavalry uniform, the dark blue coat and white breeches fitting him with faultless perfection. Gold braid decorated his broad chest, epaulettes capped his shoulders, and a crimson sash defined his waist. His arms were folded, his face impassive in the shadowy candlelight. He stood so still he might have been carved in granite.

Not for the first time, Anne wished she could read his thoughts. Did he admire the pink gown with the bodice cut so fashionably low over her bosom? Did he notice the smooth curls arranged by Lady Stokeford's own abigail? Did he see the hint of rouge on her cheeks that his grandmother had applied with a deft hand?

She wanted him to be captivated. She wanted him to kneel at her feet and beg for her attentions. And then she wanted the pleasure of spurning him.

"My, she's the very picture of beauty," Lady Enid exclaimed.

Lady Faversham gave a crisp nod. "You've quite outdone yourself this time, Lucy."

"Pish-posh," Lady Stokeford said with a flutter of her gloved fingers. "I merely enhanced Anne's striking assets."

As Anne reached the base of the stairs, Mama hastened forward, her eyes misty and her comfortably familiar features brightened by a tender smile. A smear of yellow paint daubed her cheek, while more spatters decorated her apron. "How lovely you are, darling, like a fresh-blooming primrose. I wish I had the talent to paint portraits. And I daren't hug you and mar your new gown."

"I'll do the honors," Papa offered. Striding forward, he set his hands at Anne's waist and whirled her around as he'd done when she was little enough to squeal with delight. "Our daughter will be the prettiest girl at the ball."

Basking in his praise, Anne felt a flutter of anticipation. "Don't be silly, Papa. Scores of ladies will be present—all of them far more lovely and sophisticated than I."

"Oh, ye of little faith." He tweaked her nose. "As a retired connoisseur of women, I declare you exquisite. Haven't we all said so?"

No, one person hadn't.

Anne turned her eyes to Joshua, who had moved to the front door. He inclined his head in a somewhat impatient nod. Was he amused by her desire for admiration? Or was he anxious to depart, to utilize the social event as a means to find the gunman?

"You need only one last touch," Lady Stokeford said, smiling at Anne. "Joshua will do the honors." She motioned to her grandson.

Without expression, Joshua stepped behind Anne and draped a piece of jewelry around her neck. She looked down in surprise to see a diamond pendant on a delicate gold chain. The fine gemstone flashed white fire in the candlelight.

"How lovely," Anne breathed. Involuntarily, she touched the jewel that rested just above her bosom, then snatched back her hand. "It must be a family heirloom. What if I were to lose it?"

"Nonsense," the dowager said briskly. "The necklace is

a mere trifle. I found it tucked in the back of my jewel case. You may keep it if you like."

"But it's far too valuable," Anne protested. "It's . . . it's inappropriate."

Lady Stokeford laughed. "It's inappropriate on *me*. Such a simple piece belongs on a *young* lady."

Joshua's touch distracted Anne. As he fastened the clasp at the nape of her neck, his fingers brushed her bare skin. Her flesh tingled, and she was keenly aware of his closeness. She resisted a telltale shiver, partly because she didn't want to give him the satisfaction and partly because everyone gazed at them with expectant smiles. Even her parents watched benignly.

They believed Joshua was courting Anne, that they would soon become betrothed, that this was the first of many Stokeford jewels he would shower on her. It only made Anne all the more uncomfortable about her lie.

Fending off a rush of guilt, she focused on her parents. "I do wish you both were going with us tonight. It isn't too late."

Papa's warm, solid hand came to rest on her shoulder. "Your mother and I shall be quite content here in each other's company."

"We want you to enjoy yourself as we did when we were young," Mama said.

"As we still do," Papa averred, slipping his arm around his wife's thickened waist. "There's nothing more satisfying than marriage to your dearest friend."

An envious ache caught Anne by surprise. She was still grappling with it when Mama's next remark plunged her into a pit of mortification. Glancing meaningfully at Joshua, Mama said, "Perhaps tonight, darling, you'll dance with the man of *your* dreams."

The whispers began as soon as she entered the ballroom.

The vast, oblong chamber resembled a fairyland with gilded pillars, a soaring ceiling, and beeswax candles blazing in the crystal chandeliers. At one end of the room, a row of glass doors stood open to the dark velvet night. The tuning of the orchestra blended with the merry hum of voices.

No, Anne realized, the voices were more malicious than merry. As soon as the majordomo had announced Lady Stokeford and her grandson, followed by Anne, Nathaniel Babcock, Lady Enid, and Lady Faversham, an undercurrent of ugliness spread through the crowd of aristocratic guests.

Elegantly coiffed heads peered toward the great arched entrance. Ladies lifted their fans and murmured to one another. Gentlemen craned their necks for a look at the newcomers. Lips curled and eyebrows arched.

Taken aback by the stares, Anne tightened her kid-gloved fingers around the pink ribbons securing her reticule. She had hoped the new gown and diamond necklace would help her to blend in easily with the *ton*. Did everyone here already know she was a twenty-eight-year-old spinster who belonged firmly on the shelf? The Rosebuds had warned her to expect a few snubs and snide comments. No matter how impeccable her antecedents, there would be those who would sneer at a woman who had grown up in a rustic village.

As she held her head high and returned their stares, bits of conversation reached her ears. "A disgrace . . ." "It just isn't done . . ." "How dare he show his face after what he did to Timberlake's daughter . . ."

Joshua, she realized with a start. They were gossiping about Joshua, not her. That seven-year-old scandal was very much alive.

She felt a flash of relief at having escaped the wagging tongues. Yet a different sort of tension gripped her bosom, and she shifted her gaze toward Joshua.

He was gone.

His grandmother and Nathaniel Babcock greeted a stout, mustachioed gentleman. Lady Faversham conversed with a formidable-looking lady who wore a diamond tiara in her steel-gray hair. Lady Enid flirted with a dapper, elderly man in an old-fashioned periwig.

Dismayed, Anne scoured the crowd. How could she have lost Joshua already? He had the list from the boot-maker, the list he wouldn't share with her. She desperately needed his help in identifying the suspects.

Then she spied him.

Like a prince among rabble, he stood alone by a pillar and coolly surveyed the murmuring multitudes. Her heart beat faster at the handsome picture he made in his military uniform, the white breeches and knee-high black boots emphasizing his long, muscular legs.

She wasn't the only one who had observed his uncommonly fine figure. Despite the disapproving glares from the older matrons, the younger ladies cast admiring looks at him, giggling and talking among themselves.

Joshua took no notice of them. Either he was unaware of his notoriety, or he chose to ignore it. Anne suspected the latter.

Then he looked across the ballroom and narrowed his eyes, and the intensity of his stare galvanized her. She glanced in the direction he was gazing, but couldn't see over the heads of the crowd. Had he spied one of the men? The only one she would recognize was Arthur Cummings, but she didn't see the politician's stocky form or ruddy features anywhere.

She hastened toward Joshua, drawn as much by her purpose as the irresistible tug of attraction. He had already started across the room when she caught up to him. "Wait," she murmured. "Where are you going?"

For the barest moment, annoyance touched his features. Then he gave her a polite smile. "To fetch a glass of champagne. Would you care for one?"

"No, thank you. I intend to keep my wits about me this evening."

He cast her an obliquely amused glance that encompassed her fashionable gown, his gaze lingering a moment on her décolletage and making her skin tingle there. "A pity," he said. "Wine has a rather charming effect on you."

She blushed at the memory of their scorching embrace on the beach. Did he want to kiss her again? For as long as she lived, she would never forget the pressure of his mouth on hers or the thrill of his hand brushing over her bosom. The mere thought sent the warmth in her face spiraling downward, settling low with the persistent ache of longing.

Not that she would tell him so.

"Are any of the men on the list here?" she asked coolly. "Samuel Firth, perhaps?"

He shrugged. "It's possible, I suppose."

"But you did see someone just now. You were staring across the ballroom."

"I saw a footman with a tray of drinks."

"At least tell me about your interview with Firth. What did he say? Do you believe he's guilty?"

Joshua shot her a moody, assessing look. "There's no evidence one way or the other. Beyond that he had the motive and the opportunity." He shifted his gaze beyond her, and his demeanor lightened. "Ah, here's Grandmama."

Frustrated, Anne turned to see Lady Stokeford gliding toward them. With diamonds glittering in her white hair and a pale blue gown hugging her slender form, she looked like a fairy godmother. If only she had a magic wand that could make Joshua tell the truth.

Better yet, Anne would have liked to use the wand to flog the information out of him.

The dowager smiled with determined gaiety. "You two look so serious," she murmured. "Be happy, lest anyone think you're bothered by the scandalmongers."

It's your grandson who bothers me, Anne thought waspishly. As penance for that petty thought, she shaped her mouth into a pleasant smile. "My lady, I assure you, we aren't troubled in the least."

Crossing his arms, Joshua wore a cynical expression. "Let the snobs say whatever they please."

"I most certainly will not," his grandmother retorted. "Just now, Lady Wallingford had the effrontery to question your presence here to my face."

"No doubt you told the old walrus to mind her tongue," he said.

"I did inquire as to the health of her son's mistress," Lady Stokeford said, a hint of humor flashing in her blue eyes. "She's a dancer in a London music hall."

Joshua gave her a sarcastic look. "If you know that, it means you're not above listening to the gossips yourself."

"Pish-posh, there's a difference between staying informed and spreading nasty rumors. Should anyone dare to criticize my family, they deserve a dose of their own medicine—"

A loud blast of trumpets resounded through the ballroom. Startled, Anne looked around for the source of the sound. "What was that?"

Lady Stokeford gave a negligent wave at the great archway. "Dorothy and Freddy Angleton, no doubt. No one else would make such an audacious entrance."

Into the ballroom marched six muscled servants dressed in Roman togas and carrying a litter with a curtained compartment. As the guests watched and murmured, the men set down their burden on a red-carpeted dais.

From within, a gloved hand parted the shimmery gold draperies. Then a skinny woman with gaunt features and lacquered brown curls emerged from the litter, followed by a middle-aged man with a jovial, round face and a balding pate.

The buzz of conversation built to a crescendo as the guests thronged forward to greet their host and hostess, hiding them from Anne's sight.

"Well," Lady Stokeford said dryly, "that should divert the gossips for a time."

"And while the gossips are diverted," Joshua said, "I'm

going to the refreshment table. If you ladies will excuse me."

"I'll go, too," Anne said swiftly. "A glass of punch sounds heavenly."

But Lady Stokeford linked arms with both of them. "Neither of you are going anywhere but the dance floor," she said in a tone that brooked no argument. "The orchestra is about to begin the first dance. Joshua?"

A scowl flitted across his brow; then he extended his hand to Anne. "May I have the honor, Miss Neville?"

She ought to refuse his grudging offer. The fact that he had to be prodded by his grandmother stung her confidence. Only the need to promote their sham courtship could induce her to slip her hand into the crook of his arm.

His muscles felt firm and hard beneath his sleeve. A spark flashed through her, igniting a glow in her foolish, feminine heart. Anne hid the reaction behind a composed countenance. It was unnerving how a mere touch from Joshua could make the candles burn brighter, the music sound sweeter, the air itself hold a delicious aura of adventure.

Anything could happen tonight, anything at all . . .

She brought her imagination firmly back to earth. She might find the man who had shot her, that's what. *If* she kept her mind from straying.

She gazed over the sea of unfamiliar faces. There were gentlemen of all sorts, plump and skinny, balding and curly-haired, dignified and dandified. Which one of them had Joshua been looking at across the ballroom? She was determined to find out.

He led her to the two lines that were forming in the center of the dance floor, ladies on one side, gentlemen on the other. Once again, she felt the stares boring into them. She caught the two older women beside her whispering to one another, their avid eyes flashing disapproval at Joshua.

Anne coolly met their glare. "Have we been introduced?" she asked with exaggerated politeness.

"I don't believe so," the scrawny one said, her pointy nose stuck in the air.

"Do forgive me, then," Anne said. "It must have been Lord Joshua Kenyon you were staring at so impolitely."

The ladies harrumphed and turned away to converse in hissing whispers. The music commenced, and Anne dipped the obligatory curtsy to Joshua. When she rose, she saw his mouth twitching as if he held back a grin.

"The gossips aren't the only ones with their claws bared," he said. "It's a novelty to hear you defending me."

She didn't quite understand it herself. As they circled one another in accordance with the dance, she said over her shoulder, "I won't tolerate rudeness in any form. Not even toward a knave who deserves his fate."

"You do know how to put a man in his proper place."

"There's nothing proper about you, m'lord."

"Quite so. It's an image that suits me."

His handsome face held a hint of mystery. Was he dastard or hero? According to the Rosebuds, he had never spoken an unkind word against Lily. He had kept silent when a few well-chosen innuendos could have placed the burden of guilt on his former fiancée. After all, Lily was no longer here to defend herself.

"Lady Stokeford believes your scoundrel's image is undeserved," Anne murmured so that no one else could overhear. "She said you must have had a good reason for ending your betrothal."

Joshua's expression turned cold. As the steps brought them around face to face, candlelight glinted on the metallic gold flecks in his dark eyes. "My grandmother has no right to speculate."

"She has every right. Surely you can't condemn her for wanting to restore your good name." Anne paused, burning to know the truth. "She also says she trusts in your integrity. Apparently, you were an extraordinary boy who would walk five miles to return a nail to the village blacksmith."

"Grandmama has been known to twist the facts to suit her purpose."

Was there a faintly ruddy flush to his face? "Then you're saying she's wrong? That you have no honor?"

Joshua gave her a flinty glare. "You're also skilled at twisting words to suit your purpose."

"I'm merely trying to understand what happened. If you're truly a disreputable man, then you should be blaming Lily. You should be telling the world that *she* spurned *you,* that she did something to betray your love for her."

"Enough," he snapped. "Your reasoning is ridiculous and futile."

Vexed at being shut out, Anne thinned her lips. But at least his answer proved her point. Not even when pressured would he take the easy way out.

The dance required her to raise her arm and walk around him, giving her a moment to compose herself. Considering her need for his help tonight, she resolved to lighten his mood.

When they faced one another again, she flashed him a coquettish smile. "You're scowling, m'lord. If you aren't careful, your testy manner will betray our courtship ruse."

The quirk of his lips didn't quite qualify as a smile. "Give me a better reason to be charming, Miss Neville."

"You'll make your grandmother happy."

"Only to disappoint her later when I don't fall on bended knee and beg for your hand in marriage."

Anne's wayward imagination took the fantasy to heart. Annoyed with herself as much as him, she fluttered her lashes outrageously. "Who knows? Perhaps you *won't* disappoint her."

He stared at her with incredulous eyes; then a genuine grin chased away his cheerless look. His gaze flicked to her diamond pendant. "You'd like an excuse to keep that necklace."

Anne touched the diamond. "How did you guess?" she

said flippantly. "As your wife, I'd demand lots of jewels. Cartloads of them."

"You'd especially demand the family jewels." His outrageous smirk hinted at another meaning, but she couldn't ask him, for the progress of the dance required that they move apart.

The rows of men and women glided in opposite directions, and Anne found herself partnered by a bashful young gentleman with buck teeth, then a corpulent old fellow who ogled her bosom. Subduing the impulse to smack him over the head with her reticule, she concentrated on the elaborate steps, determined to be a credit to her parents and Lady Stokeford. Only as the last notes died away did she find herself face to face again with Joshua.

He must have decided to play her game, for his expression was tolerably indulgent. "Did you enjoy your first dance?"

"I'm pleased I didn't tramp on any toes." Out of the corner of her eye, she noticed several young ladies casting fervent glances at him. Instinctively, Anne edged closer to him, commanding his full attention. "Let's take a stroll, shall we?"

He cocked an eyebrow. "It's a bit early in the evening for an assignation."

"Assignation—?" Her cheeks flamed as she caught his meaning. "Take your mind out of the gutter, m'lord. I'm merely proposing a turn about the ballroom so we might see who's here."

He bent closer, his scent of soap and spice surrounding her like a loving embrace. His eyes held a twinkle of deviltry. "A charming prospect. Alas, fate conspires to thwart you."

He glanced over her shoulder, and she swiveled to see the Rosebuds bearing down on them like a trio of warships.

"What a delightful couple you two make," Lady Stokeford said, smiling from her grandson to Anne. "But do run along now, Joshua. It's time for Anne to secure another partner."

"If it pleases my lady," Anne said quickly, "we had hoped to take a stroll—"

"Out of the question," Lady Faversham said, her lips curled sternly. "The ball has only just begun. You must dance."

"And never with the same man twice in a row," Lady Enid added, with a nod of her raspberry-turbanned head. " 'Tis only fair to give the other gentlemen a chance."

"The man never stands a chance," Joshua said with an appropriate amount of regret in his tone. "You ladies set far too many rules for us."

Anne noted the gleam of victory in his eyes. But before she could devise a way out of this dilemma, Lady Stokeford took her arm.

"Come along, Anne." The dowager had a surprisingly firm grip for one so old and dainty. As they walked away, she added in a conspiratorial whisper, "Don't be disheartened, my dear. If you wish to attract my grandson, it's best to let him see other eligible gentlemen paying court to you."

"Many gentlemen," Lady Enid said with a smirk Anne would have called wicked in a younger woman. "As they say, the more, the merrier."

Lady Faversham walked at a stately pace with the aid of her cane. "Jealousy is a tried-and-true scheme," she said. "You'll soon see that for yourself."

Jealousy?

Over her shoulder, Anne caught one last glimpse of Joshua as he swaggered away into the crowd, his shoulders squared and the candlelight bathing his raven-dark hair. The cad looked entirely too relieved to be shed of her.

But, of course, the Rosebuds didn't know the courtship was a fraud.

Lady Stokeford steered Anne toward a lanky man with protruding eyes, wild blond curls, and yellow pantaloons topped by an ill-fitting green coat. He looked several years younger than she, perhaps the age of her brother Isaac.

"Good evening, Your Grace," Lady Stokeford said. "If I might present a dear family friend, Miss Anne Neville. Anne, this is Clarence, the Duke of Nunwich."

Taking the quizzing glass that dangled from a gold chain pinned to his lapel, Nunwich inspected her, his blue eye magnified to ridiculous proportions by the little circle of glass. "One of the Abergavenney Nevilles?"

"Not at all," Anne said. "I'm one of the Merryton-on-Sea Nevilles."

Sinking into a curtsy, she saw Lady Stokeford shake her head in exasperation. Instantly, Anne regretted her irreverent tone. But what difference did it make, really? Surely a nobleman of the highest rank wouldn't bother with a woman of so few social connections. And when Nunwich disdained her, then she could go off in search of Joshua . . .

To her surprise, the duke made a courtly bow. "We would be honored to have the favor of a dance with Miss Neville."

We? At his affected speech, she gulped back a laugh. "How very kind of you, Your Grace."

He poked out his elbow, and she was obliged to accept it. As they headed to the dance floor, she found herself comparing his bony arm to the hard, sculpted musculature of Joshua's form. Joshua didn't reek of cologne, nor did he walk with the mincing steps of a hen. He possessed an aggressive masculinity that called to her deepest, most feminine longings . . .

"Does Miss Neville follow the hounds?"

"Follow—?" Anne blinked, realizing the duke was watching her with polite expectation. "You mean hunting. I'm afraid I haven't had the opportunity—although my brothers tell me I'm an expert shot."

"Truly?" Nunwich's manner changed dramatically to an almost rapturous interest. His bulbous gaze swept over her. "Perhaps, one day, we might persuade Miss Neville to join our hunting party." As the music commenced, he launched into a litany about the attributes of each hound in his stable. At the same time, he performed the hopping steps of the dance like a chicken pecking at its food, his head bobbing up and down with the melody.

Anne kept an amiable look fixed on her face. She hadn't meant to encourage the duke. In truth, she couldn't imagine why he was bothering with her at all.

The dance seemed to drag on forever, and this one required them to stay together rather than switching partners. She watched surreptitiously for Joshua, but couldn't see him anywhere. He was probably already interrogating another of the suspects. Well, if she had to endure this buffoon, she would at least use the time to her advantage.

As the lively dance slowed to an end, she seized her opportunity. "May I ask you a question, Your Grace?"

"Clarence," he said with the indulgence of a man bestowing a favor on a lesser being. "Do call us Clarence."

"Clarence." Though she disliked encouraging his too-forward manner, she batted her lashes as the Rosebuds had taught her. She would act demure and flirt if he would help her accomplish her purpose. "Perchance, are you acquainted with a man named Samuel Firth?"

Chapter Sixteen

Finding Firth

Josh wended his way through the clusters of guests outside the ballroom. A few men nodded to him, though none approached with a friendly greeting or a genial jest. His ignominy suited him in a peculiar way. Though he despised the tarnish to his honor, the scandal served as a barrier to conversations that would have distracted him from his purpose.

In the staircase hall, an older lady guided her dewy-eyed daughter in a wide detour around him. He noted cynically the moonling stare the girl sent him from under her lashes. Silly twit. Like so many others, she was fascinated by his notoriety. He couldn't imagine being attracted to a juvenile straight out of the schoolroom, a girl young enough to be his daughter. He far preferred the company of a mature woman who could match him, wit for wit.

A woman like Anne.

His chest tightened at the thought of her gliding downstairs earlier in the evening. For a moment he hadn't recognized her. Gone was the scraped-back bun, the spinster's cap, the drab, high-throated gown. Gone as well was the sallow complexion and sour-mouthed look. As she'd descended the stairs, he'd stared in idiotic surprise at a radiant vision in a pink gown that clung to her womanly curves.

It was bloody lucky he'd been standing behind the others, else the tight cut of his breeches would have betrayed his instantaneous arousal. Disciplined as he was in all other matters, he had no defenses against the memory of that lithe, feminine body clasped to his. He wanted to hold her again, to have another long taste of her mouth.

Hell, why not be honest? He wanted to haul Anne into a deserted chamber and make love to her, the consequences be damned.

That compulsion grew like tentacles around his sense of purpose. He had to find the sniper. To punish him and then get out of Anne's life, to seek peace and solitude on his estate. Already, she knew too much about him. About his dreams.

About his nightmares.

The war—and Lily—had taught him to stay aloof. In order to ensure the safety of the men under his command, an officer kept his emotions under strict control. Josh didn't intend to risk himself again on the battlefield of love, either. Ladies like Anne were for wedding, not bedding. He had given his heart once, and the scars would last him a lifetime.

Tense, he paused in the entrance to an enormous drawing room. An excess of gilt decorated the Corinthian columns, the mantelpiece, even the pseudo-Renaissance panels on the high ceiling. Swags of draperies in the same crimson hue as the carpets decorated the tall windows. Intent on their games, groups of guests played cards at tables by the light of candelabras. White-wigged footmen offered trays of drinks. The chatter of genteel voices and the clink of glasses mingled with the distant music from the ballroom.

Then Josh spied his quarry.

In a dimly lit corner of the chamber, two men stood by a long table covered in green baize. They took turns tossing a pair of dice, the result of each throw greeted with groans or cheers. Intent on their game, they didn't notice Josh at first.

One was Anne's cousin, Edwin Bellingham, staggering when it was his turn to throw. His partner was a dark-haired stranger who stood in the shadows.

Though his back was turned, there was something vaguely familiar about him. With a lean, lupine grace, he lounged against the wall, nursing the glass of brandy in his hand. Unlike his companion, he looked alert and controlled.

Stepping forward to take his turn at the table, he sent the dice flying with a neat flick of his wrist.

Edwin groaned. "Anotha' seven," he slurred. "I shay, old boy, you've the devil's own luck tonight."

"You might say I'm on hiatus from Hades." The man scooped up the dice and tossed the pair to Edwin, who dropped one and had to scramble for it on all fours under the table.

That deep, cynical voice had struck a welcome chord in Josh. Smiling, he strode swiftly forward. "I'll be damned if it isn't the devil himself."

Brandon Villiers, the Earl of Faversham, spun around. The scar beside his mouth lifted in a sardonic grin. "Josh Kenyon. I see you're back from hell, too."

Josh clasped him in a swift, back-pounding embrace. The other players stared. But Josh didn't give a damn about the gossips.

He and Brand had grown up a few miles apart, their friendship bolstered by the frequent visits between their grandmothers. Brand had been like a fourth brother to him. Of course, Michael had been of an age with Brand, but Josh had tagged along with the older boys on many an occasion. Together they'd roamed the vast acres of Stokeford Abbey, making forts in the woods and digging for lost treasure on the island in the lake. Once, they'd stayed out all night, and when they'd returned the next morning, bleary-eyed and bedraggled, the Rosebuds had soundly punished them.

Brand stepped back to give Josh a measuring look. Then he drained his glass and set it down. "I know where the

Angletons keep their best brandy. Unless, of course, you've sworn off the French variety."

"The war soured me on a lot of things, but not good liquor."

"Or French women, I trust."

Josh smiled tightly. Perhaps another time he'd describe the long hours spent training in mud and rain, the lack of privacy in a camp of thousands, the punishing treks through the countryside, chasing Napoleon's troops. Over the past fifteen years, he had enjoyed his share of women. But in the fight for survival, personal pleasures came last.

As they started toward the door, Edwin Bellingham grabbed the sleeve of Brand's maroon coat. "Hey, where're you going? We hash t' finish our game."

Brand gazed down at those soft fingers on his arm. Then he looked at Edwin until the man blanched and released his hold. "We're finished," Brand said. "You owe me five thousand."

Edwin staggered backward, reeling for balance. "F-five—?"

"I'll be by for the money tomorrow."

Edwin gawked for a moment, then swung around to confront Josh. "Thish is all your fault, Kenyon," he said bitterly. "I was jusht about t' win big."

"A pity, that." Josh had intended to ask Edwin about the nature of his other debts. But already, a few of the cardplayers had turned to eavesdrop openly. He'd have to delay his questioning until later.

"I've been meanin' t' talk t' my cousin," Edwin rambled on. "Tell her t' shtay away from you."

"What a coincidence," Josh said. "I've given her the same advice about you."

"I'm no murderer. Not like you."

Every muscle in Josh tightened. "Mind your tongue, man."

But Edwin was too stupidly drunk to heed him. "You killed Timberlake's daughter—whashername—Lilac or

Lily or somethin'. Now you're pantin' after my cousin.
Anne might be a bloody damned shrew, but I won't shtand
for you t' go after my father's money—"

Josh swung his fist and connnected with Edwin's face.
The force of the blow reverberated up his arm. Edwin collapsed like a broken marionette, blood dripping from his
nose.

People gasped. A lady screamed. The buzz of conversation rose to a crescendo as the guests commented on this
scandalous diversion.

Brand clamped a hand on Josh's shoulder. "He isn't
worth a set of skinned knuckles, my friend."

Josh said nothing. Brand didn't know the whole story.
He didn't know that Edwin might have lurked in the bushes
and fired a shot at Anne.

Then a thought wormed its way through the murk of his
anger. Why would Edwin warn him not to harm Anne? Her
death would benefit the toad, clearing the way for his inheritance. He should be encouraging Josh.

Unless he'd purposely taunted Josh before a roomful of
witnesses. To set the stage for his own claim to innocence
in the event of her untimely death . . .

His blood ran cold. He wondered if the drunken sot
knew that Anne was here tonight, dancing in the ballroom
under Grandmama's watchful eye.

Edwin moaned piteously. He fumbled in his pocket for
a handkerchief to dab at his bloodied nose. He looked
wretched, incapable of harming a flea. But Josh wasn't taking any chances.

He grabbed Edwin by the scruff of the neck and hauled
him to his feet. Edwin stumbled as Josh forced him toward
the doorway of the drawing room with Brand strolling
alongside them. The aristocratic guests parted way, talking
among themselves in shocked whispers.

So much for blending unobtrusively into the crowd.

Edwin yanked against Josh's grip. "Where're you takin'
me?" he whined. "Lemme go."

"All in good time," Josh said, turning down a corridor lit by candles in shell-shaped sconces. In the tunnel of marble, the echo of their footsteps mingled with the voices of the guests, who had poured out of doorways to watch the spectacle.

"Help!" Edwin bleated. When no one stepped to his aid, he switched his panicked gaze to Brand. "He's gone mad, Faversham! You—you won't get your money if he kills me."

The earl's mouth curved in a sinister smile. "It might be worth five thousand to watch you die."

"I'd be happy to oblige," Josh said.

He thrust his captive into the entrance hall. More noble guests spied them and shrank back, muttering in appalled tones. From the ballroom lilted the notes of a sprightly song. Intent on his purpose, Josh disregarded the watchers.

A footman saw him coming and hastened to open the front door. The cool night breeze rushed inside and made the candles flicker.

"What are you men *doing?*" a lady screeched. "You're *ruining* my ball."

Draped in a white gown more suited to a debutante than a scrawny, middle-aged hag, Mrs. Dorothy Angleton came charging toward them. Her stout, ruddy-faced husband trudged at her heels like a well-trained pug instead of a rich merchant who had earned a fortune in coal.

"Do something, Freddy," she ordered him. "Tell them to release Mr. Bellingham at once."

Mr. Angleton cleared his throat. "See here now. Let the poor fellow go."

"With pleasure," Josh said. On a forward thrust of his arm, he released his hold on Edwin's collar.

Edwin staggered out onto the porch and bumped into a pillar, clutching it for support. His gaze was bleary but venomous. "I'll get you, Kenyon. I shwear it."

Not deigning to reply, Josh closed the door on Edwin's sullen features. Then he turned to face his host and hostess.

Behind them loomed a throng of disapproving, avid-eyed guests.

But Brand had already taken control of the situation. For all his bad reputation, he could charm the hairshirt off a cloistered nun. "Our deepest apologies for alarming you," he said, taking Mrs. Angleton's hands in his. "The fellow was drunk, and we'd hoped to spare you his boorish behavior."

Mrs. Angleton looked nonplussed. "Are you quite *sure*? Someone rushed into the ballroom to report a fistfight. And there was *blood* on Mr. Bellingham's face."

"He insulted a lady," Josh said in a tight voice.

Mrs. Angleton's quick brown eyes gleamed with interest—as did the eyes of all the onlookers. "*Who,* pray tell?"

Everyone leaned closer to hear his answer.

Josh forced a regretful smile. "For her own protection, I can't say."

"No, of course not." Her gaunt features showed a piqued disappointment.

"But I'm sure the mystery will keep people talking about your party for months to come," Brand said in an undertone.

"Mmmm. Quite right." Her face brightening, she elbowed her husband. "We owe our gratitude to their lordships, don't we, Freddy?"

Mr. Angleton bobbed his balding head. "We do, indeed."

Her husband at her side, Dorothy Angleton led a troupe of ladies back toward the ballroom, their voices buzzing with excited speculation.

Brand stared pensively after them. "I can't say I appreciate what you've done here, Kenyon."

"Pardon?"

"You've managed to upstage me. I've a reputation for notoriety to maintain, you know."

Josh chuckled. "Rest assured, I don't aspire to your crown."

Brand sent him a speculative stare. Abruptly, he asked, "Is Anne Neville the cousin who inherits everything in old Lord Bellingham's will?"

His senses on the alert, Josh asked, "You've met her?"

"No, but Edwin Bellingham spoke of her . . . Ye gods!" Narrowing his eyes, Brand scowled across the staircase hall. "Tell me that isn't my grandmother—and yours, too."

The two old ladies came hurrying out of the ballroom, one tall and stately, the other small and dainty. Lady Faversham and Grandmama must have left Lady Enid to play guard dog to Anne, Josh guessed. With a sinking feeling, he watched as they marched toward them like soldiers on a mission.

"They arrived yesterday," Josh muttered. "Took me by complete surprise, too."

Brand swore through his teeth. "Look at those hellfire glares. They've heard about your little altercation."

"And something tells me they won't be as easy to maneuver as the Angletons." Not wanting the entire assemblage to witness the inevitable lecture, Josh veered into a dimly lit antechamber beneath the grand staircase.

Close behind him, Brand gave a low chuckle. "You're in for it now, Kenyon—"

His gloating words ended in a yelp. Without preamble, Lady Faversham had entered the room and whacked his thigh with her cane.

"Shame on you," she snapped, her features cadaverous in the shadows. "Engaging in fisticuffs in the midst of a social event."

Glowering, Brand rubbed his leg. "I'm happy to see you, too, Grandmama. And kindly remember that I'm not ten years old anymore."

"Really? One could never tell from the way you behave. Or rather, *mis*behave. Why are you in Brighton, anyway?"

Leaning against a marble pedestal, Brand assumed his characteristic half-smirk. "It was best to leave London for a time."

"Up to your old tricks, I see."

"I'm incorrigible. You've said so yourself."

"You need a wife," Lady Faversham pronounced. "A clever girl who will twist you in knots and teach you humility."

"There's not a woman on earth who could do that."

"Charlotte Quinton could."

Brand's insouciant look froze. "She's in disgrace. I wouldn't have her if you stripped her naked and tied her to my bed."

"Don't you dare speak of Enid's granddaughter that way." Lady Faversham lifted her cane as if to strike him again.

Taking pity on Brand, Josh put his hand out to stop her. "Regarding the fight, you've punished the wrong person."

"What's this?" Lady Stokeford exclaimed, stepping forward. "*You* struck Lord Bellingham's son?"

Her look of disappointment cut into him. "I did, ma'am."

"Merciful heavens! Have you gone mad?" Through the gloom, Lady Stokeford shook her forefinger at him. "Have you any inkling how hard I've worked tonight to repair your reputation? And then you destroy it all by behaving like a cretin."

"I'm sorry."

"Apologies are easy to make," his grandmother said sternly. "I'll have your promise that you won't behave so imprudently again."

"As you wish."

Josh spoke readily, letting his grandmother draw her own conclusions. In good conscience, he could promise not to pummel Anne's cousin again—at least not at a social gathering.

But elsewhere was another matter entirely.

When Anne heard the commotion outside the ballroom, she was trapped with the verbose Viscount Godolphin, who was in the midst of a monologue about the economic woes facing England now that the war was over. She couldn't see the Rosebuds anywhere in the throng. People turned to other people, and the gossip spread across the assemblage like the rippling of a wave.

A stout lady barreled toward them. "My dear Geoffrey," she exclaimed, ignoring Anne. "Have you heard what's happened?"

"About the gold standard being challenged by those vile Tories? Horrifying, Mama. Simply horrifying."

"Silly boy," she said, shaking her head impatiently. " 'Tis the news about the fight between Bellingham and that rascal Lord Joshua Kenyon."

Aghast, Anne made her apologies. "Excuse me, I really must go. Edwin Bellingham is my cousin."

Leaving them to stare disapprovingly, she hastened toward the doorway. It took some time to thread her way through the crowds of guests. When she reached the staircase hall, only a few scattered people remained. She didn't see Edwin or Joshua anywhere.

Who had started the fight? More importantly, where had they gone? Had they been banished from the party?

She hoped not, at least in regard to Edwin. Searching through a maze of reception rooms and corridors, she chided herself for not thinking of her cousin earlier. Edwin had friends in low places. More than anyone else here, he might know where to find Samuel Firth.

Thus far, she had been stymied in her search. Though His Grace of Nunwich had admitted to knowing of the moneylender, he had refused to introduce her and had lectured her to stay away from the rapscallion. Her subsequent dance partners had delivered variations on the same reaction. Several had seen Firth during the evening, so she knew he had to be here somewhere. Yet the man remained elusive, as if this vast, opulent mansion had swallowed him.

Joshua was missing, too, blast him. What madness had induced him to attack Edwin? In front of a throng of avid-eyed nobles, no less. Had Joshua found out that Edwin was guilty of the shooting?

Pausing in the doorway of the drawing room, Anne surveyed the throng of gamblers. Neither Joshua nor Edwin occupied the tables; the cardplayers were mostly gentlemen with a very few ladies. Across the room, Lady Stokeford's friend Nathaniel Babcock played whist in a quartet of elderly men. Anne stepped back behind a fern on a pedestal. She didn't want him to report to the Rosebuds that she'd been wandering, unchaperoned, around the house.

When a horse-faced countess walked by and gave her a nod, Anne remembered being introduced to her. "Pray excuse me, Lady Wentworth. I'm looking for my cousin, Mr. Edwin Bellingham. Have you seen him?"

The countess snorted. "That one! He's scuttled off in disgrace. A pity we can't choose our blood relations, eh?"

As Lady Wentworth proceeded into the drawing room, Anne privately agreed with that pithy assessment. She retreated to the corridor and leaned against a gilded pillar. If Edwin had left the party, how was she to locate Firth?

"I know where to find Bellingham."

The deep male voice emanated from behind her. Startled, she whirled around as the tall figure of a man appeared in the shadows of a doorway. He looked vaguely familiar. For the barest instant, before he stepped out into the golden light of the corridor, she fancied he was Joshua, and her heart took a mad leap of yearning. But the glow from the wall sconces illuminated the suave features of a stranger.

Broad-shouldered and darkly handsome, he wore a charcoal-gray coat, silver waistcoat, and black trousers. His alert blue eyes stirred an uneasy sensation in the pit of her stomach.

Before she could inquire about her cousin, a woman emerged from behind him, her raven-black curls tilted downward as she adjusted the bodice of her gown. The diaphanous white muslin barely covered her ripe breasts.

"Don't leave, darling. Nothing could be more important than—"

Spying Anne, she glowered. She slipped her hand into the crook of his arm as if to stake her claim, and her pouty expression drew attention to her reddened lips. Mortified, Anne realized the man and woman had been engaged in a romantic tryst.

A tryst even more intimate than the one she and Joshua had shared on the beach.

Under normal circumstances, Anne would have discreetly excused herself. The Rosebuds had warned her not to speak to anyone without a proper introduction. But she couldn't pass up this opportunity. Addressing the man, she asked, "If you please, sir, where is Edwin?"

Instead of answering, he looked at his companion and gave her a nod of dismissal. "Run along, my lady."

Her thin black eyebrows clashed in a tempestuous frown. "You dare to banish me?"

"Yes."

That single, softly spoken word, coupled with his cool stare, ended the woman's protests. Flashing Anne a sullen look, she stalked away down the corridor, her swaying hips communicating her pique.

But the man wasn't watching his lover. His eyes intent on Anne, he strolled toward her. "Pray forgive Lady Vane. She's been rather testy since her husband left for Scotland on business last month." While Anne groped for a response to the outrageous implication, he went on in a pleasant tone, "So you're Miss Neville."

She eased in a breath. "How do you know my name?"

"It's a logical assumption since you're Bellingham's cousin."

"Kindly tell me where I might find him."

"He left for home nigh on half an hour ago."

Indignation sharpened her voice. "Sir, you led me to believe he was still here."

He smiled slightly. "I merely said I knew where he was."

"But you implied—" She broke off, realizing the futility of playing semantics with a trickster. What was it about some men that made them enjoy duping women?

"I'm truly sorry to disappoint you," he said, sounding almost sincere. "I'll be happy to order your carriage if you'd care to go after him."

Anne bitterly shook her head. "It's no use. I wanted him to introduce me to someone."

"Perhaps I can be of assistance."

Perhaps he could, she thought, grasping at a slender thread of hope. Though with the way her luck had been running, this stranger too would refuse her request. "I'm afraid I don't even know your name."

"Quite the contrary. Rumor has it that my name has been on your lips quite often this evening." His keen gaze rested a moment on her mouth, and she felt an uneasy prickling over her skin. Then his smile returned. "I'm Samuel Firth."

"There's something peculiar going on," Lady Stokeford told her two dearest friends as they sat sipping sherry. The dimly lit antechamber where she had scolded Joshua a short time ago now provided a view of the arched entrance to the ballroom, while affording them a bit of privacy. She didn't want anyone else to overhear what she had to say.

Olivia, Lady Faversham, gave a regal nod. "I know what you're thinking, Lucy. If Anne has gone to the ladies' retiring room, she should have returned by now."

"Perhaps Joshua declined that drink with Brand," Enid suggested, her hazel eyes sparkling. "Perhaps he arranged a secret rendezvous with her."

"My fears precisely. As her chaperones, we're shirking our duty." Tall and thin as a lamppost, Olivia levered to her feet with the aid of her cane.

Lucy waved her back into her chair. "Please, Olivia, sit down and listen for a moment. I've had distressing news."

"More distressing than that fight?" Enid asked.

"Yes."

Her friends gave her their unwavering attention, Olivia's stark features taut with strength, Enid's cheerfully plump face offering a steadfast support. A swell of affection washed through Lucy. Whenever she faced a problem, no matter how big or small, Olivia and Enid were there for her, just as she was for them. Sometimes, despite all the wrinkles and pains of old age, it hardly seemed possible that fifty years had passed since their debut.

"A short while ago," she said, "the Duke of Nunwich told me that Anne has been seeking an introduction to a moneylender. A vulgar man named Samuel Firth who's bought his way into society."

Enid gasped. "Is the dear girl in debt?"

"Impossible," Olivia stated. "The Nevilles may lead a simple life, but they're hardly poor. Mr. Neville didn't so much as blink an eye when we told him the cost of Anne's new wardrobe."

"His income is quite adequate for a gentleman of his station," Lucy concurred. "That's why I'm so puzzled about Anne's interest in Firth."

"Her cousin is a gamester," Olivia pronounced, her upper lip curled. "If Firth is pressing him to repay a loan, then perhaps she intends to intercede on his behalf."

Enid gave a vigorous nod of her turbanned head. "It's just the sort of thing Anne might do. She's such a dear, kind-hearted girl."

Lucy agreed. She had prayed for Joshua to meet a woman like Anne, someone who could heal him with her love. He had returned from the war blessedly whole in body, yet wounded in spirit. She didn't know how much of his cynicism was caused by his tragic parting with Lily Pankhurst and how much by his undoubtedly horrific experiences on the battlefield. To her despair, he wouldn't confide in her. But she did know that without the love of a good woman, he might fall into a pit of bitterness and misogyny, never again to find joy in life.

Lucy couldn't allow that to happen.

Now, she had the nagging sense of having missed something vitally important. Sipping her sherry, she ruminated on several peculiar facts. "The problem is more than the moneylender. There's the matter of how my grandson has spent his evening."

"Fighting with Anne's cousin," Olivia said dryly. "Over a game of dice."

"I wonder if that *was* the reason," Lucy said, pondering aloud. "Remember what Mrs. Neville told us? Edwin Bellingham has been cut out of his father's will in favor of Anne."

Olivia frowned. "I see where this is leading. He must resent her for that."

"And Joshua was defending her honor," Enid said with an excited gasp. "That must be it."

"Perhaps," Lucy mused. "Yet I'm puzzled. Joshua professes to be courting Anne. So why did I have to prod him to dance with her? And why did he go off with Brandon for drinks just now?"

"They're catching up on all the news," Olivia said. "It *has* been seven years, you know."

"Pish-posh. My grandson should be with Anne, vying for her attention. That was the whole point of having her dance with other men. But he doesn't appear to be jealous in the least. Have I been too hasty to think he cares for her?"

Leaning forward, Enid patted Lucy's hand. "Really, dearest, you mustn't fret. Haven't you noticed the way he looks at her when he thinks no one is watching? With so much passionate feeling."

"Humph," Olivia said acidly. "We all know what men are thinking when they look at an attractive woman. It has little to do with romantic love."

"Physical love can lead to romantic love," Enid averred. "I'm hoping that Joshua seduces Anne. Then he'll have to wed her."

"Good gracious," Olivia said, thumping her cane on the

carpet. "Isn't that a bit premature? They met less than a fortnight ago. A hasty betrothal served him ill with Lily Pankhurst."

"But remember the night of *our* debut?" Enid teased. "All three of us met the man of our dreams. And all three of us allowed our future husbands considerable liberties that night. Including you, Olivia."

In the dim light, Olivia's lined face appeared a bit flushed. "All the more reason for us to find Anne and determine what she's up to."

Lucy was inclined to concur. Yet, at the same time, she sensed that it wasn't the right time for meddling *too* much.

Ignoring her creaky bones, she rose to her feet. "I believe," she said decisively, "the person we must find is my grandson."

Chapter Seventeen

An Unwanted Proposal

"Mr. Firth," Anne said, concealing her surprise.

She had expected a man with the manners of a street rat, not this polished, urbane gentleman in the tailored garb of an aristocrat. His cool blue eyes were keen and intelligent, and she knew intuitively that she must not underestimate him.

Nor let him get the upper hand.

"If you heard I was looking for you," she said, "you should have identified yourself straightaway."

"And spoil the game of hide-and-seek? Anticipation is half the fun." In a smooth move, he took her arm and steered her down the opulent corridor.

She realized in alarm that he was leading her away from the party and into a dark, deserted area of the house. Deftly extracting her arm, she turned to face him. "I'm not playing games. I merely wish to ask you a few questions."

"How intriguing. I suggest we find more comfortable surroundings."

Firmly pressing his palm to the base of her spine, he guided her through a doorway and into a music room complete with harp, pianoforte, and rows of chairs. His touch unnerved her. Again, she twisted away from him.

From a table in the passageway, he had taken a silver

candelabrum which he placed on the mantelpiece. The wavering glow of the flames threw eerie shadows over his face. Along with the fragrance of beeswax, the scent of his cologne drifted to Anne. Sandalwood. The exotic aroma brought to mind mystery . . . and danger.

Warily, she regarded Firth. Only moments ago, he had been making love to a married woman. He was a moneylender who bailed desperate men out of debt, charged exorbitant interest rates, and then threatened them when they couldn't repay. But was he also the cloaked man hiding in the bushes, firing a gun at her in the belief that she was Lord Timberlake's son?

Her scalp prickled. Fingering the diamond pendant like a talisman, she felt a cowardly longing for Joshua's presence.

"I've alarmed you," Firth observed. "If you like, I'll leave the door ajar for propriety's sake."

"Leave it wide open."

"As you wish."

His manner was indulgent, as if her apprehension amused him. In an effort to appear at ease, she walked to the harp and pretended to admire its graceful curves. "You'll be wondering why I sought this meeting," she said. "You see, I'm very curious about your business enterprises."

"I've tea plantations in Ceylon, gold mines in Africa, sugar cane in the West Indies. Which one of them interests you?"

"Your business of making loans to those in need."

He lifted an eyebrow. "Are *you* in need, Miss Neville?"

Somehow, he made the question sound sordid. "You mistake me," she said coolly. "I'm inquiring on behalf of a friend."

"I see." Firth strolled to the sideboard and lifted a decanter. "Care for a glass of Madeira?"

"No, thank you." To steady her nerves, she gripped her reticule. "Perhaps I should come straight to the point, Mr.

Firth. I'm referring to the debt Lord Timberlake owes to you."

His face inscrutable, Firth maintained a half-smile. "Did the old drunkard send you here to plead on his behalf?"

"No, I've reasons of my own."

Glass in hand, he prowled toward her and stopped on the other side of the harp. "And what might those reasons be?"

She deemed it prudent to sidestep the question. "His lordship claims that you've threatened to retaliate if he fails to repay you. Is that true?"

"It's a wise businessman who expects prompt repayment of his loans. If I ran a charity, I'd end up in debtors' prison myself."

His patronizing manner grated on her, making her bold. "But how far would you go in collecting your due?" she asked. "Would you harm Lord Timberlake? Or his son?"

"You're referring to the aborted duel."

"Yes." Either Joshua had told him—or Firth knew because he'd been there. But did he also know that she had taken David's place? "There was a man lurking nearby who took a shot at David Pankhurst."

"Have a care, Miss Neville. That's quite an accusation you're making."

His long fingers idly glided over the strings of the harp. The heavenly notes only increased her nervous tension. "I'd like to hear what you have to say to it."

"I'm innocent, of course." He smiled, looking as guileless as a fox in a henhouse. "But then, I would claim so anyway, wouldn't I?"

Was he lying? His unwavering gaze met hers. She studied his bland expression through the strings of the harp, but he was as difficult to read as Joshua. "May I ask, where were you that morning?"

"At my place of business. Alas, I have no witnesses to testify on my behalf." He strolled around the harp and stopped in a pool of shadow. "Now it's my turn to ask the questions. Tell me about this quarrel between David Pank-hurst and Joshua Kenyon. Is it true that Pankhurst's sister took her own life after Kenyon abandoned her?"

The unexpected switch of subject knotted her insides. Firth was merely repeating gossip, the same tale she had heard from David for the past five years. And yet she couldn't bring herself to denounce Joshua to this man. "I'm afraid I don't know the whole story."

"You should. Kenyon is your houseguest."

He made it sound improper, and she felt compelled to say, "My parents invited him to stay. He's a physician, and he administered to me after I fell from my horse."

"The morning of the duel. You suffered a head injury."

Again, she had the uneasy impression that he knew the true source of her wound. If Mama and Papa found out how she had risked her life . . . Her throat dry, she asked, "What exactly has Joshua told you about my accident?"

"Very little."

"Then how did you find out about it?"

"Here and there. While I was investigating Kenyon." Watching her, Firth savored a sip of Madeira. "You look surprised. He accused me of a crime, and I don't take that lightly."

Did Joshua know he'd been watched? Aware that Firth had deflected her from her purpose, she said, "About Lord Timberlake—"

He cut her off with an intolerant wave of his hand. "Un-derstand one thing about me, Miss Neville. I don't speak about my clients. Not even to pretty ladies."

She wasn't fool enough to take his compliment at face value. Geoffrey and Francis had been sneaky that way, praising her as a means to distract her from some trans-gression. "Understand one thing about *me,* Mr. Firth. I don't give up easily."

"Then we're two of a kind." His movement unhurried, he closed the distance between them and stopped in front of her. "A pity Kenyon is courting you."

So he knew that, too.

His proximity rattled her. She could smell his subtle sandalwood scent, and see the arrogance in his gaze. Her fingers icy inside her gloves, she nervously pulled at the ribbons that fastened her reticule. "I very much doubt we're alike in any way, Mr. Firth."

"That remains to be seen. Has he declared himself yet?"

"Declared—?"

"Kenyon. Has he offered you a proposal of marriage?"

Startled, she stammered, "No . . . not that it's any concern of yours."

"It is, indeed. It means I'm free to call on you myself. Free to court you and send you flowers. Do you prefer orchids or roses?"

"You're certainly *not* free to court me without my permission," she snapped. How had the conversation taken this abrupt turn? As much as she wanted answers from Firth, she shuddered to think of him as a suitor. "I'm afraid it's time for me to return to the ballroom. If you'll step aside."

He moved, but only to place his wine glass on a nearby music stand. Then he turned to her, his eyes intense. "Suppose I canceled Timberlake's debt?"

"Pardon—?"

"We'll strike a bargain, you and I. I'll let his lordship off the hook. In exchange, you'll become my mistress."

Staggered by his audacity, she blurted out, "No!"

His features tightened briefly, his only betrayal of emotion. "Perhaps you prefer a man of noble blood. I'm afraid I can't oblige you there. I was born in the gutters of London."

Stiffly, she said, "I really must go before my chaperones come looking for me."

She tried to step around him, but he blocked her path. "The renowned Rosebuds," he said. "I suspect old Lady Stokeford and her two cronies have handpicked you to be Kenyon's bride."

"I make my own choices, sir."

"Then I trust you'll have the sense not to let Kenyon abuse you as he did Lily Pankhurst. If he tries to, I want you to come straight to me."

Was Firth presenting himself as her protector? How ludicrous!

His gaze dipped in a bold survey of her, pausing on her bosom, where the diamond pendant rested. His eyebrows lowered in a frown. In a sudden move, he extended his hand as if to grab her.

She panicked. Dodging to the side, she plunged her fingers into her reticule, drew out her pistol, and pointed it at his chest. Her heart pounded as she cocked the hammer. "Don't come any closer."

He went still. Angry astonishment flashed in his eyes. He glowered at her a moment, then gave a bark of laughter. "Don't you think your reaction is a bit extreme, Miss Neville?"

"Perhaps. Or perhaps not."

"You hold a gun as if you've used one before."

"I'm an excellent shot. At this range, I can scarcely miss."

Firth eyed her speculatively. "If you must know, I meant you no harm. You've a pin in your bodice. I thought it might stab you."

"I have nine brothers, and I know that trick. You want me to look down so that you can catch me off guard."

He shrugged. "Have it your way. I make a point of never arguing when a woman points a weapon at me."

"Then proceed to the rear of the room and sit down at the pianoforte."

With calm, measured steps, he did as she commanded and seated himself on the bench. "Now what? Do you mean to tie me up?"

He sounded amused, as if he once again derived enjoyment from their encounter. Tightening her fingers on the pistol, she said, "Turn around and play a tune while I depart."

"Only ladies play. It's one of those silly, society rules."

"Bang on the keys, then. And continue to do so for the next five minutes."

"You're a hard woman, Miss Neville. But I suppose I've no choice."

He turned to face the pianoforte and flexed his hands. Then he lightly caressed the ivory keys in a trilling prelude before launching into a powerful melody that arrested Anne on her retreat to the door.

Surprise reverberated in her along with the beautiful music. She'd meant only to occupy him while she made her escape; the cessation of sound would give her a moment's warning if he came after her. But his mastery of the instrument made him more of an enigma than ever.

She shook off her curiosity. The point was not to linger and listen. The point was to depart unscathed.

Pivoting on her heel, she made for the door. At that moment, the white panel swung all the way open and Joshua strode inside.

Her heart gave a leap of gladness even as she realized the potential danger of his presence. A fierce expression hardened his face. In his cavalryman's uniform, the gold braid shining and black knee boots gleaming, he looked ready to do battle.

His flinty eyes took in the situation at a glance. He ran his hands over her as if searching for injury, and her skin tingled wherever he touched her. "Are you all right?" he demanded.

"Yes. I was just leaving. Let's go."

His gaze swept from her to Firth, then returned to the pistol in her hand. His features sharpened with a frightful violence. "What the devil did he do to you?"

"Nothing. We talked—"

Before she could explain further, Joshua stormed past the maze of chairs, past the harp and the music stand, making straight for Firth.

Anne dropped her pistol and reticule on a chair and

darted after him. The music stopped in mid-note as Firth whipped around on the bench to face him. Both men looked intent, conscious only of each other.

Anne knew that look. She had seen it often enough when her brothers had squabbled. Without sparing a thought, she thrust herself between them and braced her forearms against Joshua's chest. She was no match for his rock-hard strength, but she might delay him long enough to make her point.

"Listen to me, Joshua. You've no cause for alarm."

"You drew a pistol on him."

"As a precaution, that's all."

"I wonder."

Joshua tightened his hold on her waist as if to move her aside. Banking on the hope that he wouldn't attack while she stood in the way, Anne locked her arms around his neck. "I won't let you brawl. You've caused enough scandal for one night."

From the corner of her eye, Anne saw Samuel Firth rise from the bench. "She's wiser than you, Kenyon," he taunted. "She knows I can trounce you."

Joshua's muscles contracted, and she felt his rage ripple along the length of her body. She maintained her desperate grasp on his neck. "Leave him be, Joshua," she said sternly. "You'll draw undue attention to yourself. You'll disappoint your grandmother. She's worked hard to get you accepted back into society."

"Damn society."

"Careful," Firth drawled. "You mustn't reject your birthright."

A powerful animosity emanated from Firth. Anne didn't understand it, but she knew it was there, cold and ugly, a shadowy pall in the air.

"Get the hell out of here," Joshua growled. "Now."

"I'll leave, but only in deference to the lady's wishes." Firth strolled to the door. Before departing, he turned to add, "You've excellent reflexes, Miss Neville. A pity you didn't kill him in that duel."

So he did know about her masquerade. Had Lord Timberlake told him?

The thought flickered through her mind, superseded by the certainty that Firth meant what he said. He hated Joshua enough to want him dead. *Why?*

Shivering, she couldn't bring herself to relinquish her hold on Joshua. She stood on tiptoe, her body molded to his, her cheek pressed to his cravat. Her bosom absorbed the powerful beating of his heart, and she felt his every harsh breath as if it were her own. He had a strength, a vitality, that tempted her to touch him all over, to know him as well as she knew herself. The dread of him being harmed made her shudder again.

With his thumb and forefinger, Joshua brought up her chin so that she met his brutal brown eyes. His lips formed a line of fury. When he spoke, his anger was directed not at Firth, but at her. "What in blazes were you thinking, to bring a gun into a crowded ballroom?"

She stiffened under the lash of his voice. "For protection, of course."

"Protection?" he said on a harsh laugh. "A gun is a deadly weapon. If it had gone off by accident, you could have killed someone, maybe even yourself. Have you ever seen a gunshot wound?"

She tried to step away from him, but his arms were like iron bars. "No, but if you'd listen—"

"No, you listen." His fingers flexed around her waist, and he held her back a few inches. "I can't begin to count the number of shattered bodies I've seen. I tended to many of them myself, and watched helplessly as men died." His bitter gaze bored into her as he described in lurid detail the damage that a bullet could inflict on the human body.

Sickened by the fearsome darkness in him, she took his face in her hands. "Joshua, let me finish. The pistol wasn't loaded."

For a long moment, he regarded her with shadowed eyes. Unexpectedly, her heart ached for him. He was in a place where no one could reach him, a place of death and destruction, the stuff of nightmares. She stroked his cheek, gliding her fingers over the bristly trace of whiskers and willing him to step back into the light.

By degrees, his muscles relaxed. His chest expanded and contracted in several deep breaths. Releasing her, he walked away and combed his fingers through his hair. "I didn't know," he muttered, his back to her. "I should have let you explain."

She took a step toward him. "It's all right. I'm glad you confided in me, even a little."

He swung toward her, his expression frosty. "Glad to hear about maimed men and agonizing deaths? You've peculiar tastes for a lady."

For the blink of an eye, his hostility sliced into her. Then she realized his antagonism was meant to discourage her. He didn't want her—or anyone else—to see the excruciating memories he kept locked behind that brusque façade. Perhaps he viewed it as a weakness that he was so affected by the horrors of war.

The realization filled her with an aching tenderness. Whatever his sins, he shouldn't have to suffer this.

Closing the distance between them, she slid her arms around his waist to prevent him from turning his back on her again. "I'm glad to listen, that's all," she said. "I mean that, Joshua. If I can take some of your burden, even for a moment, I'm willing to do so."

Chapter Eighteen

A Glimpse of Light

Arrested in the throes of anger, Josh stared down at her earnest expression. She should have rebuked him, instead of offering support. She should have run from him in revulsion, rather than enfold him in a loving embrace. But of course, Anne had a habit of acting contrary to his expectations.

She had the face of innocence. Pure. Clean. Untainted by human atrocities. She had never looked into the beardless features of a terrified young soldier and had to kill or be killed. She had never heard the desperate cries of the dying, never smelled the stink of blood and gore, never witnessed the carnage of bodies stretching as far as the eye could see.

Nor would he ever enlighten her. Only a puling coward would drag her down into the abyss with him. Only a rogue would want to sully her.

Yet he could think only of doing just that. And then, when he yielded to temptation and lowered his mouth to hers, he couldn't think at all.

Her lips were warm and soft and welcoming. He turned his head to one side and then the other, testing different angles, cupping her cheeks in his palms. She tasted of candor and goodness, of delicacies he hadn't known for more years than he could count. As his hands followed her lithe curves down over her waist and hips, he had enough presence of mind to keep his lustful impulses in check. At least until her throat vibrated in a melodious little purr.

He drew back slightly, saw her dreamy face, and recognized a passion that matched his own. His veneer of control vanished like smoke. Holding her close, he walked her backward to the wall, using its solidity as a brace so that he could fit his aching loins into the cradle of her hips. She arched her body to meet his and moved her hands over him in random caresses. He rained frantic kisses over her face and throat, and she did the same to him. Their lips met again, their tongues stroking in a deep, reckless kiss that left him gasping for breath.

Brushing aside the diamond pendant, he rubbed his cheek over the satiny area above her bosom. He inhaled the rosy fragrance of her skin. His fingers delved into the shadowed valley of her décolletage, worked their way beneath the stiffness of her corset, and cupped a warm, rounded breast. Her nipple stiffened as he passed his thumb over it. A shiver went through her. She whimpered his name, the sound inciting his desire.

"Anne." His voice sounded raw and needy, torn from him. She maddened him; he felt drunk on the wine of her passion.

Reaching behind her, he fumbled with the tiny buttons of her gown, working each free of its mooring, until her dress lay halfway open at the back. He was too impatient to undo any more, and that proved to be a mistake. Her sleeves slid down her arms, but her bodice resisted him. While working at it, he covered her with kisses, nibbling at her neck, licking the hollow of her throat, tracing his tongue over the delicate shell of her ear. He slid his hands over her bosom, grasping the silk and peeling it downward.

Something sharp pierced his finger.

"Damn!" He reared back to see a drop of blood well on the tip of his forefinger. The sight jolted him back to reality.

Closing his hand into a fist, he stared down at her soft, corset-clad breasts and fought to master his breathing. What the hell was he doing, undressing Anne in the midst of a party? Had he lost all semblance of decency?

He must have.

Clinging to him, she opened her slumberous eyes. She spoke his name on a shuddering sigh. "Joshua—?"

"Something jabbed me." *Thank God.* He examined the outside of her gaping gown, spied a glimmer of metal half-hidden by the decorative embroidery at the edge of her bodice, and drew forth a straight pin. "This."

Anne blinked. Morosely, he watched her come to an awareness of her disheveled state. A flush stained her cheeks, and she brought her bodice back to its proper height. With her other hand, she took the pin from him and held it up to the candlelight. "The dressmaker must have forgotten it." A little pucker appeared between her eyebrows as she added in a contemplative tone, "So he wasn't lying."

Josh dragged his gaze from the enticing glimpse of her bosom. "Pardon?"

"Mr. Firth noticed the pin, that's all."

Her words punched him in the gut. That bastard had been staring at her breasts. He'd lusted for her.

That Josh himself had done the same—and far more—did nothing to pacify his rage.

He took the pin from her and flung it into a darkened corner, where it landed with a tiny ping. "That's all? Blast it, Anne. It shows where his attention must have been. You were a fool to come here with him."

Her lips made a prim line. "If you'd included me in your investigation, I wouldn't have had to interview him alone."

The truth of that was inescapable. When he weighed the risk of losing her against the danger of his desire, he had no choice.

He acknowledged her words with a curt nod. "Point taken. Henceforth, we're partners." As her eyes lit up, he added sternly, "But you'll stay away from Firth. You're damn lucky he didn't seduce you tonight."

"And how would you describe *your* actions?"

"Irresponsible. Reckless." Glancing at her reddened lips, he added gruffly, "Inevitable."

Tilting her head to the side, she regarded him with a steady gaze. "What are you saying, Joshua? That you regret kissing me? Or that you were only punishing me for prying?"

"No," he bit out. "It was inevitable because . . ."

"Because?"

His palms felt cold with sweat. He couldn't tell her that he found her irresistible, that she had tied him in knots, that he craved her even though it might earn him a place in hell. "Because of lust," he said bluntly. "Because this is all I want from you."

He ground his hips against hers in a crude pantomime of coitus.

Any other virgin would have recoiled or swooned in shock. But not Anne. She caught her breath through parted lips. Her lashes lowering to half-mast, she tipped her head back against the wall, exposing the column of her throat. She moved her hands to his chest, and her fingers pressed into the fabric of his coat.

Heat seared his groin in an instantaneous combustion. Desire for her blinded him to all logic and propriety. Forgetting the threat she represented, he bent his head to take her mouth in another hard kiss.

Even as their lips made contact, she brought the heel of her slipper down hard on his instep and gave his chest a mighty shove.

Josh staggered back, more irate than injured. Unslaked hunger bit at his groin. His foot didn't hurt as much as his pride.

"Blast! Why did you do that?"

"If it doesn't overtax your *lusty* brain, I'm sure you can find the answer for yourself."

"You wanted me to kiss you."

"I wanted to catch you off guard. The ploy worked, didn't it?"

Her smug look irritated him. "I've never forced a woman. There are plenty who are willing. Next time, just tell me to stop."

"There won't be a next time." Reaching around to her back, Anne worked at refastening the long row of buttons. "I can't kiss you anymore."

He should have welcomed the mandate. It was exactly the barrier he needed to keep himself from acting on his base impulses. But he found himself bristling instead. "Why not?"

"Isn't it apparent?"

The rosy blush on her cheeks mitigated his anger somewhat. Yet he wanted to hear her admit she wasn't as unaffected as she professed to be.

He walked closer to help her with the buttons. "It's cowardly to answer a question with a question. So tell me why I can't kiss you."

Anne stiffened at his touch, her spine a steel rod. "Because all you want from me is something crude and illicit."

"Crude? You certainly seemed to enjoy it. Or aren't you honest enough to admit so?"

She stood silent a moment. "All right, then. If you want honesty, here it is—when you kiss me, I can't bear for you to stop."

Her candid admission stirred him more than he cared to admit. He fastened the last button, resisting the temptation to lean down and nuzzle the tender nape of her neck, to whisper an apology for his boorish behavior.

But it was better this way. Better to keep her at arm's length. "You should have expected that," he said silkily. "I'm a scoundrel. Seducing women is my forte."

Over her shoulder, she gave him a brief, eloquent look of mingled doubt and confusion. Then she walked away, past the harp and the music stand, her posture straight and dignified. For all that she had grown up in the company of nine brothers, Anne moved with an innate feminine grace. His gaze fell to the flare of her hips and the hint of rounded bottom beneath her skirt. He knew the contour of those curves now. It would only make his erotic fantasies all the more vivid.

Feeling like a randy buck chasing a reluctant doe, he paced after her. He hoped Anne was too inexperienced to recognize how much she was torturing him. He watched in moody silence as she bent down to pick up her reticule where she'd dropped it on a chair.

The sight of the small pistol brought a chilling reminder of the lapse in his restraint. He had reacted like a madman, revealing far too much of himself. It must never happen again.

Tucking the small pistol inside the reticule, she turned toward him, her gaze troubled. "Joshua, there's something I haven't told you."

You want me. You need me. "What?"

"Samuel Firth despises you. I don't understand why, but he does."

"It's obvious," Josh said impatiently. "I challenged his character. No man takes that lightly."

"But he had you investigated. He knows all sorts of things about you, even that Lady Stokeford is your grandmother."

"That's hardly a secret."

"Perhaps." Her small white teeth worried her lower lip, and Josh found himself watching the action with the appetite of a starving man. "He asked me to be his mistress."

"What?"

"Calm down. I'm only telling you because his offer supports my point. He believes you're courting me. And it's quite clear that he wishes to steal me away from you."

Josh didn't give a bloody damn about that bastard's motives. His fingers clenched, he started for the door.

She sprang into his path and snared his wrists. "I forbid you to fight him."

"He insulted you."

"That's the least of my worries. And yours." She paused, her gaze roving his face. "I'm troubled, Joshua. *Very* troubled. I have the feeling he's trying to maneuver you for some purpose of his own."

The soberness of her expression pierced his anger. Her eyes were huge beneath her furrowed brow. She truly believed that Firth was plotting against him. "Your imagination is running wild," Josh said. "I've been out of the country for much of the past fifteen years. He can't possibly have a personal vendetta against me."

She stubbornly shook her head. "I don't care if it's illogical. When Mr. Firth speaks of you, there's something frightening in his eyes."

"He's ruthless. He wants you. And he thinks I'm standing in his way."

"Yes," she said dryly, "all the handsome men are fighting over me. That's why I'm a spinster at twenty-eight."

In spite of his foul mood, he was struck by her unconventional beauty. It was her inner strength as much as her outer appearance that attracted him. Her skin had the natural glow of a woman who liked the sun. Tawny lashes fringed her bold violet-blue eyes. With her chin tilted up, she had the wild splendor of a lioness. "You're a spinster because you never went into society."

Anne didn't look convinced. She moved her hands to his chest, her fingers curling into the gold braid of his coat. "You'll be careful, won't you? Promise me you won't provoke Mr. Firth?"

Her concern burrowed deeply into Joshua, making him aware of the powerful discord within himself. Why was she suddenly on his side? Was it possible that under all that starch and straitlacedness she cared for him?

Though it was the height of folly, he wanted to stake his claim on her. He craved her innocence—and in more than the physical sense. He wanted to use her in the impossible hope of regaining his own innocence.

The bitter irony was, if ever he committed the unpardonable sin of seducing Anne, he would destroy all that was good in her. He would damn her to his own hell. That must never, ever happen.

"I'll provoke whomever I please," he said curtly. "And I'll thank you to keep your shrewish fears to yourself."

Turning his back on the hurt in her eyes, he walked out on her.

Chapter Nineteen

The Tin Soldier

" 'My brethren, be strong in the Lord, and in the power of his might. Put on the armor of God, that ye may be able to stand against the wiles of the devil . . .' " As a shaft of sunlight illuminated his brown hair and tailored black suit, the Reverend Cummings read the long epistle from his prayerbook. His powerful voice echoed in the stately church.

Trying to concentrate, Anne sat with the choir in the balcony overlooking the congregation. Toward the front of the church, her parents were seated beside the Rosebuds. Dorian and his brood of four occupied the next pew along with Hugh, Isaac, and Nell. Behind them sat Benjamin, Genevieve, and their five children. Joshua had the aisle seat, presumably to guard against escapees.

Four-year-old Mary fidgeted beside him. She tugged at her pink bonnet and swung her legs, tapping the pew in front of her. Benjamin flashed several quelling glares her way, but the little girl didn't appear to notice.

Then Joshua bent his head down to whisper in her ear. Sliding his arm around her, he drew the girl closer. Mary nestled quietly against him.

Anne frowned, resisting the treacherous softening inside

herself. Just when she'd closed her heart to him, he did something to pry open the door.

In the two days since the ball, Joshua had been irritable and short-tempered with her. Yesterday, when they'd gone together to question several men on the list, the fruitless interviews had only served to worsen his foul mood. She had done her best to ignore him. Though his bad-tempered behavior made her want to snap at him, she had clenched her teeth in favor of cool composure. Quarreling with him would only invite more insults like the one he'd flung at her at the party.

Shrewish, indeed!

At least he had been civil to her family. At breakfast, he and Papa had had a friendly debate about politics. Upon arriving at church, he'd greeted her brothers with enthusiasm. Now he offered comfort to her niece.

Seeing the two of them together, the small girl leaning so trustingly against the big man, Anne was unable to halt the thawing of her heart. Until this moment, she had never seen Joshua behave as a father. She'd never imagined him showing kindness toward a child. From out of nowhere, her mind conjured the images of him soothing his daughter's tears and teaching his son to fly a kite.

No, she told herself firmly. He was a rude, vexing man who couldn't be trusted to nurture a flea. As soon as he completed his business here, he would go back to his home and resume his civilian life. And good riddance. She would never see him again.

" 'Take the helmet of salvation, and the sword of the Spirit. . . .' " The admonishing voice of the Reverend Cummings underscored the empty feeling inside her.

As the rafters rang with the vicar's thunderous volley, Joshua glanced up over his shoulder at the choir loft. He looked straight at Anne, caught her staring, and arched an eyebrow. Then he returned his gaze to the pulpit.

She blushed from her head to her curled toes. A case of the flutters took hold of her insides. She felt breathless and light-headed and utterly distracted. For the past two nights, he hadn't had nightmares—but she had. In the darkness of her bed, she'd awakened damp with perspiration, her heart racing. Always, she'd had the same disturbing dream of Joshua caressing her . . .

Instantly ashamed of her irreverent thoughts, Anne steepled her hands and closed her eyes, silently saying a prayer for her own redemption. It was troubling enough that Joshua could stir carnal longings in her away from church; to feel an illicit desire in this holy place was utterly sinful.

She resolved to keep her attention off Joshua and focused on the Reverend Cummings for the remainder of the service. But another sight diverted her. Hunched over the prayerbook in his hands, Lord Timberlake sat alone in his family pew at the front of the church. With his balding head bowed and his shoulders slumped, he looked like the very picture of defeat.

Had Samuel Firth threatened him again? How far would the moneylender go in collecting his due? Recalling his cold, merciless eyes, she felt a tremor of worry.

Across the aisle from Timberlake, Arthur Cummings sat straight and proud. His impeccably tailored coat and white cravat couldn't disguise a robust form like that of a stevedore on the docks. His hawk nose and strong chin jutted out as he gazed up at his son in the pulpit.

As a respected politician, Arthur Cummings was dedicated to keeping his name—and his son's name—free of scandal. Were his morals so lax that he would try to murder his son's lover?

She meditated on the letter that Joshua had purloined. Now that she had recovered from the shock of its revelation, she could consider its contents with a clear head.

You understand me as no one else does . . . I beg of you, do not speak of forsaking our arrangement . . . I miss the touch of your hand and count the moments until we can meet again . . .

She cast a surreptitious glance at David, who stood in

the garb of the choir director at the far end of the balcony. His long white surplice and golden hair gave him the aura of an archangel. A rather gloomy archangel.

Grasping a hymnal to his chest, he stared fixedly at the Reverend Cummings. To anyone else, David would appear to be devoutly listening. To Anne, he looked . . . miserable.

Unhappiness etched the corners of his downturned mouth. His skin had an unhealthy pallor. His stiff, motionless posture hinted at an inner tension.

Forsaking our arrangement. Had the Reverend Cummings ended the liaison?

The supposition made Anne sit up straight. Someone coughed in the congregation; a baby wailed and was shushed. His voice full of fervor, the vicar intoned the litany. Despite his small stature, he had an authoritative presence like that of his father.

She glanced back at David, and his despondency supported her growing suspicion. He had the aspect of someone pining for a lost love. Although he had courted her on false pretenses, she felt a glimmering of sympathy for him, the concern for a suffering friend. Her grief and anger had already subsided; perhaps David had never been more to her than a girlish infatuation.

At least now she could accept his need to deceive her. The exposure of his secret life would bring dishonor and public humiliation to him—and to the Reverend Cummings.

But if indeed the vicar had brought an end to their forbidden love, then the letter was proof that David wasn't ready to accept the circumstances. How persistently had he been pressuring Richard Cummings to relent?

Her thoughts leapt to another chilly conclusion. What if the cloaked man had been the Reverend Cummings himself?

She gripped the hymnal in her lap. It had to be sacrilegious even to consider such a theory about a man who had dedicated his life to the church. But her mind refused to let go of the notion. She kept returning to the possibility, mulling it over, examining it from all angles.

At a signal from David, the choir rose for the closing hymn. He seated himself at the massive pipe organ, adjusted his voluminous sleeves, and began to play. Anne joined in the song without sparing a thought to the words, barely noticing Mrs. Peavy's off-key warble and Mr. Foster's booming bass. All the while, uncertainties gnawed at her concentration.

When the music ended, the congregation poured out of the pews and headed down the aisle to the front doors. Anne glanced down at her family as they walked out of the church. Joshua carried Mary in his arms; the girl had her head tucked into the crook of his neck, fast asleep. Again, Anne felt that little catch in her bosom, but she focused her mind on her purpose. If Joshua was occupied, he wouldn't come looking for her. She had a few moments to speak to David without any interference.

The other members of the choir filed out, heading down the stairway that led to the vestry. Lagging behind, Anne waited until the last person had vanished through the doorway.

David gathered up the music sheets from the organ and tucked them into a wooden box on a shelf. Then he unfolded the protective cover that she had sewn for him years ago and arranged it carefully over the keys. His brow was furrowed in the manner of a man withdrawn into his own thoughts.

She stepped to his side. "May I have a word with you, David?"

He spun around, his mouth slack with surprise. Then he cast an uneasy, furtive glance down at the emptied church. "I'm sorry, I haven't the time to chat. My father is waiting for me downstairs."

"This won't take long. I only need to ask you a few questions."

"And why should I even speak to you? You're carrying on with Kenyon."

His words were a verbal slap. She pursed her lips, knowing that he blamed Joshua for the loss of his beloved sister—but also knowing that David had no right to criticize her. In a sharp whisper, she said, "I won't tolerate your condemnation. For five years, you let me believe we were courting. I considered you such a friend that I took your place in a duel and nearly died. At the very least, you owe me some honest answers."

David's blue eyes wavered. He plucked at the cloth cover, lining it up perfectly over the keyboard. His tone subdued, he said, "I'm sorry for all that's happened. I meant to fight that duel myself. If you hadn't dosed my tea with laudanum . . ." He paused and sighed. "Ask me whatever you like."

"I must know. Are you and the Reverend Cummings still . . . ?"

All semblance of color fled his face, leaving his handsome features a pasty white. With agitated hands, he straightened a pile of hymnals. "How can you link our names?" he said in a barely audible tone. "I can't speak of this here."

"A simple yes or no will suffice."

He closed his eyes, his breathing harsh in the quiet church. In a strangled whisper, he admitted, "No. We are not."

His profile had the classic beauty of his namesake sculpture, except for the anguish on his features. She placed her hand on the sleeve of his choir robe to soften the blow of her next question. "Did he jilt you?"

He gave a jerky nod, and his eloquent expression of grief told the truth.

"When did it happen?" she murmured. "Was it before or after the duel?"

"Several days prior . . ." He whipped his head around to stare at her in shocked consternation. "I know what you're thinking, Anne. But you're wrong. Richard wouldn't try to kill me. *No*."

If only she could be so certain. A man desperate to hide a scandalous secret might well attempt murder. "You haven't offered me any other possibilities. If it wasn't Richard, then who?"

David was silent a moment, his lips twisted. "Look to his father," he said with sudden bitterness. "Arthur Cummings caused our separation."

"What do you mean?"

"He and Richard had had a terrible row the previous week. Arthur threatened to cut off Richard's quarterly allowance if he didn't stay away from me. Since the living here pays only one hundred pounds per annum, Richard had no choice." His eyes watery, David blinked hard. "I offered him money from my own pocket, but he wouldn't take it. He refuses to provoke his father."

Arthur Cummings sounded like a cruel, controlling man. The news of the quarrel made an even stronger case against him. But Anne couldn't so easily discount his son. "You wrote a letter to the vicar. Have you tried since then to discuss matters with him?"

"Many times, but it's no use. No use at all." His voice cracking, David turned away and busied himself with straightening the already tidy stack of hymnals. "Please, Anne. I—I want to find who shot you as much as you do. But I can't speak of this anymore."

Her heart ached for him. There was nothing she could do to assuage his torment, nothing she could say to offer him hope. Yet she couldn't just walk away, either. She thought of all the pastimes they'd shared, collecting shells on the beach, practicing for the choir, delivering baskets to the poor and sick of the parish.

"If I could," she murmured, "I'd give you a bit of beauty."

"Pardon?"

"You used those words once to explain why you added

ribbons and flowers to the baskets for the needy. Even the poor need a bit of beauty."

The ghost of a smile flitted across his face. "I suppose I'm wretchedly poor in spirit these days."

"I'm truly sorry for that."

He nodded wearily, and for a moment, the old camaraderie surrounded them again. Regretfully, she knew it couldn't last. "If I may, I'd also like to ask you about your sister."

David's eyes widened. "What can Lily possibly have to do with this matter?" he said. "She's dead and buried."

His defensiveness made Anne choose her words with care. "Lady Stokeford believes there's a reasonable explanation for the broken betrothal. She says that if her grandson was truly a cad, he would have told everyone it was Lily's fault."

David dropped the pile of hymnals onto the wood floor. Consternation chased across his face in the instant before he crouched down to clumsily pick up the books. "The Rosebuds," he groused. "They're still meddlesome busybodies."

Anne knelt down to help him gather up the books. "Look me in the eyes, David." She waited until he lifted his guarded face to her. "Did Lily do anything at all to drive him away?"

He huffed out a breath. "That's an outrage. I've told you what happened. Kenyon tried to dishonor her. When he failed, he went after Lily's companion."

A few weeks ago, Anne would have been outraged, too. Yet now, too many doubts crowded her mind. "Are you certain of that? Perhaps Lily misconstrued an innocent situation. What exactly were they doing?"

David scowled. "You must have lost all sense of propriety to ask such a question. Has Kenyon beguiled you so much?"

Anne wanted to deny it. But the events of the past days

had stirred a turmoil of confusion in her. She resorted to saying, "I'm asking the questions, not you."

But David was like a dog with a bone. "He *has* beguiled you. You've disregarded my sister's experience. You've let that knave use you."

"No, I haven't! He'll be leaving soon, and—"

"A lot can happen in a few days, Anne. Believe me, I know."

"Well, he doesn't want *me,* so I suppose you've nothing to worry about."

That didn't satisfy David. A grim fervor etched on his face, he took her hands in his for the first time that she could ever recall. "I beg you to remember this: when it suits Kenyon, he'll abandon you as he did Lily."

The large, boisterous party returned to Merryton-on-Sea for the midday meal. The adults gathered around the long table in the dining parlor, enjoying a measure of peace while the children ate their dinner in the morning room. In between courses, Anne kept busy overseeing her nine nieces and nephews, sopping up spilled soup, fetching more bread from the kitchen, and resolving the inevitable quarrels.

More than once, she caught Joshua's moody gaze following her out of the dining room, and in defiance of David's warning and her own prudent nature, she felt an involuntary thrill. She was glad to be wearing another of her new gowns. Sewn of royal-blue silk with an embroidered design along the hem and sleeves, the dress deepened the color of her eyes and enhanced the natural pink of her skin. The diamond pendant sparkled just above her bosom.

Did Joshua find her pretty? She hoped so.

She had always thought herself sensible, outspoken, and strong, hardly the qualities a gentleman desired in a lady. All her life, she'd had to be forceful in order to deal with her brothers. Between the cleaning and mending and tutoring, there hadn't been time to fuss over her hair and clothing the way other girls did. But now the intensity of

Joshua's gaze made Anne revel in her femininity. She felt alive in an earthy way, aware of the rush of blood through her veins and the acuteness of her senses. Though he could be rude and unfriendly, there was no denying his attractiveness. With his sun-browned skin and ruggedly handsome features, Joshua had an uncompromising masculinity that fascinated her.

It was ridiculous, she chided herself, that he could make her blush simply by looking at her. Ridiculous that her body could ache for him in the midst of a family dinner. What would her brothers and her parents say if they knew he didn't intend to marry her, but she lusted for him, anyway?

She stopped in the deserted passageway to press her fevered brow to the cool wall. Why was she torturing herself? Her decision had already been made. She could allow him no more liberties. No more kissing. No more touching. No more yielding to the wild urges he aroused in her.

He was a scoundrel. He could offer her nothing beyond a fleeting pleasure—and ultimate ruin. In that, at least, David was right.

Joshua himself had made it plain that his only interest in her was carnal. His ungentlemanly conduct the night of the party served as proof of his wicked character. While guests danced in the same house, he had unbuttoned her gown and cupped her breast in his hand. Under the stroking of his fingers, her body had melted like butter, ready to be shaped to his will. He had taken shameless advantage of her naïveté.

But Anne knew there was another side to him, too.

How could she reconcile the rogue with the serious man who sat talking with her brothers, who had showed kindness to a child, who had embraced his grandmother with genuine affection? How could she reconcile the scoundrel with the tortured man who had witnessed so many untold atrocities? If Joshua were truly as callous and coldhearted as he made himself out to be, the sight of dead soldiers and mutilated bodies would have had no effect on him.

But he suffered from nightmares. He became crazed at the notion of a gun in a crowded ballroom. He couldn't speak of the horrors he'd seen on the battlefield, though another man might have bragged about his own exploits.

The more she grew to know him, the more she suspected him capable of intense, heartfelt emotions. To protect himself, he hid all sentiment behind the cold mask of a miscreant.

It was that vulnerable man who challenged her fortitude. She could turn her back on the surly ne'er-do-well. But she feared she wouldn't be able to shut out Joshua when—if—he could admit to needing her.

When the meal was over at last, the men remained in the dining room to drink brandy and wine, while the women retired to the parlor. Mama poured cups of tea and encouraged the Rosebuds to tell stories of their debut season in London half a century ago. Genevieve retired upstairs to put three-month-old Henry down for his nap.

Anne took one of her father's shirts from her overflowing basket of mending and set to work repairing a rip in the cuff.

Isaac's wife, Nell, sat down beside her. A pretty brunette, Nell wore a gown of pale blue muslin in the latest style, yet her eyes were envious as she admired Anne. "Your new wardrobe is exquisite," she said, fingering the silk. "Madame Daumier does the finest work in Brighton. I do wish I could afford her prices."

"Don't you shop there, too?" Anne said, realizing she finally had the chance to fulfill her promise to Isaac.

"I haven't been there in weeks," Nell said on a sigh. "Not since Isaac told Madame to refuse me credit."

On Joshua's advice, Anne remembered. Cautiously she asked, "That doesn't anger you?"

"Well . . . it did at first. Isaac and I had a frightful row." Her blue eyes filling with tears, Nell looked as woebegone as a child instead of an eighteen-year-old married woman. "But when he said he'd end up in debtors' prison if he couldn't pay my bills, I—I realized how selfish I'd been. I can't let my darling be locked away for years in a dank cell just because of a few gowns and hats."

Relieved, Anne patted Nell's hand. "Of course not. You made the right decision. I'm proud of you."

"Are you?" Nell ducked her chin. "I've always wanted to be like you, Anne. You're so sure of yourself."

If only Nell knew the truth. "Perhaps I could teach you how to refurbish some of your gowns from last season."

"Would you? But I'm all thumbs with a needle and thread."

"Sewing just takes patience and practice. Come, I'll show you."

Using an old chemise of hers from the mending basket, Anne demonstrated various ways to turn up a hem to hide a frayed edge, or to add a length of lace and a few tucks to give a garment a new look. She was holding up her handiwork for Nell's inspection when the men trooped into the parlor.

Big, broad-chested Hugh was at the forefront. "Make haste, fellows," he called out behind him. "Annie is showing off her underclothes."

Instantly, Joshua appeared beside her brother. His gaze scanned the plain cambric chemise, and he grinned as Anne hastily rolled it into a ball. She was tempted to hurl it at him, but thought better of letting him touch her unmentionables. Settling for a glare, she buried the chemise in her workbasket.

Her brothers hooted with laughter, even stern-faced Benjamin.

A smile tugging at his mouth, Papa clamped his hand on Hugh's shoulder and chided, "Don't tease your sister."

"That may be asking far too much of them," Anne said dryly. "Perhaps you *boys* should run up to the nursery to play with the other *children*."

"That won't be necessary," Dorian said, his head cocked

toward the doorway. "I believe the nursery is coming to us."

A clamor of shouts and pounding feet down the staircase preceded the influx of children. Pandemonium erupted.

At the lead, Benjamin's oldest boy, Peter, came running into the parlor. On his heels, his younger, tow-headed cousin Stephen chased after him. Clutching something in his fist, Peter dashed around in a madcap circuit of the room. The other children crowded inside to call out cheers and jeers.

Benjamin bellowed at the boys to stop. Hugh tried to grab Peter, but stumbled over a chair and fell flat on his rump. Dorian and Papa held back the other boys and girls. Nell squealed and clung to Isaac. The Rosebuds and Mama called out remonstrations to no avail.

Leaping over a footstool, Stephen caught up to Peter and tried to wrestle the object out of his hand. Peter held his clenched fist above his head and taunted his younger cousin.

Springing to her feet, Anne seized Peter by the scruff of his neck. At the same moment, Joshua clamped his hands onto Stephen's shoulders to stop him from lunging at his older cousin. As Peter wriggled angrily, he knocked over Anne's sewing basket.

Spools and buttons went flying. Pins and needles spilled onto the rug. Ribbons and lace landed in a tangled heap.

Benjamin planted his hands at his thick waist. "That's enough!" he roared.

The room fell silent, but only for a moment.

"He stole Napoleon from me," Stephen accused.

"He cheated," Peter asserted. "*I'm* Wellington, and *I'm* supposed to win."

"Hah. My men beat yours, fair and square."

"Did not."

"Did, too."

"Silence," Dorian snapped, devoid of his usual witty

manner. "You're only making matters worse for your-selves."

Benjamin held out his hand to his son. "Give it over."

Peter slowly unlocked his grubby fingers to reveal a small tin soldier. His face screwed up with reluctance, he extended his hand toward his father's open palm.

But Joshua intercepted the tin soldier. "As a former member of the royal cavalry, I'll claim Napoleon as my prisoner. He'll be exiled until such time as he and his troops can learn to behave."

Both boys stood up straighter, shoulders thrust back and faces sober. Their widened eyes followed the tin soldier as it disappeared into Joshua's pocket.

"Yes, sir, Captain," Peter said, giving a smart salute. He poked Stephen, who blurted out, "Aye, sir."

"Very good," Joshua said, pacing with his hands clasped behind his back. "Henceforth, you men must improve your conduct. It isn't enough to practice good manners only when there's an officer in the room. If a soldier becomes lax in his habits, it could cost him his life—and the lives of his comrades—on the battlefield."

While Joshua lectured them, Benjamin stepped to Anne's side. "Quite ingenious," he muttered, flashing Joshua a look of approval.

"Kenyon has the natural instincts of a father," Dorian said shrewdly.

He and Benjamin glanced at Anne. So did Hugh and Isaac. For the space of a heartbeat, she stood pinned by the speculative stares of her four brothers.

Then Benjamin strode forward to take hold of Peter's arm. "It's time to make your apologies to your grandparents and their guests."

Freed of her brothers' scrutiny, Anne released the breath she'd been holding. Blast that sham courtship! With each passing day, she sank deeper and deeper into a mire of lies. Although her cause was righteous, she heartily despised tricking her family. What would they think of Joshua when he left without making her an offer of marriage?

They would think him a knave and a bounder.

She ought to look forward to that eventuality. It was nothing less than he deserved for being rude to her. Yet her mind turned the thought over and over while Peter and Stephen made their rounds of apologies. Then the boys collected the spools and buttons and other paraphernalia, returning everything to the sewing basket.

"To the entrance hall, children," Benjamin said when the boys were done. "We've overstayed our welcome. And Peter must go home to face his punishment."

"You, too, young man," Dorian said, snapping his fingers at Stephen and pointing to the doorway.

Chins lowered and feet dragging, the boys trailed their fathers out of the parlor.

As the other children trudged after them, Mary tugged on Joshua's coat. She tilted her small face up to him. "Must we go, sir?" she asked plaintively. "I wanted Auntie Anne to read me a story."

Joshua crouched down and took the little girl's hands in his. "You should always do as your papa says. Besides"— he cast a cryptic glance at Anne—"your auntie won't be here. She's going out for a ride with me."

Mary pursed her rosy lips, then nodded. "You must promise to take very good care of her. So she doesn't fall and hurt her head again."

"You have my solemn vow."

As Mary scampered out of the parlor, everyone smiled. Everyone but Anne.

Her momentary softening toward Joshua vanished beneath the sting of resentment. He might have consulted with her before announcing to one and all that they were going out together.

But no one else blinked an eye at his peremptory manner. Papa stood smiling, his arm around Mama. "You two needn't hurry back," Mama told Joshua. "With the children gone, I fear the company will be rather dull here."

"Yes, do take your time," Lady Stokeford added. "We Rosebuds are attending a dinner party this evening at Lord Hampton's. Nathaniel will be joining us, too."

As Nell and Isaac and Hugh took their leave, Joshua strolled to Anne's side to murmur in her ear, "Run upstairs. You'll want to wear your riding clothes."

She gritted her teeth to keep from snapping at him in the presence of others. "Where are we going, pray tell?"

At her too-sweet tone, his gaze fell briefly to her lips. Then a grim coldness swept over his features. "To pay a call on your cousin Edwin."

Chapter Twenty

The Gun Collection

Half an hour later, they were cantering down the road to Brighton, Anne on her chestnut mare, Miss Emmie, and Joshua on his big black gelding, Plato. Anne relished the brisk ride. The breeze carried the chilly tang of the ocean. A kestrel hawk soared against the cloudy sky. The ripening berries of the hawthorne and wild privet foretold the imminent approach of autumn.

She'd had to wear her old brown riding habit with the frayed hem, but she wasn't altogether sorry to relinquish her new gown. There was a certain comfort in being clad up to her throat in spinsterish armor.

Especially when she was about to start a quarrel. As they neared town, she said, "Are you ever going to tell me why we're off to see Edwin?"

Joshua's dark gaze swung to her. His brows were drawn in a preoccupied frown. "Actually, it's your uncle I want to see."

"Why?"

He slowed his horse to a walk, and she did likewise. "Early this morning," he said, "I returned to the site of the duel. I dug this out of a tree trunk." Reaching into his pocket, he drew out a tiny piece of flattened metal and held it out for her inspection.

Anne drew in a sharp breath. "The bullet that struck me."

"Precisely. Seeing your pistol the other night reminded me that Lord Bellingham owns a gun collection. That *is* where you obtained the weapon." One eyebrow cocked, he sent her a faintly sarcastic glare.

"How astute of you," she said coolly. "If ever you wish a change of career, you could join the Bow Street runners in London."

"Hardly. It took me nearly a fortnight to remember the bullet."

A frisson of interest raced over her skin. "And you know what type of gun it came from?"

"An old-fashioned flintlock musket."

"I should have thought of that," she said, chiding herself. "My uncle has several."

"If Edwin was careless, he won't have properly cleaned the piece. I'll be able to tell if it was recently fired."

In a smooth motion, he tossed the bit of metal in the air, caught it deftly in his gloved palm, and slid it back into his pocket. It was on the tip of Anne's tongue to scoff at his showmanship. But she couldn't deny a flare of admiration for him. He sat straight and tall in the saddle, the wind ruffling his black hair and stirring the tails of his dark green coat. He held the reins in one hand, his other hand resting on his firmly muscled thigh.

She thought of those hands touching her, strong yet tender, stroking over her face and throat and bosom . . .

He turned to her, his face faintly mocking. "I'm not the only one who's been holding back. Are you ever going to tell me what you and Pankhurst talked about this morning?"

Somewhat giddy, she focused her thoughts. "Oh, that."

"Yes, that. You two lingered in the choir loft for a good fifteen minutes after services ended."

"I asked him about the letter." Quickly, she related the news that the Reverend Cummings had ended the forbidden liaison after an ultimatum from his father, but that David had been pressuring the vicar to relent.

"So the good pastor has cause to want Pankhurst dead, too," Joshua mused. His keen gaze sharpened on Anne. "Excellent work. You'll have to join me at the Bow Street station."

His teasing praise brought a blush to her cheeks, an undeniable pleasure that warmed her, inside and out. She looked away quickly and saw to her relief that they had arrived at her uncle's once-elegant old mansion across from the square. As always, the place appeared deserted, with weeds choking the garden and the windows darkened by shutters.

"We're here," she said unnecessarily.

Joshua dismounted and came toward her. But with the ease of practice, she unhooked her knee from the pommel and jumped lightly to the ground.

He stopped, a faint frown of exasperation furrowing his brow. "Don't you ever allow anyone to help you?"

Belatedly, she remembered that a lady always waited for the gentleman to assist her. "Why should I? I've been riding since I was five years old. I'm perfectly capable of getting down by myself."

"I'm referring to more than just this." His attention on Anne, he secured Plato's reins to the iron fencepost. "You never ask for help at home, either. It's something I've observed. You do everything for everyone."

"Then the next time I want the table cleared or the floor scrubbed, I'll be sure to ask you."

Joshua didn't laugh or scowl at her impertinent jibe. With a gravity of expression that made her more uneasy than a display of temper, he said, "On the day of the ball, while you were busy getting ready, you made a special trip into town to return your father's books to the lending library. The walk would have done him good."

"He was engaged in looking at his new atlas," she said

coolly, not telling Joshua what her real purpose had been. "And the walk did *me* good."

"Yesterday evening, you wrote out your mother's correspondence, eight letters in all. She could have set down her paintbrush and dipped a pen into ink herself."

"She prefers to dictate her letters," Anne said, bristling. "She says it helps her to think."

"Then today at luncheon, you kept jumping up to help the children in the next room. That task ought to have fallen to your sisters-in-law or brothers."

"They have the children day in and day out. When my brothers and their wives come to visit, I like to give them a rest from routine."

He took a step toward her. "And who gives you a rest, Anne? My God, you even took Pankhurst's place in the duel. And when you were in bed recovering from the bullet wound, you insisted on getting up to help your mother."

"Her lumbago—"

"Isn't serious. I've examined her myself, and she's in fine health for a woman of her age."

"Are you saying she's lazy? I won't have you criticizing my family this way."

"I'm not." He brought his hands down onto her shoulders. "They're fine people, and I've enjoyed their company very much. But I suspect they've grown accustomed to your doing everything for them."

Anne stiffened. "Of course. They need me."

"Do they?" he questioned, his eyes intent on her. "Or do you need them more?"

If he'd shown the slightest hint of sarcasm or mockery, she could have lashed out at him and thought no more of it. But the warm weight of his hands emphasized his seriousness, and the sober look on his face planted the seed of doubt in her mind. *Was* there any truth to what he said?

Certainly not. Most people would find her helpful nature admirable. So why did she feel guilty for taking her uncle's parcel out of the saddlebags, all too aware of Joshua's gaze on her?

She held the brown paper package like a badge of honor. "Of course I need them. They're my family and I love them. Though perhaps *you* can't understand what it means to need anyone."

He lowered his eyebrows in a frown, but the rattle of an opening door pulled her attention to the house.

A man walked out onto the porch. His dark clothing accentuated his tall, lean form, and a scar lifted one corner of his mouth in a faintly sinister look, as if he were sneering at the world.

Joshua strode up the steps to greet him. "Brand. I thought you came to collect your winnings yesterday."

"I took pity on the fellow and gave him an extra day. Let's hope his cheque is worth the paper it's written on." The stranger turned his gray eyes on Anne, who had followed Joshua up the steps. His impertinent gaze raked her prim riding habit, passing over the parcel she held by its strings. "I'll wager you're Miss Anne Neville."

Joshua introduced them. "Brandon Villiers, the disreputable Earl of Faversham."

"It's a pleasure to meet you," Anne exclaimed, shaking his hand. "I like your grandmother very much."

That sardonic look deepened. "At least someone does."

Absently, he rubbed his thigh, drawing her attention to his shiny black footwear. On impulse, she said, "By chance, are your boots from Quincy's?"

"No. Why do you ask?"

"Never mind," Joshua said tersely, taking her by the arm and steering her to the front door. "If you'll excuse us, Anne has to visit her uncle."

"And I have a lady to meet in London," Faversham said mysteriously. "Adieu to both of you. It may be some time before I see you again." After giving Anne one last, penetrating look and Joshua a sly smirk, he headed down the street.

With more force than necessary, Joshua rapped on the door. "Brand isn't on the list."

"How was I to know? You haven't shared the list with me. *You* don't like to depend on anyone else."

Joshua gave her a blighting look just as the door opened a crack and Uncle Francis peered out, his white eyebrows forming a shelf over his squinty eyes. Seeing his visitors, he yanked the door wider and motioned them into the gloomy hall.

"Well, well, 'tis past time you came to visit," he said, rubbing his crabbed hands with glee. "What did you bring me there?"

He grabbed for the parcel, but she held it out of his reach. "How do you know it isn't for Edwin?" she teased.

"Because you're too wise a girl to pamper that nitwit." He squinted up and down at Joshua. "You're that bill collector, ain't you? I suppose you want my son again." He jerked his thumb down the corridor. "He's at his favorite pastime. Getting drunk in the study."

"Actually," Anne said, "this is Lord Joshua Kenyon. I fear he was playing a little trick on you last week."

"Eh? Is he your young man, then? He certainly has that look in his eyes."

Anne blushed. As she turned irresistibly toward Joshua, Sir Francis lunged, snatching the package from her. His fingers, misshapen from rheumatism, plucked open the string with surprising dexterity. He unfolded the brown paper and bent down to smell the contents. "Damson cake," he said, the nostrils flaring on his beaky nose. "My favorite."

Anne hated that her enjoyment of his pleasure was tainted by defensiveness. "It's a gift," she said, glaring at Joshua. "I like doing things for other people."

"I wonder what you'll do for me," he muttered.

She caught him staring at her bosom. Her skin tingled in an instantaneous reaction, the sensation traveling downward to heat her loins and weaken her knees. While her uncle was distracted by the cake, she whispered sharply, "I'll help you pack your bags, that's what."

Oblivious to their quarrel, Uncle Francis motioned them toward the great, gloomy staircase. "Come upstairs, you and your young man. You can read to me while I have my tea and cake. If ever that Grafstone would answer the bell. Been yanking the cord in my chamber for the past hour."

On cue, the cadaverous old butler shuffled out of the shadows beneath the staircase. Anne would have jumped in fright had she not known that a small door there led to the dusty, hidden passageway used by the servants—all two of them. Though her uncle could afford to pay a full staff of retainers, he was too parsimonious to employ more than Grafstone and his doddering wife.

"The bell cord has been broken for over a decade, sir," Grafstone said, not a muscle moving in his long-suffering face. "If I might be permitted to hire a man to repair it—"

"Robbers, all of 'em!" Sir Francis cut in, shaking his fist. "Wanting two shillings for an hour's work. You'd think money grows like weeds in the garden."

"With all due respect, sir, if you refrained from badgering the fellows, they'd be more amenable to bargaining."

Grafstone reached for the damson cake, but her uncle guarded it jealously. "Keep your opinions to yourself. And I'll keep *this* in my chambers."

"You'll draw mice," the butler intoned. "Remember the ginger biscuits."

Grumbling, Sir Francis relinquished the gift, and Grafstone walked away with the cake on the brown paper as if he were carrying the crown jewels.

"While Grafstone fetches your tea," Anne said, "I wondered if we might show Lord Joshua your gun collection."

His face alight with fervor, Sir Francis swiveled toward Joshua. "Guns? You like guns?"

"I served the past fifteen years in the cavalry."

"In the Peninsula and at Waterloo, eh?"

"Eh," Joshua confirmed.

The old man gave him an assessing look. "My name-sake, Francis, he's in the infantry. So's his twin, Godfrey."

"Geoffrey," Anne corrected. By the twinkle in his eye, she suspected her uncle knew that. But he seemed to enjoy letting people think him dim-witted. "The collection, Uncle."

"Follow me." With his peculiar, crablike shuffle, Sir Francis led the way up the staircase, and their footsteps echoed in the dismal hall.

Within moments, they had gone down a dimly lit corridor and reached the room that adjoined her uncle's apartments. He pulled a ring of keys from his pocket and fumbled to open the lock. Anne knew better than to offer to help him. This time, it wasn't Joshua's criticism she feared, but injuring her uncle's pride.

At last the door swung open, and they walked inside. The spacious chamber originally had been quarters for the mistress of the house, but after his wife's death in childbirth nearly thirty years ago, her uncle had tranformed the space into a museum of sorts. The wavering flames of a pewter candelabrum that Joshua fetched from her uncle's bedchamber illuminated the sad disrepair of the place.

At the windows, the pale blue draperies hung in tatters. The Chinese wallpaper was stained and peeling. The fancy plasterwork on the ceiling housed cobwebs for a colony of spiders. The smell of gun oil overlay the musty odor of neglect.

But at least the gun cases were reasonably clean and free of dust. At her uncle's insistence, Anne spent half a day each week helping him tend to his collection, although she had neglected that task since the duel.

His coat pushed back and his hands at his waist, Joshua took in the accumulation of guns in a slow sweep of his gaze. His impassive face revealed nothing, and she wondered if it disturbed him to see so many weapons of destruction enshrined in glass-fronted cases.

"Look at this four-barreled combine," Sir Francis said

eagerly, opening one of the cases. " 'Tis German, fifteenth century. A man could fire twenty-nine shots without reloading."

"Unless it exploded in the gunman's face first," Anne said dryly. She moved the candelabrum so the men could see better. "This is one of the very few examples that survived."

"Then you know all of these weapons," Joshua said, his gaze piercing her.

"Know 'em?" her uncle said before she could speak. "Why, she can take 'em apart and reassemble 'em blindfolded. From that old-fashioned fowling piece to the new Baker rifle."

"A remarkable woman, your niece," Joshua said.

"She can shoot, too, so you'd best watch your manners," Sir Francis said, cackling. "I let her borrow my guns for target practice from time to time. Why, just last Friday, she brought back the French dueling pistols and exchanged 'em for my Italian pistol. 'Tis small enough to fit into a gamester's pocket."

Joshua's eyes narrowed on her. "Friday. She must have stopped here on her way to the lending library."

Anne avoided his gaze. Anxious to change the subject, she put her hand on the sleeve of her uncle's coat, the tattered blue satin that had gone out of style some forty years ago. "I believe Lord Joshua is interested in the flintlock muskets."

"Muskets? Used one myself back when I headed the Sussex militia. This one here belonged to my grandpapa."

Sir Francis veered toward a case in the corner of the room. Anne followed with the candelabrum. Her uncle brought out several pieces, pointing out all the significant features.

"May I take a look in better light?" Joshua said. At a nod from her uncle, he opened the shutters and examined the gun in the cloudy daylight, turning it over in his hands.

Anne brought over another musket and looked inside the

barrel, then at the powder pan and hammer. "Mine is clean," she murmured. "How about yours?"

"The same."

They examined the other muskets, but to no avail. Anne didn't know whether to be relieved or disappointed that there were no signs of powder or grease.

"The muskets look in fine condition, Uncle," she said. "Have you been cleaning them recently?"

Sir Francis shook his head. "I've been working on the wheel lock pieces. Come here, Kenyon, and see the stock on this one from Austria. 'Tis inlaid with mother-of-pearl and stag antler."

His jaw set, Joshua dutifully examined the gun. With a casualness she knew was calculated, he asked, "Who else besides the two of you has access to this collection?"

"Nobody, not even Grafstone. Especially not that vile excuse for a son of mine." Sir Francis bristled, his mouth pursing in a sour pout. "Did I tell you, Anne, I found the rascal snooping in here?"

Anne exchanged a look with Joshua. "When?" she asked. "How long ago was that?" If it had been the morning of the duel . . .

But her uncle destroyed that hope. " 'Twas yesterday. That good-for-nothing had the cheek to say he wanted to sell the guns for a tidy profit and claim his legacy." Sir Francis bared his yellowed teeth in a caustic grin. "Told him I'll blast his breeches with buckshot if ever I catch him in here again."

A short while later, Grafstone delivered the tea tray and they went through the connecting door to her uncle's bedchamber. The cavernous room was as gloomy and ancient as the rest of the house, though Mrs. Grafstone kept the place tidy. The shuttered windows blocked the daylight.

They took their tea in the sitting area, on moth-eaten chairs that Anne had rescued from the attic. While her uncle happily ate cake and she read a chapter aloud from *Gulli-*

ver's Travels, Joshua strolled around the chamber. He stopped at the fireplace and tilted his head back to study the bell rope, a frayed length of brocade that hung askew. Pulling over a chair, he stood on it and fiddled with the mechanism where the rope joined the ceiling.

Anne had difficulty keeping her attention on the pages of the book. She cast surreptitious glances at him, admiring his long legs and the virile muscularity of his form as he stretched his arms upward. He was masculine grace personified. With all the composure of a silly schoolgirl, she felt her heart flutter in her breast. He gave the bell rope a few tugs, stepped down, then resumed his restless pacing of the chamber.

A few minutes later, as Anne finished her reading, Grafstone burst through the doorway. The butler looked rather dazed. "You rang, sir?"

"Have you gone daft?" Sir Francis said irritably. "That bell hasn't worked for a decade."

"It does now," Joshua said. "The cord had snapped, so I tied the two ends together. It's only a temporary repair, of course."

He shrugged away her uncle's thanks and declined the old man's offer to have another look at the gunroom. As they took their leave and went out into the corridor, Anne murmured, "So you can lend people a helping hand, but I cannot?"

His gaze slid away from hers. "It was a simple matter. I didn't have anything else to occupy me."

"Or perhaps you really do have a heart beneath all that bluster."

His brow descended in a scowl. "I never said it was wrong to perform an occasional good deed for someone. Only that you do *too* much."

Did she? "I like keeping busy," she asserted. "What else am I to do with my time?"

"Take up a hobby. Write poetry. Go for walks. Do something for yourself—"

His voice stopped abruptly. As they arrived at the balcony overlooking the gloomy entrance hall, Anne followed his gaze. Edwin was stomping up the staircase, a crystal decanter clutched in his hand. As he drew nearer, she could see the black and yellow half-circle that underscored his left eye. Belatedly, she remembered that Joshua had struck him at the Angletons' ball.

"I heard you were here," Edwin groused at Anne. "Catering to the old man again?"

Her ire rose. "Perhaps if you catered to him yourself, I wouldn't need to come so often. He is *your* father, after all."

"He's a bloody skinflint. And you're a—" Glancing at Joshua's thunderous face, he amended, "You're a goody two-shoes, that's what."

Anne bristled at being compared to an overly virtuous character in a children's tale. "And you're drunk. As usual."

She stepped forward and wrenched the decanter from his hand. In his befuddlement, he lunged for it, tripped, and clutched at the balustrade for support. "Hey! Give that back!"

Joshua claimed the decanter. He uncorked it and took a deep, appreciative whiff of the contents. "French brandy. I'd like to know how you can afford it, Bellingham. That, and the cheque you wrote to Faversham."

Edwin's face took on a crafty sneer. "I'm not without my resources. There's money to be had if a man knows how to get it."

"If your shady dealings cause harm to Anne, you'll answer to me."

Edwin gingerly touched his black eye as if it pained him. He shifted his gaze to Anne. "I didn't shoot you, Anne. I swear it. *He's* the one you should watch out for. He'll wed you just to get his hands on my . . . *your* inheritance."

"Mind your tongue—" Joshua began.

"Don't be ridiculous—"

They both spoke at the same time. Their gazes clashed,

but only for an instant. Anne didn't know why she felt so embarrassed, her cheeks flushed. But she couldn't meet his eyes.

Joshua aimed a pointed stare at Edwin. "She's under my protection. If you value your sorry life, you won't ever forget that."

Edwin kept sullenly silent. He didn't argue even when Joshua took the decanter with him. As they went down the stairs, Anne looked back to see her cousin standing at the balustrade, watching them. He didn't look angry so much as . . . smug.

In their youth, when she had seen that turned-up corner of his mouth and the flaring of one eyebrow, she had known to beware of a snake in her bed or pepper in her tea. Now, his nasty expression raised her suspicions.

Had Edwin shot her? Had he been crafty enough to clean the gun before returning it to her uncle's collection? And what mischief was he planning now?

As they left the house, she was surprised to see the gray light of dusk. The yellow glow of lamps shone in the windows of the nearby houses. A chill wind whipped in from the sea, and the charcoal clouds foretold rain.

Then she was jolted by the sight of Joshua drinking straight out of the decanter. His head was tilted back, his throat working as he swallowed. Lowering the container, he released a sigh of relish and wiped his mouth with the back of his hand.

"What do you think you're doing?" she asked sharply. "You're as bad as Edwin."

He flashed her a roguish grin. "A pity to let it *all* go to waste." Then he poured the remainder of the liquor over the weeds.

That grin turned her insides topsy-turvy. It sent goosebumps over her skin and warmth to her loins. It caused a hitch in her breathing and a softness in her bosom. For heaven's sake, all he'd done was swig brandy like a reprobate and then smile at her.

But his rare smiles infused him with an enticing allure. She couldn't help wondering what he would have been like if he hadn't suffered the shadows of scandal and the torments of war. A charmer, for certain. The ladies would have been after him in droves. Would he have married already? Would he have had a troop of children to train and love?

Banishing her foolish speculation, she pulled the first coherent thought out of her head. "What did you and Edwin fight about, anyway? You never told me."

Joshua hesitated for a second. Then he placed the decanter on the porch and strode down the walk to their horses. His face averted, he muttered, "Bellingham called you a name."

"What name?"

"A shrew."

Anne huffed out a breath. "Ah, I see. You alone reserve the right to call me 'shrewish.' "

A dull red flush crept up his neck. He bent his head to untie Plato's reins. "I apologize for that remark. I was angry."

He stalked over to her horse to give her a boost, but she had already put her foot in the stirrup and hopped up on her own. Wriggling into a comfortable position, she gazed down at him in irritation. "Angry about Mr. Firth wanting me to be his mistress?"

"Yes." He answered quickly. Too quickly.

"But I refused the man. You hadn't any reason to be angry at *me.*"

His gaze was guarded. "Quite so. It won't happen again."

As they rode through the gathering dusk on the path home, she mused on what an irksome man he was. Joshua called *her* contrary, yet he blew hot and cold, smiling at her one moment and scowling the next, kissing her and then lashing out in anger. At times, he seemed to enjoy her company, while at other times, he acted snappish and rude. He accused her of having too much heart and claimed to have none of his own. Then he turned around and repaired her uncle's bell cord. He also comforted Mary in church and helped her nephews understand the importance of proper behavior.

A contradictory man, indeed. But not entirely unfathomable.

Anne glanced at his profile, so austere and proud in the fading light. He rode a short distance apart from her as if to certify his self-sufficiency. She felt a melting inside herself that had as much to do with tenderness as illicit desire.

His boorishness and name-calling was a way to keep her at arm's length, she could see that now. He could be certain of stirring her wrath with such a ploy. Certain of pushing her away. If he made her shun him, she wouldn't burrow out his secrets, the painful experiences that had shaped him into a hardened loner.

Joshua nurtured the image of scoundrel, even sought it out. His callous conduct had caused the abrupt end to his betrothal—or perhaps there was more to the story than he let on. Was he protecting Lily's reputation? Was she the guilty one, perhaps?

Anne told herself not to speculate. More likely, Joshua *had* betrayed his bride-to-be. But she could no longer condemn him as a shallow, heartless villain. Whether it was foolish or not, she wanted to believe that a good man lurked beneath his irascible behavior. And if there was any possibility of that, she couldn't allow herself to contribute to his wicked reputation.

They were almost home when Anne guided the chestnut mare closer to him. The dull thudding of hooves and the creak of saddle leather mingled with the distant rumble of thunder. "I've been thinking," she began.

Joshua glanced obliquely at her through the gloaming. "So have I. We need to find out if Arthur Cummings or his son owns a flintlock musket. Tomorrow, we'll pay a call on them. Along with Samuel Firth."

"Yes." But Anne didn't want to consider that now. Gathering her courage, she said, "However, I've been thinking about something more personal. Something about us."

"There is no us," he said, his voice turning as cold as the evening air. "I thought I'd made that perfectly clear."

"Just hear me out, please. You'll be leaving here soon, once we find the gunman. But before you return to Stokeford Abbey, there's something I'd like for you to do."

"Do?"

Tensing herself for the explosion of his wrath, she broached the ticklish topic. "I'd like for you to ask my father for my hand in marriage."

Chapter Twenty-one

Surprise in the Stables

"What?"

The word exploded from Josh. Inside his gloves, his hands felt frigid. In the deepening twilight, he could see the earnestness on her features. Anne was serious. Dead serious. She wanted him to marry her. A treacherous swamp of fear and desire sucked at him. He ought to kick his heels into Plato's flanks and run hell-bent for leather.

"You needn't look so appalled," Anne said peevishly. "I'm not trying to entrap you. It's just that . . . then I can refuse you."

He took a deep breath of chilly air to clear his head. Understanding her purpose was like trying to follow a maze without a map. "Refuse me?"

"Yes. You see, if we take our courtship ruse to its logical conclusion, and you ask me to be your wife, then my family won't think ill of you. Instead, they'll remonstrate *me* for spurning your offer. And I'll tell them that I can't marry a man whom I don't love. It's as simple as that."

Simple?

Her convoluted plan struck him harder than a punch. *She* wanted to protect *him*? He plucked anger out of the mire of emotions inside himself. "That is the most *il*logical, idiotic plan I've ever heard. Even from you."

Her lips pursed into the firm line he so craved to soften. "It's perfectly sensible. My parents married for love and so did my brothers. They'll accept my explanation."

"This is exactly the sort of misguided help that you do too often."

"I haven't ever asked a man to propose to me before," she said flippantly.

He gritted his teeth. "Heed me, Anne. I don't need you to make explanations on my behalf."

"But you shouldn't want another black mark on your reputation. People will *expect* you to make me an offer. When you don't, they'll gossip. They'll call you a knave and a bounder."

"Let them. It's none of their damned concern."

"But it's my family's concern. Don't you care what *they* think of you?"

She had him there. He had grown to appreciate her family for their warmth and sincerity, Mrs. Neville asking his advice about her paintings, Mr. Neville always ready for an intellectual discussion, and Anne's boisterous brothers trading jests and telling stories. The thought of disappointing them, perhaps even earning their animosity, chafed him like a hairshirt.

But it was no more than he deserved.

"The answer is no," he snapped. "I will not approach your father under false pretenses and ask for his permission to marry you. That is final."

She didn't appear ready to accept his edict. A stubborn little line appeared between her eyebrows, and the corners of her mouth turned downward in a sour expression that begged to be sweetened with a kiss.

"Well, then, you leave me no recourse," she said in a lofty tone. "If you wish to be stubborn enough to leave without speaking to my father, I'll tell everyone that you *did* ask me for my hand, and that I refused you. And *that* is final."

Him, stubborn?

The notion suddenly struck him as the height of absurdity. He threw back his head and laughed. The action released a measure of his tension, enough that he could look at her and allow a small grin. "Blast, but you're an obstinate wench. Don't you ever give up?"

She looked at him from beneath her lashes. "Never."

At that come-hither look, his fingers tightened convulsively on the reins. Desire clamped him in a vise. He wanted to snatch her down from her horse and make love to her right here in the deep shadows of the meadow. He wanted to delve into her chastity and claim it for himself.

A cold droplet struck his cheek and awakened his wits. "We'd best hurry. It's starting to rain."

He urged Plato into a canter. Anne's mount kept pace with his, and when they reached the dirt lane and spied the faint outline of her house on the outskirts of the village, she bent low over the saddle. "I'll race you."

Her mare took off like a shot, and with a curse, he chased in her dust. Fear for her clutched at his chest. His heart pounded like the hooves of their horses. More raindrops peppered his face, but he scarcely noticed the wetness.

He caught up to her in the stableyard behind the house. Dismounting, he seized hold of the mare's bridle and glowered up at the rider. "Dammit, Anne. It's dark. You could have killed yourself."

Anne jumped lightly to the ground. "It was only a short distance. Besides, I could find my way home blindfolded."

"You took a foolish risk. What about your horse? What if you'd injured the mare?"

"Stop grousing. Miss Emmie knows the way as well as I do."

With that, Anne led her horse toward the stables. He clenched his jaw and followed, his gaze on the saucy swaying of her hips. She had entirely too much spark for a spinster. She confounded him, teased him, angered him. And she made him lust as he'd never lusted before. He had lost interest in going into town to seek out a woman who'd relieve his itch in exchange for a few coins. All of his carnal cravings were fixed on Anne. Only Anne.

He burned for the one woman who had the power to unlock his secrets. The one woman who threatened to pry into the horrific memories buried inside him.

Yet as they entered the stables, he could think only of taking her in his arms and pressing her down into the sweet hay inside a stall. He wanted to undress Anne, inch by slow inch, to taste her bare breasts and hear her moan with passion. He wanted to slide his finger inside her and prepare her for his entry . . .

He did nothing of the sort, of course. By the faint light through the opened doors, he and Anne unsaddled their mounts. He concentrated on currying Plato, closing his mind to the woman in the stall beside him. Plato was restless, pawing the ground with his front hoof. Since the gelding wasn't afraid of lightning or thunder, Josh could only surmise that Plato sensed his master's incendiary mood.

"Where is Harrington?" Anne asked suddenly.

"With Peg, no doubt."

"Peg?" A wealth of incredulity enriched her tone. "I thought they despised one another."

Josh gave a humorless laugh. "Not in every way."

Anne fell silent for a moment. Then she ventured, "Do you mean they're . . ."

"Yes." *They're swiving their brains out, the lucky sots.*

"Oh." It was a breathy sound, part disapproval and part fascination. He could imagine the conflict in her, the prim old maid versus the ardent virgin.

He shouldn't be obsessed with satisfying her curiosity. Or with encouraging her budding sensuality.

They emerged from their respective stalls at the same moment. They stopped in the darkened corridor, face to face, and stared at one another. Tension filled the air, as thick as the rain that splattered the roof. He told himself to turn away from her, but couldn't find the strength to move.

Lust burned in him. His heart drummed in his chest, as strong and fast as the pulsing in his groin.

Compelled by the irresistible force of desire, he slowly raised his hand, anticipating the softness of her skin. She leaned toward him, her lips parted. Lightning flashed, chased by the boom of thunder.

In that brief flicker, he saw movement from the corner of his eye. From out of the darkness, something rushed straight at him.

Savage instinct roared to life. As he spun around in a crouch, the intruder struck him down. His teeth rattled as his cheek met the dirt floor. He seized his attacker and buried his fist in a soft belly. Hit in the solar plexus, the man wheezed out a stinking gasp and doubled over, moaning in pain.

Josh rolled to his feet in one motion. He had only one thought. "Anne—!"

A shadow in the darkness, she struggled with another man. He held her from behind and dragged her toward the door.

Black rage choked Josh. An animal snarl vibrating in his throat, he sprang.

Anne screamed. "Joshua, behind you!"

He spun on his bootheel. His foe had staggered to his feet. In a burst of lightning, Josh spied the wicked glint of a knife.

Josh charged him. He caught the man's arm and thrust back the knife. Simultaneously, he threw him to the floor. His assailant got in one good punch to Josh's jaw. Then Josh squeezed the man's wrist, his other hand going for the throat in a throttling clamp. The man gurgled and bucked in vain.

Driven by an inhuman fury, Josh increased the pressure on the man's windpipe. Slowly, those fingers went slack. The knife dropped to the ground.

Anne. Awareness penetrated his blood lust. His breathing

harsh, Josh stumbled to his feet, but he couldn't see her in the gloom.

He surged forward in a panic. Out of nowhere, something struck the back of his head. His ears ringing and his senses reeling, he clawed at consciousness.

But the world slipped from his frantic grasp. He fell into fire and darkness.

Frantic with fear, Anne dropped to her knees beside Joshua. She could scarcely discern him through the gloom. The flashes of lightning revealed him lying on the floor, his eyes closed, his head tilted to the side. Pressing her palm to his chest, she felt his heart beating strongly and breathed a shuddery sigh of relief.

At least he was alive. But dear God, how badly was he hurt?

Recalling her terror at seeing that ruffian leap at him with a knife, she ran her fingers beneath his coat, searching for injuries. His muscled torso felt warm and blessedly undamaged. But when she touched the back of his head, her fingers came away sticky with blood.

With jerky movements, she tore off her jacket and folded it into a makeshift bandage, which she flattened against the laceration to stop the bleeding. He shifted position and groaned. The deep, painful sound tore at her heart.

Gliding her fingers over his bristled cheek, she bent her head to him. "Joshua, wake up. Please."

His eyelids moved slightly. His arm lifted as if to bat her away. His hand fell onto her thigh, his fingers curling into the folds of her skirt. The unconscious touch had an instantaneous effect on her. In spite of her anxieties, in spite of her nervous trembling, she felt the deep, unmistakable resonance of arousal. Gathering his fingers in hers, she kissed them, rubbing her cheek against the back of his hand.

"Joshua," she said again, more forcefully. "Hear me. You *must* wake up."

His eyes opened slowly. He blinked through the darkness at her. Joy as sharp and sweet as she'd ever known
rushed through her.

He sat bolt upright. "My God," he muttered, his hand
going to her face. "Are you all right?"

"I'm fine. Not a scratch. But your head—"

"Where are they?" He turned to scrutinize the shadows.

She stroked the side of his neck soothingly. "Gone.
There were three of them, but I chased them away."

"Three—?"

"Yes. There was another man hiding in a stall who
struck you down. The one who caught me bears the marks
of a pitchfork on his posterior." Anne couldn't stop a note
of unladylike satisfaction. "The others feared it in an even
more tender place."

Breathing heavily, Joshua stared at her another moment.
Then he rolled away and got to his feet. He staggered
slightly, catching hold of a stall door to steady himself.
Plato thrust out his equine head to nuzzle his master. Paying
the animal no heed, Joshua fumbled with the latch.

Alarmed, she snatched her folded jacket and leapt up to
catch his arm. "You're bleeding. You need to lie down."

He shook off her hold. "I'm going after them."

His feral tone chilled her, made her cling all the more
tenaciously. "You most certainly are not. You must have a
concussion. That ruffian knocked you hard."

"Get out of my way, Anne."

"No. It's a fool's errand. They're gone, and the rain will
have wiped out their tracks by now."

His muscles flexed beneath her fingers. "Then I'll go
after Firth."

Anne shook her head vehemently. "How do you know
he hired those men?"

"He wants you. They were abducting you."

"No, they *weren't*. Why would you think that?"

"The bastard was dragging you toward the door."

"No, *I* was dragging *him*. I knew the pitchfork was there by the wall."

He pressed his hand to his brow as if struggling to clear his thoughts. That knock had to be causing him considerable pain. Fearing for his safety, she had to convince him to give up his search, at least for the night.

"I don't doubt that Firth *might* have hired those villains," she said quickly. "But it might as easily have been Edwin. He looked rather smug when we left, as if he were planning something."

"Then I'll go question him."

"No! What if I'm wrong, and it was Arthur Cummings? He wants that letter back. Or perhaps it was his son." She blew out a breath. "My point is that you can't go haring off in the middle of a thunderstorm. Like it or not, you need a good night's rest before you go after them."

As she spoke, she placed an arm around his waist and guided him toward the doorway. Their hips brushed as they walked. He leaned a little on her, a testament to his wound. "Blast you," he grumbled. "You're being bossy."

"I'm being sensible. Whenever men take charge, they're admired for being masterful."

He dipped his head closer to her. "Do *you* admire me, Anne?"

His breath warmed her cheek. The unexpectedly lascivious note in his voice made her insides clutch with desire. Willing strength into her weakened legs, she looked out at the storm. "I admire a man who can admit when he needs help."

He grumbled at that, but allowed her to support him as they dashed across the yard to the house. The deluge soaked them to the skin. Leaning against the door, he waited while she lit a taper at the banked fire in the kitchen.

They took the back staircase and made their way up to his bedchamber, just off the stairwell. Anne went inside with him. "Quiet," she whispered as she closed the door. "I don't want my parents to hear us."

His gaze swooped over her dampened gown, lingering a moment on her bosom. Rainwater slicked his hair and molded his clothing to his body. He turned away from her. "Get out of here," he said tersely, taking up a towel from the washstand and drying his face and neck. "You've done your duty."

"Not yet. I want to have a look at your head." Though her wet, chilly riding habit stuck uncomfortably to her skin, she carried the candle toward him.

"Don't you ever do as you're told?" He dragged the towel in an irritable swipe over his head, giving his black hair a rumpled, rakish look. "Never mind, that's a rhetorical question."

"Snap at me all you like. I know that your bark is worse than your bite."

"You should also know that I'm a physician. I can heal myself."

"Not even Hippocrates could see the back of his own head." She pointed at a stool. "Sit down."

He glowered at her another moment; then much to her surprise he obeyed. The wound must be hurting more than he was willing to admit. That thought made her fingers gentle as she parted the damp strands of his hair. "Bend your head down, please."

He did, albeit grudgingly. "It's not a concussion."

Frowning, she examined the angry, swollen lump by the light of the candle. "How can you be certain?"

"No dizziness. No double vision. No nausea."

Her own stomach twisted at the thought of how easily he might have been killed. The ruffian who'd grabbed her had been trying to keep her from going to Joshua's aid. Pondering that impression, she took the towel from him and used it to dab at the blood. "Then you must have a harder head than I do."

He swiveled on the stool and snatched the towel from her. "If you're done making jests, the door is over there."

"We need to talk first."

"We'll talk in the morning. You should change out of those wet things before you catch a chill." Again, his brooding gaze flitted over her bosom, causing an involuntary tightening there.

But Anne was distracted by a nagging, troublesome thought. "Suppose they weren't after me at all, Joshua. Suppose they were after you?"

"I wasn't shot in the duel. You were."

"A flintlock musket isn't the most accurate of weapons. Especially at that range. Perhaps the gunman was aiming at you and missed."

He stared at her, his eyes narrowed. "I'll give some thought to the matter," he said dismissingly. "Go away now. I'm weary."

Rain drummed against the windowpanes. It was a cold, lonely sound that made her shiver. More than anything else in the world, she yearned to stay here with Joshua, to lie down with him in bed and feel his muscled arms around her . . .

She forced herself to say, "I'll leave, then. But I'll have your word that you won't go out tonight."

"Giving orders again, Miss Neville?"

Too worried about him to take offense at his curt manner, she said, "Kindly heed this: if you sneak out on some wild, heroic quest, I'll follow you. I'll get into trouble, maybe even get myself killed. And it'll be all your fault."

He muttered something that sounded like a curse. He stalked to the hearth, seized the poker, and stirred viciously at the kindling. Calling on every scrap of her fortitude, Anne turned on her heel and left the room.

It was too early to sleep.

After drying off and changing into her nightrail and dressing gown, Anne sat in her chamber to read by the wavering light of a candle. She listened for Joshua, to make certain he didn't leave the house. But the book of dry essays couldn't hold her attention, so she set it down and picked up one of Hugh's shirts to repair, the mending always in plentiful supply. The mindless needlework allowed her thoughts to turn over and over, to examine the attack from every angle.

Three men, one in hiding until the last moment. Why hadn't all three leapt on them at once? Unless that third man had been someone they would recognize.

In the darkened stable, she hadn't had a good look at him. The moment she'd gone after him with the pitchfork, he'd taken off running into the rain, on the heels of the other two cowards. Yet she had seen enough to know that he wasn't a tall man like Samuel Firth nor a stocky one like Arthur Cummings. He was about the size of the Reverend Richard Cummings.

But what possible reason could the vicar have for attacking Joshua? Would he try to frighten him off from asking so many questions in town?

It was the only explanation she could think of.

Rain tapped at the window as if begging to come in out of the cold. Normally, she liked the cozy act of sitting by the fire on a blustery night. But an inner agitation banished any hope for serenity. She had to tear out her stitches numerous times, until finally she let the whole mess lie in her lap in a tangled heap. She felt restless and aching, yet she had no wish to go downstairs and join her parents, who customarily took their nightly tea in the parlor, while Papa read aloud to Mama as she arranged flowers for her next painting or sat at her knitting.

Joshua was right. They didn't need her as much as she needed *them*. She needed someone in her life. Someone to love, someone to care for, someone who belonged to her alone. For a long time, she had deluded herself into believing that David was that person. But now she knew how wrong she'd been to pursue such a pallid dream. Never before had she experienced the wild desire that she felt for Joshua.

Joshua with his moody nature. Joshua with his devilish smile.

Her insides curled warmly, and her heartbeat quickened. The mere thought of him created an instantaneous yearning in her, body and soul. She craved his strong embrace as much as she craved his quick wit and his rare laughter. In his company, she felt vibrantly alive. How desperately she longed to go to him and find out if he cared for her, too, in his heart as well as his flesh. She was a twenty-eight-year-old spinster who had yet to know a man's intimate touch.

But she could. She had only to walk down the corridor to his chamber.

Anne stayed firmly in the old wing chair by the hearth. She rested her head and stared out at the dark, rainy night. If she were selfish enough to indulge her desires, she would disappoint so many people. Her parents. Her brothers. Her extended family. She would bring shame to all of them.

And Joshua would feel obligated to offer for her. For a moment, she let herself imagine the joy of being his wife. Seeing him across the breakfast table each morning. Raising their children together. Having someone to talk and laugh with on chilly autumn evenings. Then brutal honesty came to the fore. Joshua didn't *want* to marry her. His appalled expression when she'd suggested he go to her father bore witness to his total lack of enthusiasm.

And yet . . . at times she sensed a heartfelt connection between them, when he grinned at something she'd said or when he looked into her eyes . . .

Her restless fingers plucked at the shirt in her lap. She mustn't be so foolish as to think he had changed. She mustn't forget that he had abandoned beautiful, gentle Lily.

After a time, Anne heard the sounds of her parents coming upstairs, her father's low teasing voice and her mother's laugh. The door was ajar, and Mama popped her head inside to smile at Anne. "Are you back then, darling? It's a nasty night, isn't it? I do believe the Rosebuds must have

decided to stay with their friends in Brighton for the night."
Her hazel eyes danced with interest. "We wondered if you
and his lordship had been caught out in the storm."

Anne summoned a smile. "We did get a little wet. That's
why I didn't come downstairs and sit with you and Papa."

"It's no matter. We were quite content." Mama tilted her
head to the side. "Did you two have an enjoyable outing?"

"Yes." *Until we were attacked by ruffians. Until Joshua
sent me away.* Because her mother was waiting expectantly,
Anne added, "We went to visit Uncle Francis."

"Oh." Mama looked puzzled for a moment, then her
smile returned. "You'll have to tell me all about that
naughty brother of mine in the morning. Sweet dreams,
darling." After blowing her a kiss, Mama left, and Anne
heard the click of her parents' door closing.

She felt utterly alone, utterly dispirited. The incessant
rain made her feel all the more isolated. As if drawn by an
invisible cord, her thoughts kept returning to Joshua.

Was he awake, too? Did his head ache? Did he pace his
chamber like a grumpy bear in need of soothing?

He hadn't had any dinner, nor had she. Although she
was too tied in knots to feel any hunger other than the
carnal sort, perhaps she should go down to the kitchen and
fetch him a tray. He'd bluster and complain, but she'd see
to it that he took some nourishment.

Glad to have something constructive to do, she rose to
her feet. Would that she could find nourishment, too. From
him.

Chapter Twenty-two

Into the Fire

A groan awakened her.

Disoriented, Anne opened her eyes and wondered how she'd fallen asleep, curled up in her chair. She felt chilled and stiff. Rain pattered on the window, and the wind rushed around the eaves of the house. On the table, the candle guttered in a pool of wax.

Then she looked across the dim chamber and saw Joshua lying in bed. *His* bed.

The events rushed back at her. She had brought him a tray of food, but he hadn't answered her knock. Fearing he'd either suffered a relapse from his injury or had gone out like a manly fool, she'd opened the door, only to find him fast asleep. The sight of him had sorely tempted her, so she had poured herself a cup of tea and had sat down to watch him. It was a rare treat to look her fill at Joshua without having to parry his biting wit. The last thing she remembered was feeling a small measure of contentment at being near him . . .

A muffled sound of agony came from Joshua. She sprang up, the floorboards icy against her bare feet. In the shadows beyond the reach of the candle, he thrashed in his sleep. Was he in pain from the lump on his head? Or from a nightmare?

She carried the candle closer and set it on the bedside table. He lay facing the wall, his arms thrown over his head as if to ward off an attacker. The sheets covered him to his waist, and the muscles of his bare back and arms stood out in taut contours.

A nightmare, then.

He moaned again, the bleak sound raising the fine hairs on the nape of her neck. He'd had a violent reaction the last time she had awakened him from a bad dream. But Anne didn't think twice about that. Bending closer to him, she gently rubbed his shoulder, and his skin warmed her cold hand. "Joshua."

He didn't respond. His body jerked, and as he rolled toward her, she saw that his face was contorted in anguish. His eyes were squeezed shut, and his cheeks glimmered wetly in the faint candlelight. Her heart wrenched as she glided her fingertips through his tears.

The need to comfort him overwhelmed her. Sparing no thought for the consequences, she lay down and slid her arms around him. His chest was thick and brawny, his skin damp with perspiration. He had a long, jagged scar along his breastbone, a legacy of the war, no doubt. Snuggling as close to him as humanly possible, she kneaded his rigid muscles in an effort to relax him. She stroked his face and kissed his jaw, all the while murmuring meaningless words of comfort.

Gradually, he grew quieter. He ceased groaning and thrashing, though his breathing remained deep and heavy, his chest rising and falling against her breasts. His body warmed her, inside and out. His scent of leather and spice made her giddy.

No, it was desire that caused her senses to swim. She wanted him with a fierceness that made her tremble. To lie with him like this felt utterly right.

He shifted slightly, bringing his arm around her so that it lay heavily over her waist. His fingers brushed against the back of her nightclothes. He nuzzled her hair sleepily. "Anne," he muttered.

She could tell that he hovered in that gray world between slumber and wakefulness. She wanted him to stay right there, lest he send her away. "Yes, darling, I'm here," she whispered soothingly. "I'm here with you."

He released a shuddering sigh that stirred her hair. His arm tightened on her, the palm of his hand sliding to her bottom, bringing her flush against him. Through the thin cotton of her robe and nightrail, she felt the unmistakable thickness at his loins, and a quiver of response consumed her.

She should leave. While he lay half-asleep, still dazed by his ghastly dreams, she should heed the vestiges of propriety and return to her own chamber. He wasn't truly aware, and when he did awaken, he would be furious to find her here.

But the fleeting thought slipped away under a torrent of longing. He had unfastened her gown at the party, sought her naked bosom. She burned for his touch there again ... and in another unmentionable place. The compulsion proved stronger than her scruples.

With trembling fingers, she untied her dressing gown. She unbuttoned her nightdress, slithered out of it, and let both garments drop to the floor. The linen sheets glided against her bare skin, cold at the edges of the bed, but deliciously warm where he lay. She snuggled into the heat of his body and tipped up her mouth to his. At first, his lips moved drowsily over hers, then the pressure increased with a growing passion.

His arms flexing, he rolled her onto her back and covered her. His mouth took hers in a deep, hungry kiss that surpassed her wildest imaginings. Embracing him eagerly, she returned his kiss with all the fervor inside her. She caressed his neck, his back, his face, unable to get enough of him. Heavy and welcome, his powerful body moved against hers.

His breathing ragged, he slid his mouth to her throat. His hand roved possessively over her breasts. Bending his dark head, he kissed the tip of one, his lips and tongue creating sensations that made her gasp. She closed her eyes, tilted her head back on the pillow, and arched her spine to offer herself to him. Her hands alighted on his broad shoulders in wordless encouragement. He moved his mouth to the other breast and lavished attention on it. She felt the rasp of his whiskered cheek against the underside, the lick of his tongue against her skin.

His flattened palm slid over her belly to the juncture of her thighs. In a bold act that wrested a gasp from her, he delved inside to caress her secret folds. Her initial twinge of embarrassment lasted only a moment. Then she succumbed to his skilled touch, hardly aware of her hips moving, her legs opening in shameless abandon. She was enthralled. Her world narrowed to the maddening pleasure he aroused in her, an urgency that she couldn't define. Just when she felt she could bear no more, he stopped, but that wasn't what she wanted, either. Uttering an inarticulate protest, she groped for his hand to bring it back.

But he had braced his palms on either side of her, and his iron muscles were immovable. In the next moment, another perception arrested her. A probing at her center. A thick, hot pressure. A powerful thrust that split her asunder.

She cried out and he went still. His mouth caught the sound and soothed it away. As her body adjusted to his, the burning discomfort melted into an incredible sense of fullness and an unprecedented joy that they were one.

"Joshua," she whispered. Her giddy mind couldn't gather the right words to describe how perfect he felt sheathed inside her.

He pulled in heavy breaths. His half-closed eyes watched her through the shadows. He muttered, "Anne . . . *mine*."

At that savage growl, her womb contracted in a quiver of excitement. With slow deliberation, he withdrew to her entrance, only to bury himself inside her again. Enraptured by the exquisite sensation, Anne lifted her hips to take him deeper into herself. She couldn't get enough of him to satisfy herself. The compelling friction of his thrusts made her heart beat out of control. Whimpering in desperation, she blindly clutched at him, seeking surcease to the madness.

Without warning, the extremity of passion broke into spasms of pleasure so intense that she cried out in rapture. He gave one final, pulsing plunge and shuddered, his deeply satisfied groan reverberating against her bosom. Sensing him right there with her, she gave herself up to bliss.

The fire that had consumed him burned down to embers, and Josh came to awareness by slow degrees. His closed eyelids made his other senses more acute. Outside, rain beat onto the roof, dripping down from the eaves. He felt drained, replete, contented for the first time in longer than he could remember. Her warm breast filled his hand. Lithe and slender, she lay beneath him, her breath soft on his neck. Her skin smelled like rose-scented soap. Her long legs cradled him, her tight velvet channel harboring him.

Anne. He was inside Anne.

Shock resonated through him. He had known it was Anne all along, of course. He could never mistake her supple form, her eager kisses. Yet he had been dreaming, too. Lost in a fantasy so intense, so erotic, so *real,* he had come out of it to discover himself buried inside her.

Inside the one woman who could destroy his defenses.

Battling an incipient panic, Josh raised his head slightly. The knot on the back of his head throbbed, but he was too taken by the sight of Anne to care. Strands of tawny hair trailed across his pillow. Her eyes were closed, her breathing measured. She wore a faint smile . . . and nothing else.

He rolled onto his side, bringing her with him, his hands gripping her bottom to hold himself inside her. She felt too damned good for him to relinquish her just yet. "My God," he said on a groan. "What have I done?"

She opened her eyes, and her face bore the soft look of a satisfied woman. In the feeble light of the candle, her skin had a rosy glow that made him want to kiss every inch of her. Again and again. "*We,* Joshua," she said, a hint of anxiety in her expression. "I participated, too."

"I've ruined you."

"No!" She placed her finger over his lips. "I don't feel ruined. I feel . . . wonderful."

He wouldn't let her words gratify him. "*Wonderful?* You should be outraged. I took your virginity."

"I *gave* it to you. If you're intent on placing blame, then blame *me*. When you cried out in your sleep, I climbed into bed with you. I knew what might happen—and I—I even hoped for it."

His mind had stopped on the words *cried out*. The nightmare came rushing back at him. *Gunfire. Cannons booming. Men screaming for help. He waded through a river of blood, but the shoreline kept receding. He couldn't reach them. They were dying. And it was his fault . . .*

He emerged from the trance to feel Anne's fingers pressing into his arms. She was frowning oddly at him. "What are you saying, Joshua? It *wasn't* your fault. That's what I'm trying to tell you, if only you'd listen."

He'd spoken aloud? Horrified, he turned his face to her throat lest she glimpse his chilling fear. His memories lurked too close to the surface. He could never admit to her his shame at being alive when so many had died. Or his guilt at having had to ignore mortally injured men in favor of saving those who might live.

But his defilement of Anne was one misdeed he could make right.

He raised his head to meet her fretful eyes. Closing the gates against an onslaught of emotions, he forced out, "We're getting married. I'll ride to London in the morning to procure the license."

She shook her head, stirring the fine tendrils of hair

around her face. "No. I won't let you wed me out of duty. It isn't necessary."

Her stubbornness incensed him. "It *is* necessary, dammit. I've compromised you. What kind of man do you think I am?"

"An honorable man. A tempting man." She stroked his chest in a slow, solicitous manner that wreaked havoc with his concentration. Then her hand dipped lower, circling over his flat belly. "But also a very foolish man."

Sucking in a breath, he wrapped his fingers firmly around her wrists. "Stop."

"Why? You aren't a prig. Seducing women is your forte, remember?"

Through his teeth, he said, "I don't seduce proper ladies."

"My point precisely. What happened isn't your fault. *I* seduced *you*." She moved her hips to great effect, proving herself a quick study.

Her infernal logic annoyed him as much as her natural sensuality invigorated him. Deciding to use his own brand of persuasion, he feathered his fingers over her breast and the tip contracted into a bead. "But I encouraged your desires."

As he continued to touch her, Anne caught her breath. "You've made love to other women without marrying any of *them*."

"Those women weren't virgins," he said, granting her other breast the same attention. "They knew from the start not to expect anything more."

"So did I." Catching hold of his wrist, she contemplated him through the screen of her tawny lashes. "You've no obligation to me, Joshua. You should be pleased about that. I'm letting you go free."

Free. Yes, he needed freedom to preserve his sanity—and to protect Anne from the darkness within him. The scars on his heart prevented him from giving her the love she deserved. He needed to return home, to be alone in the desperate hope that he might find peace in physical labor and the normality of life.

Yet the prospect held less allure while lying here with Anne. It was difficult to think while holding her in his arms. He couldn't comprehend why she would allow herself to be debauched *without* demanding marriage . . .

Assaulted by insight, he drew back his hand. "I understand now. You're trying to help me. You're sacrificing yourself to give me what you think I want."

She shook her head. "Quite the contrary. You told me to do something for myself. So I did."

Taking his hand, she brought it back to her breast and cupped his fingers around her pliant flesh. Heat rushed through him. Damn, every time he thought he understood her, she knocked him off guard. For a woman of indomitable spirit, Anne was soft and rounded in all the right places. His palm engulfed the rapid beating of her heart. He felt its pulsing all the way down to his groin.

Impossible that he could be primed for her so soon. It defied the laws of nature. But why the hell shouldn't he have her again? The damage had already been done.

Turning her onto her back, he embedded himself to the hilt, angry and aroused all at the same time. Her hands met his chest as if to stop him. Her eyes widened a moment, then drifted half-closed in a look of dreamy enchantment.

"Shall we do this again?" she asked breathlessly.

Upon withdrawing to her opening, he very slowly entered her again. She was tight and slick, a perfect fit. Though she moaned her appreciation, he said silkily, "If you want me."

Anne clutched at his shoulders. "*Yes.* But . . . your head must ache."

"Not as much as another part of me."

With another thrust, he showed her again. She strained upward to take him in deeper. But he wanted more from her. He wanted her to make the connection between bedded bliss and wedded bliss.

Rolling over, Josh brought her with him. Their bodies separated, but he knew the anticipation would only intensify their ultimate pleasure. As she perched astride him, her eyebrows winged upward in a startled look. Her opened legs granted him a tantalizing glimpse of paradise. "Is this . . . customary?"

He moved his palms up her firm, bare thighs. "When you're with me, you leave all conventions and customs at the bedroom door."

She gazed at him in thoughtful concentration. Then her lips parted, and she murmured, "I've only ever seen a little boy in nappies. If you don't mind, I'd like to look at you."

A chuckle caught him by surprise. "I don't mind."

Her hands braced on his thighs, she scooted back to give him a frankly admiring inspection. "You're so large. Who would have thought I could accommodate you?"

Her attention caused him to grow to painful proportions. "I would. I've thought about it quite a lot."

"May I . . . touch you?"

"As you desire," he said hoarsely.

At her first naïve caress, he nearly exploded. He held himself in check while her fingertips circled the cap and glided down the shaft, swirling lightly as she learned the heat and texture of him. "I never dreamed this part of you could give me such pleasure," she whispered.

Then her hand moved lower, to cup the sensitive sacks beneath. At that, he closed his eyes and sucked in a breath, letting it out in a groan.

Her touch vanished. "Did I hurt you?"

He brought her hand back, wrapping her fingers around him. "It's a very enjoyable pain."

"Ah." Her eyes lit with sultry understanding. She explored him in earnest, rubbing and stroking until he could bear no more torture.

"Enough," he said raggedly, catching hold of her slim waist to bring her back over him. "Or I'll be done too quickly."

In a graceful sweep, she lowered herself so that her long hair formed a veil around them and her breasts hovered enticingly close to his mouth. "I don't want this to end soon, either," she whispered. "So how else might I torture you, m'lord?"

His throat went dry. "Ride me, my lady. Like this."

He moved his hands to her bottom to guide her, but with her natural propensity for lovemaking, Anne required little instruction. She accepted him into herself, a torturously sweet slide into heaven. A faint smile on her lips, she contracted her inner folds like a velvet fist. "I confess, you're like no horse I've ever ridden."

His own smile was little more than a grimace. "Take me through my paces, then. Slow or fast. Easy or hard. However you like."

After an initial adjustment, she found the rhythm and pursued it with wanton leisure. She braced her hands on either side of him and swiveled her hips. With torturous indolence, she moved up and down his length. The cords in his neck clenched with the strain of holding himself back. Craving her pleasure before his, he suckled her breasts, bringing both to pebbly hardness. Then he brought her head down and claimed her mouth in a deep kiss that mimicked their coupling. Increasing her tempo, she moaned and panted, riding him harder now.

Seeking to intensify her enjoyment, he slid his thumb into her nest and stroked her dampness. With a swiftness that gratified him, her slim body quivered and arched in the throes of climax. Her parted lips released a sob of joy.

That cry destroyed his discipline, and he took his own pleasure in one strong, upward thrust that sent his seed pouring into her. He wanted it to bear fruit, to see her rounded with his child. He wanted Anne to love him and no other man.

In the quiet aftermath, as she lay over him in utter exhaustion, that incoherent thought returned to him. But he rejected it. Lust was all he wanted from her. She had forced him into making her an offer of marriage, and at least while he held her delectable body, he couldn't say he was entirely sorry.

However, physical union would be the extent of their closeness. They would enjoy each other in bed. But he must never allow himself to drag her down into the darkness of his heart.

Chapter Twenty-three

Mr. Neville's Fist

Upon leaving her bedchamber the next morning, Anne paused a moment at the top of the stairs to compose herself. She smoothed the skirt of her blue gown and checked her hair for the umpteenth time. It was vital that she appear perfectly normal to her parents, even though she was aware of a pleasant soreness in private places.

Exhilaration and despair warred within her. How many times had she and Joshua come together? Three? No, four. She had reveled in every thrilling moment. His mouth on her breast. His hand between her legs. His presence inside her, transporting her to rapture. Yet their night of passion also had rendered her unstrung and somehow forlorn.

She gripped the balustrade. It wasn't the act itself she regretted, but the knowledge that their tryst was over. In the cold light of day, Anne knew she could never again be with Joshua like that. She couldn't carry on an affair right under the noses of her parents. Already, she dreaded the thought of lying to them.

In all her imaginings, she had never really considered the aftermath. She had wanted the experience of intimacy without realizing how it would change her. She'd always been the caretaker, and for once, he had made her feel like the center of the universe. Most astonishing of all, her passion for Joshua hadn't gone away like an itch that had been scratched. Her desire had increased tenfold . . . or more. Even now, she longed to be joined with him in the warm circle of his embrace.

She turned resolutely and started down the stairs. After their last slow and tender coupling, she had cautioned Joshua again that she would not marry him. He had said little, only gazed at her with those dark brooding eyes and promised to think on the matter and let her know of his decision.

She *would* convince him; she must. She loved him too much.

The stunning realization had come to her during the night. She loved Joshua with the same deep, abiding love that her parents shared. Rather than alter her resolution, the discovery made her all the more determined to shun him. She couldn't bear to be trapped in a marriage founded on duty and obligation. He had once loved Lily with all his heart. But he had offered Anne only his name.

Reaching the bottom of the stairs, she paused again. Henceforth, she must keep her thoughts centered on her daily tasks and tuck her memories away to warm her in private moments. She must not be daunted by the possibility of facing Joshua at breakfast with her parents. Preparing herself with a deep breath, she summoned a smile and walked into the dining parlor.

Thankfully, he wasn't there.

Sitting alone at the long table, Mama added a sprinkle of brown sugar to her bowl of porridge. She gave a sweet, somewhat distracted smile that meant she'd been lost in thought, probably planning her next painting. "Good morning, dearest. Did you sleep well?"

Anne managed a nod. She had slumbered in Joshua's arms, awakening toward dawn to find her back nestled to his front, and the pressure of his shaft sliding into her. The sensation had been exquisite, almost like a dream . . .

Blushing, she went to the sideboard to fetch bread and

butter. If she allowed such lascivious thoughts, she would give herself away at once. Her parents knew her facial expressions too well.

Over her shoulder, she asked, "Where is Papa this morning?"

"In his study," Mama said, stirring cream into her bowl. "Something has transpired that may be of interest to you."

Anne's stomach jumped. Turning around, she searched her mother's face. "What happened?"

"Well, no sooner had your father sat down to take his breakfast with me than Lord Joshua came striding in here, wanting to speak to him at once."

"Joshua—?" Anne's mouth felt too parched for speech. The butter knife slipped from her nerveless fingers and clattered onto the sideboard. "They're in the study? Together?"

" 'Tis a matter of great importance, his lordship said." Smiling, her mother wagged a finger in mocking reproach. "Do you know what this is about, then? Is there something you withheld from me last evening? Perhaps the truth about his lordship's intentions toward you?"

"No—yes—oh, *bother!*" Abandoning her plate along with her dignity, Anne picked up her skirt and dashed for the door, paying no heed to her mother's gentle laugh.

Joshua wouldn't do this. He couldn't. Not after she'd told him in no uncertain terms that she would *not* have him as her husband.

Why had she taken so long at her ablutions this morning? She ought to have made haste and kept watch for him. She ought to have guessed he would behave in his usual autocratic manner. What would Papa think of her disgraceful actions? Blast her rash, reckless willfulness!

The study door was closed. She pressed her ear to the door, but the thick oak panel muffled their voices. No, one upraised voice. Papa's.

Without knocking, she burst inside and stopped short. Joshua sat on the green carpet, his hand to his jaw.

Her father stood over him, flexing his fist.

With a gasp of horror, she ran forward. "Papa, what have you done?"

"Something I haven't done in ages. I trained as a pugilist in my youth. It's gratifying to know I haven't lost my touch."

"A wicked undercut," Joshua said, massaging his jaw. "Hurts like the very devil."

Her heart contracting, Anne dropped to her knees beside him. She stopped herself in time before blurting out that he already had a lump on the back of his skull. Her father didn't need to know that they had been attacked by three ruffians the previous night.

How long ago that seemed!

Her fingers trembled as she tilted Joshua's head to inspect his jaw. "Let me look. Judging by the redness, you'll have a bruise."

Scowling, he pulled away. "It's nothing," he snapped. "No more than I deserved."

"Quite so," Papa said sternly, his fists clenched. "Stand up and take your licks like a man."

Joshua rose to his feet, his gaze intent on her father. Anne jumped up, too, and pushed herself between them. She placed one hand on each man's chest. "Stop this right now!"

"He can strike me all he likes," Joshua said. "I won't return the blows."

Papa tapped her on the shoulder. "Move aside and let me have another go at him."

She whirled to face him. "I most certainly will not! And if you hit him again, I'll . . . I'll tell Mama what you've done."

"Tell me what?" Mrs. Neville said, frowning as she hastened into the study. "I heard shouting! Good heavens, John. Did you strike his lordship?"

His expression grim, Mr. Neville rubbed his knuckles and glowered at Joshua. "The rascal deserves more than a punch. Last night, he seduced our daughter. He admitted so himself."

Mama's gaze flitted from Joshua to Anne. Gasping, she pressed her hand to her ample bosom. "Anne? Is this true?"

Anne wanted to sink into the floor. Fraught with shame, she regretted the distress and disappointment she had caused her parents. They had trusted her, raised her well, and loved her without reserve. She had to force herself to meet their eyes. "The fact of the matter is . . . *I* seduced *him*."

Her announcement didn't improve matters. If anything, her father's face looked darker. "Who seduced whom will not alter the outcome."

"I intend to do right by her," Joshua said. "Immediately. With your permission, of course."

"Granted," Papa said.

The two men shook hands while Anne watched in consternation. "*I* don't grant *my* permission. I only wanted to sleep with him!"

Her mother shook her head chidingly. "There is no *only*, my dear. It's all or nothing."

"But I won't let Joshua be forced into such a marriage."

"Why not?" her father asked. "I know you well enough to say that you wouldn't have allowed the knave liberties unless you loved him."

Anne's throat closed. If ever she admitted her feelings to Joshua, it would be in private, with just the two of them. "Joshua isn't a knave. If he was, he wouldn't be here."

Mama rubbed Anne's back. "I quite agree, darling. I'm sure your father knows that, too." She sent her husband a quelling look.

Papa grumbled, his face set in implacable lines. "You're marrying him, young lady, and that's that. I won't tolerate having any surprises in nine months."

Once again, Anne was rendered speechless. A baby. How foolish of her to put that possibility right out of her mind. Now she could think of nothing else but her tender yearning to harbor Joshua's child inside herself. She ached to hold his infant to her breast, to see him cradle their child in his strong arms, too. Unable to stop herself, she looked up to find him watching her with an intent, unsmiling stoicism on his face.

Papa cleared his throat. Mama had moved to his side, and they stood observing Anne and Joshua. Papa wore a rather bemused expression, while Mama smiled tenderly. Were her feelings so plain? Anne wondered.

"We may as well discuss the marriage settlement," Papa said, going to his desk and sitting down. He picked up a quill and found a piece of parchment. "I have three thousand set aside for Anne's dowry. Considering that—"

"There will be no marriage," Anne interrupted in a panic. She pressed her hands to the desk and looked pleadingly at her father. "Please, Papa. You must listen to me."

"There are consequences that must be faced," he said sternly. "Run along, now, and leave me to arrange matters."

Mama linked her arm with Anne's and gently tugged her in the direction of the door. Anne racked her brain for a way out of the dilemma. Joshua looked cold and distant, a man facing his duty with fortitude. He didn't *want* to marry her. He was offering only out of obligation.

Her eyes prickled with unshed tears. By her impetuous actions, she had forced him to take her as his wife. How he must despise her for that.

His attention was fixed on her father. "Under the circumstances, I can't accept the money," Joshua said. "But if you like, you may set up a fund for Anne's personal use."

"A generous concession," Papa said, making a notation on the paper. "However, you are aware that Anne is heiress to a considerable fortune."

Joshua grimaced. "I've no need to live off your daughter's largess. Any inheritance will be placed in trust for our future children. I'll be happy to sign a legal document to that effect."

At the doorway, Anne drew her mother to a halt. "Mama, do something," she whispered. "Please."

Mrs. Neville shook her head. "Your father knows best," she murmured, patting Anne's hand. "I know it seems over-whelming, dearest. But you'll find happiness with Lord Joshua. You'll see."

Anne wanted to latch on to that hope, but it sank like a stone. Less than a day ago, when she had suggested that he ask her father for her hand in marriage, Joshua had been revolted by the notion. She would never forget his expres-sion of appalled distaste. His opinion could not have changed so quickly.

Her father was regarding Joshua. "What precisely are your assets?"

"I own an estate in Hampshire with over a thousand acres of prime farmland," Joshua said. "My investments include a lump-sum inheritance that yields close to eight thousand a year. And there's my pension, of course." He paused. "I also intend to practice medicine."

Mr. Neville nodded in grudging approval. "An ambitious man. I trust you'll keep my daughter in comfort. I won't tolerate her being unhappy."

"You have my word, sir."

The two men reached across the desk and shook hands again. "I'll have my solicitor draw up the papers immedi-ately," Papa said. With the matter settled, he stood up, look-ing more like his old cheerful self. "Will you join me in a brandy to toast the betrothal?"

Joshua got to his feet and shook his head regretfully. "I must leave at once. It's a long ride to London and back. I'll likely have to stay overnight as it is." He hesitated. "If you don't mind, though, I'd like to speak to Anne in pri-vate."

"Yes," Anne murmured, her throat taut. "I'd like to speak with him, too."

Papa's scowl returned. "Alone? Hardly. Neither of you

will spend more than half a minute together until you say your wedding vows."

"Five minutes is not inappropriate," Mama said, going to the desk to slide her arm through his.

"Five minutes is all they need."

"Yet every newly betrothed couple should have at least that long to celebrate in private."

"But given the circumstances—" Papa blustered.

"John, come with me," Mrs. Neville said firmly. *"Now."*

Muttering under his breath, Papa obeyed. At the door, he stopped and placed his hand on Anne's shoulder. "I'm pleased for you," he said on a gentler note. "He's a good man, albeit a trifle hasty in claiming the rights of a husband."

He took her into his embrace and kissed her cheek. She clung to her father, desperate for his warmth and safety, but knowing she no longer belonged to him. Mama stroked a tender hand over Anne's brow and smiled her encouragement. Then her parents left the study and closed the door.

Mired in misery, Anne avoided Joshua's eyes, walked to the window, and stared out at the dreary day. Though the rain had ceased, puddles dotted the garden, the clumps of white daisies and scarlet pimpernel somewhat bedraggled by the storm. Tears blurred the image, and she blinked hard to dispel them. She mustn't make matters worse by behaving like a weak-spined ninny. Last night, she had made her choice, and now she must abide by it.

Resolutely, she turned to face him. He stood watching her, his posture stiff and his gaze intense. He looked so aloof and handsome that she had to take a deep breath to ease the tightness in her throat. "I'm sorry," she forced out. "I didn't mean for this to happen. If you would go and not return, I wouldn't blame you—"

"Is that what you want?" he cut in. Without waiting for her answer, he went on. "This marriage will happen, Anne. It will go better for you if you accept your fate."

His cold voice struck like a dagger into her heart. Where was the passionate man with whom she had shared ecstasy? Where was the tender man who had held her in his arms in the aftermath? "Accept my fate?" she felt stung into saying. "You're the one who went and tattled to my father. I offered you a way out, but you chose not to take it."

"There is no way out. I must get to London. In addition to procuring the license, I'll be investigating Firth."

"Mr. Firth?" she exclaimed, jolted by the reminder of the mystery. "But he lives in Brighton."

"He grew up in London. His mother was a stage actress who brought him here when he was twelve. She's dead now, but I'm hoping to find someone familiar with his personal history. It might reveal a clue as to why he despises me."

Torn between fear and worry, she took a step toward Joshua. "Then you believe me? Those ruffians were after you, not me?"

He shrugged moodily. "I'll admit to the possibility, that's all."

A quiver of foreboding seized her. "If you're in danger, you mustn't go off alone. Take Harrington with you."

"Harry will remain here to protect you during my absence. You'll go nowhere until my return."

"But we must find out who hired those men, and without delay. I could speak to Edwin and the Reverend Cummings—"

"Nowhere," he repeated in an uncompromising tone. "I'll have your vow not to leave this house, Anne. You owe me that much for entrapping me in this marriage."

Her legs almost buckled under the blow of his bitter resentment. Just as she had feared, she had earned his hatred. If compliance in this matter was her only form of restitution, she would take it. "All right," she murmured. "You have my word. I'll stay here."

He watched her as if gauging the validity of her promise. For the barest instant, his dark gaze dipped to her mouth, and she was swept up in the throes of a powerful yearning. If only he would grant her the slightest sign of forgiveness, the barest hope that she might win his affection . . .

He inclined his head in a curt nod. "After last night's attack, I expect whoever is behind this will lie low for a while and regroup. But you're to abide by your promise. And don't give Harry any trouble. I'll speak to him on my way out."

She took another step toward him. "Joshua, I . . ." *I love you.*

As much as she longed to, she couldn't voice those words to him. Such an impassioned declaration would sound like a mere sop to his pride. It would inspire either his pity or his scorn, and her heart might break under the pain.

"I wanted to say . . . Godspeed," she amended softly.

He said nothing. His gaze swept her one last time; then he turned on his heel and strode out of the study.

At last, her knees gave way. She sank into the chair behind her father's desk and wept.

Chapter Twenty-four

The Veiled Lady

By the time the Rosebuds returned later that morning, Anne could no longer indulge in despair. She had watched through the window as Joshua had ridden away, and her worries had returned with a vengeance. Would he be safe? If someone was out to kill him, would that person be watching the house? What if he sent his henchmen after Joshua?

A chill gripped her, and it took a moment to steady her nerves. No, she couldn't let herself think that. Quite likely, Joshua was right. Whoever had hired those men would need time to formulate a new plan.

In the meantime, she had to devise her own plan. A plan that would allow her to seek out the villain yet comply with her vow not to leave the house.

Brooding on the possibilities, she spent the morning in the parlor and attacked her cleaning with a vengeance, polishing the woodwork, getting down on hands and knees to wipe the baseboards, and cleaning the windows until the wavy glass panes sparkled and the odor of vinegar pervaded the air. When the Rosebuds finally came in, chattering and laughing, she was dusting the knickknacks on a shelf by the parlor door, out of sight of the entryway.

"My dear ladies," Mama greeted them. "I hope you had

a lovely time. You'll be interested to hear what's happened in your absence."

While her mother related the news out in the entrance hall, skimming over the seduction part, Anne clutched the dusting cloth and listened to the conversation with only half an ear. She knew what she had to do. The only problem would be to convince Joshua's grandmother to help out with the scheme.

"What a marvelous turn of events," Lady Stokeford was saying. "Where is Anne? I should like to speak with her."

Anne stepped out of the parlor. "I'm here, my lady."

She found herself the target of four pairs of eyes—the Rosebuds and Mama. Lady Faversham compressed her lips. Lady Enid wore her typical delighted smile as she handed her wrap to her footman. Mama hovered anxiously, her plump fingers gripping her paint-smeared apron.

Then Anne turned her gaze to Joshua's grandmother. Lady Stokeford had uttered the appropriate platitudes to Mama. But in her heart did she disdain Anne for seducing her grandson into marriage?

Those noble blue eyes softened. Hastening forward, Lady Stokeford enveloped Anne in an embrace that was redolent of lilacs and starched lace. "My dear girl. Welcome to my family."

The tension in Anne diminished. Although half a head taller, she longed to put her head on that dainty shoulder and pour out all her misgivings. Swallowing past the lump in her throat, she remembered her manners and curtsied. "Thank you, my lady."

"You must call me 'Grandmama,' just as my other two granddaughters-in-law do." Lady Stokeford took her by the arm. "I believe you'll get on quite well with Vivien and Kate. I'll be inviting my grandsons and their families to the wedding, of course. My coachman will convey the messages at once."

Mama clasped her hands to her round, pink cheeks. "Dear me, I must write the wonderful news to your brothers, Anne. It's short notice, but perhaps Abelard could come in from York, and certainly, Cyril from London. A pity Emmett is in India, and Francis and Geoffrey aren't back yet, but I must write to them all, anyway . . ."

"You'll need help, Mama," Anne said automatically. It was one more task for an already overburdened day. "I've a few notes of my own to send, and I can assist you shortly."

Her mother smiled. "But her ladyship will want to speak to you, I'm sure. And I must learn to do these things on my own now. Perhaps I'll sketch a few wedding bells and roses on the invitations . . ." Musing to herself, she hurried up the stairs.

Anne felt a pang of regret mingled with relief. Perhaps Mama really could manage without her. It was daunting to consider the imminent changes in all their lives. Changes brought about by her own reckless self-indulgence.

Yet she wouldn't change a moment of that wonderful night.

She turned to the Rosebuds. "Might I have a word with all of you? Unless you need to send your messages straightaway?"

Lady Stokeford eyed her keenly. "That task can wait for a few moments."

As the Rosebuds seated themselves in the parlor, Anne closed the double doors, then tarried by the shelves, absently running her dustcloth over a clay statue of a dog that Hugh had made long ago for their mother. Dare she reveal everything to the Rosebuds? Joshua would be even more furious with her, and they were already starting off their marriage on the wrong footing.

Yet he was in danger, and she couldn't go calmly about her business. She had to take action to protect him.

Lady Stokeford took the cleaning rag from Anne's fingers, set it aside, and guided Anne to a chaise. Tenderly, she brushed back a strand of hair from Anne's brow. "What's troubling you, child?"

The other two Rosebuds gathered around. "Are you having wedding jitters?" Lady Enid asked in a kindly voice.

"Everyone does, you know," Lady Faversham said.

"Yes—no—I don't know how to say this."

Her face full of wisdom, Lady Stokeford drew back slightly. "Rest assured, I don't blame you for sharing my grandson's bed. It's perfectly natural when two people love one another."

Could Joshua ever love her? Or would his resentment solidify into bitterness over the years? Tears welled, and Anne wiped them with the edge of her apron. "It isn't just that. The truth of the matter is . . . I fear for his life."

Exclamations burst from the three older women.

"What can you mean?" Lady Faversham demanded. "Does this have anything to do with that lowborn money-lender?"

Astounded, Anne asked, "How do you know about Mr. Firth?"

"You were inquiring about him at the ball," Lady Enid said, wagging a plump finger. "Several of your dance partners were eager to tell us."

"I'm sorry," Anne murmured. "I never meant to cause any of you worry."

"We've had a suspicion that you and Joshua were involved in something dangerous," Lady Stokeford said in an oppressive tone. "If my grandson is in peril, I must know the entire story, start to finish."

Haltingly, Anne related everything from the duel to the previous night's attack. "There were three of them. They hid out in the stable and surprised us just as we'd returned from our ride. One of them hit Joshua and knocked him out, but I frightened them away with a pitchfork."

Lady Stokeford's face was pale as paper. "Merciful heavens," she said in a faint tone. "Were either of you harmed?"

"Joshua suffered a bump on his head, but he professed to feel fine." She blushed to remember how well their bed-sport had proven his vigor. He had been wild, tender, insatiable. Perhaps, once they were wed, he would make love to her again, and in bodily joy at least, they might find accord.

"I'm appalled that such men would attack so close to home," Lady Enid exclaimed.

"You ought to have informed your father," Lady Faversham stated.

"No, please," Anne said urgently. "I can't involve my parents. I couldn't bear to cause them any more trouble than I already have."

"I quite understand," Lady Stokeford said, patting Anne's hand. "But this criminal must be brought to justice. And the sooner the better."

"That's why I asked to talk to all three of you," Anne said. She looked at Lady Enid, her plump face full of maternal concern, then at Lady Faversham with her prunish lips and age-spotted hands on the cane, before returning her gaze to Lady Stokeford's gently wrinkled, patrician features. "If you'll agree to help me, I have a plan to trap the villain."

By the following morning, the scheme was in place. The Rosebuds had promised to keep her parents occupied with the wedding preparations. Anne would honor her vow to Joshua—though taking certain liberties of interpretation. She had sent out invitations to the suspects, asking each of them to call on her at a specified hour. The Reverend Cummings and his father would be first to arrive at eleven o'clock in the morning.

So when a small dogcart stopped in front of the house at twenty past ten, Anne peered out in puzzlement from the parlor window. A lady in a sober gray gown stepped down and secured the pony. A veil covering her face, the woman walked with measured steps up to the porch. Was she a friend of the Rosebuds?

Anne answered the knock. The lady's features were

barely distinguishable behind the gray gauze. "Ma'am? Were you seeking Lady Stokeford?"

"No." The lady handed her a small, engraved card. *Mrs. Catherine Loftus.* "If you're Miss Neville," she said in a cultured tone, "then I've come to see you."

Anne subdued a frisson of mingled curiosity and anxiety. She needed to prepare herself for the meeting with the vicar. "In what regard, may I ask? I've another appointment very soon."

"I'll only take a few moments of your time," Mrs. Loftus said. "But I do believe you'll want to hear what I have to say. You see, I was Miss Pankhurst's companion seven years ago."

Anne's heart stopped, then resumed beating at a swift pace. *Catherine.* According to David, she was the woman whom Joshua had attempted to seduce on the day before his wedding to Lily.

Quickly, Anne ushered the woman into the parlor and shut the double doors. She expected Mrs. Loftus to put back her veil, but the woman seated herself without disturbing the facial screen. Why did she wish her features to remain unknown? Was she someone Anne had met at the ball? "May I fetch you a dish of tea?"

Mrs. Loftus waved away her offer. "Thank you, but I'll get straight to my purpose, Miss Neville. I've heard from my sources in society that Captain Kenyon has been courting you."

"Yes," Anne said cautiously, "we're to be married soon." An involuntary warmth curled inside her. How odd to think she would soon be Joshua's wife. She prayed she wasn't wrong to trust him.

"Ah." The veiled woman sat back, her gloved hands clasped in her lap. "I had feared . . ."

"Feared?" Anne prodded.

"That you might be put off by the scandal. I thought you should know that what happened seven years ago was not his fault. None of it was."

The declaration seized Anne's attention. She knew she oughtn't pry. She ought to respect Joshua's wishes. But the desire to know the truth burned in her. "How can you be so certain that I don't already know the story?"

"Because he vowed to me that he would never tell another living soul."

Mrs. Loftus's certainty stirred a quiver of jealousy in Anne. Why would Joshua make such a vow to this woman? Had he harbored such regard for Mrs. Loftus? "He's kept his promise," Anne said stiffly. "I won't have you thinking him unworthy of your trust."

A small laugh issued from behind the veil, rippling the gauze. "There's nothing anyone can say to discredit the captain in *my* eyes. But you mustn't look so suspicious, either. Although I admire him greatly, I have no designs on your betrothed. Nor did I when he was betrothed to Lily Pankhurst." Mrs. Loftus paused. "Although Lily thought otherwise."

Anne leaned forward, bracing her elbows on her knees. "I must know. What happened?"

"First, let me say that I was a school acquaintance of Lily's, but my family fell on hard times. I came to work for her when she lived in London. It wasn't long before Lily displayed her . . . unusual nature. She had periods of acute gaiety for weeks on end, when she'd go from party to party, leaving a trail of broken hearts. Then one day she would turn melancholy and accuse me of flirting with everyone from her brother to the old butler. She would spend many days weeping in her bed, and then become her gay self again overnight. It was most peculiar—almost as if there were two women residing in her."

The portrayal shocked Anne. Neither David nor Joshua had mentioned anything of this. "Then Joshua must have met Lily in one of her happier times."

"Yes." Mrs. Loftus tilted her head as if lost in memory. "He was one of many suitors. Lily was quite beautiful, with a charming manner that captivated men. Within a fortnight, they'd become engaged, and since his leave was nearly over, they decided to hasten the wedding. It was on the day before the ceremony that I saw the signs of gloom descending upon Lily."

Sitting on the edge of her chair, Anne could scarcely believe what she was hearing. "What did you do?"

"After she'd wept uncontrollably for hours, I approached Mr. Pankhurst and Lord Timberlake, but neither would say anything to the captain. They were afraid he might back out of the betrothal contract. So I took the task upon myself." Mrs. Loftus held herself straight. "Perhaps you'll think it wasn't my place to do so, but I felt strongly that he should be warned about her nature."

"Of course," Anne said without hesitation. "I would have done the same."

Mrs. Loftus nodded. "His family had come for the wedding, and I sent word to him at their townhouse. He called at once, very much concerned. We met in a downstairs room with the door closed. Lily walked in on us."

"David said . . . Joshua was seducing you."

"Merciful heavens, no! The captain was holding my hand, that was all. I was distraught, and he meant to encourage me to speak."

Relief washed through Anne, pure and sweet. "What happened then?"

"Lily flew into a rage. She accused me of trying to steal him from her. In her despondent times, she often thought I was far prettier than she." Mrs. Loftus shook her head. "It was a ridiculous accusation, I assure you."

Anne wished she could judge so for herself. Only good manners kept her from mentioning it. If Mrs. Loftus wanted to conceal her identity so that Anne wouldn't recognize her in society, then she must respect that wish.

"Didn't Joshua reassure her?"

"Of course, but it did no good. She was beyond reasoning. But at least he could see the proof of what I was telling him. The poor man had had no inkling of her dual nature until that moment." Mrs. Loftus paused, her head bowed. "He tried to talk sense into her, but she was so incoherent that finally he left with a promise to return later in the evening, after she'd had the chance to calm down. But later it was too late. Lily had already had her revenge on me." With that, Mrs. Loftus slowly lifted her veil.

Anne couldn't stifle an inadvertent gasp. Beneath a pair of solemn blue eyes and a clear, unmarked brow, the lower half of Mrs. Loftus's face was a demi-mask of scars, thick and smooth in places, pitted in others. Even her lips bore the bumpy texture of badly healed skin.

Anne felt ill, more from the revelation of Lily's vicious attack than from the scars themselves. Overwhelmed by compassion, she reached out to touch Mrs. Loftus's gloved hand. "I can't imagine . . . the pain you must have suffered."

"It was scalding water, quite a lot of it," Mrs. Loftus said in a realistic tone that said she'd overcome the horror of that moment. "Lily had procured a pot from the kitchen and heated it over the fire in her bedchamber. I'm very thankful that I was able to put up my arm in time to protect my eyes."

"Joshua tended to your burns, then."

"Yes. David Pankhurst let him into the house. Neither he nor his father would summon any other physician for fear of word getting out about what Lily had done. The captain bore me away and found me a safe place to stay."

Anne's heart squeezed. A refrain ran through her mind: *He doesn't mourn Lily. She destroyed his love for her.* In a whisper, she said, "Everyone called him a scoundrel for abandoning his bride-to-be."

Mrs. Loftus looked away for a moment. "I found that out only much later. He remained with me for a fortnight until I was on the road to recovery. Then he provided me with a pleasant cottage on the coast and a small nest egg. I would not have allowed him, but I had nothing—no hope of employment ever again—and he insisted. I've kept to myself and posed as a widow ever since."

Shaken, Anne sat back. What a burdensome secret Joshua had kept. He had shouldered the guilt that rightfully belonged to Lily. "How could David and Lord Timberlake have allowed him to take the blame?" Anne burst out. "How could they have been so cruel and selfish? David was so angry about his sister's death that he even challenged Joshua to a duel."

"Good heavens," Mrs. Loftus exclaimed. "Was anyone injured?"

Only me. "It was an aborted duel. Neither man came to harm."

"I'm grateful for the captain's sake." Her gloved fingers plucked at her skirt. "I hold myself to blame for his tarnished reputation, for I begged him to keep silent. I didn't want anyone to know what had happened to me. I've been reluctant to show my face for fear that people would turn from me in horror." She drew the gauze back over her ruined features.

"I could never censure you," Anne said firmly. "Please be assured, I'll keep your secret."

Mrs. Loftus rose to her feet. "You may tell whomever you like," she said in a voice that vibrated with sincerity. "It's the least I can do to repay such a fine man."

Shortly thereafter, as Mrs. Loftus drove away, Anne's mother came down the stairs along with the Rosebuds. Both Lady Enid and Lady Faversham were dressed for an outing in fashionable finery complete with hats and pelisses.

Mama wore her best maroon gown topped by an ivory redingote. "Did we have a visitor?" she asked, peering out the side window. "Who was that woman?"

"Just someone who needed directions into Brighton," Anne murmured. There would be time later to tell them about Mrs. Loftus, to clear Joshua's good name. And to absorb the giddy truth. He didn't still mourn Lily.

But could he ever love again? Or was his heart as scarred as Mrs. Loftus's face?

"If she'd waited a moment, she could have followed us into town," Lady Enid said, cheerful in yellow silk with a matching turban.

"I didn't think of that," Anne said. "Are you leaving straightaway, then?"

"Along with your father," Mama said. Raising her voice, she called down the passageway, "John, are you ready?"

Straightening his white cravat, Mr. Neville emerged from his study. "I'm coming," he grumbled. "Though I still say my blue coat is quite fine enough for any nuptials. It's done me well for the weddings of my sons."

"And since it was new for Abelard's wedding over a decade ago, that means it's shamefully outdated," Mama said. "We'll leave you at the tailor's shop while we ladies visit the dressmaker."

"I do hope you don't mind that I stay behind," Lady Stokeford said.

"Of course not," Mama said, giving Anne a fond smile. "You and my daughter must become better acquainted."

"You'll excuse us if we make haste," Lady Faversham said, giving Lady Stokeford a pointed stare. "We're late already, and we'll need hours in which to visit all the shops."

As the party trooped out, both Lady Faversham and Lady Enid lingered a moment to clasp Anne's hand and admonish her to take care. Anne and Lady Stokeford stood on the porch and waved as the coach headed toward Brighton.

Then Anne hastened to the kitchen to reconnoiter with Harrington. She was taken aback to find him locked with Peg in an amorous embrace. They made an incongruous pair, Peg taller and stouter than the wiry valet.

Anne loudly cleared her throat. The couple sprang apart, Peg blushing to the roots of her ginger hair and Harrington sheepishly ducking his grizzled face.

"If you're quite ready, Mr. Harrington," Anne said.

"Ready and—er—waitin' fer ye." Favoring his bad leg, he picked up his rifle from the table and stumped toward her.

Snuffling, Peg rushed in his wake and threw her arms around him. "If ye get yerself harmed, Harry, why, I'll— I'll never get over it!"

"Ye're worse'n a barnacle, lass. Now let me go do a man's duty." But he looked gruffly pleased by the maid-servant's show of devotion.

Anne was envious of their happiness. Anguish had taken up residence in her own heart, and she knew that she had been no better than the rest of society in censuring Joshua. But she couldn't let herself think of that now. As she and Harrington went to the front of the house, she turned her mind to the immediate problem and gave him instructions on his role. He and Lady Stokeford were to stay out of sight while Anne interviewed the suspects.

"The cap'n won't like this," Harrington warned, his thick brows forming a single gray shelf. " 'E told me to keep ye safe."

"And I intend to keep *him* safe," she stated. "Whether he approves or not."

The valet released a gravelly chuckle. "Methinks the cap'n's met 'is match."

Not ten minutes later, a curricle bearing Arthur and Richard Cummings drew up in front of the house. Anne's stomach contracted into a knot. "They're here."

"Mr. Harrington and I shall wait in the next room," Lady Stokeford said, her face set in an imperious expression. "Never fear, we'll be listening in case you call for help."

Harrington gripped his polished Baker rifle. "Just say the word, miss, an' I'll blast the blinkin' fools from 'ere t' London."

As a knock sounded, they vanished into the sitting room across the entryway.

Subduing her panicky nerves, Anne donned a smile and opened the door. Both men regarded her warily, ruddy-cheeked Arthur looking like a bulldog in a tailored russet coat, and pale-faced Richard, a slim man in cleric black who had the same squinty brown eyes as his father.

"Good day, Miss Neville," Arthur said in an eloquent tone. "May I say, you're looking exceedingly fine today. Blue brings out the beautiful color of your eyes."

That affable charm had earned him a seat in Parliament, Anne knew. They had only a nodding acquaintance, yet his flattering manner created the artificial aura of friendship. "Thank you. Do come in so that we might visit."

As they entered the parlor, the vicar cleared his throat. "I understand you're to be wed. Your father asked me to perform the service next Friday."

"My sincerest felicitations," Arthur Cummings said heartily, taking up a stance by the mantelpiece, his hand over his heart. "A fine man, Lord Joshua Kenyon. A captain in the king's cavalry and a hero of our victory at Waterloo. Our illustrious country needs more brave men like him—" He paused, his cordial expression sliding into a frown. "What are you doing, Miss Neville?"

Anne had seated herself at a small table and picked up the pistol lying there. She commenced polishing the mother-of-pearl stock with a piece of cloth. "I'm cleaning my gun, of course. Do go on."

"I—er—I was saying that—ah—" Arthur exchanged a sidelong glance with his son. "Perhaps you should tell us why you invited us here."

"All in good time. First, I'd like to ask a few questions of the Reverend Cummings." Anne focused her attention on the man whom David loved beyond reason. Looking distinctly uneasy, the vicar gripped the mahogany arms of his chair. She asked, "Do you own a flintlock musket?"

He blinked. "Why, no, though Father does, and I've done a bit of bird hunting from time to time on his estate—"

"Silence," his father cut in, his face ugly with hostility. "She's trying to link us to that duel. Kenyon came to me last week, making wild accusations—as if a man of my sterling reputation would hide in a hedge and shoot at people."

Anne turned to the elder statesman. "*Do* you own a flintlock musket, Mr. Cummings?" she asked, with a composure that went only skin-deep.

"Of course," Arthur said with a snort. "What gentleman doesn't? Go to any proper manor house in this great nation and you'll find all manner of guns from muskets to fowling pieces." His gaze skated over the pistol she held pointed in his direction. "If that thing's loaded, you'd best take care how you handle it."

"My brothers say I'm an expert shot. So does my uncle, Sir Francis Bellingham." Raising the pistol, she sighted down the barrel at Arthur.

He stepped sideways behind the vicar's chair. "Put down that weapon, miss. I'll not be threatened."

Affecting a laugh, she lowered the pistol. "Nor would I threaten you. I merely wondered . . ." She turned her gaze to Richard Cummings. With his slim physique, the vicar was similar in size to that third shadowed figure. "Where were you the evening before last, Reverend?"

"Why—ah—that was the night of the storm," the Reverend Cummings said. Glancing at the gun in her hands, he squirmed in his chair. "I was at the vicarage, I'm sure. Yes, I was going over the parish accounts."

"I demand to know what these impertinent questions are about," Arthur boomed. "Where is your father? I shall chastise him for allowing you such free rein."

He edged toward the doorway. She stood up, pistol in hand. Though her heart pounded, she said coolly, "I don't believe you'd care for my father to know about that letter."

Arthur Cummings came to an abrupt halt. Behind him, Richard Cummings uttered a small groan and buried his face in his hands.

A dull red flush swept over Arthur's axe-hewn features. He flashed a furious glare at his son's bowed head and then swung toward Anne. Without bothering to affect ignorance of the letter, he said, "You would dare to play the extortionist? Well, then, I'll give you two hundred guineas in exchange for that letter."

"No," Anne said. "You won't."

Keeping her eyes on him, she pulled open a drawer in the table.

"Three hundred, then," Arthur snarled. "That's my final offer."

"I don't want your money. I'll just give this to your son. That's why I called you both here."

Stepping forward, she handed the folded letter to Richard Cummings.

His face ashen, the vicar took the paper. He fumbled to open it. His brown eyes filled with cautious hope as he looked up at her. "But—this is the letter David wrote to me. Why have you given it back?"

"So that neither of you will have any reason to harbor ill will toward Lord Joshua."

Arthur strode forward. "That letter must be burned. Give it to me and I'll chuck it straight into the fire."

But when he tried to snatch it from his son, Richard tucked the letter into an inner pocket of his coat. "With all due respect, sir, it belongs to me."

"Don't be a ruddy fool! It'll fall into the wrong hands again."

Richard ignored his father. Rising to his feet, he took Anne's hands in a fervent clasp. "God bless you, Miss Neville. You can't imagine what this means to me."

Because he feared the exposure of his secret? Or because he treasured any missive from David? She couldn't be certain, but she hoped it was the latter.

"Hush," Arthur snapped at his son. "Have a care what you say to her."

"Come along, Father. I doubt Miss Neville wishes to witness our quarrel."

Straight-shouldered, the vicar walked to the front door with his father muttering recriminations behind his back.

As soon as they closed the front door, Anne leaned against it in relief. Lady Stokeford and Harrington came rushing out of the sitting room. "We heard the entire conversation," the dowager said in a huff. "What a vile man, that Arthur Cummings. I shall have to tell my friends here in Brighton how much I dislike him. If I have my way, he won't be re-elected."

"I hope I did right in giving back the letter," Anne fretted.

"Of course you did, my dear. It's a show of faith that you won't spread the gossip. That gives the vicar and his father little reason to attack my grandson."

"*If* they were behind that ambush." And would David be safe? she wondered. If Arthur had intended to shoot David at the duel, then he might go after him again.

"Two down an' two t' go," Harrington said, brandishing his gun. "Who's the next blighter?"

"My cousin Edmund." Uneasiness crept with icy fingers down her spine. "He'll be here at one o'clock."

Stunned and shaken, Josh stepped out of the seedy boardinghouse near the Strand and braced his shoulder against the rotting doorframe. All around, the sights and sounds and smells of London assaulted him.

The singsong call of a woman hawking turnips and carrots. The stink of rubbish in the gutter. Children in rags darting to and fro, laughing. Across the narrow lane, an old man sat on his stoop, puffing on a pipe.

But none of that could penetrate the shock Josh had been dealt in a dank, tiny chamber inside the building. He had found his source after half a day spent asking questions at theaters and dance halls. At last he'd been directed here, to a dirty slattern who'd cradled an empty bottle of gin. For the price of a few coins, she had spilled out her story. And he had departed in a daze.

Josh squinted up at the sky. He had a hell of a hard ride ahead if he was to reach Anne by nightfall. He tossed a shilling to the boy who'd watched Plato, and the skinny lad ran off to show the piece of silver to his mates.

Tension goaded Josh as he rode down the crowded lane. He had lain awake the previous night, tortured by the possibility that he would never again hold Anne in his arms, never have the chance to use the marriage license tucked safely in his pocket. Now he had all the more reason to fear for her.

He knew why Samuel Firth hated him. Firth could have aimed a shot at him on the morning of the duel and struck Anne by mistake. He could have attacked Josh in the stables and threatened Anne in the process.

The chill of urgency gripped Josh. What he had found out gave Samuel Firth a powerful motive for abducting Anne.

Chapter Twenty-five

Edwin's Plot

By the time her cousin arrived, Anne had paced the ground-floor rooms more than a dozen times, stopping now and then to peer out at the dirt lane that led through the village. When the rap sounded, she rushed to the door and paused with her fingers curled around the handle.

Lady Stokeford and Harrington gave her a nod and melted into the adjoining chamber. Nervous anticipation throbbed in Anne's temples. This would be the first time since before the duel that she'd faced Edwin alone. Of all the suspects, he had the strongest reason to want her dead.

Today, she would determine once and for all if he hated her enough to resort to murder.

The moment she opened the door, he pushed past her and stalked into the entrance hall. "This had better be worth my while," he snarled. "What am I, a hound to be summoned at a snap of your fingers?"

With his cravat askew and his face unshaven, he looked as dissipated as ever. The sour smell of brandy emanated from him. The bruise beneath his eye had changed to a hideous shade of yellow-green.

Anne snapped her fingers, then walked into the parlor. Over her shoulder, she said, "Heel, Edwin."

He stomped after her and grabbed her upper arm. "Hey! I told you not to do that—"

She reached for her pistol, swung around, and pointed it at his chest. "Yes?"

With a yelp, he released her and backed away. "For pity's sake! Have you gone mad?"

Anne took a step toward him. "Perhaps I have. Perhaps this latest plot of yours has made me so angry that I don't care if you live or die."

"P-plot?" He backed slowly away, putting a chair between the two of them. "I don't know what you're babbling about."

His shifty eyes faltered a moment, enough to confirm that he knew more than he would admit. Appalled that he might have hired those ruffians in the stables, she decided to continue the bluff. "It's useless, Edwin. I've found you out. You've gone too far this time."

His alarmed gaze darted from her face to the pistol and back. "You wouldn't shoot me. You wouldn't dare."

She moved closer. "Are you so certain? I can't miss at this range."

"Put that thing away." Edwin lunged toward the entrance hall. "Help! Uncle John! Aunt Lenora!"

Anne stepped into his path. "They aren't here. There's no one here but you and me. And it's time to put an end to your mischief." She cocked the pistol.

A strangled sob escaped him. "Please don't shoot! I— I'll burn the document. No one need ever know about it."

"You'll burn the document," Anne repeated, hiding her bafflement. To what document was he referring? "And how would that solve matters?"

"With the forgery gone, there's no need for you to be angry. You'll still be the heiress. Everything shall be as my father intended it."

Stupefied, Anne stared at her cousin. At last she realized what he meant. Edwin had made a falsified will that undoubtedly left all his father's assets to himself. No wonder he'd looked so smug two evenings ago.

And if he'd felt confident of his own success, he would have had no reason to hire those men. She didn't know whether to be relieved at that or angry that he would stoop so low as to perpetrate fraud.

"Burning the forgery doesn't alter the fact that you committed a criminal act," Anne stated. "You deserve to be turned over to the magistrate."

"I'll destroy the counterfeit will. You'll have no proof."

She eyed him up and down. "Then I'll shoot you right now. Not to kill, of course. Just to incapacitate you. I'll say that you'd threatened my life. Then, when the authorities search your chambers, they'll find the forgery and know what a villain you are."

His mouth twitched into a sick grin. "There's no need to be so harsh. We're family, remember? Surely you can— er—find it in your heart to forgive me."

Thinking fast, Anne eyed him up and down. "Perhaps under certain conditions . . ."

He clasped his hands in a feeble attempt to look like a choirboy. "Anything. Anything at all."

"First, you'll cease drinking alcohol."

He abandoned the pose as if she'd poked him with a pin. "What? That has naught to do with falsifying a document."

"It has to do with your general propensity for vices." She gestured with the gun. "Or perhaps you'd prefer a lead ball in your leg? A hit to the knee could cripple you for life. Of course, I could take pity and shoot you in the thigh. It'll bleed rather a lot, but at least—"

"All right!" Edwin said, his face turning a green that complemented his bruise. "I'll stop drinking."

"You'll also give up gambling."

"Never!"

"Promise me," Anne said with another wave of the pistol. "On your dubious honor as a gentleman."

He gnashed his teeth. "As you wish."

Knowing him too well, she said, "The trouble is, I can't trust you. Remember the time you promised Uncle Francis that you wouldn't ever steal his brandy again? As soon as he turned his back, you reverted to your old ways."

"I won't this time, I swear it—"

"I think I'll tell Papa about the forged will. He'll keep a very close eye on you. You'll be interested to know that he trained as a pugilist in his youth."

"He won't believe you." But Edwin's voice lacked conviction.

She smiled. "And then there are my brothers. I'm sure you can recall what happened when you tried to blame Dorian for cheating at cards, and you were the one at fault."

Edwin squirmed. "That isn't fair! There's nine of them and only one of me."

"And of course," Anne went on, "if *I* find out you've broken your word, I can still put that bullet through your leg. I'll simply say it was an accident."

"Damn you, Anne. You can't do that!"

"Don't curse. Have I also mentioned that Joshua will be livid when he finds out that you've tried to cheat me out of my inheritance?"

"Have a heart," Edwin said, an unhealthy pallor to his face. "I'll be a paragon of virtue."

She doubted that. But if she'd frightened him into making even a small improvement in his character, life would be easier for Uncle Francis. And her uncle might relent and allow Edwin at least a portion of the inheritance that Anne felt uncomfortable accepting. "I do have a heart. That's why I'm letting you go."

The moment she stepped back, Edwin scuttled toward the entrance hall, keeping an eye on the pistol. He flashed her one last glower before the door slammed shut behind him.

In the parlor, Anne sank into a chair. She felt ill at the thought of Edwin conspiring against her. They had grown up together, and although he'd been a spoiled brat and a bully, she had tried her best to keep the peace. It was a blow now to face the extent of his corruption. She didn't want the inheritance, yet she could understand Uncle Francis's desire to keep it out of Edwin's squandering hands.

Lady Stokeford hastened out of hiding and sat down beside her. "My dear, you were splendid to force a confession out of that knave. Forging a will is the act of a criminal."

"Perhaps it was foolish of me to let him go."

"You dealt admirably with a sticky situation," the dowager asserted. "Edwin Bellingham is your cousin, after all. Blood demands a certain loyalty of us, no matter how wretched those relations may be."

"If Edwin had the new will in his possession, then he would have little reason to hire ruffians to attack me," Anne mused. "But does that also exonerate him from shooting me in the duel?"

Like a sentry with his rifle, Harrington paced at the parlor doorway. "If 'twas him that morning," he said, peering out the window, " 'e were ridin' a different horse. That one was a gray."

"Edwin doesn't own a gray," Anne said.

"Horses are easily hired," Lady Stokeford said. "However, it's something that must be checked when Joshua returns."

"Yes." Anne took a deep breath. "For now, though, we must turn our minds to Samuel Firth."

"The moneylender," Lady Stokeford said, her lip curling with aristocratic disdain. "I needn't ask what manner of man *he* is."

Anne thought about the polished, dangerous man she'd met at the ball. "Samuel Firth isn't what you'd expect. I was surprised at how well he fits in with the gentry. And he plays the pianoforte as if he were born to it."

"Unusual, to be sure. But for that, at least, I cannot condemn him. My late husband played remarkably well, too, without ever having formal lessons." Lady Stokeford's eyes went misty, as if she were remembering a time long ago. Then she compressed her lips. "If Firth despises my grandson as much as you say, then I should like to meet this man."

"But our plan is to let him believe I'm here alone," Anne said.

"Men never consider an elderly lady to be much of a threat," Lady Stokeford said. "I'll admit him to the house and then leave the two of you alone."

Lucy stood at the front window and observed the man who emerged from a fine black coach. First impressions were often valuable; she had learned that from years of experience. And Samuel Firth arrested her attention.

Tall and strikingly handsome, he looked to be the age of her youngest grandson, Gabriel. And like her grandsons, Firth was a man's man, not a dandy. He didn't pause to straighten his carelessly tied cravat or smooth his hands over his black hair. His tailored blue coat and tan breeches showed a scorn for frills. His purposeful steps up the front walk exuded a confidence that bordered on arrogance.

Lucy also had the fleeting impression that she knew him from somewhere.

Pondering that, she opened the door to his knock. His eyes widened a fraction, frosty blue eyes that missed nothing. What was that brief flicker of emotion in him? Surprise? Or something darker? She couldn't tell. His face had the hard, closed expression of a man who knew exactly what he wanted and would stop at nothing to get it.

"Madam," he said, with excellent intonation for someone who had grown up on the streets. "I'm here to see Miss Neville."

She stepped aside so that he could enter. "We've been expecting you, Mr. Firth. I'm Lucy, Lady Stokeford."

"You attended the Angletons' ball."

His recognition jarred her, but Lucy kept her expression

serene. If he had noticed an old woman, that only made her all the more suspicious of him. "Perhaps you saw me with my grandson, Lord Joshua Kenyon."

"Perhaps. I understand he's gone to London for a few days."

His cold tone chilled Lucy. Raising an eyebrow, she fixed him with an imperious stare. "He'll return this evening. How do you know my grandson?"

"We met when he accused me of shooting Miss Neville."

"And did you?"

His granite features gave away nothing. "There's no point to these questions. I'll see Miss Neville now."

Lucy wasn't accustomed to being dismissed, especially not by upstart moneylenders. But for the purpose of the investigation, she held her tongue. She mustn't appear too formidable.

As she led him to the parlor, Lucy couldn't imagine how she'd thought she'd known him. Without a doubt, she would have remembered that glacial blue stare. Did Firth simply remind her of someone?

And there had been that flicker in his eyes. The impression of hatred. Intuition told her that Samuel Firth despised her as much as he did her grandson.

Anne watched as Samuel Firth followed Lady Stokeford into the chamber. In his tailored coat he looked every inch the gentleman, but she knew he would not be so easy to maneuver as Edwin or Richard and Arthur Cummings. Nor did she feel marginally safe as she had with the other men, even though Harrington was lurking out of sight in the next room.

The dowager hadn't changed her low opinion of him, judging by the grim set of her mouth as she glided out of the parlor. Firth's gaze tracked the old woman as she disappeared around the corner. His brows were quirked in a frown before he switched his concentrated stare to Anne.

Then a faint, mocking amusement played across his face. She stood with her hand resting lightly around the grip of the pistol. It felt cold and deadly, and she wondered if this time, she would have her bluff called.

He bowed. "I see that we continue to be at odds, Miss Neville. I had hoped we might become friends."

"I'd sooner befriend a black adder. Do sit down."

"Ladies first."

"I prefer to stand."

"As you wish. And I'll take you up on your invitation. I doubt you'll splatter my blood all over your parents' furniture." He settled down with his arms draped along the back of the chaise in a nonchalant pose. "I'd feel more welcome if you'd come and sit beside me."

"This isn't a social visit, Mr. Firth."

"A pity." His gaze traveled up and down her blue gown, lingering at her bosom. "I'll have you know, there are few women who could persuade me to leave my desk in the midst of a busy afternoon."

"Then I'm grateful for your sacrifice," Anne mocked. She strolled to the doorway and turned to face him. "Once again, I must question you about your activities. Where were you on the evening before last?"

He tilted his head in a quizzical manner. "Why? What happened?"

"If you're guilty, then you'll know. If you're not, then there's no reason for you to know. So where were you?"

"That depends on what time you're referring to. Early in the evening, I was at home. Later, I was in bed with the insatiable Lady Vane."

Anne fought back a blush. He wanted to shock her, and she wouldn't give him the satisfaction. "You don't strike me as a man who would hide behind a lady's skirts—"

"I assure you, the lady wasn't wearing any skirts."

"Don't be crude, Mr. Firth. I would appreciate some serious answers. Do you hate Joshua enough to send your hirelings after him?"

Firth's ease of manner vanished. Although he didn't move a muscle, he exuded the vigilance of a wolf. "Someone attacked Kenyon? Is that what happened the other night?"

She wondered if his show of surprise was calculated. "You haven't answered *my* question," she stated. "Did you pay three men to go after Joshua?"

"Absolutely not. If I wanted him thrashed, I'd do the job myself."

Anne eyed him suspiciously. Pistol in hand, she paced the length of the parlor with its collection of assorted knick-knacks, the china figurines that she and her brothers had purchased for her parents' birthdays, the battered deck of cards from long-ago family games, her mother's flower paintings that brightened the walls. Somehow, those ordinary items underscored the danger in the air. "Why do you hate Joshua so much?"

"I've told you, he accused me of a crime."

"You're a clever businessman—"

"Thank you."

"—and you don't strike me as the sort who would react with undue wrath if indeed it's a simple case of mistaken identity."

"That error could tarnish my sterling reputation."

Caressing the stock of the pistol, Anne took a step toward him. "You're toying with me, Mr. Firth. You're not telling me everything you know."

"If I have any secrets, they'll emerge in due course. You may tell Kenyon I said so." On that cryptic statement, he reached inside his coat.

By reflex, she lifted the pistol and aimed it at his heart.

"Easy, now. I don't have a gun." Smiling a little, Firth withdrew a slim black case, stood up, and strolled toward her. He opened the case to reveal a glittering diamond bracelet. "It's for you, Miss Neville."

She caught her breath in mingled surprise, involuntary

admiration, and utter dismay. "I can't accept such a gift from you."

"Why not? I assure you, it's a mere trinket."

He sounded oddly like Lady Stokeford when she'd presented Anne with the diamond pendant, now tucked safely in Anne's whatnot box. "It's more than a trinket, and you know it. I can only imagine what you'd expect from me in return."

"So can I." His gaze resting on her lips, he lowered his voice to a silken purr. "Since the ball, I've thought of little else."

Her wariness returned in full force. Only with effort did she keep herself from retreating. "Then you must not have heard the news of my betrothal."

His cold blue gaze pinned her. "Betrothal?"

"Joshua and I will be married soon. He rode to London yesterday to procure the license."

Firth said nothing for a moment. Other than a slight narrowing of his eyes, his taut features might have been chiseled in marble. His thoughts were hidden behind that impassive mask. "There'll be no reading of the banns, then?"

Again, she resisted a flush. Did he guess the reason why they couldn't wait three weeks to marry? "Joshua is anxious to return home. I intend to go with him."

Firth snapped the case shut and replaced it inside his pocket. "My congratulations. You're marrying into an illustrious family."

"His family has nothing to do with why I agreed to be his wife." She wouldn't tell this man of the love that ached in her heart or the exhilaration she felt in Joshua's arms. And especially not the pain of Joshua's bitter resentment over being seduced into wedlock.

"Let's go for a drive, shall we?" Firth said abruptly. "A breath of fresh air might clear the bad feelings between us. And you can tell me all about your wedding plans."

His proposal startled her. Was he still intent on winning

her over? "I'm sorry," she said stiffly, "but I can't leave the house. I'm waiting for Joshua to return."

"It'll do him good to wait. That way, he won't take you for granted." With a smoothness that caught her off guard, Firth lunged, wrested the pistol from her, and set it on a high shelf out of her reach.

"Give that back!" Her heart pounding, she dodged one way and then the other. But Firth had the instincts of a street fighter, and she couldn't get past his solid form.

"Calm down," he said on a laugh. "I mean you no harm. But we can't talk easily while you have a gun trained on me." As he spoke, he put his arm around her waist and propelled her toward the door.

At the touch of his lean body, alarm sizzled through Anne. "Release me at once or I'll scream."

She jabbed him with her elbow, but he deflected the blow and tightened his hold, not enough to cause pain, yet enough for her to feel his strength. "You're being theatrical," he said in a deceptively winning tone. "I merely want to talk to you without any listening ears—"

The cocking of a gun stopped him. Harrington took up a stance in the entrance hall with his Baker rifle trained on them. A white-faced Lady Stokeford stood beside him, a heavy candlestick gripped in her hand.

"Let 'er go," said the grizzled old soldier.

Firth didn't move. His hands were like iron manacles on Anne. She tensed her muscles in preparation to attack, but his grip eased suddenly. "Never let it be said that I hid behind a woman's skirts."

Anne stepped quickly out of range and whirled to face him, her hand on the newel post. She steeled herself against an onslaught of outraged trembling. "How dare you try to abduct me."

"Abduct?" He cast her a cool, sardonic smile. "That's a harsh term to describe a pleasant drive through the countryside."

"Silence," Lady Stokeford snapped. "You attempted to

coerce her when she refused your offer. I too would call that abduction."

"I appreciate the lesson in manners, madam. Having been raised in the gutter, I missed the finer points of etiquette."

Anne had had enough of his sarcasm. Despite all his smooth denials, Samuel Firth must have been the one who had taken a shot at Joshua and struck her instead. The one who had hired those men in the stables. But to her frustration she had no proof. "Leave this house at once, sir."

"Lest me finger slip and I blow a 'ole in ye," Harrington added with a menacing gesture of his gun.

Cool as ever, Firth inclined his head to Anne. "It's been a pleasure, Miss Neville."

But as he opened the door and strode outside, the rapid thudding of hooves sounded on the lane. Anne's heartbeat surged. "Joshua."

In the company of Lady Stokeford and Harrington, she dashed onto the porch. But instead of Joshua's tall form in the saddle, an older man slumped on a gray gelding.

David's horse. David's father.

Lord Timberlake dismounted, half staggering as his feet hit the ground. Firth shored him up until the baron caught his balance. Timberlake blinked in befuddlement, then backed away with his fists clenched. "You! I haven't got your money, blast you."

"Never mind that," Firth said. "What's put you in such a state?"

Timberlake shook his head as if to clear his vision. Without answering, he tottered up the flagstone walk toward Anne. "Miss Neville," he gasped out. "Praise God you're here."

Anne felt a fleeting anger that he had allowed Joshua to take the blame for Lily's vicious act. Then the baron's obvious distress tempered her hostile emotions.

She met him halfway and automatically grasped his upper arms to steady him. Detecting the stench of brandy fumes, she realized that he was drunk—and in a panic, judging by his sweaty pallor and desperate eyes. "What's wrong, Lord Timberlake?" she said. "Why have you come here?"

"There's been an accident. At home." His gaze jerked nervously toward the road as if his thoughts remained at Greystone Manor. "A terrible accident."

The breath froze in Anne's lungs. "David?"

Timberlake shook his head. "Nay, it's Mrs. Oswald. She . . . she fell down the stairs, and she's in a bad way. David is with her, but . . . you must come. Please."

"You'll need a physician," Firth said. Only then did Anne realize that he towered beside them. "I'll ride into town to fetch one."

"No!" Timberlake exploded. He ran a visibly trembling hand over his balding pate. "I—I've already sent . . . another servant on the errand. Please come *now*, Miss Neville."

His anguish overwhelmed even the thought of her vow to Joshua. Never before had David's father called on her for help, and as much as she disliked the sour housekeeper, Anne couldn't refuse a person in need. "Of course. I'll saddle my mare immediately."

She turned to leave, but Lady Stokeford detained her. "You'll go nowhere without Harrington and me."

"Take my coach," Firth said. He lifted a sardonic eyebrow at Anne. "And don't glower, Miss Neville. I'll stay behind and await your return."

Chapter Twenty-six

The Bride

The sun had dipped low on the horizon by the time Josh reached Merryton-on-Sea. He was dusty, saddle-sore, and edgy. But when he spied the Neville house on the outskirts of the village, he felt a surge of unmanly eagerness.

His gaze scanned the rambling house with its picturesque flower garden and the pillared front porch. The place looked quiet and serene. No one looked out from the windows; no one rushed forth to greet him.

Disappointment seared him. Hell, why not admit the truth? He'd hoped Anne would be watching for him. He wanted to see her expressive features light up in a smile. He wanted to know she had missed him, that she forgave him his cruelty toward her at their last meeting.

He had lashed out in anger because he had been afraid. Afraid of the softness inside himself. Afraid of the tender emotions she'd awakened in him. That fear still skulked at the edge of his thoughts, but it was overshadowed by his craving to hold her in his arms and know her love.

Did she love him?

Her father had declared that fact, and she hadn't denied it. Of course, she might have wanted to let her parents believe what they willed. Or perhaps she had deluded herself with romantic thoughts in order to justify the heat of lust.

On the long ride, Josh had found himself obsessed with the matter, examining it from every angle, thinking over their night together and reliving her every soft word. Fool that he was, he longed for an intimacy of the heart as well as the body. But he feared he was too scarred to return her love.

Besides, she probably wouldn't even speak to him now.

His barbed remarks had been for her own good, he reminded himself. Without the vow he'd wrested from her, Anne would have found a way to endanger herself. She didn't realize the darkness that could lurk in a man's soul. But he knew. He knew how easily that darkness could engulf her, drag her down into a black pit of despair. He himself posed a threat with his poisonous memories.

And so did Samuel Firth.

Josh hurried Plato toward the stables at the rear of the property. Again, he glanced at the house. Even if Anne had forsaken him, surely someone would have responded to the sound of hoofbeats. Anne's parents. The Rosebuds. In particular, his grandmother.

But the place looked shadowed, uninhabited. With the rapid approach of evening, there should be candles lit. He should see people moving around inside the chambers. He should smell the scent of dinner cooking instead of the manure of the stable yard.

As he came around the side of the house, a sight struck him hard as a fist. A man led Anne's horse out of the stables. The tall, arrogant form of Samuel Firth.

Scorched by a combustible mix of fear and fury, Josh rode swiftly forward. He swung down from Plato. In the same instant, he drew his pistol from the saddlebags, caught Firth by the throat, and shoved the barrel into his throat. "What the hell are you doing here?"

With cold calculation, Firth regarded him. "Your fiancée invited me."

Josh's finger tensed around the trigger. Hot rage encroached on his sanity. "You're stealing her mare. What have you done to Anne?"

"Nothing. But she's gone from here, and you're wasting time."

"Gone where?"

"Let me go and I'll tell you."

Josh tightened his grip, fighting the urge to choke Firth. With supreme effort, he shoved him backward. Firth staggered a step, caught himself, and glowered at Josh.

"Talk," Josh snapped. "Or I'll kill you."

Just then, the back door of the house slammed, and Peg's voice called out, "M'lord! I've a message for ye."

He turned to see the stout woman trotting across the yard. Huffing and puffing, she gripped both sides of her skirt. When she spied his pistol, her usually placid features screwed up in alarm, and she let out a squeal.

"Give me the message," Josh said testily.

"Harry told me . . ."—she gulped, bringing her eyes from the gun back to his face—"he told me t' tell ye that he took Anne an' her ladyship over t' Greystone, an' he'd keep 'em both safe."

"That's what I've been trying to tell you, man," Firth said. "Timberlake came here not an hour ago. His housekeeper had had an accident. Anne and your grandmother went to Greystone in my coach."

"That'll be all," Josh told Peg, and watched until she'd trotted out of earshot. Then he pivoted toward Firth. "You were going after them. Why?"

Firth narrowed his eyes. "It's a feeling I had, something I couldn't shake. Timberlake was more nervous than distraught. There's something odd going on in that house . . ."

"Odd?"

"A fortnight ago, I called on Timberlake in regard to his debt. Mrs. Oswald burst in on us. She was frantic, told him to come quickly. He looked every bit as panicky as he looked today."

"What was the matter?"

"I don't know. I could only deduce it had something to do with his son. Timberlake never returned, and I finally left."

Firth had to be lying to deflect attention from himself. What possible purpose could induce Timberlake to shoot Anne at the duel? Or to pay three oafs to attack them in the stables?

And if Josh was wrong?

He battled an onslaught of misgivings by using the sword of Firth's guilt. "More likely, you're looking for a chance to abduct Anne. Or to harm my grandmother."

"You're wrong—"

"Don't deny it. I spoke with Hannah Davenport in London."

Firth fell silent. A flicker of emotion crossed his features, and he stared as if trying to gauge how much Josh knew.

"We'll talk when I return," Josh said. "And by God, if you leave here, I'll hunt you down like the dog you are."

He swung into the saddle. As a precaution, he brought Plato beside Miss Emmie, snatched the reins, and led her to the edge of the yard, where he swatted her rump. The mare took off running down the lane. By the time she found her way back to the stables, it would be too late for Firth to interfere.

Josh wouldn't rest easy until he held Anne safely in his arms again. Focusing his mind on her, he spurred Plato down the road toward Greystone Manor.

"You two will have to wait down here," Lord Timberlake told Lady Stokeford and Harrington. "We can't have so many people crowding Oswald's room."

His tremulous voice echoed in the vastness of the entrance hall. Through the shadows of evening, the delicate white chairs and pleasant landscape paintings took on a spectral aspect. The grand staircase appeared to float in a ghostly curve toward the upper floors.

Anne concealed a shiver. "There's only four of us. And Harrington can wait outside the chamber."

"I quite agree," Lady Stokeford said. "You'll need help caring for the woman."

"I know a mite o' doctorin'," Harrington added. "I'll 'ave a look at 'er injuries."

But Lord Timberlake emphatically shook his head. "My physician is probably already upstairs. And Oswald dislikes strangers. I won't have her upset when she's already in considerable pain."

His pacing illuminated his agitation, and Anne's heart went out to him. She touched Lady Stokeford's arm. "I'll be fine, truly I will. There's no danger here."

A furrow marked the dowager's finely wrinkled brow. They shared a look that said they both knew Firth was the guilty party. Then Lady Stokeford gave a brief nod. "All right, then. You're to call if you need help. In the meantime, perhaps I'll find a servant to bring me a cup of tea."

"In the kitchen," Timberlake said, making a vague motion toward the rear of the house. "Miss Neville, we really must hurry. I'm terribly worried."

He gripped the newel post and started up the stairs. As Anne followed him, Harrington took up sentry duty near the front door and Lady Stokeford went to stand in the doorway to the drawing room.

Timberlake glanced down at them almost furtively. "Thank God you came with me," he muttered. "Don't know what I'd've done if you'd refused. It's the only way . . ."

"The only way?"

He blinked owlishly through the shadows. "Er . . . the only way to get to Oswald's chamber quickly is through here." At the top of the stairs, he touched the paneling along the passageway, and a cleverly concealed door swung out to reveal a staircase for the servants.

In the narrow shaft, only a feeble light came from a skylight far above them. Timberlake hastened up the wooden risers, his footsteps quick and sharp. She kept close at his heels. He was climbing so fast that she developed a stitch in her side. "How did Mrs. Oswald reach the servants' floor if she was injured?"

"David carried her," Timberlake said, his voice sounding hollow. "He insisted on staying at her side. Oswald's been with us since David was a young lad. Don't know what he'll do if . . ." His voice broke as if it were too painful to go on.

He took a flask out of his pocket, uncorked the top, and tilted his head back for a drink. His hand shook, and a few drops dribbled down his chin, but he didn't appear to notice.

Compassion filled Anne. He wasn't Edwin, drinking himself into a stupor out of sheer weakness. Lord Timberlake had suffered the loss of his daughter, reprehensible though Lily had been. How difficult it must be for him now to face the injury of a beloved servant.

"How badly is Mrs. Oswald hurt?"

"What? Oh. Hit her head, broke her arm, I think. I'm not entirely certain—" He fumbled with the cork, and it bounced down the stairs and vanished into the shadows.

But Timberlake didn't even pause. He proceeded quickly up the stairs to the top floor.

The door opened into a narrow corridor that stretched out in either direction. The baron glanced up and down, then grabbed her wrist and hauled her down the left path. "Make haste, Miss Neville. We're almost there."

His fingers were cold and clammy. His jumpy manner struck her as excessive. Of course, the master of the house would feel out of his element up here in the servants' quarters. And he was quite touchingly worried about his housekeeper.

Closed doors lined the passageway. At the far end, Timberlake halted in front of the last one. He shoved the uncorked flask into his pocket and pulled out a key. Metal rattled against metal as he attempted to open the door.

Her sense of unease grew. "I don't understand. Why is her sickroom locked?"

"Oswald likes it that way," he muttered. "She's a peculiar old bird. Come in now, there's a good girl."

He turned the handle and opened the door. It was a stout oak panel, she noticed distractedly. Like a beacon, soft golden light spilled out into the passageway. Anne craned her neck to peer past him and regarded the large, finely decorated chamber in surprise.

Masses of candles flickered on tables and the mantelpiece. Pots of roses filled the air with a heavenly scent. She could just see the end posts of a large bed that was draped in blue velvet hangings.

Lord Timberlake had spared no expense to keep Mrs. Oswald in comfort. Why? Was the sour-mouthed housekeeper his paramour? That would certainly explain his anxiety over her accident.

Anne told herself not to speculate. Her purpose was to give succor to the poor woman. Resolutely, she followed him into the chamber.

Josh didn't bother to knock.

Gripping his pistol, he strode into Greystone Manor and let the massive front door bang shut. It took a moment for his eyes to adjust to the dim light of the entrance hall. Then the scuffle of footsteps pulled his attention to the drawing room, where his grandmother emerged with Harry right behind her.

"Joshua!" she exclaimed, rushing toward him. "Thank heavens, you're back."

"There be plenty t' tell ye, Cap'n," Harry said.

Josh had only one interest. "Where's Anne?"

"Upstairs with Mrs. Oswald," Lady Stokeford said. "I don't know how long she'll be—"

"Where upstairs?" Reminding himself that his grandmother knew nothing of the attacks, he made an effort to conceal his growing disquiet.

"The servants' floor, I believe. Timberlake escorted her there."

"How long ago was that?"

"Half an hour, perhaps less." Grandmama looked at him keenly. "She's safe, I assure you. Today, we found disturbing evidence to implicate that moneylender."

Josh's mouth went dry. How the devil had she found out—?

But she couldn't know the truth about Firth. It was impossible. "What are you talking about?"

"It's no use to pretend," Lady Stokeford said sternly. "Anne told me everything. The aborted duel. Your search for the gunman. The attack in the stables. To safeguard you, we devised a plan to entrap the villain."

"To safeguard *me*." Josh hissed out a breath. He didn't know whether to be more furious at Anne or at his grandmother.

"Today, she invited the men, one by one, to the house," Lady Stokeford went on. Her voice shaking with indignation, she added, "Mr. Firth attempted to kidnap her. Harrington and I stopped him, of course."

Josh clenched his teeth around a curse. Damn Firth! He wanted to head straight back and kill that treacherous liar. But his need to find Anne overrode even his anger. Though he doubted every word Firth spoke, Josh couldn't forget that description of Timberlake's nervousness. He couldn't rest until he held Anne tight against him.

And then he'd give her a lecture she'd never forget.

"Wait here," he said abruptly. "I'm going to see Anne."

Grandmama placed her frail hand on his arm; her fingers felt remarkably strong. "Timberlake said his housekeeper doesn't want strangers in her sickroom."

"To hell with Timberlake."

Shaking off her hold, he surged up the staircase, taking the steps two at a time.

"They went through the door in the paneling at the head of the stairs," his grandmother called out, her voice ringing in the vast hall. "A servants' staircase, I expect."

She sounded almost amused, as if he were driven only by his eagerness for his beloved's company. Let her think that. He couldn't give voice to the foreboding that gnawed at him. Nor could he shed his gut instinct that Anne was in danger.

Running his fingers over the paneling, he found the tiny latch and opened the door. He could barely see through the gloom. As he raced up the wooden stairs, he brooded on Timberlake, seeking a reason why he would harm Anne.

Lily. It all came back to her. To avenge his sister's death, David Pankhurst had challenged Josh to the duel, his anger possibly fueled by his father. But Anne had dosed Pankhurst with laudanum. And if Timberlake had wanted to ensure Josh's demise, he might have donned a cloak and lain in wait. When he'd missed and struck Anne instead, Timberlake had run away like a coward. Only to try again in the stables.

Now, the wretch must have discovered that Anne was Josh's weak point.

The plausible scenario made his blood turn to ice. Until today, he'd never even considered the older man. Timberlake had appeared to be too dispirited, too feeble and drunken to pose a threat. But on the day that Josh and Anne had questioned him, he had made his resentment over Lily's death plain enough.

It was a terrible blunder to underestimate a man, Josh knew. Even a weak enemy could rally and deal a death blow. And if Anne came to harm, he would never forgive himself. He might slide into that black pit forever.

He reached the top of the stairs and found himself in a narrow corridor of the attic. Closed doors stood in both directions. Gun in hand, he stood unmoving, listening for a sound to betray Anne's whereabouts. He heard nothing but the thunder of his own heartbeat.

Turning to the right, he quietly tried doorknobs. Most of the rooms were outfitted for servants with narrow beds, a washstand, and little else. But the simple furnishings bore a coating of dust. He brushed away a sticky cobweb that dangled from a doorway. The musty scent of disuse pervaded the quiet air.

Where did Timberlake house his staff? In the cellars?

That meant his housekeeper's room wasn't here in the attic. He had no reason to bring Anne up to this floor. Unless he intended her harm.

As he continued to search, Josh tortured himself. Perhaps they weren't here at all. Timberlake could have overpowered Anne. He could have taken her anywhere in this vast house. Every moment was of the essence.

With swift urgency, he completed his inspection of the right half of the corridor and turned his attention to the left. He found more of the same, rooms that had been unoccupied for a long while. Then, as he neared the end, he noticed a pale sliver of light leaking out from beneath a door.

He made haste to examine it. A thick oak panel, built unusually strong. He crouched to peer through the keyhole.

On the wall directly opposite, the mantelpiece held groups of flickering candles. In the center stood a huge vase of hothouse roses tied with a white ribbon. He could see little else. But the indistinct murmur of voices drifted to him.

Anne was here, he knew on a surge of furious hope. She had to be.

Galvanized, he stood up and stealthily tested the handle. It gave way, the door opening under a push of his hand. Going inside, he took a swift look to get his bearings.

It was a large, oblong chamber with a high sloped ceiling. The furnishings were straight out of a French château, white with gilt trim and too dainty for a man. Several fine carpets scattered the polished wood floor. And everywhere, more candles and flowers, the scent sickening him.

His pistol ready, he pushed the door shut without latching it. There was another doorway at the far end of the room. As he started toward it, he noticed someone lying beneath the covers in bed. A woman with a beak nose, graying hair, and closed eyes.

Mrs. Oswald.

Keeping close watch on the doorway, he made his way to the bed. He knew without feeling her pulse that she was dead. By her cold, waxen skin and rigid muscles, she had died many hours ago.

Long before Timberlake had come to fetch Anne.

A black rage honed Josh's senses. The primal urge to kill banished his scruples. Curving his forefinger around the trigger, he started toward the next room. And froze.

A woman stepped into the doorway. A gown of pale blue satin draped her slender form, and a circlet of rosebuds crowned her black hair. Petite and delicate in her bridal raiment, she stood gazing at him as if in wonder.

Stupefied, he stared at the face of a ghost: dainty nose, high cheekbones, pouty lips. Blue eyes that flashed with excitement . . . and madness.

She stretched out her arms and laughed, the sound a sweet chime that resonated from the shadows of his memory. "My darling Joshua," Lily said. "I knew you would come to our wedding."

Chapter Twenty-seven

A Dance with Death

Anne heard Joshua's voice in the next room. From where she sat, bound and gagged, against a wardrobe in the spacious dressing room, she couldn't see Joshua—or Lily.

Her flash of joy was drowned by dread. He didn't know about Lily's knife. But Anne had seen Lily slip the blade into her long, white glove.

Lily Pankhurst . . . alive. Anne could scarcely believe it.

Tugging in vain at her bonds, she fought off the miasma of a nightmare. David's sister possessed a cunning cleverness and a wiry strength that defied her aura of fragility. With Timberlake's aid, she had overpowered Anne from behind, binding her wrists behind her back.

A wood chip struck Anne's cheek, and she flinched involuntarily. Standing beside her, Lord Timberlake dug feverishly with a penknife at the lock on the wardrobe. Lily had given laudanum to David, then locked him inside the massive cabinet. She had threatened to kill her brother if her father didn't cooperate.

Shivering, Anne eyed the flintlock musket that lay on the floor beyond Timberlake. With an eerie chill, she realized that it must be the gun Lily had used the morning of the duel. Anne had to get hold of the weapon. But how?

The knot was so tightly cinched that her fingers were

going numb. Joshua's deep baritone reached her from the bedroom. He sounded shocked, disbelieving.

"Your brother said...you were dead. I saw your grave."

Anne pictured the crypt on a hill overlooking the sea. David and Lord Timberlake had been so determined to hide Lily's madness that they had constructed an empty tomb. Lily wasn't the only mad one.

"They've kept me a prisoner," Lily complained. "They said it was for my own good. But darling, I've waited and waited for you to come back and rescue me."

"You know why I left." His voice changed, grew harder.

"We quarreled," she said in a soft, dulcet tone. "I thought you were flirting with Catherine. But it was *her* fault, not yours. She tried to take you from me."

"So you maimed her."

"It was an accident, I swear it. I was boiling water for tea, and she was standing too close. You must forgive me, darling. It's our wedding day."

"Where is Anne?"

"That tall, ill-favored witch?" Lily said resentfully. "Father is guarding her. He'll shoot her if she tries to beguile you again."

"I want to see her."

As if he hadn't spoken, she said, "Look, I've been working since dawn on the decorations. Isn't it lovely? I sent Oswald down at first light to clip every last rose in the greenhouse."

"And then you killed her," Joshua said in a cold, flat tone.

"No, she fell down the stairs! Oh, perhaps I bumped her, but only because she wouldn't let me go get more flowers. She shouldn't have stood in my way."

Goosebumps skittered over Anne's flesh. That would be Joshua's fate—and hers, too—if she didn't get free.

Her fingers aching, she yanked at the knot with renewed desperation. Joshua could easily overpower Lily, but Anne knew he wouldn't do it. Not until he felt certain of her safety. She tried to scream, but the wad of cloth in her mouth made the sound almost inaudible. Timberlake didn't even look at her.

"Where is Anne?" Joshua repeated. "Is she in the room behind you?"

"Why do you keep asking about her? She tried to kill you in that duel. But I shot her and saved your life."

"Then you struck *me* in the stables."

"That witch frightened my men away. I needed their help in getting you away from her."

"Let me see Anne now."

"No," Lily said, her voice rising with incipient hysteria. "She'll trick you into shooting me. She'll cast a spell on you."

Anne willed him to be more conciliatory, to play along with Lily's scheme. At any moment, the woman could draw her knife . . .

A pause stretched out. Then, as if he had read Anne's urgent thoughts, he said in a milder tone, "I can look at no other woman but you."

"Your word can't be trusted. You went away and left me." Her voice wobbled. "You made me weep. For days and days and weeks and weeks."

"Forgive me," he said with a show of stiff sincerity. "Let me make it up to you. Did you want Anne to witness our wedding? Let me bring her in here."

"Put down the gun first. If it goes off, you'll get blood on your clothes. You'll ruin everything."

Anne prayed he wouldn't obey. Leaning over, she tried to get Timberlake's attention by bumping his leg with her shoulder.

But the baron paid her no heed.

"All right," Joshua said. "I'm setting the pistol right here on the bed. But you must let me see Anne."

No, Anne thought. *Don't put down the gun!*

Lord Timberlake glanced wildly at the doorway. When

they didn't enter, he kept at his work, quietly gouging the wood around the lock. His panting breaths attested to his fear.

"Where is your brother?" Joshua asked, his voice sounding closer. "Is he guarding Anne, too?"

"No, David's a fool. He refused to abduct her. Father only agreed to help me after I locked up David." A note of aggrieved bitterness entered her voice. "No one *understands*. No one realizes that you and I belong together."

"I understand," Joshua said. "Anne can't trick me anymore. Not while you're here." He sounded as if he were reciting lines in a bad play. "But we'd better check on your father. What if she beguiles him and gets away?"

Lily gasped. "You're right. I didn't think of that."

Timberlake dropped the penknife and snatched up the musket, pointing it at Anne. Joshua stepped through the doorway.

His gaze locked with Anne's. Savagery leapt in those dark, inscrutable depths. In the candlelight, he took on the guise of a stranger, his face all hard angles and rigid resolve. He looked ready to kill.

Lily hovered directly behind him. Her exquisite beauty was that of a china doll, with features too perfect to be real.

Anne despised her own helplessness. What a complacent fool she had been. She had thought herself invincible, strong, able to protect herself. Believing Samuel Firth to be the villain, she had let down her guard. In trying to do the right thing, she had put Joshua in danger.

Wretched, she lowered her gaze. Now she might never have the chance to show him how to love again. Then she spied the penknife lying on the blue carpet.

Stung by hope, she wriggled closer, trying to make it look as if she were simply struggling against her bonds. Her fingertips brushed the metal, still warm from Timberlake's hand. But she couldn't quite grasp it.

"There now, you see?" Lily said. "The witch can't get away. She hasn't given you any trouble, Father, has she?"

"N-no." Timberlake's hand trembled visibly, making the musket shake.

Anne forced her gaze away from the small, deadly circle of the barrel pointed straight at her heart. Again, she reached surreptitiously for the penknife, and this time, she managed to pick up the implement. She maneuvered the blade into position against the knot and began to painstakingly saw at the cloth.

"You don't need that gun," Joshua told Timberlake. "She can't run away."

Timberlake glanced at his daughter. "Lily doesn't want to take any chances."

"You must guard her very carefully," Lily said. "She's sly and cunning. She tried to steal Joshua from me, but now he's come back."

"Righto," Timberlake said in a falsely cheerful tone. "Go into the other room now. The Reverend Cummings should be here soon."

"The vicar has agreed to perform this wedding?" Joshua asked on a note of incredulity.

"Not yet." Lily smiled. "But he'll do it so long as David is my prisoner."

Timberlake shuffled his feet. "Hurry along, then. I—er—have matters under control here."

Lily sashayed toward her father. "There's one more arrangement to be made, Father. For the ceremony, Miss Neville must sit beside Oswald."

Anne's stomach lurched. She kept slicing at the stubborn knot, her fingers tingling from the restricted flow of blood. If she could free herself, then she could grab the musket.

Joshua strolled forward, looking benign except for the burning darkness of his eyes. "I'll carry her into the other room."

"No! Stand back!" Lily snatched the musket from Timberlake and aimed the muzzle at Anne.

Joshua froze.

"Father will move her. I told you, she's an evil temptress. I can't trust her not to put a hex on you again."

His face ashen, Timberlake looked from his daughter to Joshua. Then he stooped down to pick up Anne.

In desperation, Anne forced the little blade into the knot, the cloth separating fiber by slow fiber. She glowered at Timberlake in the faint hope of awakening his conscience, but he avoided her gaze.

He slid his arms beneath her. "Come, Miss Neville. There's a good girl. If we cooperate, David will live. We'll all be fine—"

Lily let out a screech. "Father! What have you done?"

Timberlake looked over his shoulder, and his grip slackened. Lily was staring at the damaged wood on the wardrobe, where he had been digging around the lock.

While she was distracted, Joshua lunged. He seized the musket and thrust the barrel toward the ceiling. A shot exploded, setting off a rain of plaster.

The penknife slipped from Anne's nerveless fingers. Inhaling the choking dust, she strained against the half-severed knot. In one final wrench, the binding gave way, and Anne scrambled to her feet.

Timberlake cowered in paralyzed shock as Joshua grappled with Lily. The small woman fought like an enraged tigress, kicking and scratching and biting.

Anne stripped off the gag as she raced into the bedchamber. Snatching up Joshua's heavy pistol, she dashed back to the dressing room.

In those few seconds, Joshua had managed to flip Lily around, imprisoning her back to his front and rendering her teeth and nails harmless. Kicking and thrashing, she extracted the knife from inside her long white glove. The candlelight gleamed on the sharp metal blade.

"Joshua, watch out!" Anne screamed.

He saw the knife too late. In a flash, Lily swept her arm up and back, and the knife sliced into his shoulder. He cursed as blood welled down his sleeve.

Lily jerked around to face him, the blade upraised.

In that same instant, Timberlake charged from his crouch on the floor. He grabbed his daughter around the legs and pulled her off her feet.

Lily tumbled to the floor. Instantly, she scrambled to her knees. Her features twisted into a grotesque snarl, she turned on her father and brandished the bloodied knife. Without thought, Anne took aim and fired. The bullet struck Lily, sent her staggering backward. A red patch appeared on her bosom, spreading over the pale blue fabric in an ever-widening circle. But madness had her in its grasp. In a final burst of frenzied force, she plunged the blade into her father's chest and collapsed beside him, her eyes open and staring.

The pistol slipped from Anne's nerveless fingers. She darted to Joshua, who leaned against the wall. He yanked off his cravat and stuffed it inside his coat, pressing it against the wound. His face was pale, his lips thinned with pain.

She slid her arm around his waist. Shuddering, she realized how easily he might have been killed. "How badly are you hurt?"

"Never mind me."

He brushed past her and dropped to his knees beside Timberlake.

Anne went after him. Sickened, she averted her eyes from Lily's sprawled form. "Lie down, Joshua. I want to look at your wound."

"Later. Hold this compress in place while I check Timberlake."

She flattened her palm against the pad at his shoulder. "Is he . . . ?"

"He's dead," Joshua said in a low tone. "The blade must have pierced his heart." Then he turned to Lily and closed her eyes.

Gazing at that pale face, exquisite in death, Anne trembled and her teeth chattered. She swallowed the sourness in her throat. "I took her life," she whispered. "I killed her."

Standing up, Joshua pulled her into a tight embrace. His lips met her hair. "Don't grieve. You had no choice. She would have come after you next."

"But I should have wounded her. I should have winged her. Why didn't I?"

"You had the courage to do what needed to be done, Anne. That's all you could do."

For once, his authoritativeness brought a measure of comfort to Anne. The heat of his body warmed the cold place inside her, and she breathed a shivery prayer of thanks that she hadn't lost him. Anxiously, she tilted her head back. "Your shoulder needs tending."

"I'll survive." Dark and deep, his eyes drank her in. "Anne, when I knew you were in danger, I—"

The clamor of voices intruded on whatever he'd intended to say. The outer door banged open. Anne recognized Lady Stokeford's commanding tone.

"Don't come in," Joshua called out.

Grandmama didn't obey. She stopped in the doorway, her blue eyes wide with alarm as she looked at the bodies lying on the floor.

Three other faces appeared behind her. Harrington, his grizzled features thunderstruck. The Reverend Cummings, clutching a prayerbook to his chest. And Samuel Firth, his hair wind-tossed and his expression grim.

"What on earth!" Grandmama exclaimed. "Joshua, are you all right?"

"I'm fine."

"He's injured," Anne amended. "Lily stabbed him in the shoulder."

"Lily? Lily Pankhurst? Dear heavens!"

Lady Stokeford tried to walk forward, stumbled, and Samuel Firth caught her by the waist. He looked stiff and uncomfortable as he led her toward a fringed stool. "Sit down before you swoon."

Flashing him a glower, she refused his assistance. "I've

never swooned in my life, thank you. I must see to my grandson."

Firth grimaced and let her go. Joshua met her halfway, his hard gaze trained on Firth. "There's nothing more to be done up here. We'll go downstairs and wait for the magistrate."

"But where's David?" the Reverend Cummings asked in a quavering voice. "Has he been hurt?"

Anne gasped. "Lily locked him in the wardrobe. She put the key . . . inside her glove." Her flesh crawled at the notion of retrieving it.

"I'll fetch it," Firth said.

In short order, he had the wardrobe opened and lifted out David's limp form. David snored in deep slumber, and Anne couldn't help but note the irony that she too, had given him laudanum on the night before the duel. Never had she imagined that Lily Pankhurst was alive, watching and listening.

Firth carried David downstairs to a chaise in the darkened drawing room. The vicar drew up a chair and waited for him to awaken. The rest of the party moved to a grouping of chairs at the other end of the chamber. Grandmama, Harrington, and Anne had brought candles down from the attic, and the wavering light played over the elegant French furnishings.

Samuel Firth stayed in the shadows. Anne wondered that he didn't leave while he had the chance. Joshua would be furious when he found out about the abduction attempt. But Firth wasn't the villain they had sought.

It had been Lily Pankhurst who'd escaped the morning of the duel. Lily Pankhurst who had dropped that calling card—to lead Harrington astray. Lily Pankhurst who had hired two men and had hidden in the stables.

Still struggling to absorb the shock, Anne took hold of Joshua's uninjured arm. So many feelings crowded her heart, but first and foremost, she had to assure herself of his health and comfort. "Sit down," she said. "I'll have a look at you now."

He lowered himself to a chair near the fireplace. "Harry will do the honors. You and Grandmama can wait in the next room."

"No. I won't leave you. Take off your coat, please."

"And don't be as stubborn as a two-year-old," Grandmama added.

"Ye've got no choice, Cap'n," Harrington said with a broad wink. "When a woman's got that look in 'er eye, ye'd best swallow yer pride an' obey."

Chapter Twenty-eight

Firth Revealed

Josh knew when he was outnumbered. Swearing under his breath, he allowed Anne to help him ease out of his coat. His arm burned like hellfire. "I warn you," he said grimly, "it won't be a pretty sight. You'll faint."

"We'll see about that."

Anne pulled the torn edges of his sleeve, and the linen ripped readily. Examining the wound, she pressed her teeth into her lower lip. From his shoulder halfway down his upper arm, the deep cut oozed blood. But if the sight made her ill, she didn't show it.

"I'll need towels and water, along with a needle and thread," she told Harrington. "And enough cloth to bind the wound and fashion a sling."

Harrington saluted her. "Aye, Miss Cap'n."

Traitor, Josh thought darkly.

"I'll find the sewing supplies," Lady Stokeford said. Taking a candle, she and Harrington disappeared into the corridor.

Firth, of course, didn't offer to help. He watched from the shadows, his arms folded and his gaze cold. Anger roiled inside Josh, but he forced himself to wait. When they had their confrontation, he wanted Grandmama present.

Anne distracted him with a touch to his cheek. "You're

looking rather pale," she said. "You ought to lie down."

"Stop fussing. I'm fine."

"I'll fuss as much as I please," she retorted, holding the compress in place to slow the bleeding.

He clamped his teeth together. The pain made him snappish. So did the fact that she had witnessed his stupidity in failing to dodge that knife. He wasn't angry at her, but at himself for failing to protect her. For a few horrifying moments upstairs, before Lily had allowed him into the dressing room, he had descended into the depths of fear.

The fear that Anne was dead. The fear that he was too late to help her. Now, even in agony, he wanted to kiss her, to hold her close and rejoice that she was safe.

Out of the corner of his eye, he noticed Samuel Firth pacing toward the door. Josh shot to his feet. "Where are you going?"

"To get some salt to rub into your wound."

"Very amusing," Josh mocked. "Don't leave this room. I'm not through with you."

"And I'm not through with *you*," Anne said, taking hold of his good shoulder and thrusting him back down into the chair.

"Believe me," Firth said, "I wouldn't miss this show for all the gold in Barclay's Bank." He went to a cabinet, removed the stopper from a decanter, and filled two glasses. Over his shoulder, he spoke to Anne. "You *are* going to sew him up yourself, aren't you, Miss Neville?"

"Of course—"

"Harry will do it," Josh interrupted. "He's had experience."

"So have I," she said. "Geoffrey fell out of the tree house once, and I had to stitch the gash in his forehead. Then there's Isaac, who sat on a rake and cut open his thigh. And Emmett sliced his foot on a piece of glass. Their scars are barely visible."

"*I* don't doubt you're good," Firth said as he walked

toward them. "Brandy, Miss Neville?" Taking a sip from one glass, he offered the other to her.

"No, thank you," she said primly. "Give it to Joshua. He'll need it."

"I'm fine," Josh said through gritted teeth. "And keep your distance from Anne."

"I'll leave it here," Firth said, placing the glass on a nearby table. "Just in case you stop playing the hero."

Josh wasn't fooled by that show of benevolence. Firth was goading him. He knew how much Josh craved that brandy. How much he needed it to dull the throbbing in his arm. And how much it galled him to accept anything from Firth.

Harry trotted in with a bowl of water and an armload of towels. Grandmama brought a whole basket of sewing supplies, which she deposited near Anne.

"Planning to embroider flowers on me?" Josh asked.

"If you're making sarcastic jests," Lady Stokeford said, "you can't be feeling too poorly."

"Just be careful not to provoke *me*," Anne warned him. "I'll be the one wielding the needle."

For all her warning, her touch was gentle as she cleaned the cut. It burned like hell, and he set his jaw. To keep from coveting that glass of brandy, he focused his gaze on her bosom, her throat, her lips. She leaned closer, filling him with the clean scent of woman. Then a flash of pain made him wince.

Her hands paused a moment. Her gaze met his. "You really should have that brandy."

"No."

"Suit yourself."

As Anne threaded the needle, Harrington left to fetch the magistrate.

Grandmama sat down near Josh. Her brows drew together in a troubled frown. "I confess, I'm baffled by all that's happened. Why on earth did Timberlake lead us all to believe that Lily was dead?"

"She went mad," Josh said tersely. "He and Pankhurst kept her locked in the attic all these years."

"And lest you think Joshua drove her out of her mind," Anne said, "Lily had shown signs of melancholy long before he met her. Her companion, Catherine Loftus, told Joshua the truth on the day before the wedding."

Thunderstruck, Josh twisted on the chair to scowl at Anne. "How do you know that?"

"I'm ready to start, so sit still," Anne warned. "If I take a bad stitch, I'll have to tear it out."

He obeyed—and gripped the arms of the chair at the first sting of the needle. To occupy his mind, he growled, "Tell me."

Her breath wafted lightly over his skin. "Mrs. Loftus came to see me this morning. She'd heard you were courting me and didn't want me to be put off by your tarnished reputation."

He hissed out air, both at her disclosure and at the pain.

"Ah," Lady Stokeford said, watching the proceedings with stoically thinned lips. "She was the woman in the dog-cart."

Anne paused to look at his grandmother. "I'm sorry, Grandmama. I do hope you'll forgive me for not telling you earlier."

"Of course, you had far too much on your mind at the time. But I should like to hear the story now."

As she stitched—with light, neat strokes that hurt less than Harry's rough sutures had in the past—Anne proceeded to relate the story of Catherine's burns. "Joshua took Mrs. Loftus away and tended to her. He also provided her with a cottage and a small annuity. And he abided by her desire to keep the matter quiet."

In a haze of pain, Josh wished he could read Anne's reaction. Did she understand why he couldn't tell her? Did she admire him? He had fallen hard for her, he had to admit. He had never cared so much what a woman thought of him.

Grandmama cleared her throat. "Though I'm outraged that Timberlake would sacrifice your reputation, it's a relief to learn the truth at last. I've known all along that you couldn't have been at fault, Joshua. I didn't raise you to be a cad."

"You raised him to be a damned saint," Firth said from the shadows.

Fury sliced into Josh. "Why don't you tell Grandmama about *your* upbringing? She'll be interested to hear about it."

"Nothing about him interests me," Grandmama said, coldly eyeing Firth. "In truth, I'm surprised he's still here. He's a coward who preys upon women."

Firth drained his glass of brandy and set it on a table. Then he took a step toward her. "I'm also your grandson."

Both women gasped. Anne ceased sewing to stare at Firth. Grandmama's posture turned rigid, her nostrils flaring.

Josh regretted the need to shock them. But they had to understand just how great a danger Firth posed in his thirst for vengeance on their family.

"What nonsense," Grandmama said in a thin, high voice. "How dare you suggest—"

"That your son had an affair?" Firth said. He walked closer, his eyes frosty. "Let me tell you how it happened. My mother was an actress, an innocent girl from the country who had the misfortune of meeting George Kenyon, the Marquess of Stokeford. He swept her off her feet with gifts and promises. She knew the wretch was married, but she fancied herself in love with him. When she told him she would bear his child, he walked out on her and never returned."

"This can't be true," Grandmama stated, slowly shaking her head. "I don't believe you."

"My mother wouldn't lie. The marquess left her to raise me alone. She never stopped hoping he would come back.

Even twelve years later, on her deathbed, she spoke of him."

Grandmama held her fist pressed to her bosom. "Have you any proof of this tale?"

"I needn't prove myself to you—"

"I have the proof," Josh interrupted tersely. "Just this morning, I tracked down his old nursemaid in London, a woman by the name of Hannah Davenport. She told me the whole story. His baptism is recorded at St. Martin's Church."

Lady Stokeford stared at Firth. "At least this would explain why you tried to abduct Anne. You wanted revenge by stealing Joshua's bride."

Reminded of that aborted attempt, Josh sprang to his feet again. "I'll thrash you for touching Anne—" A sharp twinge seared his arm. He looked down to see he was still attached by a thread to the bloodstained needle Anne held between her forefinger and thumb. "Let go."

"I most certainly will not," she said tartly. "This is no time for a brawl."

"As always, Miss Neville, you're the voice of wisdom," Firth said. "It was stupid of me to frighten you this afternoon. Please accept my sincerest apologies."

"No, she doesn't accept," Josh said.

"Yes, I do." Anne pushed Josh back into the chair and resumed her sewing with a vengeance. "For heaven's sake, show a little compassion. He's your brother."

He sucked back a groan. "*Half* brother. He might have had a rough life, his mother might have died in poverty, but that's no reason for him to threaten *you*."

"Have some brandy," Firth taunted. "It might soften your ill humor."

"It's *your* ill humor that wants softening," Lady Stokeford said sternly. Rising, she walked to Firth and inspected him from head to toe. "I knew you looked familiar when we met today. And no wonder. You have my son's eyes and mouth."

"Then I curse my eyes and mouth. George Kenyon was a drunken sot and a bloody philanderer."

Lady Stokeford drew back her arm and slapped his face. "I'm well aware of my son's weaknesses," she said. "But that is no excuse for your crude speech."

His hand to his reddened cheek, Firth glowered at her. "I'm a crude man. What else can you expect from the son of a common stage actress?"

"So you would denigrate your mother, too. I suspect she would be ashamed of the man you've become."

A muscle worked in his jaw. In a dangerous undertone, he said, "You know nothing of my mother."

"Quite so. I wasn't given the opportunity. But I *will* know you."

Josh came up out of his chair for the third time. "*What?* You can't associate with him."

Once again, Anne made him sit. "Let your grandmother handle the matter."

Firth loosed a harsh laugh. "Don't fret, Kenyon. She'll never turn me into another adoring grandson."

"I agree, that's quite impossible." Lady Stokeford paced with measured deliberation. "But however loathsome you are, Mr. Firth—*Samuel*—you are also a member of my family. You will attend me at Stokeford Abbey in one month's time."

"You'll see me in hell first, madam."

She went on as if he hadn't spoken. "In addition, your other two half brothers will be arriving in a few days for Joshua's wedding. You'll arrange time in your schedule to meet them."

"I'd sooner make a pact with the devil."

"Apparently, you've already done so. Nevertheless, you'll behave civilly when you're in the company of your brothers—"

"Enough, Grandmama," Josh exploded. In all his zeal to expose Firth, he hadn't imagined that she would welcome him like a lost lamb. "Next, you'll be inviting him to my wedding, and I'll be forced to run him out of the church."

Anne tugged harder than necessary as she tied off the knot. "Don't be rude."

"Of course he'll not be attending the wedding," Grandmama said, her austere gaze on Firth. "He'll have to earn the honor of being accepted at family functions."

"Honor?" Firth jeered. "I don't want your charity or your acceptance."

"You want something from us," Grandmama retorted. "You rode here to warn me that Timberlake was up to no good. You could have left just now and let Joshua break the news. But you didn't."

"I wanted you to see what your son had spawned."

Lady Stokeford arched a silver eyebrow. "I see an angry man in need of a loving family."

Firth stiffened visibly. "Then you're blind, madam. I'm a cold-hearted bastard. I don't believe in love."

Turning on his heel, he strode out of the drawing room. A moment later, the outer door banged shut.

Grandmama wilted into the nearest chair. Tears glossed her blue eyes, and she looked old, almost haggard. "I handled that badly."

"You were magnificent," Anne said, washing her hands in the basin of water. "You were taken by surprise, that's all."

"Yes . . . I'm astonished. I'm still shaking. How could I never have known of his existence? How could George have never told me?"

Josh wondered that, too. He'd always known his father was a weak man, prone to drinking and complaining about Josh's mother, who had spent most of her time at prayer in the chapel. As a boy, he had learned to avoid his parents lest he get pulled into their quarrels. To know now that his father had kept a mistress was an unpleasant revelation. Worse, his father had abandoned his own son.

Josh could allow a certain sympathy for Firth in that. But it wasn't enough to absolve his actions.

"You've suffered a dreadful shock on top of a difficult day," Anne murmured, sounding strained herself. She brought Lady Stokeford the untouched glass of brandy. "Please, drink this. It'll help restore you."

As Grandmama took a sip, Josh gave vent to his antipathy. "Forget about Firth. He went after you once, Anne, and he could do so again. He's not going to forget his desire for revenge so easily."

Anne wheeled on him. "Be silent. Can't you see your grandmother is distraught? You're behaving as badly as Mr. Firth."

Stung, Josh compressed his lips. Dammit, she couldn't think him so ruthless and disreputable. He wasn't anything like Samuel Firth.

His half brother.

A black thought struck him. Upon their marriage, Anne would become sister-in-law to the scoundrel who had tried to abduct her. If Grandmama had her way, Anne would encounter Firth time and again.

Josh watched morosely as she comforted his grandmother. Anne had less incentive than ever to want him as her husband. He had accused her of entrapping him when, in fact, he was the one who had compelled her into the marriage. Overriding her objections, he had settled the matter with her father and treated her with cold disdain, as if she deserved no voice in her own future. Now, he had soured her toward him all the more, and he didn't know how to win her heart.

But he did know that he could never let her go.

Chapter Twenty-nine

Wakebridge Hall

On a beautiful day in early October, Anne became Joshua's wife. She wore a pale blue gown and the heirloom diamond pendant. She walked up the aisle on her father's arm without knowing if Joshua still resented her, without knowing if he could ever set aside his bitterness and love her.

The five days since his injury had been hectic. Her brothers had come in from out of town, Cyril from London, and Abelard and his brood of five from York. Then Joshua's brothers had arrived with their families, and the house rang with the laughter of children. Michael and Vivien had three youngsters under the age of ten, while Gabriel and Kate had one, with another on the way.

In all the excitement, Anne hadn't had a moment alone with Joshua. He had avoided her company, befriending the children and catching up on news with his brothers. But at odd moments, she'd caught him staring at her with a brooding intensity that stirred an unmistakable desire in her. He wanted her, and for now, that thought sustained her.

After the ceremony and the ensuing breakfast, the entire family gathered in the front yard to say goodbye to the newlyweds. They would ride to Wakebridge Hall, Joshua's estate in Hampshire. As much as Anne loved her family, she felt a deep yearning to be alone with Joshua.

Her husband.

Mindful of his injury, she stood on the other side of him. He wore his cavalry uniform, the buttons gleaming in the sunlight. The sling added a certain flare to his dashing good looks. Gathered together, he and his brothers all possessed that virile, dark-haired handsomeness.

"Perhaps we should travel with you," Michael suggested with a sly grin. "Wakebridge Hall is on our way home. We'll make a party of it."

"A fortnight would be good," Gabriel concurred. "How about it, Josh? Surely you and your bride won't be too busy to entertain a houseful of guests."

Joshua gave his brothers a grim look. "If either of you shows up on my doorstep anytime in the next month, I'll send you on your way with a swift kick."

The men shared a ribald chuckle. Anne blushed as they glanced at her. At the same time, she felt a curl of anticipation, the longing to find accord in the marriage bed. She intended to do everything in her power to convince Joshua to love her.

Then it was time to depart. Time to hug her parents and her brothers and take one last look at the rambling old house where she had grown up. Where she had become a woman on a rainswept night of passion.

"It's only five hours to your new home," Mama said, smiling as she wiped her tears, and then Anne's. "We'll see one another often."

"Lucy has invited all of us to Stokeford Abbey for Christmas," Papa said. "The boys, too." He shook hands with Joshua, then caught Anne in a tight embrace.

A lump in her throat, she mounted Miss Emmie. Anne had disdained a carriage, preferring to ride beside Joshua. Her boxes and trunks had been sent ahead with Harry and Peg, who had shocked everyone by announcing their own impending nuptials. Amid a refrain of goodbyes, Anne and Joshua set off at a brisk pace toward the west.

It was a glorious day, the sky a sharp, clear blue. The

foliage was beginning to show the colors of autumn. Alongside the dirt road grew the scarlet berries of the guelder rose and the black fruit of wild privet and elderberry. Flocks of migrating birds gathered in the marshes and meadows, geese and jays and thrushes.

Even more glorious, Anne was alone with Joshua. She drew the mare closer to him and asked, "How was the meeting with Samuel Firth yesterday? What did Michael and Gabriel think of him?"

Joshua shrugged. "They're wary, of course. Firth doesn't exactly endear himself. It was tense for a while."

"You three were gone for hours. What did you talk about all that time?"

"Business, mostly. It seems moneylending is only a small part of Firth's interests. I'll admit, he's made some impressive investments overseas, everything from gold mining to sugarcane plantations."

"Then you'll make peace with him?"

Joshua grimaced. "He tried to abduct you. I can't forget that."

Anne leaned toward him. "But you must forgive him, Joshua. It isn't wise to let such a matter fester inside you. It'll make you bitter and unhappy."

He sent her a long, penetrating look. Then he nodded. "If it pleases you, I'll get along with him."

If it pleases you. Would he overcome his intolerance simply because she had asked it of him? Surely that meant he harbored tender emotions for her. Anne felt a giddy surge of hope that bordered on euphoria. She would win his love. She would make him happy . . . if only he would allow her.

He shifted the conversation to mundane matters, entertaining her with stories about Michael and Gabriel. In turn, she talked of her own brothers and their many escapades. He also described Wakebridge Hall in terms so glowing that she could picture the large Tudor house and the rolling hills of the countryside. It was clear that he loved the estate.

But Joshua never spoke of love for *her*.

She wouldn't let herself feel disappointed, not on her wedding day. Fondness would grow in time, she assured herself. He had agreed to wed her out of honor and duty. And tonight, she would make him glad of their forced marriage. As selfishly glad as she herself felt.

Josh had always fancied himself a patient man. Even in the heat of battle, he had acted with cool deliberation. Impetuous conduct could cost a man his life.

But on his wedding night, he couldn't wait a decent interval for Anne to ready herself. He had abided by her request to have a dinner tray in her chamber. He had ordered hot water sent up for her bath. He had arranged for a maid to assist her at her ablutions.

But after spending half an hour pacing his chamber, he could tarry no longer. He had to settle the churning emotions inside him. Foremost of which was . . . uncertainty. Could he ever win her heart?

There was only one way to find out.

He quietly opened the connecting door, entered his wife's dressing room, and found Anne at her bath. Transfixed, he stared past the screen that partially shielded her from his view. He could see enough to set his imagination on fire.

Ensconced in the brass tub before the hearth, she lifted her arm and ran a soapy cloth over her creamy skin. Droplets coursed down her naked limbs, and water lapped at the undersides of her breasts. The candlelight glowed over her upswept hair and graceful curves, glinting on the gold chain of her diamond pendant. How had he ever thought her prim? She was a nymph, too beautiful to be real. And she belonged to him—in body if not in heart.

Beyond the screen, Eliza, an elderly maidservant, waited with a towel. He put his finger to his lips and walked barefoot across the rug to take the towel. He motioned his head toward the door. Beaming, Eliza tiptoed out, closing the door.

Josh forced himself to stand behind the screen. He could hear Anne humming as she rinsed herself. He'd never known the sound of splashing water could be so erotic.

She called out, "May I please have my towel, Eliza?"

Unfurling the thick cloth, he moved around the screen and stood behind her. She stepped out of the tub, her back turned modestly. Josh enveloped her in the towel, bringing his arms around her middle and his mouth temptingly close to the dewy skin at the nape of her neck.

She gave a squeal of surprise, then caught her breath. "Joshua."

To his gratification, she tilted her head back and kissed his jaw. She was soft and warm from her bath, delectably scented. He burned to lay her down on the rug in front of the crackling fire. Anne possessed an earthy sensuality, and he had no doubt she would enjoy his lovemaking. The swift beating of her heart attested to her arousal.

Yet for the first time in his life, he wanted more from a woman than her soft, willing body.

She tried to turn toward him, but he wouldn't let her. He let his fingers drift over the diamond pendant, so close to her breasts. "You forgot to take this off."

She shook her head. "I like it. It was your first gift to me."

"It was Grandmama's gift. I'll give you finer jewels."

"I don't need any other," she said firmly. "This is quite sufficient."

But he resolved to shower her with jewelry anyway. A treasure trove would scarcely be enough to make up for the hell he'd put her through. For the wretched, black moods that were bound to try her patience as his wife.

He led her out of the dressing room and into the bed-chamber. A branch of candles on the bedside table illumi-nated the shabby furnishings, the dark green draperies and heavy mahogany furniture. The place was clean and tidy, and that was all he'd ever required on his infrequent visits here. But now he was chagrined to see the old-fashioned chamber through her eyes.

"The house may not be all you were hoping for," he said. "You may redecorate as you please. We'll visit the shops in London. You can buy whatever strikes your fancy."

She frowned slightly. "I don't want to change anything, do you? It's a perfectly wonderful old house, and I adore it already."

Knowing her penchant for pleasing people, he said sternly, "This is your home, too, and I want you to be happy here."

"I *am* happy," she asserted. "I can't wait to go exploring tomorrow. I especially want to go up in the tower room. The view must be magnificent."

He dragged his gaze from the glimpse of her breasts through the folds of the towel. "Magnificent," he agreed, his throat dry. The tower room had a chaise where they could make love. If he had his way, they'd christen every one of the forty-some rooms.

He maneuvered her across the threadbare rug, and she stopped beside the massive bedpost. Gripping the towel like a shield around her, she studied him from beneath her lashes. "Joshua, I must know. Are you still angry at me?"

"Angry?"

"For seducing you. For trapping you in this marriage."

He winced to hear his brutal words on her lips. By way of amends, he kissed her with restrained fervor, not permitting himself to move his hands from her shoulders, not allowing himself to press his body to hers. Dragging his mouth away, he said huskily, "I hope that answers your question."

A wicked smile curved her lips. Then she released her hold on the towel and let it drop to the floor. "I hope this answers your dreams."

She stood before him in proud, naked glory. The candleglow gilded her, the full breasts, slender waist, womanly hips. Reaching up, she drew the pins from her hair and shook her head so that her long locks came tumbling down like a veil.

Heat seared his loins. His muscles trembled. Anne was his wife. Totally, completely his.

Or was she?

"Lie down. On your belly." He could barely get the words out.

"Why?" she asked impertinently, even as she sat down on the edge of the mattress. "What will you do to me, m'lord?"

"I'll massage your muscles," he said, taking a small jar from his pocket. "You must be sore from five hours in the saddle."

Anne glided onto the sheets, giving him an enticing view that tested his resolve. "That sounds . . . interesting. But doesn't your arm hurt?"

"I can't complain." That dull ache was nothing compared to the agony in his loins. "Do as I say now. Remember, you vowed obedience to me today."

"I had my fingers crossed beneath my bouquet." But she rolled onto her stomach and nestled her head on the feather pillow.

From his vantage point near her feet, she was a feast for his pleasure. Her form had a supple grace, strong and inherently feminine, his perfect mate. Her long, slender legs led his gaze to the gates of heaven. He took several deep breaths to clear his head.

Then he poured a small amount of oil onto his palms. Using a firm pressure, he kneaded her slim calf. "We have to talk, Anne. There are things I must tell you."

She wriggled in sensual indulgence. "Mmm. Can't it wait until later?"

That sultry tone scored a direct hit on his resolution. Before he could surrender, he said hoarsely, "For many years, I've seen only the ugly side of life. Because of that,

I've let myself become bitter and bad-tempered."

"Oh, really?"

He slapped her lightly on the rump. "Be serious. You should know that I was prepared to die at that duel."

She lifted her startled face toward him. "For heaven's sake, why?"

Josh glanced away, reluctant to speak. But if he craved true intimacy, he had to share his thoughts. "After the war, I was . . . ashamed to be alive when so many men had died. I'd intended to return here to Wakebridge Hall. If I had to live, I wanted to be alone, to hide from the world."

"While I condemned you for being cynical," she whispered. "Joshua, I'm so sorry—"

"Hush. Let me finish." He massaged the tight muscles of her thighs until she sighed and relaxed. "Everything changed when I met you, Anne. You wouldn't let me retreat to my own cave. Even when you believed me a bounder, you wanted to help me."

"There's nothing wrong with helping people."

"I know that now. But I also want you to know there are memories I'll never share with you. Memories that are better left buried. I hope you can accept that."

"I understand," she murmured in a subdued tone. "Truly, Joshua, I do."

His chest wrenched. He knew she was thinking about Lily, and he would have given his own life to have spared Anne that ordeal. He went on doggedly. "I'll be sullen and quick-tempered at times. I'll have nightmares. I won't be an easy man to live with." He smoothed his palms up the lissome curve of her back. "But I pray you'll put up with me because . . ."

Her head tilted watchfully, she prompted, "Because?"

His heart thundered. He had to say it. He had to open a part of himself that had been locked up forever.

No, not forever. Forever was . . . Anne.

"Because I can't live without you," he admitted roughly. "Because that night you came to my bed was the best night of my life. And because I love you with all my heart."

Sitting up, Anne gazed at him with the softness of yearning. "I love you, too, Joshua. So much." She paused, her lips curving upward. "But surely the *best* night of your life is yet to come."

The sensual promise of her smile banished the vestiges of darkness inside him. Chuckling, he reached out and drew her to him. "I did consider sharing that bathtub with you tonight. But I didn't want to behave like a scoundrel."

"Lately, I've discovered a liking for scoundrels," Anne said, opening his robe with deft hands. "And you, darling, will always be my hero."

EPILOGUE

FEBRUARY 1816

Snowflakes swirled outside the frosted windows of Villiers Hall, the family seat of the earls of Faversham. The storm-swept elms were barely visible along the front drive. An icy draft seeped into Lucy, but she scarcely noticed the ache in her old bones. Drawing the blue merino shawl snugly around herself, she enjoyed the cozy feeling of being indoors on such a wintry afternoon.

She also relished the contentment of knowing her grandsons were happily wed—three of them, at least. Alas, Samuel had scorned her efforts at a reconciliation. But she ignored that problem in favor of a more pressing one.

"If the blizzard continues, we'll be snowbound," she said, returning to the fireside where her two best friends sat drinking tea. "I propose we use the time to discuss Charlotte and Brandon."

Morosely, Olivia poured a cup for Lucy. "There's nothing to discuss. My grandson is an incorrigible rake. No woman will ever tame him."

"And I fear Charlotte is far too independent to wed," Enid added, an uncharacteristic gloom on her plump, wrinkled face. "When we sent her to York in disgrace, I never imagined she would decide to stay there for good."

"My dear, you mustn't despair," Lucy said, reaching

over to pat Enid's age-spotted hand. "She and Brandon need a little push, that's all."

Olivia shook her head. "It's too late, Lucy. Remember what my grandson said: 'I wouldn't have her if you stripped her naked and tied her to my bed.' " Her lips forming a prune of disgust, she thumped her cane on the carpet. "He's irredeemable, I can see that now. The succession will have to go to that namby-pamby cousin of his."

"It's never too late," Lucy said. "Remember how Joshua resisted courting Anne? 'Tis a wonder they ever fell in love."

Enid released a wistful sigh. "But Brandon and Charlotte have despised one another since childhood. Perhaps this time, we're facing impossible odds."

"There's no perhaps about it," Olivia said. "Even if we did coax them to the altar, they would murder one another before the wedding day was over."

Wondering if her friends could be right, Lucy wrapped her cold fingers around the warm cup. Brandon and Charlotte *did* have a history of quarreling. And yet . . . there was something Lucy had observed between them, a spark of awareness that might be fanned into love.

"Matchmaking is our specialty. We can't give up without even trying." Seeing skepticism on their faces, Lucy continued. "We'll find a way to lure them back here. Once they're under the same roof, then we can encourage a romance."

Olivia arched a thin, gray eyebrow. "That's easier said than done. My grandson will see through any ploy we devise."

"As will Charlotte, I fear," Enid said.

"Not if we think of something exceedingly *clever*. Come, ladies. We must have faith. There must be *some* way we can bring them together."

While the fire snapped and the snow hissed against the window glass, the three old women ruminated on the dilemma. Sipping her tea, Lucy examined and rejected a dozen possibilities. Family celebrations, estate matters, the pretense of illness . . . there had to be a foolproof ruse to bring her friends' grandchildren home.

Lucy only prayed she wasn't deluding herself. She couldn't bear for Olivia and Enid to have their hopes dashed again. . . .

A knock sounded; then the door swung open to admit a rush of chilly air from the corridor. A tall footman, his freckled face chapped and reddened, entered the boudoir. Snow glistened on his blue livery.

Lucy set down her teacup. "Rumbold," she exclaimed. "What brings you from Stokeford Abbey in such weather, pray tell?"

"The post for you, m'lady." The servant handed a letter to Lucy. " 'Twas brung by special messenger from London." Then he bowed and left the room.

"Who is it from?" Enid asked, wriggling to the edge of her chair. "None of your grandsons are in London."

"Open it," Olivia urged.

The paper was cold to Lucy's stiff fingers. Feeling a portent of disaster, she broke the seal and unfolded the letter. Her disbelieving eyes scanned the boldly penned words as an icy weight crushed her heart.

"We must leave for London immediately," she said, rising.

"But why?" Enid cried out. "What's happened?"

"We can hardly depart in the midst of a snowstorm," Olivia argued. "Surely whatever it is can wait until the morning."

"No," Lucy said in agitation. "Samuel Firth is getting married tomorrow. To the Duke of Chiltern's daughter."

"Dear heavens!" Enid exclaimed. "She can't be more than fifteen years old!"

"It seems a Rosebud's work is never done," Olivia said grimly, using her cane to lever to her feet.

"But we're more than equal to the task," Lucy declared, taking heart from the support of her dearest friends. "Together, we must stop this wedding."